QUEEN VS QUEEN
SHE MEETS HER MATCH

BARBARA WINKES   ALYSIA D. EVANS   ANNE HAGAN

VOLUME ONE

SUNSET TO SUNRISE

BARBARA WINKES

SUNSET TO SUNRISE

Barbara Winkes

Copyright © 2023 Barbara Winkes

All rights reserved.

This book is a work of fiction. Any resemblance to actual persons, living or dead, events or locales are purely coincidental. This book or any portion thereof may not be reproduced or used in any manner whatsoever without the express written permission of the author except for the use of brief quotations in a book review.

DEDICATION

For D.

CHAPTER 1

sabel

ISABEL WINDSOR COULD FEEL her skin prickle with apprehension and anger when she walked over the threshold of the historical building, her heels clicking on the tiled floor. She wasn't supposed to be here. She didn't need to be here. Most of all, she did not want to be here.

Her supervisors might be okay with wasting company money and time, but in the meantime, she'd be stuck in these classes, missing relevant meetings and information she would have to catch up on later.

Two other women were already waiting at the reception desk, adding to her general annoyance and impatience. Isabel had chosen this city when she could have been in Paris or Rome, but she hadn't done it to save the company money. She had done her research and learned that this branch of the International Leadership Institute for Women was a newer one, which made it unlikely that she'd run into someone she knew. There was no need to add to the unexpected humiliation—and, after all, she hadn't come here for a vacation, just to get this over with as quickly and quietly as possible.

While she stood in line behind the other women, Isabel had the time to acknowledge that the context and surroundings were far from humiliating. The high ceilings, paintings and the sweeping staircase all added to a luxurious environment, even if it was a bit dark. She wouldn't hate it so much if this seminar had been her choice.

It wasn't.

Dressing it up didn't make any difference. Assisting and encouraging women into leadership positions was a noble business, but Isabel was already a leader. She didn't need assistance or encouragement, or relaxation exercises.

AFTER SECURING the most lucrative deal of the past couple of years for the company, she knew better than to expect a thank you. She had treated herself to a cruise instead, only to find out upon her return that due to complaints about her, she was being sent to an attitude adjustment seminar.

Not that anyone called it that. Isabel knew that this was what the vice president Peter Hopkins had in mind—for her to be friendlier to his conservative friends.

Not matter how irritated she was by his short-sightedness, every calming impact from the cruise long gone, Isabel knew that her only option was to agree and go through the motions if she not only wanted to keep that job but rise even higher in the hierarchy. Her initial goal had been jeopardized when the owner's health started to deteriorate, and he brought in his nephew as the new VP. Hopkins senior had no son of his own, and the latter was apparently in need of an opportunity.

Peter was itching for an opportunity to oust her. She couldn't let that happen. She wouldn't.

"*Bonjour,*" a friendly employee greeted her.

Realizing that the other guests were gone, she stepped forward.

"*Bonjour,*" she returned. "My name is Isabel Windsor. I'm here for the—"

"Yes, I know. Welcome to the International Leadership Institute for Women, Ms. Windsor. Orientation will take place on the second floor, Room 220. You can take the elevator, or the stairs if you like."

Isabel resisted the urge to wince but was vindicated when the woman's cheery tone faltered a bit. Perhaps she'd realized that Isabel wasn't going to climb stairs in her footwear, not if she could avoid it.

"Well, the elevators are right behind you. I hope you'll have a productive week, and a wonderful stay in Québec City."

"Thanks." She gave her the barest of smiles, after all, the woman had nothing to do with her circumstances. It was going to be productive, no doubt about it. She had brought work and would keep herself informed about what was going on at home.

Isabel took the elevator, catching her reflection in the mirror wall. If nothing on the outside revealed her inner turmoil, it didn't exist at all. One week. She could do it.

Upstairs, she found the room and a wardrobe area. Ten minutes to 9:00 a.m. She could hear voices from inside the room. Now, all she had to do was pass with flying colors, and of course, she would.

Isabel took off her coat and, her focus on the next few hours, handed it to the woman next to her wearing a black sleeveless dress.

"Thank you for taking this."

"I'd say you're welcome, but I don't work here," she informed Isabel, her tone icy.

Something about that voice startled Isabel, but within a few heartbeats, the person actually minding the wardrobe arrived, looking flustered even though it wasn't her who had made the mistake.

Mistakes.

"I'll take this. Enjoy your class."

Everyone who did work in this place, seemed beyond happy, which, even irrationally, only added to Isabel's irritation. To be honest, she was mostly irritated with herself at this point. Stress and unwelcome surprises had made tension settle in her shoulders permanently. It could be that the three-inch-heels were responsible, but they served a purpose. Isabel didn't like looking up at anyone.

When she turned to the woman she had slighted with her action, more curious than apologetic, her breath caught in her throat. Absent-mindedly, she accepted the nametag from the wardrobe girl and fastened it on her blouse, unable to tear her gaze away.

She couldn't believe it. The last time she'd listened to that voice, it had been the opposite of icy—warm, comforting, seductive.

The memory brought heat to her face and other parts of her body at this most inappropriate moment. She remembered how the long auburn tresses felt under her hands, how they had brushed over her thighs...Isabel wanted to shake herself out of the spell. That had been before she found out in just how much jeopardy her position was, even though she had delivered that deal. It was all coming back to haunt her now, the deal and the way she had treated herself afterwards.

In the short time they had spent together, they had used first names only. Isabel. Grace.

Grace McAllister.

She knew that name.

She knew why there was none of the passion and affection in her gaze, because likely, Grace, too, had made the connection.

Isabel didn't obsess about small, unintentional transgressions, but having mistaken her for the wardrobe girl made her cringe.

There had been no mistakes or misunderstandings that other time, but that time was long gone. It didn't even exist anymore. They both had something to salvage.

"Sorry about that," she said and turned around, leaving her standing. Under the circumstances, it was the best course of action. Whatever had brought Grace here, Isabel couldn't help her. And most of all, she couldn't indulge in what had been.

She walked into the room and found herself an empty chair in the back, willing to keep all possible complications at bay. Isabel didn't usually sit at the back of the room, not anymore, but she had come here for one reason only. She'd provide the vice president with a piece of paper that said she was more than capable of filling her position in the company, translation, handle obnoxious clients with outdated views.

Nothing else mattered.

She crossed her legs, not sure why her heartbeat couldn't seem to settle.

Grace.

Her temporary escape.

Her reality check.

One week. She wasn't fazed. Nothing much could faze Isabel Windsor, and this unexpected encounter was no exception.

CHAPTER 2

race

AFTER THE INDULGENCE of carefree and oh-so hot sex with a gorgeous woman during a short cruise, Grace had returned to a catastrophe. She had thought she could do this, pick up the pieces of her life and somehow glue the jagged edges back together to present an acceptable image to the outside world, and herself.

Move on to greater things, because there was no doubt, she was made for things greater than what had happened to her. She was ready to put in the work. She would produce results as always, and this time, she wouldn't hesitate or look back.

She had believed it until she found herself face to face with the woman who was adjusting her name tag cautiously on her silk blouse.

Isabel Windsor, the woman who had single-handedly caused Grace's crisis.

Isabel Windsor was the woman she had met on the cruise.

She wanted to turn back and run away in shame, drown her instant self-loathing in something stronger than the fruity cocktails of which they'd had plenty during the cruise, regardless of the time of day.

But Grace McAllister didn't run, from anything, so she stood, holding the other woman's gaze stubbornly. She wouldn't be the first to blink.

She didn't have to.

"Sorry about that," Isabel said, referring to the now completely irrelevant incident of her assuming Grace would take care of her coat. She turned to walk inside the room, having given no indication of whether she even remembered Grace, or if she was aware of the role she had played in the recent drastic changes in Grace's life.

Likely, she didn't care, so why should Grace?

She straightened her shoulders and walked inside as well, only to realize that the instructor and everyone else was already assembled, waiting for the fortyish-year-old woman named Marie-France Gagnon to begin.

Grace could feel all eyes on her as she made her way to the only available seat left, the seat next to Isabel Windsor.

Grace had been in similar situations multiple times. She was used to it, she excelled in them. There was no reason why this group, and this place she herself had chosen should feel like a scene out of her less than pleasant high school experience. She was here to learn and connect and had assumed the others were too.

But...Isabel. She couldn't dwell on her presence either because the whispers around her, harmless as they might be, made her skin crawl.

Chances were, they weren't even talking about her. They might be, or they could be discussing what to have for lunch. They could be talking about Isabel.

In the world most of them were walking in, Grace had

worked hard to find her footing, only to lose it to the careless actions of one woman. She might not be the only one. Isabel's name and reputation had to be familiar to more of them.

She forced herself to listen Gagnon's introductory comments but found it hard as her calm voice seemed to be drowned out by her own worries.

"You have chosen this particular curriculum..."

Not that she was paying attention, but she could tell by the minute change in Isabel's expression that it might not be true in her case. Why was she here, then? Didn't she have someone else's future to ruin?

Or hook up with another woman in an exotic location? a little voice whispered.

"...to continue and improve serving your clients' needs, but also to guard necessary boundaries," Gagnon continued. "You all have your curriculum for the week. You'll complete a number of exercises with a partner, and you'll check in with your mentor on a regular basis so they can identify any issues and help you stay on track, if necessary."

Most of the eight women in the room, Grace included, had had a lifetime of someone telling them what to do, someone who believed they knew better—and had been proven wrong. Usually, but not exclusively, men.

She could sense an air of resistance in the room, aware of her own. If she had to guess, she'd say Isabel looked bored. For sure she thought all of this was beneath her—but why was she here? The institute prided itself in supporting women in leadership positions, and those who attempted to get into one. Mentorship, connections between women entrepreneurs and CEOs...It made sense that the woman who erased jobs without thinking of the consequences for the individual, didn't care much about any of it.

Grace understood hard decisions. She'd had to make many. She made them rationally, not cruelly, even though she'd been told in not-so-subtle ways that she came across as cold. It came with the territory of often being the only woman in the room. Sexism was a part of it. Jealousy. Part of why she'd been excited for the seminar was to, for once, take out those variables, spend productive time with women who shared those experiences.

Isabel's presence confused her.

It was impossible to reconcile her with the woman Grace had met, and intimately discovered in those days that had passed in a feverish blur, desire, heat, pleasure, all of it fueled by luxurious surroundings and excellent cocktails.

She was drifting again. She had to do better. After all she was here to turn her life around. Grace forced her attention back to the instructor who had given them a bit of background about the ILIW and this particular class.

Grace would have to start from scratch. For the first time in years, she'd have to go hard after clients. She hoped that this week would help her overcome the resentment and suspicion she harbored for pretty much everyone in the world she'd once felt appreciated in.

"And now, why don't you tell me a bit about yourself?" Marie-France, obviously aware that everyone had straightened in their seats, laughed. "Don't worry, it's not like that. You all filled out the information, so we have what we need. Regardless, I'd like to hear a bit from you about your goals for this week. This is important for your assigned mentor and partner. And it goes without saying, but I will say it anyway—everything we share for the duration of the course stays here."

Grace saw agreement and relief in the other women's faces. So far, so...No, there was no way in hell she could say in front of Isabel what she intended to achieve here, at least not in any detail. That would have to wait for her partner and mentor. She assumed that once they all came back together again, she could be equally vague.

When it was her turn, she simply said, "I need to address some recent professional changes. I've heard good things about the institute...This is why I'm here."

"Could you elaborate a bit more on those changes?"

She cast a quick look at Isabel who held her gaze, though she seemed to grip the paper with the curriculum a little tighter.

"I'm afraid that at this time, no, I can't."

If she was surprised, the instructor didn't let it show.

"Okay, then we'll go to the next step. Once you have your partner, you will meet with your mentor, and discuss how to adjust the exercises for your specific needs. We'll come together later after lunch for a first test. Any questions so far?"

After she'd answered a few, she announced who would be working together. They weren't going to be drawing names out of a hat, Grace realized when the woman started to name pairs.

A catastrophe was possible, she thought when it was only her, Isabel, and two others. But not likely. No one could amass this much bad luck, and Grace didn't believe in that kind of thing anyway.

Until the other two women were paired together, smiling at each other.

For the first time since the class started, Isabel seemed a bit more interested, and she made her opinion clear.

"I'm sorry, but I don't think that's going to work."

Her tone was soft and polite, but no less hurtful. It didn't matter that Grace agreed with her. Perhaps she'd just wanted to be the first to say it.

She was aware of who Grace was after all.

"Trust me, it is," Gagnon objected. "We don't take these decisions lightly, and they always benefit our attendees."

"It's not your decision to make." There was a note of warning in the statement. Isabel was clearly frustrated when the instructor didn't budge, probably because Isabel didn't have the power to get her fired.

"I have to disagree, Isabel. I promise you, we know what we are doing."

"I don't understand why we can't just switch," Grace spoke up. "I think that would make it easier for everyone." Except for the person who had to work with Isabel. Nothing personal. Well, maybe they'd get to enjoy this time in unexpected ways.

Jealousy? Really?

"I'd like you both to give this a chance for a couple of days. If at that point, you still want to change, we can talk about the reasons. We'll have a half hour coffee break, and after that you'll meet your respective mentors."

"Unbelievable," Isabel muttered next to her, but she didn't protest any more, just schooled her gorgeous features into an unreadable mask.

Grace still wanted to run...

* * *

GRACE HAD BEEN WATCHING *the woman sitting by herself at the bar for a few minutes, certain that the blonde would have company soon. Not that Grace minded being on a cruise alone—she was an independent woman, after all.*

But her...She had to be here with someone. The minutes passed, and no one joined her. Perhaps it was her strict posture that signaled approach with caution, and the way she seemed satisfied sipping her drink in her form-fitting blue dress. It looked a little too formal for the occasion, but while the icy exterior might warn off others, it ignited heat in Grace.

Halfway through her second Mai Tai, she felt brave and ordered a Martini, the other woman's drink, to send over to her.

She wasn't sure what to expect, but this was her well-deserved vacation, and she could allow herself to be a little carefree, couldn't she? If not now, when?

After the server had left the Martini with her, the woman turned her gaze on Grace, raising a perfectly shaped eyebrow, an amused smirk playing over her lips.

Grace lifted her glass, and she did the same.

This felt like a sign.

Grace never broke the rules, never colored outside the lines. It had provided her with a stellar career, and she wasn't done yet. All she needed was a break, to be someone else for a moment. Brave or foolish, she'd be hard pressed to tell the difference. Grace picked up her glass and walked over to the gorgeous fellow cruise guest who had captured her attention the instant she entered the bar.

"Hi. I don't want to impose, but..."

"You thought you'd give it a try."

"I'm afraid you saw right through me." A younger Grace might have staged a polite retreat at this point, but she was more experienced now, sensing that her company wasn't entirely unwelcome. The other woman would have communicated that clearly by now, had it been the case. "You came here alone?"

Just to make sure.

"So did you, I assume?"

"Yes. Of course, there's nothing wrong with that. I'm enjoying myself so far."

"Yes, it's quite excellent. You'd expect that for the price."

"Right. I'm Grace."

"Nice to meet you, Grace. Isabel. Thank you for the drink."

Something clicked between them, a common knowledge, an understanding, the experience that other people often seemed to make communication so hard—while this was easy.

"You're welcome. So, what brings you here? Are you escaping the day-to-day grind? Or are you here for work?"

The latter might explain her outfit. Grace looked down at herself and realized that hers, too, looked more like casual office wear while they were surrounded by sundresses and Bermuda shorts. The realization pleased her.

"Yes and no. A bit of both I guess," Isabel replied, keeping it vague.

"Are you going to see the show later?"

"I was thinking about it. Why? Did you have anything more exciting in mind?"

Oh, Grace could think of many exciting things when it came to Isabel. She had spent the better part of the evening doing just that. It wasn't just the alcohol that brought heat to her cheeks.

Grace knew that some colleagues were talking behind her back about how she needed to get out more often. She didn't care because her hard work brought results.

However, she didn't mind how "getting out" was turning out for her so far.

"There's a bottle of champagne and a box of chocolates in my suite. Could you be tempted?"

Grace had worked hard to overcome teenage shyness resulting from years-long bullying. In the boardrooms and conference rooms no one cared, and if she didn't speak up, she would be overlooked.

Somehow it was very important for her to be seen by Isabel. The possible implications made her heart beat faster, arousal building with every pulse.

Grace also had learned to read people, and she wouldn't have asked the question if she didn't see hope for an affirmative answer.

"I was tempted from the moment I realized you were formulating an idea. I have to say sending me a drink is a bit cliché, but you, Grace, are very tempting."

Everything from there was easy as well. They sat on the couch in Grace's suite, drinking champagne and talking about the places they'd seen so far. Other places to visit in the future in the hope that once there, they'd make it out of hotels and conference rooms.

And when Isabel set aside her glass, her hand touching Grace's in a way that was deliberate, and careful and oh-so-sexy, the rest was easy too.

Exquisite would be the perfect term for the evening, and her companion.

"We can keep it casual, right?" Isabel whispered as she leaned close.

"Those are the rules when you're far away from home, in magnificent surroundings, with a gorgeous woman..."

Grace was drunk on champagne, flattery, and Isabel's touch, and they hadn't even taken off their clothes yet.

When they finally did, easy and exquisite applied as well.

That was Isabel Windsor, the woman who had taken her breath away. More than once.

AN EMAIL. Who would send this in a fucking email?

Grace sat back in her chair, trying to get her breathing and the burning in her eyes under control. She could tell from the shocked silence outside her office that she wasn't the only one who had gotten this message.

They were closing down the department. No, unfortunately employees couldn't be relocated, but the severance package would be generous.

You bet, she had thought, curling her fingers into fists, for a few seconds feeling as dejected as she had felt when hiding from her schoolyard bullies.

But Grace was a grown woman, accomplished, a hard worker.

Damn right that package would be good—she would call her lawyer today.

She would...It was too early. She wasn't ready to make that jump and go it alone. Or was she?

The bosses had followed through immediately when the consulting company they'd hired gave the recommendation to get rid of Grace's department.

That was Isabel Windsor too.

CHAPTER 3

sabel

ISABEL COULD THINK on her feet under the most trying of situations, and this didn't even come close. During the first break, her group had the opportunity to mingle with those attending other classes. She was content to stay on the sidelines and observe while she sipped the surprisingly good coffee. Isabel had high standards, and she could appreciate when they were being met, even though she wanted to be anywhere but in this place. At least there was enough space so she could be far away from Grace while forming a strategy in her mind.

Being far away from Grace was necessary, she affirmed with a hint of regret. After all, they had proven to be highly compatible, but none of it mattered anymore.

Exercises. It was hard to ignore the intruding memories. They sure had done some together, inspired by the total freedom those other circumstances had given them. It had been a fantasy, but an incredible vivid one. Warm, sun-kissed skin under her hands and mouth, appreciative sounds spurring her on...

Isabel set down her cup with enough vehemence for some coffee to slosh over the rim. She needed a different kind of motivation now. Knowing what might happen if she didn't get this right did the trick.

She left her coffee behind and went straight to the room where she and Grace were supposed to meet their mentor in ten minutes from now.

"Ms. Andrea Marlowe?"

The woman looked up from her book with an easy smile. She was in her late fifties maybe, a few silver lines in her long dark hair.

"Yes, that's me, but Andie works. Ms. Windsor." She got to her feet. "You're a bit early, but that's fine. Welcome."

"Thanks." Isabel noticed that Andie didn't speak with the same faint accent she had observed with a couple of other staff members. She didn't return the offer of first name basis. What was the point? A week from now she'd be back home and taking care of things. Catching up. Isabel never shied away from hard work, but the thought of missing one entire work week had made anxiety settle in her stomach. "I need to talk to you."

"Of course. We're here for all your questions and concerns. I see your focus will be on client interactions."

Forget about anxiety, her anger easily won once more. She didn't need a class to tell her how to handle clients. She had read the many testimonials of women who had benefited from and loved her time with the institute. Obviously, the founder and her international team knew what they were doing.

That didn't change the fact that Peter had made a grave mistake by sending her here. Now she had to bide her time until the board understood that.

"There has been a misunderstanding. I appreciate what you're doing here, and I know it has helped many women leaders. But I could serve my company better if I was actually there to do my job."

"I was under the assumption that you chose Québec City. Can I ask why?"

Yes, that had been her mistake, but what were the odds that she would find Grace McAllister here? Isabel admitted to herself that she might have too high a profile even without the inconvenient coincidence—but said coincidence made things worse.

"It's close enough to home in case of an emergency that requires me to intervene," she said with a shrug. "It's nothing against the institute, or the city, for that matter. I hear it's quite beautiful." Not that she planned to do a lot of sightseeing, but the view from her hotel room was the first thing that had calmed her some since Peter pulled that stunt. "I assume that with your exercises, you don't require anyone to go into details of their work. I handle sensitive documents every day, and you understand that leaders in the same field are also competitors, regardless of gender. In any case...Like I said, there was a misunderstanding, and all I need from you is to sign that form at the end of the week."

Andie Marlowe still wore the same friendly smile. Isabel didn't expect her to object much—after all, their business model depended on the satisfaction of their clients.

"You don't have to worry about us asking you to reveal company secrets or anything that could get you into trouble." Was there a hint of amusement to her words?

Isabel narrowed her eyebrows. She had been disrespected enough for one week. She might be playing the long game with Peter, which required her to be under the radar for a bit longer. That didn't mean she tolerated ridicule.

"Ms. Marlowe—"

"Andie, please."

"Fine. Andie. I didn't mean to imply that. I just have to make sure you understand my situation. I cannot—"

She stopped cold when Grace walked into the room, looking hurt for a moment brief enough it might have been Isabel's imagination.

"Ms. McAllister, hi. Nice to meet you. I'm Andie Marlowe. You two already know each other—so we can begin."

Isabel could have sworn that if their situation wasn't this complicated, they both might have rolled their eyes in agreement. As it was, they avoided each other's gazes, though she couldn't help casting a quick glance at Grace's hands folded in her lap.

She couldn't underestimate the potential danger. Grace was bound to have misunderstood everything, and she might be looking for a way to get back at Isabel, for any weakness to exploit. Isabel wasn't going to give her any opportunity.

* * *

DURING THE DAYS on the cruise, they hadn't talked about their jobs at all. Much had changed since then—Isabel needed to succeed here in order to keep hers. Grace had lost hers. Nevertheless, she appeared determined and goal-focused, and that was a new side to her...No, actually, it was not, Isabel remembered. She had been on the receiving end of that focus, and experienced unprecedented pleasures...damn it. This had to stop.

She could tell that Grace was equally hesitant to reveal anything an opponent might use, but she did mention that she was starting her own company.

"I'm good in a crisis, and several people had encouraged me towards that step before. But then I had a job I thought was secure." Her tone had about the same quality as earlier this day when Isabel mistook her for the wardrobe girl. A new quality she found intriguing, enticing, and for some reason, a tad irritating at the same time. Perhaps she was just too irritated with herself, and the inevitable. It was no secret that they shared certain traits and habits. It was what had drawn them to each other and put them at odds.

"You both will have to go after clients and connections in a different way than before. I have a few ideas on how we could move forward, and I'll give you some homework to do individually and together. Any questions you have we'll discuss once you've completed the work."

Grace nodded. "Sounds great to me." Now she sounded defiant, challenging.

Isabel suppressed a sigh. She would play along as much as possible, regardless of the fact that she had still work to do. She wasn't going to spend a week here without checking in on a couple of allies, and ready herself for any eventualities, like Peter screwing up even more. She could be home within a few hours. She admitted to herself that perhaps she wished for a crisis, something that would prove to the owner she wasn't the dispensable one.

"I'm curious what you'll come up with," she said, uncaring that she might sound insincere. Andie couldn't show the irritation she certainly felt, but Grace had no such reservations. The headshake was both subtle and elegant.

"Great," Andie said. "I'll leave these tablets with you, and I'd like to ask you to follow the instructions in your email, including the questionnaire. When you answer the questions, try not to think about them for too long. It's a test designed to assess your leadership style. We'll discuss the results tomorrow. They'll likely give you some interesting insights."

Isabel refrained from offering her opinion on yet another questionnaire. She knew herself well enough, didn't she?

When they could finally call it a day, relief flooded her. The first part of the homework seemed easy enough, and she didn't need anyone else to do it. After a few phone calls and paperwork that she had brought with her, she could fit it in.

Isabel was the first out of the room, but she wasn't fast enough.

"So, you're trying to sabotage this too."

It was quite the statement from Grace, made in a calm, conversational tone. Small talk. Except it was anything but.

"I have no clue what you're talking about. I'm not trying to sabotage anything, but you might be a little bit more careful about what you reveal during the course. Someone will always try to take advantage."

"Oh, you're giving me advice now. Thanks, but no thanks, Ms. Windsor. I am not new to this either, or to the fact that some people in business are less than ethical. As you know, I've experienced it."

Isabel was not inclined to deepen this conversation. As it was, they had done so much better without the talking, not that they could ever go back to that…which was unfortunate. It might have made the days go by faster, and she would have been less bored and stressing about the future…No.

"That's funny to you, I assume."

It wasn't until then she became aware of the smile she was wearing.

"Not funny," Isabel said, sobering. "Those veiled accusations you're making aren't either. If you don't understand that closing the department was a necessary move for your employer, and you don't think you could make those decisions, you might rethink starting your own business. There you have it, yes, I'm giving you advice. You're welcome. I guess I'll see you tomorrow."

She wouldn't give her the impression she was trying to get away, even if that was the truth. Lucky for Isabel, she could get into a cab right in front of the building. She didn't bother waiting for anyone, least of all Grace. Give her one more reason to hate her, Isabel didn't care. They had both made their respective beds, no need to dwell.

And why did every thought about her have a sensual memory attached to it? *This too shall pass.* She needed a drink, and soon.

* * *

ISABEL MADE a few calls and caught up on the work she'd brought with a quick snack from room service. She had ordered a bottle of wine as well, not bothering with the minibar. It would last her a few days, preferably for the duration of her stay, but she wasn't betting on it yet.

At least everything was quiet at home, according to Carla and Sam. They wouldn't lie to her in order to smooth things over. They had too much respect for her which meant they'd fear the consequences if she found out they acted against her instructions. Good enough. She put the laptop aside and cast a glance at the clock. It was late, and she should be exhausted after the day she'd had, but Isabel felt inexplicably wired and restless.

She picked up her customized schedule for the week, a mix of classes in groups, with Andie, room for exercises with her partner who was equally as apprehensive about spending time with her.

Something for the next morning caught her eye, and she shook her head with a wry grin. *No, thanks.*

Decision made, or at least, made easier, she went over to the wardrobe and chose a thin cardigan. That would suffice. Below her hotel room, there was some sort of boardwalk, the *Terasse Dufferin*. When she arrived, and again when she returned from the seminar, it had been packed with tourists, children running about, ice cream in hand.

Now, it wasn't empty, but less crowded than before. She picked up her purse, took the elevator to the lobby and stepped outside. She followed the path around the building and back to the boardwalk. While it wasn't exactly quiet, Isabel found the relative solitude, not having to engage with anyone, a relief. She walked a few steps to the guardrail that protected visitors from a steep fall.

The shiver crept up her spine like a premonition, and she focused on the beautiful view in front of her, the dark river, the bridge in the distance.

Isabel understood French well enough to translate some of the fragments that floated over to her as people passed her by. She heard a variety of other languages as well from tourists strolling along the boardwalk, enjoying the view of the river, or stopping to listen to a musician playing a saxophone. She took it all in, the fact that she didn't have pay attention to anyone, allowing her to drift, a rare occurrence.

Cruise ships docked regularly in Québec City's old port—ships like the one where she and Grace had met. Grace wasn't by far her biggest problem.

Ironic how she had thought she'd be prepared for the worst after dealing with the patriarch of the company and then, his nephew. The former believed in politeness even with those who didn't deserve it, but Peter was worse.

Isabel couldn't help frowning at the memory of the incident that had made them decide to send her away like a chastised schoolgirl. Peter Hopkins had married into a conservative family and was trying to win points with them. While he appreciated Isabel's talent for finding companies that looked healthy on the outside, but were struggling, ready to be bought and cut up, he didn't like *her*.

He wasn't so special. A lot of people didn't like her. But this was different, more dangerous. If Senior started to listen to more of his outrageous ideas, if would put everything she had worked for in serious jeopardy. She felt a bit sorry for Grace who apparently hadn't thought of a Plan B—not sorry enough to say it out loud. It had to be done, not just for the sake of Isabel's career.

Earlier, she had barely noticed what she ate. The pang of hunger signaled that it probably hadn't been enough. She could have gone for one of those soft-serve ice cream cones she'd seen, but as she walked closer to the building, she saw that the shop was closed.

Too many metaphors. She needed to sleep, and not escape into dreams of abandon and desire. That wasn't her, that had been the exception. She already had the life she wanted, didn't she?

CHAPTER 4

race

Grace had spent a mostly sleepless night, wondering how she could successfully complete the curriculum without revealing the full impact Isabel's actions had had on her. She couldn't show her any weakness, give her any advantage.

But she also wanted something to bring home, something that would help her start over. The two of them seemed irreconcilable. She finally gave up on sleep, got dressed and walked to the location of the seminar on foot. A caterer provided breakfast for everyone who didn't want to eat at their hotel, and that seemed like a good option to mull over her choices.

To her relief, Isabel didn't have the same idea.

Grace cursed her fate for yesterday's revelations, and herself for, the first time in her career, not doing her homework diligently.

How could she have known? The Isabel on the cruise had

been a different woman, passionate, empathetic, funny even. They had laughed together, and at the time it had felt so intimate, like it came from a sense of humor only the two of them shared.

Too much sun and rum—and lust—had blinded her intuition. She should have known.

Grace chose some fruit, a muffin and a coffee and found herself a table in a corner, by a window. Here in the upper town, the views were amazing everywhere, the city, the river, mountains in the distance.

Certainly, there were limitless options for romantic getaways...She almost groaned at her train of thought. No, the lack of sleep hadn't helped. Today and the rest of the week would require lots of caffeine. She needed to pay attention a lot more than she needed romance. Or foolish ideas.

The second cup brought some improvement, and so did the third.

After brushing her teeth in the restroom, she felt ready to face whatever might come her way—Isabel Windsor, and today's first block: Relaxation and guided imagery, before she and Isabel would discuss yesterday's homework with Andie. She had read over the results of the test, a personality quiz, really. Not the first of its kind HR had made her take over her latest employments, but this one surprised her.

Sociable. Inspiring. She was curious about Isabel though doubted she'd be eager to share.

Next part: Identify obstacles regarding the goals they had established, and brainstorm ideas for moving forward. Well, Grace could think of one obstacle in particular, but she wasn't so petty as to write her name on the list.

Besides, Isabel didn't have any impact on her next steps. Those were Grace's responsibility alone.

Sitting in one of the comfortable chairs, she focused on the instructor's warm voice, walking on imaginary sand. Grace appreciated the immediate effect, though she doubted that any exercises like this would find their way into her busy day-to-day life. Once she had established that day-to-day life again, anyway. Detach. Analyze mistakes. Forgive herself. Move on. She would, eventually, for not having seen this coming. The job part, anyway.

She had been a heartbeat away from giving Isabel her number on that last day, against all odds wishing, hoping…Grace wasn't sure if the fact that she hadn't done it was a blessing or a curse. She would have known sooner.

Blinking, she realized that the chair next to her had remained empty. She wasn't sure whether to be annoyed or impressed with Isabel openly defying the rules. Attendance was required.

She decided not to dwell on it and returned to the imaginary beach. Grace had always been good at retreating into herself, creating a space from where to plan her next steps. Having been a bullied teen required it.

Being a woman in business, the value of detachment couldn't be overestimated. And she understood that this wasn't just some feel-good, wellness feature, but a tool in her arsenal. Perhaps she should try harder to make time for mediation and such, but when would she sleep?

It looked like Isabel would miss the entire hour. She might have given up on the course altogether, and wouldn't that be a relief? Grace was aware that any potential sarcasm was directed solely at herself. She deserved it for that flash of disappointment. What did she think could happen during this week?

Isabel would never apologize. Grace wasn't inclined to forgive.

Then again, apologies and forgiveness wouldn't be a requirement for…She reined in her runaway thoughts, back to the beach, annoyed with herself when a remembered sensation, a scent, invited itself to the imagery. No.

Grace was finally jolted out of her semi-relaxed state when the door opened, and Isabel walked in. Grace recognized the tactic—not only had she stayed away on purpose, but she was letting everyone know that she thought of this activity as a waste of time.

Did she really think the instructors would tolerate that, that they wouldn't send her home at some point? Grace could read between the lines, and it was easy to tell that Isabel hadn't chosen the seminar—so something depended on it for her.

She watched her walk over to the instructor and exchange a few words. No one raised their voices, but the atmosphere in the room had become unmistakably more tense.

Isabel Windsor had single-handedly ended the first block of the day.

Grace suppressed a sigh. This was going to be a much bigger challenge than she could have ever imagined.

* * *

Isabel's exchange with the instructor made them three minutes late for their meeting with Andie. The latter didn't mention it.

"You're here, great, let's get right to it. How did it go with your homework?"

For some reason inexplicable to Grace, Isabel's shoulders tightened once more.

"Fine," she said. "I emailed you the results as you requested."

"Yes, I got them, yours too, Grace."

Andie spent a bit of time explaining the results and methodology. At one point, Isabel's gaze met hers, and despite herself, Grace was certain she wanted to role her eyes. Open-minded? Caring? In their world, if they had those traits, they had better hide them, or the competition would eat them alive. At this point, Grace had few illusions left, and the old boys' club was only part of the reason.

Disciplined. Isabel sure was disciplined when it came to her professional decisions. She wasn't swayed by emotions. Grace had thought that she brought similar qualities to the table, and she wasn't sure how she felt about the test revealing a more vulnerable side of hers. It made her uncomfortable, especially in the presence of the woman she had been vulnerable with.

When they moved on to the next part, Isabel wasted no time.

"What's in my way? Sexism. The fact that no matter how far I get, there are still preconceived notions reserved for me, and there's a significant gap in salary." Isabel's voice sounded quiet, pensive, as she spoke. Compelling. "Then again, none of this is new to you, I assume, and we're not going to change any of it in one week." Any gentleness Grace might have imagined was gone in an instant. "I've been working around it, of course, as we all have. That's all we can do. I'm not going to hold back the truth with ignorant clients though. They're not good for anyone's business."

"It's important to draw the line," Andie agreed. "What about you, Grace?"

Yes, what about Grace? Where did she draw the line? Sexist clients? Homophobic? Alone with her homework the other night, Grace had done some research on Isabel, finding nothing she didn't already know. Isabel wasn't out per se, though there were rumors she had clashed a few times with the more conservative vice president of her firm, especially after his marriage into a far-right religious family.

Aside from that incident, Isabel's boundaries remained vague, and she certainly hadn't missed out on anything, deals, promotions, in the past few years.

Grace couldn't figure out why she made her so angry, except for the obvious. Did she stand up for something? Erasing Grace's department, whom exactly had that served?

"What about me," she repeated, stalling. "I think what held me back before were romantic expectations about how women leaders lift each other up. No offense."

"None taken," Andie returned calmly. "Go on."

"It's a myth. At this level, everyone looks out for themselves as it seems, consequences be damned."

She cast a glance at Isabel who sat perfectly still.

"So, I won't make that mistake any longer. I have a few opportunities lined up, and I will pursue them. I know we've just started, but I can already see that clearer."

"I guess I shouldn't have missed that relaxation training," Isabel mumbled.

Well, any other person would have mumbled. Isabel *murmured*, the way she had back then, a warm whisper against Grace's skin…

"We'll circle back to that later," Andie promised. Or was it a warning?

Oddly enough, when they were back with the group and Marie-France, both Grace and Isabel presented similar conclusions. The classes were going well so far, they had done their homework and were eager to move forward.

Maybe they would let Isabel get away with missing one of the classes.

Maybe the fact that they were both still here, was a success.

"You don't know what you're missing," she told her on the way to lunch break. "If it's something the bosses would scoff at, you know you'd benefit from it."

"Suit yourself," Isabel returned. "I don't have time for this."

* * *

AT THE END of the day, Andie listened to their respective summaries, and asked, "Why are you here? Grace first, please."

"We've been over this a few times now," Isabel spoke up. The tense set of her shoulders and her cool gaze spoke of her irritation.

This time, Grace could sympathize.

"I have to say, it feels like we're moving around in circles," she admitted. "I've told Ms. Gagnon, and you, and I remember filling out different questionnaire before I came here. I'm starting my own business. I have experience in acquiring clients for my former employer, but I'll have to be even more aggressive about it. I'm looking to make connections. What else would you like to hear?"

"Isabel, what about you?"

"I tend to agree with her. We've told you…I don't think sending me here, at this moment, was a smart course of action, but here we are, and like Grace said, it's all about cultivating and securing clients. We have done the damn homework."

Andie raised an eyebrow at Isabel's choice of words but didn't comment on it.

"You see my concern? Here, we understand that given where you come from, you need a bit of time to decompress. You all worked hard for the kind of career you have, and this is work, too, but you don't have to watch your back at every moment. Everything you reveal in the context of our classes is confidential. We have enforced this, and we'll continue to do so."

Both Grace and Isabel remained silent.

"You've named general goals, but to be honest, they could apply to anyone. Nothing specific about your business, what drew you to it, and what matters most to you personally. In case that wasn't clear, I'm not obliged to send a play-by-play to anyone's supervisor. My obligation is to make sure that when you go home at the end of the week, you do so with more tools and knowing you have more support."

"How do you enforce it?" Isabel asked after an uncomfortably long pause.

Grace turned to her, her own face heating with the implications of her words. "You're unbelievable! You really think I'd use this seminar to get back at you? I can promise you, I'm not that juvenile. I didn't even know you'd be here!"

Grace took a deep breath, willing herself not to reveal that the accusation hurt.

"You said it yourself. The sisterhood is a myth. I believe you."

"Grace, Isabel. I understand that there are complicated dynamics at play, but they don't have to hinder you in your day-to-day business, especially in the future. In fact, you can make them work for you. Believe me, we get the need to be cautious, but you need to trust somebody."

I trusted her. And how did that work out for me?

"If you say so." Isabel didn't sound convinced. "So, what you do suggest?"

"Take a look at the schedule together, and if there's something you need to talk about without me, I suggest you do that," Andie said. "And get specific. Tell me exactly what kinds of problems you've run into, and how you're going to deal with them in the future. Shake it up. Do a river cruise or a ghost tour tomorrow, but when you come back, I want you to tell me without a doubt what matters to you most at this moment. Because you haven't yet."

Grace couldn't help wincing at the term cruise. She had to keep things under control, move forward. Going on another boat, especially with Isabel, was the opposite of that. Why, if she knew that without a doubt, did her fingers tingle at the thought? Those damn body memories.

"Oh, and Isabel, please don't miss the relaxation block again. It's there for a reason."

Just barely, but Isabel bristled at the woman telling her this.

Grace assumed that no client she could ever want to pursue would be harder to crack than this woman—she might as well start to put the exercises learned here, to use.

While everyone was enjoying a coffee break in the common area before the last block of the day, she approached Isabel who stood by herself, holding the coffee cup like she was ready to use it as a weapon. It was perhaps because she'd seen another facet to the enigmatic woman that Grace was unafraid, or maybe she could see something they had in common if she looked past the resentment.

She wasn't going to bother dressing up what she had to say either.

"Look, it's already the second day, and I can't help thinking Marlowe has a point. You don't have to like me, but I get the impression that the outcome of this week matters to you too. So why don't we forget about everything that happened..." *Liar. Like you could.* "...for a few days and focus on the work?"

That was bold, and nearly impossible. It was also the only way they'd manage to move ahead.

Isabel's expression was pained, and her shoulders still looked so tense it made Grace want to wince. Surely, she could get a massage somewhere around here?

"You have this all wrong. I barely know you. It's not about liking or disliking you."

"Then we're going to do this? It's just one week, and since I'm paying out of pocket, I know this class isn't cheap. Your bosses must have had something in mind when they sent you here."

"Yes, they did." She gave a bitter laugh. "To have me out of the way for some time, so their conservative buddies could cool their heels."

"It was that bad? What did you say to them?"

A hint of a smile played over her lips—delectable soft lips. Grace had to remember that this woman was responsible for the drastic changes in her own life. She wasn't going to indulge her, just investigate enough to make sure she had an angle, so they could complete this seminar. She had observed the other women earlier, and none of their classmates seemed to struggle like this.

"You know as well as I do that you don't have to say much with these folks, just be a woman in their space, and it irks them." This time, the smile was more pronounced. "I might have told them to keep their homophobic attitude to themselves, or it would be difficult to work with them again in the future...I might have used different words." She shrugged. "My direct supervisor backed me up at the time. However, I was called into the office the next day, and he and the vice president informed me that I was supposed to brush up on my social skills. They would not have treated a man that way."

It was almost enough for Grace to sympathize with her, but those moments of mutual understanding never lasted long with Isabel Windsor.

"There you have it. Do with it whatever you want."

So, nothing Andie or Grace said had tampered down her paranoia. At this rate, she would feel sorry for herself sometime soon.

"No matter what you think, that was never my intention—"

"Are you ready to come back in?" Andie asked behind them.

Grace turned to her, practicing boundaries and a tone that usually left the recipient without a doubt.

"Could you give us a moment?"

Even being jobless and somewhat disheartened, it still worked.

"Please don't be too long. I'll wait for you inside."

"Thanks."

When she and Isabel had relative privacy again, Grace didn't hold back.

"Frankly, I am offended by all the things you keep accusing me of pre-emptively. I lost my job because of you, and so did many other good people. I don't expect you to show your regret, or apologize, but I do expect you to work with me or get out of my way, so I can find a partner *I* can trust." This time, she left Isabel standing. It didn't feel like triumph or even a small win, but Grace saw no alternative. Talk about hard decisions.

CHAPTER 5

Isabel

So, Grace might not be planning to exploit every piece of information she could get out of this seminar. The realization didn't come with the expected relief. She had been under so much tension for some time now that it was hard to determine anything that could help with that. Realistically. Her body had other ideas, reminding her of a time, albeit short, when she'd been able to leave it all behind.

That wasn't real anymore. Maybe it never had been. At her hotel, she was about to call Carla for an update, but paused, going over the events of the day. Nothing would convince her that the time spent here wasn't…misused at best. But contrary to what Grace believed, it wasn't her intention to ruin her personally, not with what happened at her former employer's, or at the seminar.

While she was stuck here, she might as well make sure Grace understood that. Tomorrow, they'd have to do a presentation in front of their fellow attendees, including some sort of roleplay.

She would, well, play along if Grace thought that helped her future business.

Because they thought of Isabel as arrogant and unapproachable, people often assumed she hated equally as many. It couldn't have been further from the truth. Isabel didn't hate many, or all that often. She reserved that emotion for a few deserving individuals and directed it at them with deadly precision.

Some might misunderstand. For some reason it was becoming more important to her that Grace didn't. Isabel went over her notes from the day, and the scenario they had agreed on. It wouldn't be that hard.

No matter what Grace or Andie said, she wouldn't attend that first block. She needed that time to work, and besides…Sitting in a room with other people, eyes closed, it was…A waste of time. Her willingness to see this through went only so far. Isabel laughed bitterly as she remembered Andie's suggestion to do a ghost tour. She had enough ghosts of her own, no point in looking for more.

It was time to call Carla.

Isabel could tell right away from her tone that she had news. Not the best news either, judging from the way she was trying to stall.

"Why don't you tell me what happened?" she asked in that mild, slightly patronizing tone she had perfected over time. Isabel didn't use it on women all that often, but she needed Carla to get to the point, and it was a bit more complicated since they weren't face-to-face.

"Nothing…yet," Carla admitted. "I hear that Peter wants to bring someone new on the board, a friend of his he offered the position to…but no one can tell me who it is. I swear. If I knew, so would you."

"Why would he do that?" It wasn't idle musing. Her heart was hammering. Isabel had no illusions as to why Peter made that move now while she was conveniently out of the way. If he planned to bring some of his wife's relatives into the company, Isabel's chances of ever moving up were in jeopardy. Worse, her days with Hopkins might be counted. When Carla didn't answer, she said, "You get me that name, right? You can call me any time, day or night."

"Yes, I know. I'm sorry."

"Is there anything else? Did he say anything?"

"No. It all seems very hush-hush."

"What about the Crawfords?"

The family owned a large chain of hardware stores, and they hadn't been too fond of Isabel commenting on their discriminatory practices against employees. Short-sighted fools like Hopkins' in-laws. You could explain to a child that employees were more productive and loyal if you treated them like human beings.

She could almost see Carla shrug. "They've been quiet. I think according to them, you have been appropriately punished."

"Thank you. Let me know if you find out more."

Carla's words lingered, making Isabel wonder who was making the mistake. She had reason to be cautious given this abrupt action by Peter. He knew that she was coming for his job, and he couldn't care less about women in leadership. But what could she do from here other than keeping herself informed?

In a few days she'd be back home. Did she really want to hole herself up in her hotel room for all of that time?

So, she didn't come here on a vacation—definitely not for a ghost tour around the old town—but perhaps she could take a little time for some sightseeing tomorrow. They would have a half day to themselves, to catch up, to discuss the curriculum with their respective partners, and, according to Marie-France, to explore.

Even though the classes, their content and the requirements were quite clear and precise, there was still something about this setting Isabel found confounding.

Perhaps a good Martini would help clear her mind.

After a quick shower, she changed into appropriate clothing for the bar located on the ground floor of the hotel and took the elevator to the lobby. She could dine in the gourmet restaurant if she wanted to, but Isabel wasn't feeling it tonight. The more muted tones of the bar suited her, and the menu was quite exquisite as well. She asked for a table by the window and ordered her drink.

When it arrived and she took her first sip, Isabel nearly sighed with pleasure. Clearly it was having the desired effect. She leaned back in her seat and glanced outside where once more tourists were strolling by. She still hadn't managed to get that ice cream. Maybe tomorrow.

Now you're really letting your hair down, that sarcastic inner voice commented. Screw that voice popping up no matter what she did, telling her that nothing was ever good enough. For the moment, being here and sipping her drink was the best, most pleasant course of action.

The sound of laughter made her turn, but the two women coming in and choosing to be seated at the bar hadn't noticed her. One of them was in the class where they'd do their presentation tomorrow, the other one...Grace.

How was it possible that the realization came with an instant pang of jealousy? Neither of them had been thrilled about getting partnered together. Grace had the right to...*associate* with whomever she wanted. She felt her face flush at the multiple directions her mind was going, all of them making her self-conscious in a way she wasn't used to and didn't appreciate. She finished her Martini with a too big sip, barely avoiding a coughing fit as the alcohol burned in her chest.

When she looked up, the other woman had slipped off her barstool, greeting a newcomer...Her partner in the seminar. The two of them left together. Isabel quickly averted her gaze when she realized Grace was studying her. For how long had she been doing that? Why, when she had made it clear earlier that she was single-mindedly focused on launching her business, and warned Isabel to stay out of the way?

She tensed when Grace left her seat at the bar and walked over to her, unsure what to expect.

"Would you keep me company? Or are you too worried about the secrets you might reveal under the influence?"

Her tone was conversational, but Grace's eyes challenged her the way they had that night on the cruise ship. Isabel thought of the mysterious new board member, the bigger picture, and regrets she'd had in the past. She hung on to those thoughts so long she worried Grace might walk away, but then again, the woman had a patient side to her. Isabel had experienced it. A few times.

"You'd be so disappointed. I'll tell you a secret—I really don't have that many."

"No, you're pretty much an open book."

Grace set her drink on the table and sat down across from Isabel, her beautiful features softening when she spoke.

"Maybe Andie was right, and we do have some things to talk about, whether we like it or not. I do understand what's business, and what's personal. I want to benefit from the time we spend here. Don't you?"

It's hard to benefit when the intention behind it was punishment, Isabel wanted to say.

"I was thinking of visiting *Petit Champlain* tomorrow, and *Place Royale*," she replied instead.

"I hear it's very touristy, but beautiful," Grace commented.

How ridiculous was it that she wanted Grace to approve of her choices? They didn't owe each other anything. Regardless, when the waitress came by, she signaled her and ordered another Martini, and "another one if this, *s'il vous plait*," she pointed at Grace's glass. When they were alone again, she said, "Let's see about which secrets *you* reveal under the influence."

Grace's small content smile was dangerously sexy, stealing her breath.

"I appreciate the gesture, but I'm afraid you'll need more than a cocktail and a half to get those from me."

"Can't blame me for trying…"

Grace reached for her glass again. Was she uncomfortable with where the conversation was going? She had come here. Isabel couldn't figure out her emotions, an unnerving mix of irritation and attraction. Drinking that first Martini so fast hadn't helped.

"You have to admit, it makes a difference, having some distance from work. Even if it wasn't what your bosses intended for you."

It was still to be determined what they had intended…

"It's nice," she said, allowing a note of wistfulness to slip into her tone, the complete opposite of the attempt at…what? Seduction? Did she really think they could go there again? "You don't have to feel sorry for me. I did cost you that job after all."

"Yes, you did. And maybe you did me a favor."

Isabel sat up even straighter. "Why are you saying that? Yesterday you made it look like I destroyed your life's dream."

"You certainly destroyed something, but things are always different when dreams come true, aren't they?"

"What do you mean?" It might be the alcohol. It might be something else. Isabel vowed to put Carla and Sam to work—more work—when she talked to them tomorrow.

"Nothing. Everything. I'm starting my own business, and I know I'll be good at it. I got my ducks in a row. No more answering to people who feel like they need to correct your attitude…You of all people know what I mean."

The sense of alarm she'd felt a few moments ago, slowly vanished, and her chest didn't feel as tight anymore.

"I do. I guess that means we have something to celebrate. Champagne would be appropriate."

"You don't have to…" For emphasis, Grace laid her hand on Isabel's, thumb brushing over her knuckles.

"I think I do." Even the few words were too much, too revealing of her state, her heart once again racing for a different reason, the warm pulse between her legs telling. Isabel shifted on her chair as Grace said, "Fine, but we need something to eat then. I haven't had *poutine* yet, and I've been told I have to try it here in Québec."

"*Poutine?*" Isabel repeated. "How's that different from loaded fries?" Let alone messy. She had never appreciated messy in her life, and food was no exception.

"I don't know that it is, but it sounds decadent, and the one they have here is supposed to be even more special. How about we share?"

"Wow, I'm starting to see what those deep dark secrets of yours are," she commented, and Grace laughed.

She had missed that laugh.

She was in trouble.

"So, we go with it?"

"Champagne and *poutine*. Let's do it."

CHAPTER 6

Grace

THRILLING. Surprising. Grace tried to tell herself that after everything they had already shared, then and now, laughter, the drinks, and the realization that they might have a lot more in common than either of them had thought...It was predictable too, that air of desire between them. Aloof, defensive Isabel irritated and intrigued her at the same time.

The setting, more reminiscent of their first encounter, made it easier to be forgiving. This shift to being her own boss wasn't easy, no matter how much of a knack for business she had, or how many clients would follow her in a heartbeat.

She needed allies. If Isabel Windsor was no longer the enemy, that would be a start, wouldn't it? Could she really be an ally to Grace, or was it delusional to imagine?

She wanted to touch her again, the notion turning into a

physical need with the minutes passing by, and so she ran her fingers up her bare arm.

Grace all but shrank back at the realization of what she had done, what line she had crossed. Fantasizing, reminiscing, it was one thing. Acting on it...something else altogether. It was dangerous.

"I'm sorry," she said with an awkward laugh, her heart hammering.

Too late, she had opened that door, Isabel's eyes meeting hers, the room spinning with the flash of desire. No one else had this effect on her.

Reason for celebration...

"Don't be," Isabel started, and then they both straightened when the waitress came by to fill their glasses from the bottle in the ice bucket, not ready to be this obvious.

Then again, how much more obvious could they be, sharing a bottle of champagne, sharing looks that made heat gather at her core? Isabel did that so effortlessly, she envied her for it.

"Shall we take this upstairs?" she asked softly. Gone was the sarcastic attitude she had exhibited for most of the time here, her demeanor now gentle.

There was nothing Grace wanted more, go with her, have more champagne maybe, and forget about all the reasons why she resented her. While she seemed to have resigned to her fate and the seminar in particular, Isabel still hadn't offered an apology.

Instead, Grace had assured her that she understood, that she would be fine even without the job she had worked so hard for to get.

Did it matter, right here and now? Or in the long run?

"Yes," she said. "Let's do that."

They stayed in different corners of the elevator, aware that there could be cameras.

Isabel's first swipe of the key card didn't open the door, and she mumbled a curse. The second attempt worked, and they were in a room much like Grace's, though she didn't notice much of it as Isabel lightly pushed her up against the wall and kissed her.

So here they were again. Those tender but determined hands awakened her memory in a heartbeat, and they awakened her body at a speed it made her head spin. Isabel's mouth on hers, her hands starting to unbutton her top, made it easy to forget all the areas of conflict still between them. Yes, she wanted to leave it all aside for the prospect of more shared intimacy.

She wanted it with an intensity that scared her, because they weren't just strangers on a fun adventure anymore, first names only. Contrary to what Isabel had insinuated, they both had their secrets, and a lot to lose.

Excuses? Cold hard reality? Whatever it was, it was making her sober up, and quickly.

"I'm sorry," she rasped and hastily buttoned her blouse again.

"What's wrong?"

Grace turned away from Isabel's inquisitive gaze.

"I don't think it's a good idea. I'm sorry," she said again and fled.

What was she trying to prove? Who was she trying to punish?

* * *

GRACE DIDN'T FIND any answers as she sat by the window, cursing herself for her loss of control. First, she should have never gone over to Isabel. What did she think would happen?

It wasn't a surprise that attraction still flared easily between them, but under the circumstances, that wasn't enough. Grace hadn't been looking for a relationship on the cruise, and she wasn't now, though she had come home wondering...She tried so hard to avoid these kinds of entanglements, so why had Isabel such an easy way of drawing her back in?

Grace would celebrate once she had secured a number of clients to come with her, once she had signed a few contracts.

The fact that her department had been closed down for alleged lack of efficiency didn't help. It was still Isabel's doing, and she had been willing to forgive her because she…What? Had the hots for her? Grace frowned at her own phrasing. That seemed rather…pedestrian. The facts didn't change though. She couldn't throw herself into this, get distracted, the way she had been on that cruise when she didn't realize what was to come.

Isabel was angry, and she was vulnerable, something they shared, and Grace doubted anything good could come out of it. No matter how much she would have loved to allow those hands to go further, pleasure her the way they had before…

She needed a glass of water, a cold shower and a good night's sleep.

Tomorrow she'd make smarter choices.

* * *

THIS TIME, Grace barely made the morning's first block on time. As the day before, the chair next to her remained empty, and she caught the instructor giving it a slightly frustrated glance.

Grace could relate, though she was aware she might be the one responsible for Isabel's absence. Would they ever find a way to talk to each other, without the innuendo and suspicion?

"Good morning, everybody. Welcome to Day Three of—"

To the surprise of Grace and everyone else in the room, Isabel walked inside and hurried to get to her chair, mumbling an apology as she passed the instructor who gave her a welcoming smile despite the disruption.

Something was different about Isabel.

Grace needed a moment until she realized that in lieu of her usual neat buns, she was wearing a ponytail, the way she sometimes had during the cruise. Her clothes weren't exactly casual, but as close as Grace had ever seen. Even on vacation, she had worn those form-fitting sheath dresses, the t-shirt and linen pants she had chosen this morning, quite the contrast.

Grace was still irrationally, helplessly attracted to her, even though she had slammed on the brakes last night.

"For what it's worth, I'm sorry too," she whispered. Isabel's smile was as pained as it had been the other day.

"It's fine. Don't worry about it."

"Before we start, is there anything you'd like to say?" the instructor asked, much to her credit, not a hint of impatience to her tone.

Grace wordlessly shook her head.

She found it harder to relax and focus, which was ironic since the day before, she'd been wondering why Isabel was missing the class. Beside Grace, she was sitting in her chair stiffly, the opposite of someone about to delve into pleasant imagery.

Until now, Grace had the impression that Isabel was pretty much unshakeable, especially when it came to what she considered useful or not in this seminar. If she didn't know better, she'd think Isabel was nervous. About the upcoming presentation?

Truth be told they hadn't talked about it much outside class, and certainly not after a bottle of champagne. This couldn't be anything new or nerve-wracking for the woman who determined the fate of a company and its departments with the stroke of a pen?

It didn't take Grace long to realize that it was the present class that seemed to bother her.

She leaned over to her and whispered, "Don't worry, this is kind of fun." It wasn't that Isabel Windsor didn't know how to relax, in fact, Grace knew from experience that it was just one more thing she was excellent at. Her imagination might go to interesting places today...and why did she seem to forget all of her caution around her, again? Maybe it was because Isabel looked close to frightened.

"Is everything okay?" The instructor had come over to them.

"Yes. Please, proceed," Isabel said coolly.

"Are you sure?"

"I am. Let's get going."

"All right. Let me know if anything changes."

This time, Isabel closed her eyes, but the tension radiating off of her made Grace wince. She wanted to reach out, but in order not to startle her, she resisted the impulse.

* * *

The presentation revealed a different side of Isabel, almost chameleon-like. She portrayed the "difficult" client with ease, making Grace forget about the questions she had been harboring since the morning. If anything, she knew how to handle difficult, and she could tell their work impressed both Marie-France, her colleague Louis, and their fellow attendees.

Every once in a while, Grace needed to remind herself that high school was long gone, and that her plan had worked out—those who had tormented her daily had no more power over her life, and for sure they had nothing to do with her losing her job. The business world could feel like a frat house sometimes, but she was an adult with skills and power of her own.

As much as Isabel's actions had set her back, at the moment, she was reminding Grace of these facts.

She couldn't help thinking back to last night with regret, not even completely sure what had held her back. Isabel had her own demons, but she wasn't one of the mean girls. Could she be an ally, of the kind Grace had hoped to find here? And could they reconcile those goals with that undeniable attraction?

It would be difficult to say the least. None of them had ever even raised the question of a relationship. They hardly knew each other beyond…well, that. Intimately.

"Great job," Marie-France praised. "I see you've done your

homework. We'll use all of that in tomorrow's starter block. Have a great afternoon, and I hope you'll enjoy exploring the city. Isabel, could I talk to you for a second?"

Isabel looked startled at the request. Grace wondered, if given everything, she still wanted to do sight-seeing. She looked tired, but then again neither of them had gotten a lot of sleep, last night, or since the day they'd arrived here.

"Sure," she said.

Grace left the room but lingered in the vicinity. She didn't mean to eavesdrop, but she felt that she and Isabel still had some issues to resolve, despite the successful presentation. Regarding the curriculum, they were on the right track.

Everything else…that was yet to be determined.

CHAPTER 7

Isabel

Isabel hated surprises. Having to face them in a state of sexual and otherwise frustration made them worse, not that she couldn't have predicted what would happen. At least she hadn't run from the class, like that other time. Like Grace had all but run from her hotel room, but that was something to be dealt with another time. If at all. The timing never seemed to be right for them.

Marie-France asking her to stay behind was one of those unwelcome surprises, and the timing couldn't have been worse. She suppressed a sigh watching Grace leave the room, not that she had anything to say to her.

"You know we take attendance seriously, and sometimes we ask guests to leave their comfort zone. Isabel, I want you to know it's not our intention to force anyone to do something they're not comfortable with."

"I understand that."

"Is there something that is important for us to know?"

Marie-France was only being kind, Isabel could see that. She still didn't appreciate being singled out. Here, it didn't matter so much because she was among strangers. Back at home, she couldn't be seen as someone who had *issues* when everyone else just went with the program. It might not be right, or just, but that was her reality.

"I'm fine, really."

The woman's patience was as endless as it was irritating.

"The kind of accommodations that employers rarely ever make, we can make them here."

"I appreciate it, but..." Isabel got to her feet, signaling she was done with this conversation. "There's no need. I have a lot on my mind, that is all."

"All right. If you change your mind, please let me know."

"I will. Thank you."

Isabel forced a smile and walked out of the room slowly, not like she was fleeing from anything. She couldn't deny the relief at seeing Grace standing outside. That in itself was disconcerting, but she needed things to stabilize themselves again.

"You're still here," she commented. "Are you sure you're not spying on me?"

Grace didn't seem to get the joke.

"I just wanted to make sure you're okay."

Isabel hadn't fooled her, unfortunately. She didn't think it had shown, or that anyone else had guessed that she had been uncomfortable, to say the least. That was a mild interpretation.

To the instructor's soft voice, she didn't slip into the scenery of a mild summer night, a comforting place to detach and take in her successes. Her mind slipped right into dark, cold waters, no surprises or secrets there, at least not to herself.

But they only had a few more days, and after that she'd get the piece of paper she needed to present to Peter, and she could move on with her life.

He'd be placated. He had no idea what he had unleashed. She realized Grace was still waiting for her to speak, so she did.

"I'm fine. And don't worry—*we're* fine. You were right. We both have a lot to consider and don't need any distractions."

If Grace was disappointed Isabel was letting her off the hook, why had she run? Isabel wasn't naïve or fooling herself. The champagne might have encouraged them, but they were headed in that direction anyway.

"Okay. I've been thinking about what you said yesterday."

I said many things yesterday, Isabel thought. Maybe she should have stayed in her hotel room and worked, but if she was honest, she had enjoyed every part of the evening. The local delicacy, the champagne, their heated kisses up against the wall of the room... The memory caused a rush of sensation and arousal, contradicting her earlier words sharply. But the part where Grace left had not been enjoyable.

She couldn't take so many risks, take her eyes off the prize. She wouldn't mind something to help her take her mind off those cold, dark waters. Isabel suppressed a shudder.

"What part?"

"The sightseeing. It sounded nice."

A nap sounded more pleasant at the moment, and besides, what did it mean? Did Grace want to invite herself?

"Yeah, but I'm not sure I have time. I'll have to take care of a few things first."

"Me too, but then we could go? Honestly, I'd hate to go home without seeing anything of the city."

Isabel hadn't intended to socialize with anyone here, let alone go sightseeing together—least of all with Grace McAllister. She could be flexible if the situation required it.

"As long as you don't run away before the good part..."

Grace's smile was worth it. "I promise. And I'm really sorry. How about we meet in an hour?"

"That works for me."

They weren't friends, or lovers. For the remainder of the seminar, they'd be, well, friendly.

* * *

IF THERE WAS anything Isabel had learned in the past few days, it was that Grace had more of a Plan B than she had expected. She had been opening up more and mingling with the other attendees during the break.

Isabel knew that everyone in that room and their employers could be helpful, or they could crush her endeavor before it had even begun. She believed in pre-emptive strikes, so she texted Sam and let him know about a promising new enterprise he could spread the word to their contacts to.

Grace might never know, but that would make them even. It mattered to Isabel, to start on a clean slate, darker waters notwithstanding. Whatever they were or weren't ready for at the moment, it wouldn't hurt to keep tabs on her.

Any news on the new board member?

Not yet, Sam texted back. *We'll let you know as soon as we know. How's Québec?*

Full of surprises, Isabel sent and tossed her phone into her purse.

She had enough time to get ready for an afternoon, possibly evening, in town. She was living dangerously, but the sights of the city, not to mention exquisite Grace McAllister, would chase away the remnants of darkness. Everything was under control, the way she liked it.

Grace waited for her in the lobby. She too, had changed from business attire for something a little more suitable for their visit, the sundress, and her hair falling down to her shoulders reminiscent of unusually lighthearted times. Isabel suppressed a sigh, the longing irrational and futile.

"Hey. You're ready?"

Grace got to her feet. If she found Isabel's tone unusually cheery, she didn't comment on it. Isabel wasn't exactly faking it. She'd need a little time, and perhaps their shared activity for today would be the reset she needed.

Normally, the streets crowded with tourists would make her cringe. To her surprise, her usual claustrophobia she felt around a lot of people, familiar or strangers, big or small crowds, didn't kick in full force. Instead, the chatter around her, in many different languages and accents, presented a relaxing white noise. The people around her looked happy, eager to explore, and they would do the same.

They took the funicular to the lower level of the city where they visited small boutiques and art galleries, and eventually came up to the *Place Royale*, the location where the city had been founded. The market square and surrounding buildings reminded her of European cities she had seen.

"*Notre-Dame-des-Victoires*," she remembered the name of the church from a flyer at her hotel she had leafed through. "The oldest stone church in North America."

"Marie-France wasn't kidding," Grace said. "You did your homework. Do you want to go inside?"

Isabel hesitated for a moment. It had been years since she'd last been inside a church which was less an expression of rebellion and more the reality or her devoting all her time to her career. With few close relationships since her parents had passed away, there had been no obligation either.

Grace seemed interested though, and it was hot, so she agreed. "We could have a coffee afterwards," she said, pointing to the café behind them.

"That sounds good, though I might go for ice cream. I saw someone getting soft serve close by."

They went inside. Isabel had to admit that her attention was more on her companion than on the history of this place. Adoration. Infatuation. She usually had a better handle on her emotions, and she had disliked the worried look Marie-France had given her earlier. Along with the concern, she had offered encouraging words, but Isabel wasn't sure she truly understood what the goal for her was.

The walls she'd built around her served a purpose, one that the cool somber stone walls around her reminded her of. She had to be careful about who to let in.

A weeklong seminar, a stroll in town, even their blazing hot connection, it might not be enough. Time would tell.

But she really wanted that ice cream now.

She also wanted to take back some of the words she'd said earlier.

* * *

"What are your plans for the evening?" Isabel asked when they finally had that ice cream in front of them.

"You still haven't gotten enough of my company?"

It wasn't working as well as it used to, she reflected. Grace could see through a lot of her tactics. Which was scary and exciting at the same time.

"Forget about it. It's fine." Isabel was doing a terrible job hiding her disappointment.

"Come on! I apologize."

"Apology accepted." That was all it took to regain her confidence. "You must excuse me for being cautious," Isabel continued. "The last time I was deprived of your company rather abruptly."

"You're going to hold that over me forever? I thought we had agreed."

Had they? At the same time, Grace's words had intriguing implications. Isabel wasn't fooling herself. Not the forever part, but at least they had this evening. Maybe tonight, or was she getting ahead of herself?

"So, did you have anything in mind for tonight?"

"Actually, yes," Grace confirmed. "There's a revolving restaurant called *Le Ciel* I wanted to try. It's not far from the institute, and a few of the others went to lunch the other day. They loved it."

"Revolving? At what speed?"

"Not too fast, but apparently you can go around once easily during a meal. What do you think?"

She definitely couldn't get enough of Grace's company, especially in moments like this when her enthusiasm shone through the caution that they all had adopted as a means of survival in a cutthroat world.

Maybe she was fooling herself, but realistically, what bad could happen? They'd go their separate ways soon enough. She would have to deal with Peter soon enough.

"Why not?"

"Great. Before we go back, let's go into one of those tourist traps."

Isabel couldn't help it, she was probably wrinkling her nose. "Why?"

"Because I need to buy overpriced maple syrup and candy to bring back. Perhaps a hat." She laughed at Isabel's expression. "Okay, maybe not a hat, but I would like a reminder. I had fun today."

Isabel had to admit it. "Me too. So, let's see if we can make a reservation at that restaurant."

As they walked back to their hotel, reservation made, she had to say it again.

"Thank you. I really enjoyed this afternoon." Including that ice cream. When had she last allowed herself to stop for such a trivial, sweet indulgence?

She had done some sightseeing in various cities, but that almost exclusively happened in the context of having to entertain clients. Certain famous restaurants and museums. At the time, Isabel saw no reason to complain, because every one of those outings brought her closer to her goal. This was the life she wanted.

Her forced time-out came with unexpected consequences. The good ones were all because of Grace.

Isabel pushed aside the pang of guilt. There was no reason. She had paid her dues. Grace's business would be successful.

CHAPTER 8

Grace

It made her ridiculously happy that Isabel had moved on from whatever it was that had bothered her this morning and enjoyed their shared tourist experience. She had to be careful. With the alcohol. With her heart. The structure of the seminar had provided some protection from her runaway emotions, but a few hours outside of it…

She still thought that she had a point, and Isabel was on the same page. They were going to make the best of this time, then Grace would go back to her still young consulting business, going after clients, while Isabel returned to chopping up companies.

Part of her still wanted to ask why, because none of the higher-ups had given her anything but vague excuses when the department was closed. They hadn't held back with their opinion on Isabel Windsor though, and looking back, she wondered who had been telling the truth.

Regardless, tonight, she wanted nothing but enjoy the view, the one right in front of her, and the one outside the huge windows that wrapped around the entire restaurant. Office towers nearby, mountains in the distance, the ever-present river, and currently, Plains of Abraham, and the Joan of Arc Garden below. Isabel tore her gaze away from the sight to focus on the cocktail menu.

They decided to start with one of the restaurant's signature cocktails, a spin on Tequila Sunrise.

Isabel gave her glass a wistful glance.

"Yeah. I didn't expect to find so many reminders here either. We had fun, didn't we?"

That elicit a wry smile from Isabel.

"Some people have told me I don't know how to have fun."

"I don't know that that's true at all."

Grace had the eerie impulse to apologize again. What had she been thinking? And what had she been afraid of? Isabel didn't want to do her harm. In fact, all the harm she could do was already done.

As she held Isabel's gaze, ambience and insinuations shifting, Grace came to a new, somewhat terrifying conclusion. Maybe her problem wasn't that she worried Isabel might use their brief but intense connection against her. On the cruise, she hadn't known who Grace was. The reason why she had run from her hotel room the other night might be something completely different. The same reason why Grace had invited herself to Isabel's sightseeing afternoon and was taking her to dinner now. If she took another step, she might not be able to go back, be in too deep, unable to detach.

And perhaps she didn't care.

Especially when Isabel reached out to brush the back of her

hand against her cheek, right here in public, something that was uncharacteristic. Her smile softened.

"Thank you. I'm glad you think so."

Before Grace could process what had just happened, a friendly and engaged server brought their wine and appetizer plates, breaking the spell.

Everything was on the table.

Maybe she was letting Isabel off the hook too easily, for being gorgeous and sexy, and the memories they'd shared not knowing their paths would cross again in a less amiable way. Maybe Grace had been overdue to reassess her priorities, working harder than everyone else in the department, never finding time to stop and *think*. She had *thought* she'd be up for a promotion soon, that her qualities were valued. Her direct supervisor was, impossible to dress it up nicely, lazy. Much of the work he should have done fell to Grace and her colleagues, though they rarely got the credit for it.

She wasn't going to let anyone exploit her that way again, and the connections and conclusions formed during the seminar would help her achieve that goal.

Isabel might have had a point. But she had done the same thing to other companies, and not everyone involved could fall on their feet like Grace had.

"Do you like it? Your job?" she asked.

"I do," Isabel returned to her surprise. "I know you probably don't see it the same way, but I help companies survive. Be better equipped for the challenges they face. There's a reward in that."

"Regardless of the collateral damage." She didn't mean to provoke, but she was curious.

"That's not the best part," Isabel admitted. "Sometimes, it's impossible to avoid. I stand by my decisions. I didn't think you wanted to discuss that tonight."

"I really don't. But I was serious when I said there's an opportunity for me here. I'm not going to waste it. Just don't take too much credit."

This time, she had hit the right note. Isabel's smile brought heat to her face, and other places.

"I promise I won't, not for this, anyway. I know my areas of expertise."

Grace drank another sip of the wine, too hasty, too much. More heat.

"You sure do," she returned. "To be honest, I had heard a few things about Isabel Windsor, and I had no idea she was so good at...fun."

There was a sparkle in her eyes that suggested she accepted the challenge.

And they had barely made it to the main course, a *Coq au vin*-style dish for Grace, and the catch of the day fish, halibut, for Isabel.

"Maybe it would be a good time for a reminder then."

Isabel gave a polite smile to the server who refilled their glasses with the wine they had chosen, from a vineyard in the area. When the woman had left, she continued in the same soft, conversational tone, "Given that you're prone to disappear on me, I might have to employ new strategies. Make sure you don't run away again."

She took Grace's hand and ran her thumb over the inside of her wrist, the implication clear.

"No, you don't have to do that, tie me up," Grace told her, a little amused, and aroused beyond measure. No, she didn't, but if she wanted to, maybe Grace would let her... "I promise you, I won't go anywhere."

She was willing to accept the inevitable, the beauty of her surroundings and her company having sent her senses into overdrive. The cuisine they were experiencing, was excellent, the wine light and delicious, and the view...They were treated to a spectacular sunset.

"Good. I've had other plans. After dessert and coffee?"

"Agreed. I don't want to miss any moment of this experience."

She wasn't entirely sure, but she thought they were on their second rotation of the restaurant, a spectacular sunset accompanying their culinary experience. Isabel hadn't complained about the speed either. What if for once, the timing turned out to be right?

* * *

BY THE TIME they were enjoying their dessert, a full moon had risen over the city. The name of the restaurant didn't promise too much. It was indeed a heavenly experience, though the woman across from her was as responsible as the setting and delicious food and wine.

Grace remembered distantly that their class started early tomorrow, but she didn't care. She had already learned a lot during this week, most of all that some chances didn't come back.

She didn't want to go back and obsess about the fate of her department, the incompetence of her supervisor and how it cost them. As far as she knew, he had left the company too, and that might have saved them.

As for another kind of chance, right in front of her, at her fingertips…She was supposed to go more aggressively after what she wanted, what she deserved. Tonight, hers and Isabel's goals were aligned.

"Let's go get a cab," she said after paying the bill, including a generous tip for the attentive server who had made this an even better experience.

Isabel looked more at peace than she had ever seen her. It filled Grace with an unexpected sense of pride, and affection.

So be it.

CHAPTER 9

Isabel

IT MIGHT BE SILLY, but for a few heartbeats, Isabel still entertained the fear that Grace might change her mind, again. She was no stranger to being disappointed or even left behind by people who mattered to her. If that had led her to project a cold and uncaring image, it had served her. In her job, as well as in brief and inconsequential relationships that were more stress relief than anything else.

The stress and the pressure to perform would always be there.

Grace wasn't going to run tonight, and relief didn't even come close to describing what she felt when they walked into Grace's suite, pretending to be unhurried, exchanging glances that made her overly aware of the heat at her core. She had enjoyed the moment, each moment, but memory and fantasy blended easily. She needed more. Isabel wanted everything she could get from the present because she doubted it could last. Few good things did.

A bottle of champagne sat in an ice bucket. Grace's light touch to her waist made her flinch with a jolt of desire, an echo warm and wet between her thighs. Imagining them together, remembering, had made her wet moments ago.

"Do you want some?"

She held on to Isabel's hand.

"Yes," she whispered and leaned in to claim her mouth in a heated, unmistakable kiss. She let go in order to cup Grace's face in her hands, leading, controlling the encounter. Isabel was well aware she didn't control much else at this point. Her knees were weak, her body thrumming with the sweet ache, the need for release growing with each second.

She'd been in a state of constant need since the moment Grace had left her room, but she didn't have to worry about that now. Grace reached behind her to pull down the zipper of her dress, her hands warm and confident on her back before fingertips graced the lace of her bra. Isabel's nipples tightened under the careful touch, and she couldn't hold back the moan.

"Don't worry. I'm here."

With her dress on the floor, she was almost naked in front of Grace. The affection in her gaze caused too much emotion, nearly bringing tears to her eyes.

"You're overdressed too."

Before she could do anything about it, Grace opened the clasp of her bra and leaned in to suck a nipple into her mouth, eliciting a breathless gasp. Isabel allowed herself to get lost in the sensation for a few heartbeats, before she said, "Let's go over there. And I want you out of your clothes. I mean it."

With an amused gaze, Grace pulled her top over her head, revealing a strapless bra. She stepped out of her skirt.

"Better?"

"Yes," Isabel breathed. She needed a soft surface underneath her, because her legs wouldn't hold her up much longer, but instead of making the few steps, she pulled Grace close to her, kissing her again as her hands roamed over tempting warm skin. Reliving those memories hadn't even come close to what she was experiencing now.

On shaky knees, they finally made it to the bed, removing the last pieces of clothing between them. The moment their bodies came together, entwined in a sensual embrace, last reservations vanished into thin air. The sensations of feeling Grace against her, arousal coating her thigh, her breasts pressed against Isabel's, took her breath away.

Grace shivered with pleasure, moving beneath her, encouraged by the sounds Isabel couldn't seem to stop making.

She reached between Isabel's legs, fingers meeting warm wetness as they played and teased. She wanted more. Everything. She didn't want it to be over so soon, so she gently disengaged herself and began to explore Grace's pliant body with lips and tongue.

Grace tried to protest, but her resolve didn't last when Isabel's tongue dipped into her navel, hands caressing her breasts. Exploring her, tasting her, Isabel couldn't lie to herself any longer—about the many times she had sat at her desk, slipping back into the memory of their brief encounter on the cruise.

Peter's decision to send her away to learn proper etiquette around unbearable people had been a harsh awakening, and maybe a part of her had believed it could be punishment for having abandoned all rules for a couple of days.

The guilt and constant worry couldn't touch her now. She placed her hands on Grace's thighs, applying gentle pressure. Grace obliged happily, and Isabel leaned in, a brush of tongue against her clit. Encouraged by soft moans and gasps, she increased her efforts, guiding on the steady climb to a deep intense climax.

Grace trembled beneath her. Isabel moved up her body placing kisses as she went and pulled her into her arms. She, too, was shaking, caught between a sweet tenderness she couldn't remember feeling for any of her partners before, and a feverish desire. Come to think of it, she likely hadn't experienced the other part before either, before Grace.

"Take a second," she mumbled when Grace reached for her, because she wanted her to take the time she needed, but she also feared it would still be too quick. Not that she could wait or hold back any longer, and Grace sensed her state of mind correctly. She could read Isabel in a way that was almost scary. Isabel's body remembered the caresses, the magic those fingers could do.

"Please," she whispered, contradicting her earlier statement.

Teasing, stroking, too much sensation yet not enough.

"I got you." Grace's confidence shone through in her quiet tone. "You don't have to beg with me." She proved her statement, action following swiftly. Isabel bit her lip, to hold in a sound, a sob, when she felt Grace's fingers glide into her, moving just at the pace she needed. Between deep possessive kisses, a bit of hair-pulling and those lips touching her breasts, she found relief in giving in—and she finally found the release she'd been craving since she got home from that cruise.

They didn't speak, just listen to each other's rapid heartbeat, the sounds melding.

If they only had a short time again, Isabel was determined to make it count.

Despite the short night, they didn't oversleep, waking up with enough time for another heated encounter before the alarm.

"I should go to my room and get ready," Isabel said, though with Grace in her arms, half on top of her, she couldn't bring herself to move, too comfortable and sated.

"We could have breakfast at the institute," Grace suggested. "Though I'd almost be willing to skip relaxation. She traced a finger down Isabel's arm, making her shiver with delight. "You are a bad influence."

"Am I? That's fine. I've been called worse."

She hadn't meant to kill the mood, but Grace's expression had turned pensive.

"Why don't we get ready and have breakfast here? I could even lend you something. No one will know."

Last night had been truly joyful, though Isabel would draw the line at wearing another woman's clothes. It was too much, too intimate.

"I'm just one floor below," she said. "How about I go, and we meet downstairs for breakfast?"

To her relief, Grace didn't argue. "There's an idea," she said, her smile reassuring Isabel that they were okay. "Unless you'd like to…"

"I'd like to, but I need to be able to walk for the rest of the day." She laughed, then leaned in for another kiss before she got up and gathered her clothes. "I'll see you in twenty minutes, breakfast, and then we can head over there?"

"Works for me. And I'm glad to know I have that effect on you."

"You have no idea."

Isabel still had that smile on her face when she headed to her room. In her world, it was rare that she expected a day to be without complications, but she had to admit that in the context of today's plans, she felt safe.

When could she last say that? Her phone vibrated in the pocket of her dress, and she checked to see a text message from Carla. She'd deal with it later. Shower, get dressed, have breakfast…even that first block wouldn't be so bad with Grace by her side.

CHAPTER 10

Grace

SHE WOULD BE CRASHING LATER, but for the time being, Grace was carried by adrenaline, unexpected jolts of happiness, and caffeine. They made it just in time for the first block to start.

"At least that's not me this time," Isabel whispered when a couple of women came in after them, Ariel and Chantal. With the class about to start, Grace noticed that she'd gotten tense again. She understood the instructors wanted attendees to take advantage of every part of the program, but maybe this part wasn't for everyone.

She assumed that eventually, the creators of these courses would make some adjustments. Grace wasn't sure if Isabel would appreciate a public display of support, or if she even needed it. To be on the safe side, she stole a few glances during the guided imagery. One time, Isabel caught her and gave her a strained smile.

If there was something to share, she would when the time is right. Grace vowed she would at least let her know that she'd listen if Isabel needed to talk.

For the rest of the morning, the instructors were shaking things up and mixing the pairings for the exercises. At first, she was a bit disappointed, but she soon realized that this enabled her to a different perspective on Isabel Windsor.

It was smart, Grace reflected, what the institute was doing, analyzing their strategies and approach to the day-to-day reality of their work in a space as safe as it could be.

Isabel…She was still Isabel *take-no-prisoners, don't-mess-with-me* Windsor. She also appeared more comfortable and confident.

It's for us, Grace thought. She too had stepped into many conference rooms holding herself so straight her back hurt at the end of the day. It wasn't about being nicer or putting a client at ease when they had gone over the line. Her conclusions made her smile. This was exactly what she had hoped for…With the additional bonus of mind-blowing sex, and…what? A beginning romance? She wasn't that naïve, but this time, she might suggest that they meet elsewhere. It didn't have to be a date. It could be anywhere…

As Isabel was obviously warming up to the seminar and her fellow attendees, perhaps they could study the schedule some more. The institute had branches in Paris, Rome, and various other places all over the world. Neither she nor Isabel liked to be idle for too long, so that might be a good compromise. The ILIW had many more interesting classes they could benefit from. Exploring more cities together would be a definite benefit. Landmarks, history…hotel rooms.

"Where would you like to go? I'm starving."

Grace took a moment to answer, realizing she had missed the end of the class when Isabel sat back down next to her. Despite the long night and the seminar day starting off with her least favorite block, she seemed energized.

"You don't want the buffet?"

"No. I want to be somewhere alone with you," Isabel stated bluntly. "There are many smaller restaurants not far from where we were yesterday. I'm sure we could get lunch somewhere around there."

"Okay. Let's go."

Grace hadn't expected that on their way out, Isabel would open the door to an empty room, pull her inside and kiss her deeply.

"I thought you were hungry," she gasped, every thought of food rapidly fleeting from her mind.

"I am," Isabel returned, her smile all but predatory. Grace shivered in anticipation of familiar pleasures.

"Oh, good. Lunch can wait."

She couldn't, she realized, breathless with desire, liquid heat pooling between her legs. Isabel kissed her again when she slid her hand beneath the waistband of Grace's skirt and panties. Grace closed her eyes, her attention split between the incredible sensations, the hot mouth claiming hers, fingers massaging her clit, finding the pace and pressure Grace needed.

Isabel's kiss stifled her moan when she shuddered against the perfect touch.

She loved everything about this, she thought when she was struggling to catch her breath, righting her clothes with trembling hands. What Isabel and Grace, what all the women coming to these classes had in common was that they had to project a perfect image most of the time, or at least chase it. It was elusive, because they could never please everyone.

It was true in a professional context, at least. They needed to take charge. Grace was happy to step into that role every day, and at the same time it was an unbelievable relief to abandon all control for moments like this.

"Thank you," the words, unintended but truthful, came out in a breathless whisper.

"You're welcome." They shared another kiss, but before Grace could even think about reciprocating, Isabel opened the door.

"Let's go. Now I'm really starving."

So that was how she wanted to play it? "Fine. As long as I'll have another opportunity?"

"You will," Isabel promised, her voice warm and dark with an unmistakable emotion. "Now we need to go, or we'll be late."

Predictably, all the restaurants in the vicinity were busy during the lunch hours, but the managed to get a table in a corner of a terrace, under a sun umbrella, at a reasonable distance from the never-ending throngs of tourists walking by.

The restaurant advertised excellent seafood, and they weren't promising too much. Grace wondered if it was a good opportunity to bring up certain subjects. Her mind was still reeling from the earlier experience, but Isabel seemed very much in the moment, enjoying her scallops. Grace had gone with an octopus *carpaccio*.

"Is it good?" Isabel asked.

"The best I had since Portugal," she confirmed. "You'd like to try?"

She found it adorable how Isabel hesitated for a heartbeat, just like she had when Grace suggested sharing the *poutine*—as if that was the first thing they'd shared. Finally, she picked up her fork and stole a bite from Grace's plate.

"You're right," she said. "It's delicious. Have some of mine too."

Before she could do that, Grace had to get another subject out of the way. It was now or never.

"I know we're both going to be busy back home. I'll have to put everything I've learned to good use, but…I think I could take a weekend every once in a while." When Isabel didn't respond right away, Grace continued, "Neither of us expected to meet again, but now we're here, and—"

"It means something?" Isabel interrupted her. Her question

didn't sound sarcastic, more pensive, but still Grace understood that she had to tread carefully.

"Maybe? No matter what anyone thinks, we know how to have fun, and we definitely have a lot of fun together. I'm not saying we should—" All of this had sounded better in her head. "I'd like to see you again. There are other ways than leaving it all to chance again."

Did it make sense at all? She didn't mean to suggest an occasional, casual hook-up, but she didn't want to spook Isabel either. Or herself, not when she knew that she was already in too deep.

"I'd love to see you again," Isabel said, her smile warm and caring, putting Grace out of her temporary misery.

"Good." She suppressed a sigh. Some things didn't need to be so hard. "Now I'd like a piece of one of those scallops."

"What did you think I was going to say?" Isabel asked, curious and a bit amused.

"I don't know, but I'm glad we're on the same page."

"Me too." In a couple of words, Isabel revealed a startling vulnerability, making Grace wonder if she had hoped Grace would raise the subject, because there was no way she could have done it herself.

CHAPTER 11

Isabel

WHAT WAS HAPPENING TO HER? Something unexpected, amazing, and scary. Isabel didn't do scared well, and whenever she came close, she usually slipped into the persona that had shaped her and had served her best during darker times of her life. It kept the darkness at bay, dissolving it into nothing more than shadows.

She was still struggling with the innocent approach of getting her to relax first thing in the morning, though she didn't blame the instructor, Marie-France, or Andie. Or any of the women who were taking to it so well, imagining beautiful calm sceneries that provided a distance from the neck breaking speed in which the business world moved.

Grace being close by made it better, and how could anyone know how hard it was for her if she kept pretending she was fine? Isabel had bigger and more important things to do than to rehash the past, she was single-mindedly focused on the future.

Delivering that final blow she had prepared for so long, only to be stalled by Peter.

It might be for the better. She had been holding back, but not with everything. If she had scoffed at Andie's praise in the beginning, she could now feel a shift within herself.

Caution was all too often warranted in her job, but she didn't need to be defensive all the time. Certainly not with Grace who wanted to see her again.

Isabel wasn't yet sure how the logistics of this plan would work out, but they were both smart and efficient. They'd figure it out.

As they wandered along the cobblestone streets that night, past antique shops, and more small restaurants, she did something else unusual for her: She took Grace's hand.

Grace didn't miss a beat, but her smile told Isabel she appreciated the gesture.

For some reason, Isabel's appreciation and approval had come to matter a lot to her, or perhaps she'd been a lost cause from the first night they had shared together.

She realized that she had never called Carla back. She'd take care of it tomorrow. They had another day of the seminar, and the weekend. Isabel would keep in touch and mail the work she had done to finalize her latest project, so she'd have something more to present to Peter come Monday.

But until then, she'd be right here.

* * *

THEY SPENT another night in Grace's room, but this time Isabel had the foresight to bring a change of clothes so they wouldn't have to hurry as much in the morning. Tonight was different from the series of rushed, heated encounters, the pace slow and gentle.

They fell asleep in each other's arms, until Isabel woke abruptly, unsure of the reason.

Whatever the reason, she was wide awake now, with the unsettling feeling that she had forgotten about something important.

Nothing had changed from a few hours ago. Grace was still snuggled in her arms, but the warmth of her body and the steady beat of her heart failed to comfort Isabel. She carefully disengaged herself and got out of the bed. After putting on a robe, she poured herself a glass of bottled water from the fridge, shivering as she cold liquid washed down her throat.

Typical. She had to doubt something good that was happening to her. Even—or especially—something that could have gone a lot differently.

She had her reasons, good reasons for doing her job the way she had in the case of Grace's former employer. Things had worked out for the better, for the company, and for Grace who was putting all her efforts into her consulting business. Isabel was determined to make sure that said efforts would be rewarded.

They were fine. They were going to see each other again, on occasion, sharing ideas, laughter, pleasure.

It was real.

Seeing that Grace was still fast asleep, Isabel picked up her phone and went to the living area where she sat in an armchair by the window. Isabel, too, had a view of the river and the bridge whose name she had yet to learn. Smiling wryly, she remembered that one of the seminars the institute offered was something along the lines of "making friends inside and outside of business."

Maybe it was what she needed, because her line of work, and her life didn't lend themselves to making and maintaining friendships. At this moment, she wished there was a friend she could call, to share with them that maybe for the first time in her life, she was truly happy.

"Couldn't sleep?"

She flinched, almost dropping the phone at the sound of a quiet voice. Grace, now wearing a satiny negligee, had appeared out of nowhere.

"I'm fine," she said, putting the phone aside. "Just relaxing."

"Well."

She loved the mischievous smile that came with the one word. Grace's offer didn't disappoint. "Maybe I could help you relax enough to go back to sleep."

Isabel might not have had the same thing on her mind, but she could be persuaded. Grace never seemed to have a problem doing just that.

"What did you have in mind? I'm open to suggestions."

"That's a good start."

Grace put her hands on Isabel's knees, gently opening her thighs before she dropped to her knees. Isabel held her breath long enough to feel lightheaded for a few heartbeats.

"Don't tease," she warned. "I might not be responsible for my actions."

"Don't worry about it. I know you've been patient all day."

Isabel leaned back into the chair, her sigh seeming obscenely loud in the quiet of the night. True to her promise, Grace didn't make her wait, and a moment later, she felt the warm soft pressure of her tongue against her clit. How could she have ever hesitated when Grace suggested they should see each other again?

Isabel knew one thing for sure: This time, fantasies and memories wouldn't be enough. She wanted Grace in her life, the laughter, the ideas, the deep sensual connection she'd never had with anyone before.

It was never too late to see the light. Grace's timing was perfect as usual.

As her body came down from the high, Isabel thought that she might be able to sleep.

* * *

SHE MANAGED A FEW HOURS, but the day was still just dawning when she sneaked out of bed again, reassured, ready to tackle another day. They would only spend a couple of hours on Saturday. For the rest of the time, they could do more sightseeing…or never leave this room. So many attractive options in her future.

She checked her messages, frowning at finding several from both Carla and Sam, her stomach starting to flutter. This couldn't be good. She was also convinced that they wouldn't send this many if it was just about supporting the business of a woman who was asleep in the room next to her.

Why now? She had only just begun to feel comfortable here, going far beyond making the best of a bad situation.

Even if she hadn't told Marie-France and Andie the whole truth, she had clearly benefited from the distance. From Peter, the company…

She had plans. Isabel wouldn't let anyone stand in the way.

Determined, she opened the first message from Carla.

Call me back. URGENT.

She went back to the first one, feeling the color drain from her face as she read.

It's Joel Abbott. I think you're familiar with him?

Isabel was. And she could have told Peter that Abbott was the worst possible choice for the company. In fact, Peter should have known himself, given the fact that it was Abbott's department that Isabel had last slashed. For good reasons other than a personal vendetta.

She got up and started to pace, then silently stepped back into the bedroom where she picked up her clothes, got dressed and left. It was much too early for that conversation, not that she intended to have it with Grace, ever.

They might see each other again, spend some time untainted with necessary decisions and shadows of the past.

Back in her own hotel room, she went to the bathroom and splashed cold water on her face. Some of her plans might need to be implemented sooner than expected. It would be better to go home on Sunday, meet with Carla and Sam to strategize.

They had no idea what was about to happen, and Isabel planned to keep it that way, but she needed to know without a doubt what she was going to walk into on Monday.

Damn it. She stared at her reflection in the mirror, her shell-shocked expression. Her eyes were burning, but she wasn't going to give in to the impulse. Taking a deep breath, she went over the things that needed to be done now. They would just happen faster, but they would still happen.

Isabel had no doubt now why Peter had sent her here, have her out of the way as he invited his buddy to the board. Abbott shouldn't be sitting on any board or be in any position of power again. She had worked towards that goal for almost five years, and she'd make sure she would succeed.

First, she needed some caffeine. She ordered a small breakfast from room service, then called Carla's private number.

Carla picked up right away.

"So, you finally checked your messages."

"I check my messages when I have time to check them," she returned and almost apologized. But Carla had moved on already.

"We were stunned to say the least. I mean, everyone knows his department wasn't efficient, and it went poof because you—"

"I know the story, thanks," she interrupted, not feeling apologetic any longer. "What are you hearing? When will he start, and did Peter mention anything about me?"

"He just told us that while the department certainly wasn't viable, Abbott was a good friend and an excellent addition to the board. He said it wasn't his fault that productivity was down."

Isabel scoffed.

Joel Abbott was the ultimate archetype of a mediocre and lazy man coasting on his privilege for most of his life. Isabel would have done away with his department even if she didn't have personal reasons. They hadn't even mattered much in her previous decision. They mattered now.

"The department might have been salvageable if it hadn't been anyone but him in charge. He was the one responsible." Isabel took a deep breath. "Check Peter's calendar and let me know if he can see me first thing on Monday morning. I have a few things to tell him that might change his mind."

She had no illusions that Peter would consider most of Abbott's transgressions as dealbreakers, but some of them might make him worry about the company's reputation. Isabel knew him, knew without a doubt that he cared about the bottom line most of all, his friends, maybe next. Just like the rest of them, he had to keep connections in mind, so she'd have to choose her steps carefully. If she played her cards right, next week could make all the difference.

It would be her time.

Isabel wished the realization could come with more of a sense of triumph, rather than urgency and apprehension that made her shoulders tense up again.

"I'll call you," she said when she heard the knock on the door. Her breakfast. Isabel got to her feet to open, freezing when she saw her visitor. Not the room service.

"Can I come in? And good morning."

Grace didn't wait for an answer but went inside instead. As much as Isabel had come to cherish her, she didn't think she could handle her presence at the moment. Or the questions she likely had.

Isabel had too much to think about. Too much at stake.

"When I realized you were gone, I decided I wasn't going to wait," Grace explained, her gaze open and hopeful. "I don't want any secrets or games, not after...everything. Please, just tell me what happened, what's on your mind."

Oh, where to begin.

"Nothing," Isabel said. "Don't worry, it's nothing. I just needed a bit of alone time to get ready for Monday."

Grace cast a look at her desk where her laptop, tablet and phone sat, together with a neat pile of folders and papers.

"Is that why you couldn't sleep?" she asked, her gaze softening. "Are you expecting any trouble? You did the class like they asked you to."

"I can't talk about this right now." She didn't want to be rude, but she needed her to leave. Right now.

"I'll see you at breakfast then."

A knock on the still open door made both of them spin around.

With a friendly greeting, the hotel employee pushed her cart inside.

Isabel knew the exact moment Grace realized that she had ordered for only one person. The disappointment.

"Okay. I see. We'll talk later, I assume." She walked outside. Isabel had to rein in the impulse to call after her and ask her to stay, all of a sudden terrified that Grace had completely misunderstood.

CHAPTER 12

Grace

She got Isabel. She had promised her, and Grace did understand her, better, she assumed, than most people. The connection they had wasn't just sexual, they shared a way of life and a certain approach to it—so why was she still worried?

The past few days had been intense, the seminar, the two of them, emotions running high. Isabel needed her space, and it wouldn't harm Grace to stop and think either.

Think, rather than obsess. The week was coming to a close. It made sense that Isabel was redirecting her focus to work, and so should she. Grace couldn't help going back to last night's bittersweet intimacy. If Isabel had received bad news, she apparently didn't consider Grace the person to share it with. Not yet.

It didn't mean whatever had begun between them was already over.

Grace decided to have her own breakfast at the institute's

catering table, mingle, do what she had come here for in the first place. Everything else would resolve itself sooner or later. Grace wished for it to be sooner, and she would do her part, but first, she needed food and caffeine.

She hoped she had made it clear enough to Isabel that she could reach out to her.

Deep in thought, she left the hotel and took a cab to the institute where a few women were already assembled in the breakfast area. She recognized Ariel and Chantal who sat at a table together but were each engrossed in something they were reading on their cell phones.

Chantal looked up when Grace passed her by on her way to the buffet. She had a faint headache. Caffeine had become somewhat of an urgency.

"Hi, Grace. You have to try those crêpes. They are amazing."

She was going to have a buttered toast and black coffee, not in the mood for a treat, but she smiled and nodded.

"Thanks for the tip."

Over Chantal's shoulder she caught a glimpse at an article on her phone, something about her former boss. Grace suppressed a sigh. He was connected, so it wasn't a surprise that he'd fall on his feet and right into a well-paying position. The old boys' club worked. More than ever, she was determined to take away from this week as much as she could. The institute's mission statement didn't say it in so many words, but Julia Baker-Zucchero's intent was clear nonetheless: Enable women to shatter glass ceilings and form bonds than made them competitive in the cutthroat world they inhabited. To pick their battles, and then go home and detach, knowing that they deserved every bit of their success.

"Would you mind if I sat with you?" she asked.

"Of course not," Chantal said, and Ariel nodded with a smile.

She was going to find out more. It might be connected…With Isabel being involved in the department's shutdown, Abbot might try to go after her. She had to do a few inquires of her own, and then she needed to talk to Isabel. Her insights might be valuable, and they could likely prevent a battle from becoming public and ugly.

Instead of going with Chantal's suggestion, finally, she chose a croissant, butter and jam, and some fruit, and the biggest size available for her coffee.

"Short night," Ariel remarked with a knowing smile when Grace sat down at their table. Ariel laid her phone next to her plate, a picture of Joel Abbott, Grace's former boss, smiling smugly on the screen.

It made her a little less excited for her breakfast.

"Aren't they all?" she returned. "There's a lot to learn, and we have to keep an eye on things at home."

"That's right, you started your business already. I hope it will do well. I don't wish *him* well."

It wasn't a huge surprise to Grace that Joel was well known, and not all that well liked. She had often found him disrespectful, especially to younger women. Looking back, she remembered how she had hoped for this job to be a steppingstone. An opportunity might arise when he messed up and the higher-ups would appreciate that it was mostly her who did all the work.

"I guess I don't wish him anything, and that's the nicest thing I can say about him," Grace acknowledged.

"Did you hear he's going on the board of Hopkins'?"

Chantal let her words hang in the air, obviously wanting to gauge Grace's reaction before she said anything else.

"Really?" All of a sudden, Isabel's abrupt retreat made sense. Not only was Abbott likely looking for revenge, but he might also be trying to turn others in Isabel's company against her.

"I'm sorry," Ariel said.

"Well, I don't have to work with him anymore. I wish it wasn't so easy for people like him, but other than that, nothing I can do about it."

Except she could help Isabel improve her position.

"You're okay with this? I think someone might owe you an explanation." She cast a meaningful look at the door. Isabel had walked in, but she didn't acknowledge any of them, just walked past the area to the seminar room.

"Isabel? I don't think she invited him to the board. What?"

Her stomach turned before Chantal explained, "I'm not sure about the source of this article, but I've seen a few others this morning. They say it was a done deal, kill your department, wait it out and then get him on the board. Everyone else who lost their job, who cares?"

She didn't want to believe what they were insinuating.

"I wasn't too happy about it, but I still don't think it's entirely Isabel's fault. She was making her decision based on the numbers."

"They say she asked for this project specifically. Are you sure she didn't know what was about to happen?"

Grace had been sure, until now, when the thought sprang to mind that Isabel's odd behavior might have another reason. What did that mean? For Grace? For the two of them?

"I'm sure there's an explanation. In any case, it's her who has to deal with him now, not me."

Another, less polite reaction flashed on her mind. *What. The. Fuck?*

But she wasn't going to get ahead of herself. She couldn't believe that Isabel would go along with a plan to let multiple skilled employees go and secure a sweet deal for frat boy Joel Abbott at the same time.

Grace contemplated skipping this morning's classes, but she had too much invested at this point, on every possible level.

She would get to the bottom of this.

CHAPTER 13

Isabel

"Is there any particular reason?" Andie asked softly, far too sympathetic, when Isabel told her she had to leave. Isabel wasn't completely oblivious to the kindness of people around her, the mentor who had shaped and enhanced her and Grace's efforts, or Marie-France who possessed mad coordination skills, Louis and the others. That didn't change the facts.

"I can't talk about it. I might be able to come back for the rest of the day, but there are a few things I need to take care of." She shrugged. "You know how it is. Little fires to put out everywhere."

"Many of us are in that situation," Andie acknowledged. "It's too bad that the powers that be can't leave us alone for five minutes, even if we work on something that they benefit from, too."

"Yeah." Isabel couldn't deny it. This was all Peter's fault to begin with. First, he had given her no indication that he had a problem with the decisions she'd made regarding Abbott, then he invited him in and made her look incompetent, or, well, oblivious. She was aware of the nervous fluttering of her stomach, too much caffeine. She hadn't been able to eat anything.

It had to stop. It would. The tables had turned a long time ago. Abbott just didn't know it yet.

"Okay. You take care of what needs taken care of and come back whenever you can. I'll notify the others. *Bonne chance*, Isabel."

"Thank you." She could use all the good luck she could get, even if the outcome depended on so many more factors. Most of all, on her keeping it together and sticking to the plan.

"And remember, if there's anything else you'd like to talk about, we are here for you. If it's something we can't solve here, you know we have a network of professionals to connect you to."

"Thanks."

Isabel could tell from Andie's genuine smile that she might have been up for a little more talk, but there was no time to waste. "I have to go."

Outside the door, Isabel quickened her step, hoping to avoid more helpful conversation and concern, especially from Grace. She hurried past the breakfast area and back to the elevator. After she arrived in the lobby, she marched straight to the door, down the stairs and towards one of the waiting cabs…only to change her mind.

Another sunny day, she might as well take advantage while she still could. Isabel kept walking in the direction of the hotel, past restaurants and bars, a few of them serving breakfast, most of them closed at this moment.

She wasn't sure how much time had passed, but she found herself back in parts of the old town she and Grace had visited. Isabel remembered how treacherously light she'd felt. She should have known it couldn't last.

There was another voice, protesting that assessment, pointing out that she could still talk to Grace once she had sorted out this giant mess. Only for that, she would have to start sorting, not walking around aimlessly.

She wasn't ready to do any of it yet, at least the heavy parts. Peter had forced her hand, and she had to react accordingly, but it might be a good idea to finish the seminar, not to tip him off. Or Joel. As long as they thought she was here working on her social skills, they'd be clueless as to the storm that was coming.

Better that way.

Next week around this time, revelations would rise to the surface, and all hell would break lose.

She might just as well enjoy the scenery until then.

Eventually the smells from restaurants getting ready for the lunch crowd started to tempt her, and she found a table with a view, where she could set up a mini workstation.

Isabel resisted the urge to go with nachos—too messy—and ordered a salad and some fries instead. A glass of *Cabernet Franc* too. Who could blame her? There was no one around to judge her anyway, for missing the dreaded parts of the seminar, for avoiding Grace.

Come to think of it...

She sent a text message, *I'm sorry. We'll talk later*. Isabel could breathe a bit easier afterwards, which was ironic. She had successfully escaped the trap so many women found themselves in, which meant that in a business context, she rarely apologized. This time...It might just be necessary.

She was surprised to find her phone ring seconds after. Wasn't Grace supposed to be in class, the same class Isabel had excused herself from earlier?

"I'm surprised," she greeted her. "Don't tell me you're skipping class."

"Actually...I am." Grace sighed. "Isabel, I need to see you."

"I have to take care of something now. Later—"

"No, not later."

Isabel was taken aback by the hint of...anger? Sure, she had sneaked out on Grace this morning, and all but run from the institute earlier, but she had to understand there was a reason? Andie had, apparently.

"Okay," she relented. It had been a long time since she had felt like this for anyone, butterflies in her stomach a sign of affection or anxiety, she wasn't sure. "I'm at..." She read the name of the restaurant from the menu the server was handing to another patron. "*Sapristi.*"

"I'll be there in a few. I'll see you then."

She couldn't afford to get nervous—too much depended on her staying calm. Determined, Isabel called another number right away and got to work.

* * *

WHEN GRACE WALKED into the restaurant fifteen minutes later, Isabel felt a little more reassured that things were under control. She had talked to Carla and Sam and outlined a plan for how to proceed.

Come to think of it, a small part of it might interest Grace, in case Joel felt like sabotaging her business. Small minds operated like that and given the power he'd have on the board of Hopkins, she wouldn't put it past him. But they had a few days before everyone would settle into the new balance. She hoped.

"I'm glad you're here," she said, her smile as genuine as it could get on this mostly awful day. "Please, have a seat. I'm sorry I started without you, again." The fact that Grace had sought her out, even skipped class to do so, made it a little less awful, though she couldn't let her guard down yet.

"That's fine." Grace sounded pensive. Disappointed?

Isabel did have a few things to make up for, although she was certain Grace remembered the previous night as fondly as she did. That seemed like forever ago.

"I have to ask you something. When you shut down our department…"

"It was necessary," Isabel returned, wondering where this was coming from. She had thought they were past it. Grace was happy where she was now, wasn't she? They had toasted to her venture with champagne, and unbeknownst to Grace, Isabel had put safety measures in place.

"So you keep telling me. Why did you want that project? This one, specifically?"

"What? Where did you get that?"

Oh, it had been true. Being the one responsible for Abbott's firing had been a fleeting, but most welcome moment of satisfaction.

"Does it matter? You said it's not personal, but you asked to be put on the project. Could you tell me what I should make of that?"

"Nothing." She was aware her answer had come too quickly for Grace to believe her, though she was far off. "Everything I told you is still true. It wasn't personal. I assume that you weren't privy to all the numbers. I didn't know you, or the others." It was mostly true. She had names and numbers, but Abbott was the only one she had known in person at that time. "I make my decisions based on the facts."

She couldn't help wincing at another lie hidden between truths. She wasn't ready. If she wanted any chance at striking first, something she had prepared for years, she needed to steer Grace away from the pressure cooker that would be her workplace come Monday.

She might be going back tomorrow, to have the weekend to prepare, or obsess.

"Why do I have the feeling you're still not telling me everything?"

Isabel had to make a decision, and she had to make it quick. A necessary sacrifice? One she could live with? Time would tell.

"Grace, I'm sorry, but I don't have to justify my professional decisions to you. I told you everything I could. See, this was exactly what I was worried about when I came here. Everyone at the institute has good intentions, but it's a small world, and people are talking."

"I thought that I was more to you than the outcome of a professional decision. I don't know. Maybe this was a mistake."

"Wait," Isabel said, cringing at her despair coming through clearly in her tone. "Could we just postpone this? You see I'm really busy. Things are moving fast, and I have to prepare for Monday."

"Sure. I won't keep you."

"Grace, please."

She had already turned and walked away. Isabel watched her, regret familiar and bitter in her heart.

CHAPTER 14

Grace

Isabel eventually returned to the seminar, finishing her tasks —individual, group, and the ones she and Grace had to do together. She was different from the woman Grace thought she had come to know in the recent days, doing and saying everything that was expected of her, but really just going through the motions.

Grace realized she was starting to come to the end of her own line, struggling to deal with this new development after the intensity they had shared.

Or maybe it was that intensity that represented a problem? If Isabel hadn't set out to destroy her department out of personal revenge, why was this rumor floating around? Why wasn't she even trying to dismiss it?

She and Isabel had another session with Andie where they were starting to compare their initial goals to their achievements during the week. She could tell the other woman was frustrated with both of them though she did her best to hide it.

Grace didn't blame her. She, too, felt like they were going backwards. She understood emergencies, and there was obviously something Isabel felt needed fixing, but why wouldn't she talk to her?

"Is there anything else you'd like to add?" Andie asked after a nearly two-minute silence.

Grace had thoughts, but she had no intention of sharing them. *So stupid and naïve of me to think that this was more than sexual.* Because that's what it meant if Isabel used this workplace situation to conveniently shut her out, didn't it? What else could it mean?

"Grace?"

"No, thank you."

Isabel shook her head.

"Okay. I'd like you to write down a few points we can discuss at the end, about how you plan to go forward. Be as specific as possible. You don't have to use real names if you're more comfortable that way, but I want you to have something concrete on paper. You will have the afternoon, and we'll get together at the end."

When she still got no reaction, Andie added, "That will be our last session this week. As you know, everything tomorrow will be with the entire group. For any comments or critique you'd like to share in person, this would be the moment."

"Thank you," Isabel told her. "I appreciate everything you've done for us. This has been very…insightful."

Was she serious? There had been a time when Grace was sure she could tell, but now she wasn't, and it bothered her. Certainly, not everything was Isabel's fault. From the moment she realized Isabel had been her short-time companion on the cruise, she had been too eager to leave their differences aside. It hadn't been that hard, she had to admit, when they had so much more in common.

When they later sat at their respective desks in the sun-filled room, she wondered if she had been fooling herself about that too. There was a reason why she had kept her head down and done the work, not realizing that Joel was single-handedly making sure they'd be out of a job. Maybe she wasn't as detached and driven as Isabel. If that was the lesson of this week, she would have to work even harder to make her new business venture work.

She remembered what the other woman had said about not wishing Joel well. She understood their sentiments. She didn't think he had paid enough attention to her to consider her competition or an obstacle in any way…but she might have to be prepared for that regardless.

She looked up to cast a glance at Isabel who had her gaze hefted to the paper she was writing on.

Longhand. Grace allowed herself to get lost in her observations, Isabel's handwriting as elegant and sexy as the movement of her hand…hands that had touched her with passion, and tenderness.

She couldn't go there. If Isabel didn't want whatever it was between them to continue beyond this place, there was nothing Grace could do. And she had to protect herself.

* * *

GRACE CONTINUED what she had set out to do. She finished her assignment, and later that day, she told Andie in detail about her hopes and expectations.

"I have a list of clients I need to follow up on, and a couple of others that are already scheduled for Monday. I think I had to remind myself why I was doing this, that it's really worth it."

Isabel nodded. She hadn't said much, and Grace thought she hadn't gotten all that specific about her Monday plans either, though she had actually written a few pages. Whatever was on her mind, it was sharp and organized, because she hadn't stopped once.

"Isabel?"

"I have enjoyed this week." Isabel arranged her papers, so they overlapped in a perfect congruent rectangle. "And I think my employer will be happy with the results. I'm sorry, but I'm waiting for an important phone call. Is there anything else, or could I leave now?"

"That's fine," Andie said. "I'll see you tomorrow."

Grace guessed it meant that she could leave too, but instead she remained seated, wrestling with all those emotions she couldn't afford to have. There she thought she could give Isabel some insights about her former workplace and the new board member…Isabel obviously had it under control, and she was no longer interested in anything Grace had to offer her.

"You two did well together," Andie commented, ever supportive.

Not well enough, Grace thought. "I should go too."

She got to her feet, all of a sudden fighting stubborn, embarrassing tears.

"I'm sorry. I think I'm just tired…I've had a few short nights."

Her face heated when all the ways Andie could possibly interpret this came to mind.

"I swear this is not a case of TMI." So, she had lied, but it was necessary to save the last shreds of her dignity.

"I get it," Andie reassured her as they both got up to walk out together. "All this introspection is intense, and it can be taxing. But it's important going forward. The more you know about yourself, the easier it will get for you to determine a path forward."

"It's not me you have to convince." To her surprise, the smile came easily.

Andie returned it. "I gathered that much. We do our best to

tailor our efforts to every attendant, but sometimes there are dynamics at play that we are not privy to."

"Or that attendees don't want to share."

"That too." They had reached the lobby and were walking towards the front door. "I see you at dinner tonight?" Andie asked.

Grace remembered only now that one was scheduled for the last night, with everyone in the group, attendees, mentors, and instructors. It was supposed to be fun. Earlier, she had been hoping to make one last attempt at talking to Isabel, but it didn't look good for that.

She likely wasn't going to show up tonight either, given the fact she had run from the last session.

"I think I'll be there," she said.

* * *

Isabel's seemingly frosty exterior intrigued and challenged her environment, Grace observed during the few moments they were out together.

One night, they visited the casino, playing around with a few of the machines, losing some, winning some, it didn't matter so much to Grace, but Isabel seemed to get frustrated with the randomness.

"Let's try something that requires actual skill, shall we?" she asked. Grace had no objections, distracted by the tone of Isabel's voice and the memory of other skills she had masterfully applied the night before. And just this morning.

"Poker?"

"Sure."

A couple of men had overheard them and possessed the confidence to invite themselves.

"You wouldn't mind if we joined you, would you? We could teach you some tricks."

The corner of Isabel's mouth just barely moved. Grace was about to tell them off, so her jaw nearly dropped when Isabel said, "Yeah, let's see what you have."

They found a table, and one of the men, Jake, who looked like he might know his way around a surfboard, ordered a round of drinks. Grace whispered to Isabel, "Do you know how to play?"

Isabel had the perfect poker face. "I think so..."

They might be in trouble. Grace had been quite good in her postgrad days, but that was a while ago. A challenge, no doubt.

It turned out that the biggest challenge was not to get distracted by Isabel who stayed calm and cool even when it seemed like she was backed into a corner. Grace was ready to quit when the men's expressions reflected something akin to pity. One of the lessons she'd learned in life and business was that you couldn't win them all. Literally.

"Isabel, how about we call it a night?"

"Not yet." The warm whisper against her ear instantly took her mind off potential losses.

"We're not entirely heartless," Jake's companion, likely an investment banker or something of the kind, joked. "Let's go back to the bar and have some drinks? On us."

"One more round." Isabel smiled sweetly, and that moment, Grace knew. Her? Discipline was an immense turn-on to Grace, and it was no surprise that they stumbled into her suite half an hour later, giddy, bringing back a substantial amount of money, even given their salaries. At least Grace assumed that Isabel's salary had to be in a similar category, since she could afford this cruise.

"You are amazing," she enthused, kissing her deeply.

In Isabel's expression, she could read a rare show of emotion.

"I would seem that you bring me luck."

"Look at all that money! I want to make it rain all over the bed."

Grace laughed when Isabel's face contorted into a display of disgust.

"You know how many people touched that?"

"Okay, you might have a point. Besides, there's only one person I'd like to touch tonight."

"Is that so?"

The sexy smile, as Isabel stood, arms crossed over her chest, went straight to her core.

Discipline. That summed her up regarding most things, and it made Grace desire her with an intensity bordering on feverish.

* * *

Discipline. Whatever was disturbing Isabel right now, she had chosen not to share it, to let it show, and there was nothing Grace could do but wait.

That was driving her crazy too.

CHAPTER 15

Isabel

IN THE SITTING area of her hotel room, Isabel finally closed her laptop. Outside, dusk had fallen, the lights of the bridge connecting the city with the Île d'Orléans now a familiar sight.

Alone with her thoughts, she could admit that she hated to leave things like this, leave Grace wondering about her true reasons. She couldn't tell her yet, couldn't tell anyone before setting her plan in motion.

It was too risky, because she would only get one chance, to leave the past behind, rid herself of any demons lurking.

She would not accept any position in which she'd have to answer to Abbott in any capacity. When she talked to Peter on Monday, she had to be precise, make sure he knew what kind of risk he was taking. Should he not see reason, it would be time for Phase Two.

If she had to put it in motion, many things would happen fast, and she would have to be ready to step in, not be distracted by...

What exactly? A flirtation? An affair she couldn't seem to let go of?

Bad timing, bad coincidences, perilous emotions she couldn't ignore or erase.

After next week—would it be too late? Would Grace resent her since she'd once again be the last to know?

Was there any alternative?

She couldn't be off her game. Once the smoke had cleared, she might be able to do some damage control. All she could do in the meantime was drown her sorrows. It would come to an end like all things did, and if the memory of those nights together were all that remained, she had to live with that.

So be it.

She picked up the phone to call room service but changed her mind. Isabel left her room and went to the now familiar door. What would she do, say? She had no idea. A desperate one-last-ditch effort to make Grace see she hadn't lied to her where it counted?

Isabel knocked on the door, waited, then repeated the action when laughter floated over to her from the distance. She saw Grace standing with Ariel waiting for an elevator. The two women didn't notice her.

Self-conscious, and abhorring the emotion, Isabel waited until they were gone, then returned to her room and ordered her dinner after all. She should be more disciplined than to give in to the lure of more wine and that local delicacy, basically the gourmet and more expensive version of a tasty fast-food dish. Isabel would have iron discipline come Monday, but she needed to let go a bit first.

It wasn't like she hadn't taken anything away from this week.

* * *

She had fallen asleep only to be jolted awake by the nightmare, wiping angry tears from her face. *Fine. Get it out of your system.*

Isabel hadn't found a safe place in her imagination because she didn't believe such a place existed. She knew what she wanted from life, a career, security, a certain lifestyle that enabled her to enjoy the good things and give where she could. Put her talents to good use, reap the rewards she had earned.

Long before she met Joel Abbott, she had known that there were privileged groups who would do whatever they could to keep someone like her from reaching her goals. Straight white men born into wealth, feeling entitled to positions of power without the hard work.

He had crowded her in the copy room, suggested he could help her career in exchange for sexual favors. Isabel was one of the luckier ones, all things considered. After a colleague walked in on them, she escaped with threats to her person and was forced to sign an NDA.

Isabel kept her job as a base from which to plot her master plan, biding her time. She had known that colleague would never back her up, and she wasn't willing to throw her career away, recurring nightmares notwithstanding.

Abbot had never tried to touch her again, but she was certain he had done this before and gotten away with it. Eventually, Isabel had left the company and gone with a new employer on her own terms, trying to put the incident past her best she could. When the company's file landed on her desk, she had no regrets about shutting down his department. He was a predator, plain and simple, and it was about time someone stopped him for good.

If Peter had other ideas, he would have to accept that he might end up collateral damage.

After everything, would Grace still answer her call, or had she already moved on?

Isabel Windsor was nobody's fool. One way or another, her life would change in the coming week.

She just wished it could have been with Grace by her side, in her corner.

Apparently, she couldn't have it all. If Joel was taken care of for good, she would have to take the win and cut her losses…the way she always had.

CHAPTER 16

Grace

AGAINST ALL ODDS AND REASON, Grace found herself turning her head every time the door of the restaurant opened. Every time she was disappointed—Isabel hadn't changed her mind and joined the group. She wondered if she had overreacted earlier, the questions weighing on her.

"So, some of your firm's old clients came to you. That means they did value you all along." Chantal commented.

Grace knew she wasn't simply lucky, but she didn't have so many illusions either. A few of them had simply preferred dealing with her directly rather than Joel, and she was the only one of her former colleagues who had gone into business. She did have a couple of calls out of nowhere though.

Grace didn't believe in coincidence, or anything that looked too esoteric to her, but she was convinced she had done the right thing by coming here. Julia Baker-Zucchero and her team weren't promising too much. Intense? For sure.

"And I hope they'll continue to do so. It's nice to pay the bills."

She might be exaggerating, but of course, without clients, bills would be a problem at some point. Strange to think that six months ago, she had believed herself to be in a stable, secure job.

She refrained from the impulse to shake her head. If Isabel wanted to end things, whatever they were, she didn't owe Grace an explanation. She understood the demands of the job and business as usual. Grace couldn't shake the feeling that there was more at play. She didn't think she had ever been a target, but she still had so many questions only Isabel could answer.

"Definitely. And it's nice to do it without indulging sexism and homophobia," Ariel added. "No one should have to do that."

"Oh, I agree."

She thought back to the beginning of the seminar, and Isabel's more cynical approach. She wasn't completely wrong. It was tough to shine a light on all the wrongs and still find a path, but as Andie had said, knowing her own limits and priorities would definitely help.

Where would Isabel draw the line?

Had Grace missed opportunities to call out Joel Abbott?

Some of those questions couldn't wait any longer.

* * *

SHE TOOK a cab from the restaurant back to the hotel and made a quick detour to her own room. Grace stood in front of the mirror, trying to calm her mind before she would make that step.

Would she, really? In the past few years, Grace had learned her lessons without much of a doubt. Showing weakness could be dangerous. In business. In a relationship. She had forged her path anticipating events, reactions, outsmarting opponents.

She had still been taken aback by the developments at her firm, and she had still fallen for Isabel.

It was impossible to deny. She knew who she was, and what she wanted. Priorities. She was going to take that risk.

She went to Isabel's door and knocked, only to be met with silence, save for her loudly beating heart. Just because it was decided, it didn't mean it was easy.

A couple of other guests passed her by, but it was no one from the seminar which filled her with relief. Chantal and Ariel might have figured it out, but regardless of anyone's opinion on her—association—with Isabel, Grace was a private person who appreciated the kind of discretion and intimacy they had established between them.

Was it all already in the past?

She was about to turn away when Isabel opened the door to her, and the words "Are you okay?" were out of Grace's mouth before she could come up with anything better.

Even though it was late, Isabel was still fully dressed, her make-up faded, hair bound into a loose ponytail. Grace easily interpreted her expression, because she had perfected it herself, put on a distant, neutral face when the emotions raging underneath were too much.

"Can I come in?"

"Yes. Sure." There was a hint of resignation, though Grace couldn't tell if it was for her, or the general situation Isabel was dealing with at home.

"I was hoping you might join us."

She could tell by the surprise in her expression that Isabel hadn't expected that.

"I wasn't exactly friendly earlier. I'm sorry. There's a lot going on."

"Yeah, I figured. Were you able to fix whatever it was that needed fixing?"

Isabel gave this some thought, maybe stalling, maybe trying to choose the right words.

"It will take longer to fix, but I've made some progress."

"Good." Grace walked further into the room and to the sitting area by the window. Isabel's laptop, tablet, phone and papers were neatly arranged on the desk. She was aware of Isabel's tense posture, though she didn't intend to try and catch a glimpse. "Look," she said, turning to Isabel, "I don't want to prod, but I want you to know you can trust me. I'm sorry too if I insinuated anything…"

If she had meant to protect her heart, Grace was going a terrible job at it. She couldn't stay away, couldn't let things be.

"It's okay," Isabel said, longing softening her tone.

Temptation was rising.

"Thank you. But there's something I meant to ask you. Maybe it's important to you, too, since you have to work with him. How was it possible for Abbott to be invited to sit on your company's board? You must have some insights."

"Why do you want to know? You don't have to worry about him anymore."

So Isabel did? Worry about him?

"Maybe I do, if he's petty about some of our clients liking me better."

Isabel made a scoffing sound. "For sure he'll be petty about it, but you don't have to worry about that either. Grace! You don't think I would do my job, and then open a backdoor for that asshole? If you must know, nobody asked for my opinion when they made the decision. They sent me here to be out of the way. I heard about it the same day you did."

"I'm sorry they went behind your back."

"Yeah, me too, but there's nothing I can do about it now."

Defeatist Isabel didn't sound right to Grace. In fact, her missing classes and working around the clock in hotel rooms and restaurants didn't seem that defeatist at all. She tried not to be hurt about the fact that Isabel was still stalling, that she didn't seem to consider their relationship the right context to share... Another thought came to mind, the possibility tightening her chest with sadness. What if no one had offered before?

"It's late. I thought you were having a nice evening with the other attendees." That, too, sounded wistful. "Was this question really that important?"

"It was. But most of all, I wanted to see you, because I know, that even if you try to hide it, you're upset, and you're hurting. Most people might not see it, but I do, because I've spent a considerable amount of learning how to pretend. And I don't know why you think it's hard to imagine, but I care about you."

She had almost expected that deer-in-the-headlights look from Isabel, because it was a lot to take in. It was a lot for Grace, too, who had never made a speech like this in her entire life.

"And I'm sorry if I haven't made that clear, but I'm here even for the bad stuff. I promise you."

Too far?

Isabel stepped forward and put a finger to Grace's lips.

"I know. And it's kind of amazing. I thought I'd be miserable for a week, and that meeting you here again would make it even worse. Well...Surprise."

"Maybe I can help. I have heard things..."

"I don't want to talk about this tonight." Just like that, Isabel took control again, and when she claimed Grace's mouth in a deep, take-no-prisoners kiss, she didn't try to resist. She had made her point clear, or at least she thought she had. Isabel hadn't told her to go, though Grace sensed that she had been on the verge to do so.

That wasn't going to happen now. Obviously, she, too, couldn't let go.

It was a start.

CHAPTER 17

Isabel

She hadn't meant to sleep with Grace again, not after it looked like they had both half-heartedly accepted that they needed to keep their distance, at least for a while.

Given the opportunity for few hours more of stalling, Isabel didn't stand a chance. She still needed to be careful, she mused when she drew non-sensical patterns with her fingertips on Grace's naked back. She couldn't stop touching her, as if things would be okay as long as she kept up that connection.

She had her ducks in a row, so to speak, meetings scheduled with Peter and a couple of reporters she trusted. She wasn't going to meet them at the company.

Next week, one way or another, the truth would come out, and there would be some sort of fallout. She had taken every possible measure, but she was still dealing with a few unknown variables, and she didn't want any of them to come back and possibly hurt Grace, simply for her connection to Isabel.

They would have to break up said connection, soon. But not now. At this moment she was content, no, deeply happy to experience once more the sensation of warm skin under her hands. She was tired. Grace sighed in bliss under her careful touch.

Isabel wasn't going to sleep. She needed to fill her mind with images and sensations so she could remember them in case they didn't find a way back to each other after everything.

Third chances didn't often come by.

* * *

She had moved up her flight home to Saturday afternoon, torn between regretting making that change, and knowing it was necessary. Isabel would have loved to spend another evening with Grace in town, but it wasn't possible. She had gotten more out of those last hours than she could have hoped.

Still, when Grace accompanied her to the lobby where she waited for her cab after the closing block of the seminar, she had to push back the impulse to blurt it all out. Let the chips fall where they may. They could stay for a few more days, and she would turn in her resignation…

No, she couldn't do that, to herself, or anyone who might be threatened by Abbott's new-found power. She knew how to stop him, no matter what happened afterwards. It had to be her.

"I could go to the airport with you," Grace offered. "It gets boring."

"No, I have things to do, but thank you." She kissed her softly. "And my ride is here. Thank you for everything."

Before she left, she could see Grace's eyes widen as the possible implications of Isabel's words sank in.

Was this a temporary goodbye?

A final one?

Only time would tell.

The fact that her vision blurred when she sat in the back of the cab told her which was more likely. Isabel might win this fight, but very few people could have it all. She might not be one of them.

CHAPTER 18

Grace

GRACE'S FLIGHT didn't leave until Sunday at noon, and now she regretted that she hadn't booked an earlier one. She felt restless and worried, oblivious to the beauty around her as she walked around the city alone.

She couldn't shake the feeling that Isabel's words meant goodbye, that every step forward and making love last night had been a means to an end. Making love. She shook her head. When had she started considering love?

It wasn't just that she understood Isabel. Those days with her, first when she didn't know her last name, then when she realized there was more to Isabel than the woman who had cost Grace her job.

She didn't want it to end here, but she was aware there was a limit as to how far she could push Isabel. She hadn't revealed much. Grace had read between the lines, and she knew now that shutting down the department had been about efficiency, and perhaps something else. Isabel's decision had been overturned only in one case, which meant her bosses might have a stake in the game.

Was Isabel's job at stake too?

Damn it.

All of a sudden, things made a whole lot more sense to Grace. How could she have not seen it? She didn't want to rush to conclusions, but Isabel had been so wary of the morning's relaxation exercise. Grace knew that Andie had spoken to her a few times in private. Contrary to what Isabel had been worried about in the beginning, the institute took privacy seriously.

There was no such thing as privacy on the Internet though, and perhaps she should have done her homework earlier. Grace didn't want to pry, but she wanted to be prepared. Most of all, she wanted to try and correct all mistakes she might have made.

She knew that there had been a harassment charge against Abbott at one time. It had been thrown out in court, which didn't have to mean anything. The most inappropriate he had ever behaved around Grace was to yell at her and mock her outfit a time or too—that didn't have to mean anything either.

She wondered if it would be at all helpful to Isabel if she told her about these instances. Grace found herself a place in a restaurant where she took out her phone and did a quick search.

When the server came by, she ordered a glass of wine from the menu, the first one that she and Isabel had shared. Then Grace went to work.

She didn't find much, but there was a brief mention of when Isabel had left her previous firm. Five years ago, Abbott was CEO of that company at that time.

Grace sat back, absorbing that information. Whatever happened, he was likely out for revenge now, and Isabel had known from the moment she heard the news.

Something was coming, something Isabel clearly didn't want

to talk about, or she wouldn't have tried to distract Grace with a passion bordering on desperate.

She appeared to have a plan though.

Grace needed a plan too.

* * *

She used Sunday morning to make a few phone calls and texts to friends and rescheduled a couple of Monday's meetings. Yes, they were important. This mattered more. She resisted the urge to contact Isabel again.

She had to be patient now. Forget about protecting herself. The premises had changed. There was more to protect than just one person.

After a smooth flight and a cab ride, Grace returned to her apartment, marveling at the changes that had taken place in one week. She felt a lot less anxious than she had a week ago, now that her next steps were clear, and she could give a lot of credit to the instructors and mentors at the institute. Grace knew how to deal with a crisis, but maybe she had needed a gentle push in the right direction, to see what mattered most.

And she wasn't afraid of it any longer.

I love you, she wrote. *Whatever happens, you know you can come to me.*

She let her finger hover over the send button for a few seconds, then clicked.

Grace didn't expect an answer right away. She could be patient when it was worth it.

CHAPTER 19

Isabel

IT WAS NOW OR NEVER. Her meeting with Peter was scheduled for ten, but she had been up since 5:00 p.m., going over her notes again, too wired to sleep any longer.

She had turned off her phone last night, so when she looked at it over breakfast, the message from Grace came up.

Isabel wasn't going to call her today, that she knew for sure, but the sentiment filled her with a calm she hadn't achieved since the moment she had heard the news about Abbott. Grace did that effortlessly.

Love. It was nothing she could contemplate now, a few hours away from a potentially life-changing moment.

Except this, too, changed everything. How could she be so sure? Isabel couldn't say that she had ever been in a relationship that deserved the term, or that anyone had felt for her that way. It seemed both foreign and intriguing, and she didn't know what to do with it under the circumstances.

Knowing the storm she was going to unleash, she would wear those words, *I love you*, like a protective coat.

Peter wasn't in his office when she arrived. Isabel checked in with the two journalists she had briefly spoken to. They were ready to meet with her should things move fast. She sat at her desk, time crawling by as she tried to get some work done but failed horribly.

For once, Isabel didn't blame herself. It would still be there later today.

Five minutes to ten, she got up and walked across the hall to his office. She knocked and stepped inside.

Peter was on the phone, about to end the call.

"Yes, get back to me on that right away. Bye. Isabel," he said with a jovial smile. "How was your vacation?"

"It wasn't exactly a vacation." She kept her tone light, reminding herself that she had bigger aspirations today. "But I got all the papers for you. I completed the course successfully."

"Like I knew you would. Is there anything else? I'm busy this morning."

"I'm afraid there is. We need to talk."

"That sounds ominous," he said, frowning. "Please, sit. I thought the course went well."

"Oh, it did." She remained standing. "This is about the new board member, Joel Abbott. The optics of him joining us after we just got his department closed, are a little odd, wouldn't you say?"

Ease them into it, read the room, strike at the best possible moment. Isabel had done that successfully for most of her career. She wouldn't fail now, even though the circumstances made her lightly nauseated.

"That's what you wanted to talk about? I think it's water under the bridge already. It wasn't all his fault, was it?"

Had he even read the report before he signed off on it?

"He kept information from his employees and failed to

protect them. The majority of this was his fault. Give him a prize, one that will cost the company, makes all of us look bad."

"I think you're exaggerating, Isabel. Abbott is a good man. He'll take this work seriously."

"He is bad news, Peter. If you have ever put any weight to my word, take this from me. He will harm the company's reputation."

"What makes you so sure?"

So, she had to spell it out for him. Isabel wished she had sat down.

"When we worked at the same firm, he assaulted me in the copy room. A colleague walked in, and that was it." That wasn't it at all, but she didn't have the time or room to go into details. "He made me sign an NDA, and nothing ever happened after that, but Peter, there are bound to be more. You don't want anything like this to be associated with the work we do here, with the name of the firm."

She took a deep breath. If all else failed, she had put a name to what had happened. For a long time, she had tried her best to push the memory away, convinced that since the worst didn't happen, she should be able to just move on. But the term was still accurate. And her concerns were too.

She could tell Peter was struggling with what to say, which could have various reasons.

"I have to talk to Joel," he finally said. "These are severe accusations. Why didn't you—"

"I wasn't exactly in a position to disclose," she returned, wrapping herself in the cool distant tone that had so often done the trick. "I wasn't on a personal vendetta when I recommended the closure of the department either."

"Okay. Right. I'm sorry, Isabel. Like I said, I'll talk to Joel, so we can get ahead of this."

"What does that mean?"

"I don't think the board will reverse their decision, so we might have to make the best of that situation."

"You're not serious." She wasn't all that surprised or shocked, but perhaps she had harbored the, albeit naive, hope that it might end here.

"I'm really sorry," he repeated. "But my hands are tied. All the paperwork has gone through already and trying to rock the boat now could cost us even more."

"I see."

"If there's anything I can do..."

You've done enough.

"No, that's all. I assume you'll fill me in on the outcome of that conversation?"

"Of course."

He was lying and being quite obvious about it. It wasn't the first time that he used the jovial condescending tone to determine a conversation was over. If Isabel was honest, things were going exactly the way she had expected them to go.

Worst case scenario for Abbott, he would get a few stern words and a slap on the wrist, but Isabel wasn't satisfied with that. She had waited a long time. She had feared for other employees who might be in that situation, but she was now in a position where she had everything she needed to take care of the problem. Once and for all.

After she left Peter's office, she called the two journalists. She had learned not long ago that the NDA was no longer enforceable. It was time.

* * *

Isabel had put a few safeguards in place. The information Sam and Carla had provided her with, proved that Peter's intention was to keep quiet about the incident. His first call to Abbott had been to warn him.

Assured of that, she met with Kevin and Tessa to discuss the details of their piece.

No matter how certain she was of doing the right thing, by the time she had finished, Isabel was exhausted. She would have to hold out a bit longer.

"Thank you for all of this," Tessa said warmly. "Once we're done, you'll have enough time to read it first."

"Thanks. I assume you will turn up more stories about Abbott."

The two of them shared a glance.

"Definitely," Kevin confirmed. "We already have reached out to a couple of other sources, and…I promise you, he's not going to get out of this. Not this time."

Tessa nodded grimly.

When had she last believed, truly, that someone could be on her side, that she didn't have to do it all alone? The two reporters trusted her word enough to stake their reputations on it. Carla and Sam had never once doubted her.

And Grace, beautiful, inspiring Grace. After they had excused themselves, Isabel stayed behind, sipping her latte as she opened her message once more.

Given how angry she had been to be sent there, it was ironic how the time she had spent in Québec City, with Grace, and at the seminar, had changed something profoundly within her.

She wasn't going to hold herself back any longer. And she would have to find a way to talk to Grace and tell her how much of a role she had played in this, but she couldn't do it while she was still in the eye of this particular hurricane.

When her phone rang, Isabel knew she would be called into one of many emergency meetings to follow.

She put a bill on the table and left. She wasn't sure if Marie-France or Andie were aware, but the lessons from the seminar would stay with her for a long time. She was going to put them to good use.

She was not alone.

Tomorrow, everything would change, and Isabel Windsor was ready for it.

CHAPTER 20

Grace

SHE MIGHT NOT HAVE HAD ALL the information, yet, but her instincts had been right. In everything, Grace still believed that. In the recent media circus, the truth still stood out: Abbott's tenure on the board of Hopkins was over before it had begun, only days after the allegations against him came to light. Abbott and his wife released statement after statement, all rambling and outraged.

Grace had contacted one of the journalists that broke the story, Tessa Hall, and told her about what she knew about the charges dropped in a similar case at her old firm. It spoke to pattern.

Hall hadn't revealed much to her, but Grace could read between the lines. The article had mentioned multiple sources.

For sure, when the powers that be let go of him, and his buddy, former Vice President Peter Hopkins, they had the survival of the company in mind. Grace was still cynical as to how whether doing the right thing had played into this decision, but it was done.

She had been busy, surprisingly so, her phone ringing off the hook, so she had little time wondering about what—else—could have been, had Isabel decided to answer her message.

She hadn't.

Yet.

And Grace was working in her business, so many hours that she was considering hiring staff.

Could it be that Julia Baker-Zucchero's philosophy had done the magic? The beauty of Québec City?

She smiled wistfully to herself as she sat at her desk, once again late in the evening. It had been beautiful for sure. It had been an amazing backdrop for some of her favorite memories. She was beyond lucky to have had this experience not once but twice, but deep down inside Grace knew that she was still asking for more.

Was it greedy? She didn't care. She was greedy where this subject was concerned. The subject of her dreams, and on occasion, daydreams. She knew she had to give Isabel time and space. It looked like she was weathering the storm just fine, and she hoped Isabel knew that her offer still stood, regardless of their relationship status.

Grace could only imagine how hard it had to be, doing her job and at the same time being aware of all the mud being thrown at her online. Isabel had probably expected it, but some of the comments still made Grace furious when she took a few minutes to read them.

She looked over the final bill for a client when the familiar voice, coming from the TV she had on in the background, made her look up. Grace nearly dropped her teacup when she realized it was Isabel, and the owner of Hopkins, at a press conference.

Grace couldn't help staring at Isabel who was entirely back

into professional mode, in a tailored suit, not a hair out of place in her neat bun. It was enough to make her breathless. Lost in her imagination, she missed a few words.

"…will be taking over the duties of Vice President effective immediately. Thank you. I'll be taking questions now."

Grace leaned back in her chair as she watched the rest of the press conference, thrilled for Isabel, anxious at the kind of questions she knew were going to come.

Isabel remained calm throughout, and she ended with the words, "I know there will be some who dismiss or don't believe my experience. I had plenty of questions as to why I didn't come forward earlier, or if I didn't misinterpret anything. The answer is no, I didn't, though it took me some time to understand it. And before I had the option to get the NDA thrown out, I knew I would have faced severe repercussions. I know there are many in the same situation, and if you're watching, I want you to know your experience is valid—whatever you decide, whenever you decide it."

The company's owner added a few more words about the necessity for equal rights in the workplace, and that, too, felt different. He didn't mention the fact that the former VP was his brother's son, likely so embarrassed with the turn of events he didn't want to remind anyone.

Grace picked up her phone, her fingers tingling with the urge to act, right now.

She wanted to talk to Isabel, hear her voice some more…

Instead, she typed, *I'm proud of you. And I still love you.*

She sent the message and winced, hoping Isabel wouldn't think of her as a creepy stalker at this point. Grace would trust her instincts once more.

CHAPTER 21

Isabel

"That was a brave thing to do," Carla said.

"Promoting you?" Isabel asked, and they both laughed. Yes, she had come a long way. It didn't mean she was always at ease with the recent events, yet more so than she could have ever imagined in her lonelier days.

"That was the *right* thing to do. But I'm not joking. I admire you. I've always have."

"Come on. You've had one too many of these." Isabel pointed to the colorful cocktail on the counter of the upscale bar where they were celebrating their respective promotions. In here, they were safe from prying eyes or anyone trying to shove a microphone in their faces. Isabel knew well enough what they were saying between the lines, but she enjoyed the light banter, something so rare in her life.

It occurred to her that she and Carla had never gone out

together outside of work dinners and lunches. Perhaps that should change…Along with other changes.

"All of it can be true," Carla reminded her, and she stopped arguing.

When Isabel was named Vice President, she had the opportunity to pick her team, and she made sure Carla and Sam were rewarded for their constant dedicated work. She had vowed to be a reliable supervisor, to make time for everyone's concerns, to help them unfold their full potential, and give credit where it was due, unlike many of the bosses she had before.

Vice President.

She wished that the path to this position could have been different, but she wasn't going to apologize for being here. Isabel knew she had earned it.

She found her thoughts wandering back to the seminar, her initial reluctance to open up to its potential. There had been moments of banter, moments that had not been related to the job, and yet all those exercises and roleplay scenarios had opened a world of possibilities. For the first time, she imagined she might go back, maybe even reconnect with some other attendees.

The concept worked.

Isabel could work with well thought-out concepts and scenarios, but she hadn't yet managed to solve the ever-present question.

Her days were busy, and so were Grace's, or so she had heard. Isabel felt weird for keeping tabs on her, but she wanted to make sure that everything was going according to plan. Grace had hired staff because she had a lot to do, and the clients who had already worked with her had given her rave reviews.

Everything according to plan…

"You are far away," Carla commented. "Does that have to do with a certain company landing another big client—the one you told me to check on earlier?"

"It's always helpful to keep an eye on the competition."

"Except she's not really our competition…more like a possible partner in the future. And she's…easy on the eye. But I assume you've noticed."

Isabel's glare had no impact on her, in fact she was laughing.

"Yeah, I know, none of my business. On the other hand, I'm paid for being observant, and I couldn't help noticing…You've changed."

It was true. The old Isabel would have retreated behind a protective layer of ice, a word or a look enough to stop such bold behavior from a subordinate. Amused, she thought back to the seminar and one of the classes they offered about the importance of making friends.

Apparently, she had more than she had thought.

"Thank you," she said, raising her glass to meet Carla's.

Her subordinate…companion…friend…didn't ask for an explanation. None was needed.

"Congratulations, Isabel. You have always been the best person for the job."

This statement might have been fueled by whiskey and whatever else was in that cocktail, but Isabel knew how to take a compliment.

* * *

Later that night she sat in a cab, opening the latest text message from Grace. It made her smile, and at the same time, her heart fluttered with anxious energy. She had to answer her at some point, or Grace would stop reaching out.

And if she did…

It was all so easy in her imagination, but the reality was this: Isabel had gotten Grace fired. Then, mistaken her for the wardrobe person, and once again, she was leaving her in uncertainty.

Her reasoning, to protect her from the fallout. Was it still valid?

I'm proud of you. I still love you, said the message.

Thank you, she typed, cringing. *It's been wild around here, but things are finally calming down. I hope you're doing well.*

Isabel hit send. I miss you. I love you too. It was what she really meant to say, and she still couldn't say it. She, too, had a bit too much to drink, and it was making her weepy. She had better be careful the next time. That was the only explanation, wasn't it?

There was no answer, and when she lay in her bed after a quick shower, Isabel wondered if she had been too late. Despite all the steps she had made, her timing was still off. People were still speculating if she had chosen to disclose Abbott's behavior towards her so she could oust him and her old boss.

Regarding Grace...

At around three a.m., the sound from the phone indicated an incoming text message. Bolting upright, Isabel reached for the phone.

I'm good, Grace wrote. *Busy. How are you?*

That was a loaded question. And damn it, it was all true. She had been falling for her during their heated passionate encounter on the cruise. The time spent in Québec City, working with her, exploring their surroundings together while said passion flared once more, had made the truth even more obvious.

With Grace, she had felt seen and understood like never before.

She did love her.

It seemed like the right thing was always also the hardest thing to do.

Was she really that brave?

* * *

CARLA HAD RELIABLY SUPPLIED her with the necessary information as always. Isabel had taken work with her that she wanted to take care of during the short flight. She needed to keep busy, distract herself, or she might turn around and forget about her carefully constructed plan.

Carla's report sounded good, but she had to see for herself. After that, maybe, she could figure out what to do about that message, the way it had shattered her barriers, and what to do about it.

Isabel took a cab from the airport. She arrived before check-in time like she knew she would, which wasn't a problem. She might not even stay overnight but had booked the room anyway just in case.

What Isabel needed to do first of all wouldn't take long. Carla had done all the research. Yet, she felt poorly prepared after leaving her suitcase with a friendly hotel employee and heading back out.

She checked her phone once more to make sure she had the right address. The restaurant was just down the block, a bistro frequented by young professionals from the various office towers surrounding the place.

It was light and airy inside, with big tables and comfortable chairs, something she herself would have chosen for business meetings. Or a quick working lunch.

Isabel stopped at the entrance, her gaze falling on a table at the far end of the restaurant. Of course, Carla's information had been correct. She had expected nothing else.

The longing to just walk up there and reveal herself was almost physical, but she reined in the impulse.

Grace was not having lunch alone, but with a couple of clients, from the look of it. From this distance, Isabel couldn't make out words, but she could read the body language just fine.

Grace was in her element, doing well, now that she was no longer held back by a lazy, inefficient boss.

Isabel was proud of her, and a little proud of herself. She didn't secretly lend a hand to just anyone…She had to admit it was a relief to see that in all likelihood, Grace had forgiven her.

"Good morning," the hostess greeted her. "A table for one?"

"Oh no, I'm sorry," Isabel replied and turned to leave. She cast one last glance over her shoulder, at the puzzled woman, and at Grace.

She wasn't going to interrupt. At least, that was the story Isabel told herself. She had taken so long. Did she even have the right to interfere with Grace's life again? Was it foolish to hope?

Carla had also provided Isabel with various options for her itinerary, and she could be on a flight home late this afternoon.

She walked back to the hotel, lost in thought, wondering if the past few days had used up all the courage she had. Because she didn't feel very brave at the moment.

CHAPTER 22

Grace

She wasn't sure if she should be intrigued or annoyed with the small interaction that she and Isabel had the previous night, much too late for two people who had to be up at six in the morning.

Thanks to a good amount of make-up and caffeine, Grace was making it through her day. Today she was working with her employee Sara on the new project they had signed on just last week, and she had a few interviews for another potential hire.

Focused on the multiple tasks at hand, she still couldn't help pondering Isabel's words. She was texting like that was speaking, without unnecessary frills, but with so much between the lines.

Not always easy to decipher. Isabel was guarded for a reason, but Grace hoped she knew that she was ready to try. Still. She had a collection of beautiful pieces. Grace was so eager to learn the complete picture.

"There you go, boss. Double espresso."

She flinched when Sara put another latte in front of her, realizing her thoughts had been drifting to some of that intimate knowledge she already had.

Not the right time, especially when the first of a few hopeful applicants would arrive in fifteen minutes.

"You're a lifesaver," she said with a sigh.

"That's my job," Sara returned. "Long night?"

"Like every night. We still have a lot to do."

* * *

ALL THREE CANDIDATES for the job were eager and highly qualified, though one of them would have preferred a full-time position. Between the other two, Grace had a favorite, but she wanted to hear Sara's opinion as well, and give it a day.

Regarding the new project, a consulting job for a coffee shop franchise, they had made good headway, and she had hope that both of them might be out of the office before 8:00 p.m. this time.

It was a good thing that she had had success right out of the gate, so she could offer appropriate overtime pay.

Sometimes it all still seemed like a dream, but then she would remind herself that she had worked hard for this, rolled with the punches. If there was a little luck happening to her along the way, Grace would not question it.

At about 7:30 she deemed her progress satisfactory enough to leave for the night. She stepped out of her office to where Sara still sat typing away at her own desk, suppressing a yawn. Grace could sympathize, however, she wouldn't head straight home and to her couch. She had planned to stay awake long enough to treat herself to a nice dinner.

She still made time for a ten-minute meditation every day, and her workdays were more efficient for it. It was something she had learned at the seminar too—these things didn't just work in theory. They made a difference.

There was still a learning curve as she had been employed all of her adult life, always had to answer to someone who had the final say and responsibility.

Grace was that person now.

"I'm calling it a night," she told Sara. "You should, too. There's nothing that can't wait until tomorrow."

"Thanks." Sara gave her a grateful smile. "I think I'm going to start rewatching my favorite TV series. The new season is starting soon."

"Have fun."

Grace walked back towards her own office to get her coat, lost in thought until she realized Sara was greeting someone at the door, her tone friendly and professional despite the hour.

"Oh, I'm sorry, but did you have an appointment?"

Her back turned to them, Grace froze when she heard the answer.

"No. I was hoping I could have a few minutes anyway."

She spun around so quickly she nearly gave herself vertigo. The sound of the voice she had been longing to hear...It wasn't coming from the TV this time. Grace blinked.

Isabel was here, standing in the doorway with an apologetic expression.

Sara sent her a questioning look, and Grace finally moved.

"It's fine, Sara, you can go. Good night."

Sarah hesitated the tiniest bit, curiosity written all over her face.

"Good night. Nice to meet you, Ms. Windsor."

"You too..."

"I'm Sara," she said with a smile before she left.

"Nice to meet you too."

Once the door fell shut behind her, Isabel leaned against it as she held Grace's gaze.

"Hi."

"Hi, *Ms. Windsor.*" Grace loved how the smile was tugging at the corners of Isabel's mouth. She had missed that mouth too. Everything about her. She had to be careful not to get ahead of herself, but would Isabel really come all the way to tell her to stop texting? She might, Grace reasoned. Her stance, relaxed and open, unlike the woman who had all but thrown her coat at her without looking, suggested otherwise. "What brings you here?"

"One of my employees suggested I check out this exciting new enterprise. Satisfied clients all around. She thinks we should be working with them."

"She does think that, huh?"

As if drawn by an invisible force, Grace walked closer. She couldn't help it. She was tired of being worried and afraid. *Know yourself, your priorities.*

"It's true. It was also a good excuse for why I needed to take this trip right away."

"An excuse for what?"

Isabel's expression turned sober, and a bit anxious.

"I needed to see you. Grace, I am so, so sorry I left things the way I did, and then I didn't answer when you clearly…"

"Told the truth? I did. It wasn't easy, but I'm glad I did it. I hope you feel the same…About telling your story, I mean."

Everything else would have been a step too quick.

"You are right about that. It sure brought out some ugly stuff from certain individuals, but I've dealt with that before. It's not what I meant. There was a moment when all of this could have been backfired, badly, and I didn't want you to be associated with it at all. But I believe the worst is behind us, and I have no more excuses."

Grace held her breath.

"I wanted to tell you in person that I am proud of you too. And I love you too."

The only appropriate reaction was to move in, slide her

fingers into Isabel's hair and kiss her senseless. Her patience had paid off in every way.

"I hope that means you forgive me?" Isabel whispered against her neck, making her shiver in anticipation.

Grace was no longer tired.

"I do, as long you'll join me for dinner. And then come home with me."

"I'd love to."

"Good. Just let me get my coat."

Grace stepped back, the relief on Isabel's face making her throat go tight. "I want you to know I understand. You had a lot to deal with. Still have."

"It's not a lie," Isabel admitted as she followed Grace back into her office. "But when I looked at my priorities, I realized that there was something that was more important than anything else. I still don't know if we can make this work, or how...but I want to try."

"Me too." Grace reached for her purse and coat and dropped everything when Isabel pulled her close again.

CHAPTER 23

Isabel

ACTIONS RANG LOUDER THAN WORDS. Isabel understood that more words would have to follow, but she was happy to postpone them now that the hardest part was out of the way.

They could figure out everything else, including logistics, later.

She hadn't had anything to eat since lunch, and Grace had planned to go out anyway. On the way to the restaurant Grace had promised was in walking distance, almost shyly, she took Isabel's hand.

Isabel's first impulse had always been to avoid anything that could make her look emotional in public, never to present a weakness to exploit.

Now, she didn't care about anything but the sensations evoked by the warm tender gesture. She shared a look with Grace, unable not to return the smile.

This felt so familiar. Breathing easier when she was with her.

Isabel had taken a long time to draw the right conclusions. Lucky for her, she hadn't taken *too* long.

"I wanted to hold your hand back then," Grace said wistfully. "The first morning."

"It's probably a good thing you didn't." She tightened her fingers around Grace's lightly, to assure her that it was okay now. Very much so. "I had been avoiding a lot of things."

"I can relate to that. Sometimes it's necessary in order to move forward."

"Yeah. But I'm grateful for having finally exorcised some of my demons. It's less lonely when you realize that there are some people you can trust."

"True."

They walked hand in hand down another street before Grace stopped in front of a door with intricate detail in the wood frame and stained-glass window. She moved to open the door, but then turned to Isabel.

"Could it be that this is our first real date?" she wondered out loud.

"I might be," Isabel agreed, thrilled for the turn this day had taken. Better yet, her life.

* * *

THE RESTAURANT, which happened to be the most recommended Vegan place in town, presented the perfect backdrop for that real first date, white tablecloths and intimate lighting, excellent food and vine.

"So, this is take three," Grace said, her eyes shining in the light of the LED candle on the table.

"It is. And I promise you I'm not going to screw it up this time."

"You didn't. You took the time you needed, and that's fine with me...Even though I did get a little impatient at times," she admitted. "I might have come find you. I was thinking about it, but then I was worried you might get the wrong idea."

"I think it was my turn."

Grace didn't disagree.

"You are doing well," Isabel continued. "I always knew you would."

"One of the reasons being that you made a few phone calls on my behalf?"

Grace's smile took any possible sting out of her words, so Isabel saw no reason for denial.

"You are good at what you do, regardless. It never hurts to form connections, or so some smart women reminded me."

"Yes. And I want you to know I'm grateful. I understand that before, with my former employer…You did what made sense at the time."

"I did."

The server came to bring their dessert, a vegan chocolate mousse.

"How are you doing with everything?" Grace asked, a trace of somberness to her expression.

Isabel took her time to answer.

"Still reeling with it all," she admitted. "I was so used to pushing it all down. But I don't regret what I did."

"You shouldn't. Not just because you earned the job, which you did. You deserve some peace."

It was on the tip of Isabel's tongue to wonder if something like peace could ever apply to their career and lives, but she didn't want to dismiss what Grace had stated with such confidence. And she knew it was the truth.

There were few questions left between them. From the restaurant, they took a cab to Isabel's hotel, where she checked out, and another driver brought them to Grace's apartment.

Home.

When she left her own workplace earlier today, she had imagined multiple scenarios about how this evening would go. Isabel had prayed she wouldn't end up alone in a hotel room and allowed herself fantasies of what could happen in that hotel room —or any room where they could get some privacy, really.

The past few weeks had taken their toll on both of them, but certainty lifted a lot of that weight.

Finally, back in Grace's arms, she didn't mind when after a few shared kisses and whispers, they fell asleep in each other's embrace.

Third time really was the charm.

EPILOGUE

One year later

WALKING THROUGH THE SAME ROOMS, Isabel had felt excitement and gratitude. The sense of dread, of things to come, was gone, and this place, and the people in it, had helped with that a great deal.

She had thanked Marie-France, Louis, Andie and the others by recommending their work in high places. Grace wasn't the only one whose business was booming but like for their friends from the International Leadership Institute for Women, Isabel's contribution was merely a small push—they knew what they were doing, and their success was proof.

Later that day, they embarked on a private cruise on the St. Lawrence River that allowed a breathtaking sight of the majestic Montmorency falls.

Part of their package was a visit to the Île d'Orléans before they'd have dinner on the boat.

They found themselves leisurely strolling along the main street of a small village, stopping at an art gallery. While Grace wandered away to admire large canvasses and eventually started talking to one of the painters, Isabel stopped near the entrance when a display of jewelry caught her eye.

Grace's birthday was coming up in a few weeks from now, and what better gift to get her than a reminder of their anniversary trip? It would be one of the gifts, anyway. Isabel nearly drifted off into a daydream, but she knew she had to act fast. And the perfect item was right in her sight.

She had paid and slipped the small package into the pocket of her coat before Grace joined her again, and almost forgotten it by the time they she and Grace were having dinner to a stunning sunset.

Both of them felt the need to come back, to talk to the people they had worked with here, and to spend some uninterrupted time not marred by misunderstandings and welcome surprises.

In spite of their busy and thriving careers, they had made time to return and explore places they hadn't yet been to. Like this cruise.

Everything that had seemed so far out of reach was right in front of her.

Isabel remembered watching the bridge in the far distance from her hotel room, the sight filling her with, at the time, inexplicable longing and melancholy.

She had always longed to build bridges but been afraid of what would be on the other side, anticipating opposition, and worse, betrayal.

A few people had proved to her that trust didn't always have to end up in hurt, most of all, the woman sitting across from her.

"I love you," she said, her words heartfelt, without hesitation.

Grace smiled, likely because she sensed how big a step this was for Isabel after it had taken her so long to answer a simple message.

But she was learning, they both were.

"I love you too," Grace returned easily. "And I love this. It's quite the romantic backdrop."

With the sun setting, light glittering on the waves of the river, the two of them surrounded by gorgeous nature and in relative privacy, it was.

Once the idea sprang to mind, she couldn't let it go. Isabel had made a habit to prepare for all situations, all the time. She wasn't prepared now, didn't even think they would approach the subject this week, let alone today. Yet she had purchased a *ring*.

"Marry me," she uttered, as the last rays of sun vanished on the horizon, and set the small box in front of Grace.

The emotions in Grace's beautiful expressive face changed quickly from surprised to joyous.

"Right now? I mean yes! You think the captain is going to do it?"

Isabel laughed, deeply happy in a way she'd never felt before. She had completely forgotten that getting married on a ship was a possibility. "I love you so much, Grace McAllister, but no, I didn't think right now. I'd like a bit more time to plan."

"I understand. Planning is good."

Isabel waited, a bit light-headed when she realized she had been holding her breath.

"I'll be honest. I saw this earlier and meant to give it to you for your birthday, but it seemed more fitting…"

"I love it."

"So…Could I get an answer?"

It wasn't until then that Grace realized she hadn't given one yet.

"Of course! Yes. I want to marry you. Now, later, it's all good. Not that I mind this setting for a spontaneous proposal. It's perfect."

She was right, Isabel thought as they leaned close to kiss. Very few things in life were—celebrating them mattered.

"I agree."

What a way to realize that finally, they could have it all.

ABOUT THE AUTHOR

Thank you for reading! Please consider taking a moment to leave a review. Your feedback is welcome and appreciated. If you'd like to stay up to date with new releases and sales, you can sign up for my newsletter here and receive a free novella: http://eepurl.com/dGvo_1

All my titles are available on Amazon:
www.amazon.com/author/barbarawinkes

Sapphic Crime Fiction & Romantic Suspense:

The Crossing Lines trilogy
    The Carpenter/Harding series
    The Joanna Mitchell thrillers
    The Jayce & Emma series (romantic suspense)

The Amnesia Project
    Secrets
    Amber Alert

Christmas Romance

Destination Christmas, Next Stop Love
    Christmas Cupid
    A Girlfriend For Christmas
    Bells Will Be Ringing

Contemporary Romance

Venus & Aphrodite
    Open Spaces
    The Interpretation of Love and the Truth
    The Design of Everything Perfect

Paranormal Suspense

RISE

Speculative Fiction

Cypher
    The Exodus Strategy

VOLUME TWO

ADRENALINE KISSES

ALYSIA D. EVANS

ADRENALINE KISSES

Alysia D. Evans

Copyright © 2023

All rights reserved: No part of this publication may be replicated, redistributed or given away in any form or by any electronic or mechanical means including information storage and retrieval systems without prior written consent of the author or the publisher except by a reviewer, who may quote brief passages for review.

This is a work of fiction. Names, characters, places and incidents are products of the author's imagination or are actual places used entirely fictitiously and are not to be construed as real. Any resemblance to actual events, organizations, or persons, living or deceased, is entirely coincidental.

CHAPTER 1

Meryl

I THREW myself through the doors of the Regal Duchess Hotel. A man in a striped navy suit stood by a table in the foyer, watching water drip from my jacket onto the sparkling marble floor.

"The weather hasn't improved," he said, a forced smile attached to his baby face.

I gave him a merciless scowl. Having walked from the train station in pouring rain, I wasn't ready to make amiable conversation.

His face reddened, and he stared at the clip-board in his hand. "Are you here for the International Leadership Institute for Women's conference?"

"Yes, my name is Meryl McGuire."

He ran a pen down a list, finding my name and ticking a box. "You're the last person to arrive. Here's your seminar wallet." The man handed me an envelope filled with sheets of paper. "I'm afraid you've missed lunch. I'll deposit you in the lecture theater.

They're showing a repeat of our leader's welcome video. You can watch it while you wait for this afternoon's seminar to begin. Follow me."

I yanked the handle of my Gucci cabin case and followed the man into an elevator. In silence, we traveled to the second floor, and walked into an empty art déco inspired lecture hall. I shoved my case at the man and handed him my red leather jacket. "Put my luggage somewhere safe and hang my jacket where it can dry naturally. If it becomes moldy, I'll know who to blame."

He held the jacket collar, about to protest, changing his mind when he saw the sharpness in my eyes.

I turned and entered the hall, treading quietly across the polished wooden floor, attempting to muffle the squeak of my boots. I took a seat in the middle of the room and crossed my legs, staring at a huge movie screen. A stunning female appeared, staring at me with her mesmerizing eyes.

"Good morning," the dream woman said in a sexy southern accent. "Welcome to the International Leadership Institute for Women. My name is Julia Baker-Zucchero. I created the Institute to allow women to develop the skills to achieve. The aim of the next few days is to help you fathom your issues and identify how they are negatively affecting your life. Through our seminars, you will develop your confidence, build positive attitudes, manage your emotions, and develop the ability to make and maintain effective friendships."

"I created the Institute when I discovered I was the abominable person in the office. I became the woman everyone hated. Finding this out about myself was unnerving, and I realised I needed to change. Like me, you will discover things about yourself you may not appreciate." The woman's face turned serious, and she pointed a finger at me. "You will need to change." Her eyes stared at me, then she faded into darkness.

Julia's dramatics didn't impress me; this was just a money-making activity. The cost of the conference was astronomical.

However, it had sold out. Julia Baker-Zucchero was making a fortune from her employees telling her she was a cow.

Fortunately, I hadn't paid, and was attending because I'd won my ticket in a charity lottery. If the conference was rubbish, I hadn't lost anything other than my time. Besides, attending might be good for business. My stomach gurgled with hunger. I popped my last fruit sweet into my mouth and folded my arms, waiting for the conference attendees to join me.

I sucked my sweet and watched women enter at a steady pace. The hall became noisy, filled with the high-pitched chatter of nervous, energetic women dressed in high priced designer wear, taking seats, surrounding me. When a woman sat by my side, she nudged me with her sharp elbows, pushing me out of her space.

A short, rotund woman stood on a low stage at the front of the hall. She pressed buttons on her laptop, and the institute logo appeared on the screen behind her. The woman's keen eyes gazed at the expectant audience. Her thick midlands accent boomed through the microphone. "Okay folks, let's get started. My name is Sonia Armstrong. I've worked for the International Leadership Institute for Women for five years. During that time, my job has grown from welcoming and organising delegates to presenting Julia's seminars." She studied the room, hoping her words were inspiring the eager crowd. "The ladies joining me on stage are Clara, Arabella, and Tabitha."

Each of the women presenters stood, giving a perfect smile and jovial wave when Sonia introduced them.

"Julia Baker-Zucchero, must appreciate names which end in the letter 'a,'" I said under my breath, glancing at the woman by my side.

She stared at the stage, the edge of her mouth twitching into a sneer.

Sonia Armstrong continued. "Myself and these ladies will present the conference seminars, and I will allocate one of them to act as your mentor."

While Sonia's monotonous drone continued in the background, I flicked through my envelope, trying to work out how the conference operated. There were worksheets to complete and advertising fliers for more of these courses. I removed the gaudy adverts, depositing them on the floor beneath my seat.

I stifled a yawn and glanced at my elbow jutting, sneering neighbour. Wearing a grey pin-striped suit and black biker boots, she noted everything Sonia said. When she realized I was staring at her, she turned her face to mine. Stony blue eyes, covered by large round glasses, glared at my damp flower print dress. She sniffed with contempt and shuffled her sheets of paper. Returning her gaze to the speaker, she continued to write copious notes. The woman resembled the others in the room, well-dressed, tedious and dull.

On the stage, Sonia pointed to a PowerPoint slide displaying a list of training sessions. "The motto of our Institute is *'Work hard, be smart and play hard.'* Your chosen seminars will allow you to achieve your ambitions and be successful in business and life." Her eyes wandered around the room, ensuring everyone was paying attention.

A finger tapped my back. I turned my head, meeting the eyes of a young lady. "Hi, I'm Ruby, and this is Joan." With a sharp movement of her shoulder, she nudged the identical-looking girl beside her. "We're twins."

"So I can see," I said with a grin.

Joan peered at me, a delicate smile emerging from her lips. Like her sister, she was elegant, with wavy black hair and delicate facial bone structures. She raised her hand, giving me a coy wave.

"I didn't see you at lunch," Ruby said, her eyes piercing mine.

"No, a business emergency delayed me," I said, concocting an excuse which was more acceptable than me waking late and missing my earlier train. "Did I miss anything?" I asked.

"We had to book into the hotel and decide which track we

were following," Joan said, her voice quiet, reminding me of a leaf rustling in a gentle breeze.

"Oh, okay, I'll check into my room later," I said, telling another tall tale, since I wasn't staying in the hotel. "What do you mean by track?" I leaned forward to hear Joan's whispered reply.

"In your envelope, there are sheets listing a variety of developmental tracks. Have a read of them. They tell you which seminars you need to attend."

Ruby put a hand on Joan's thigh. "I'm trying to develop my sister's confidence. I'm the outgoing, talkative type, but my sister is shy and reserved."

"Total opposites," I said, determining it would be easier for Joan to find herself if Ruby fucked off.

Turning in her seat, my neighbor nudged my arm. "Can you be quiet?" she muttered. "I'm trying to concentrate."

"Ooh, apologies. I'm working out my track. Have you chosen yours?" I asked, sounding as if I knew what I was talking about.

"Yes. I'm attending the collaboration seminars," she said, bristling her shoulders. She adjusted her position, re-arranging her papers.

"Me too," I said, sighing and stretching out my legs.

Sonia, the presenter, pressed her laptop buttons, and dimmed the lights. I stared at the screen, forcing myself to stay awake.

* * *

I WOKE to my arm being shaken. Sonia had stopped talking, and there was activity around me. "What's wrong?" I exclaimed.

My neighbour glared at me. "Nothing! I want to grab a coffee before my seminar. If you don't let me out, I'll be late. Not that my actions are any of your business," she said.

I moved my legs, creating a narrow gap for my neighbour to squeeze through. She was tall, with a slender neck and firm shoulders, features which always turned me on. Sadly, the face didn't match the body.

"By the way," the woman said, pushing past me, "you snore."

Her arm swept over my breasts, making my nipples tingle. A surge of arousal flooded through my body, making me catch my breath.

"She's not a bundle of laughs," Ruby said with a giggle.

Joan smiled in agreement and rested a hand on my arm. "Will you join us for coffee and cake in the atrium?"

I nodded, knocking my brain out of its transfixed state, and followed the twins.

In the atrium, an array of delightful pastries filled a long table. I took a plate, piling it with tasty snacks. Each time I selected one item, I sneaked another into my handbag, wanting to ensure I had enough food for an evening meal.

I sat at a circular table with Ruby, Joan, and two attractive women. My conference room neighbour took the table space directly opposite me.

"Meryl," I said.

"Polly," the woman opposite replied with a firm nod, returning her eyes to her food.

The hair of the woman on my left-hand side spiked into short peeks. Tattoos covered her arms. My eyes followed a scorpion crawling along the muscles of her lower arm, its pincers clenching the head of her ulna. On the woman's biceps, a dragon's tail slunk from the cuff of her short-sleeved grandad shirt. On her neck, a claw emerged beneath her earlobe.

"Hi, I'm Sydney," she said, offering me her hand.

"Meryl," I said, shaking her strong palm, trying not to drool.

She handed me a business card. "You should visit my gymnasium. I could develop your tone."

"I will," I said, her voice slinking around my brain, convincing me to become fitter.

Ruby leaned over and grasped Sydney's arm, drawing her

attention away from me. "Sydney," she gushed, "have you worked with any famous people?"

"Oh, sure," Sydney said, turning away from me and wowing Ruby with tales of her well-known friends.

I sighed.

"Everyone's fancying Sydney," the woman on my other side said into my ear.

I glanced at her. She was wearing a thick plaid shirt, outdoor trousers, and leather hiking boots. "Can't blame them. She's striking."

"The name's Bernie. How you doing?"

"I'm doing just fine," I said, mimicking Bernie's mid-west voice. "Did you hike here?"

Shocked by my question, Bernie squinted and furrowed her brow. "Err, this is Joan," she said, introducing her neighbour.

"We've already met." I gave Joan a wave. "So, Bernie, are you looking forward to the seminars?" I asked, tucking into my food, groaning when my stomach greeted each mouthful.

Bernie tucked an unruly red curl behind her ear. "I sure am. I need to gain a lot of skills and learn how to run my new outdoor centre."

"I could help you with your learning," Joan said, a surge of confidence emerging from her body.

"That'll be mighty fine," Bernie said, a huge smile covering her ruddy face.

I reached for a jug of water, accidentally knocking a glass. It toppled, crashing onto the floor. "Oh, shit," I said, waving to a waiter, pointing to the broken glass.

Joan screeched, curling her legs beneath her, huddling close to Bernie.

"Hey now, don't be so nervy. It's only a glass, nothing to be worried about," Bernie said, squeezing Joan's arm.

"I'm so pathetic," Joan said, unfurling herself, sobbing.

Bernie handed her a serviette.

"There's always one accident-prone person in a group," Polly said from across the table, glancing from her mobile phone and sneering in my direction.

"Are you implying that the person is me?" I asked, returning her glare.

"If the cap fits."

An administrator arrived at the table. "I'm collecting health and safety, and permission to be photographed forms," he said.

Polly handed him her completed slips.

"I'll get mine to you later," I said, biting into a tiny quiche, savoring the taste of lobster. "Oh, this is so delicious," I spluttered.

"Here are mine and Joan's." Ruby handed the man two sets of forms.

Joan blushed; the administrator gave a charming smile.

I groaned and shook my head.

"What's your issue?" Ruby's friendly demeanour disappeared with her huff.

"I can't believe Joan needs you to act as her supervisor," I said with a shrug.

"How rude," Ruby said, scowling, waving her hand around the table. "And there's me thinking the six of us could be friends."

Polly glanced at her, a look of horror on her face.

Bernie took Joan's hand and gazed into her eyes. "I'd be happy to be Joan's friend," she said. "It would be my pleasure."

"Excellent, our first sign of progress," the administrator said. "Let's give this lady a round of applause for providing Joan with unquestioning friendship." He clapped loudly, circling the area, ensuring everyone joined his exuberance.

Ruby linked arms with Sydney. "Why don't the four of us sit together at the next seminar? And get to know each other," she said, winking at her new beau.

Joan attached herself to Bernie, and they wandered away from me and Polly.

I stuck my tongue out at the departing group. "I hope I won't be seeing them again," I exclaimed.

Polly shuffled her worksheets into a neat pile. "You should consider why you're here," she said, staring around the room and sighing. "I suppose you're the same as the rest of us imperfect souls, trying to escape your pathetic life." She stood and disappeared into the lecture hall.

I shook my head. I needed to find myself some new acquaintances.

CHAPTER 2

Polly

I SAT ALONE in the lecture hall waiting to start the late afternoon session, *'Developing confidence.'* The large assembly of women from this morning had diminished, and we'd only be a small cohort. I hoped that awful Meryl woman wouldn't join the group. She was obnoxious.

The door swung open, and Arabella Arkwright, the speaker, entered, followed by Ruby, Sydney, Bernie, and Joan. Arabella stood at the front of the room, counting the attendees as they arrived, and took their seats. A body plonked itself by my side.

"Fancy meeting you here," a familiar voice said. "What's this session about?"

Turning my head, my eyes met Meryl's. "It's described on page four."

Meryl scanned her muddled worksheets.

"Give them here," I said, grabbing the sheets and re-organizing them. "There, the seminar is about how to develop your confidence. Not that you look as if you need to learn anything about that."

Meryl gave a relaxed shrug.

Arabella tapped the microphone and gave a throaty cough. "Hello, ladies. I hope you enjoyed your coffee and cakes." She glanced at a few faces and smiled at my keen eyes. "Before I plow through my slides, we need to take a few deep breaths and relax our thoughts. This will help you focus on my words and open your minds to the activities we'll be carrying out."

Activities! No-one told me I'd have to do things. I believed all I had to do was listen to the speakers and learn how to improve my communication skills.

On the other side of the room, a timid Joan raised her hand.

"Yes, Joan," Arabella said, pointing to her. "Please share your thoughts with the group."

Embarrassed by Arabella's attention, Joan lowered her arm.

With a straight back and a calm smile, Arabella walked toward her, holding out her hands for Joan to take. "Look into my eyes," Arabella said. "Now stand." She raised Joan's hands with her own, almost yanking her out of the seat, and her finger raised Joan's chin. "There, stand tall, attend the room, and speak your words."

Joan pulled back her shoulders and gazed from left to right. Myself and the entire group stared at her. Meryl gave a sardonic grin. If I was Joan, I'd want to give Meryl a kick on her rude backside.

Joan coughed and cleared her throat. "What activities are you planning?"

"Excellent question." Arabella pushed Joan back into the seat. "You'll be writing a five-minute speech and presenting it to the group, on a subject of your choice."

There were audible gasps from the attendees. Joan went pale and almost fainted. Bernie held her close, offering words of encouragement.

Arabella returned to the front of the room. "Before you plan your talk, let's discuss confidence. When Joan asked her question, what negative aspects did you notice?"

Meryl energetically threw her hand in the air. Arabella pointed to her. "She was a wuss, a big sissy. It was uncomfortable watching her shrinking into her seat," Meryl said, proud of her interpretation of Joan's actions.

"Thank you, Meryl, but let's try to speak about our group members more supportively. We could say Joan withdrew from the situation. What other identifiers did we see?"

Joan was now the main element of the discussion. I watched her fall into a pit of despair, her face reddening. People pointed out her slumped shoulders, forced smile, and quiet voice.

Meryl leaned over to me. "Joan's one of those people who'll never benefit from this sort of conference."

"Hm, maybe," I said in reply.

Arabella applauded, and pointed out how confidence grows from standing upright, looking others in the eye, and speaking in a calm, clear manner. She pressed enter on her laptop and highlighted these aspects in her PowerPoint presentation.

Meryl nudged me. "Then again, Joan and Arabella might have planned this spectacular opening? If they did, Joan's acting skills are brilliant."

* * *

ARABELLA TALKED for another twenty minutes, then sent us away to plan our talks. We'd be presenting them the following morning. Meryl was standing by the elevator holding the handle of a Gucci suitcase and wearing a red leather jacket.

I followed her into the elevator and pressed button ten. "What's your room number?" I asked.

"Eight hundred and four," Meryl said, staring at the silver control panel.

I pressed number eight for Meryl's floor and leaned my shoulder on the lift's cold metal wall. I stood in silence, admiring the bounce of Meryl's wavy brown hair and her ample cleavage. Even though she was a thoroughly annoying woman, her shapely femme figure was incredibly attractive.

Meryl winked at me when the elevator stopped, and she stepped out. "I'm not available."

"Shame," I said, when the door slid closed. My phone vibrated in my pocket, creating a sensual tremor. Pulling it out, I saw it was a text from Verona, asking me to phone her. I texted back, saying I was in a conference session, and I'd call her later.

Entering my room, I sat at my desk, tapping my teeth with the end of a pencil. I could talk about law, but it was a dull subject. To me, art was far more interesting, and a topic I could discuss effectively.

I drew squiggles on an empty page, while my mind figured out ideas. Five minutes wasn't a long amount of time. Maybe I could discuss an artist, Matisse perhaps, since the local art gallery contained a wide selection of his paintings. My talk might inspire members of the group to visit the exhibition.

On my laptop, I explored the artist's life. His work covered many styles, flitting from one art form to another; painting, drawing, cut-outs. I downloaded images and wrote about each piece, creating a decent presentation.

My phone rang. It was Verona, doubtless this was another of her begging calls. If I ignored her, she'd keep ringing. "*Ciao, bella... ci,* ...but why do you need a new phone? The one you have is brand new and works fine." Verona demanded everything she owned was the newest model. Her requests irritated me. I needed to put my foot down. "I'll think about it," I said, putting off my decision. "Yes, bye, love you."

My head dropped to the table, and I sighed in frustration. Having a girlfriend was so much hard work. The alarm on my smart watch beeped, telling me it was time to prepare for the evening meal.

I showered and dressed in a clean shirt and black jeans. Then wandered to the dining room, wondering if I'd find Meryl. Although she was arrogant and rude, her delicious body had perked my interest.

I took a seat with the fantastic four; Joan, Bernie, Ruby, and Sydney. "Have any of you seen Meryl?" I asked, looking around the dining room, and seeing no sign of her.

Ruby tutted and shook her head. "No, and I wouldn't want to hang around with the nasty woman."

Joan nodded in agreement. "She totally upset me."

"She'd better not talk like that to you again," Bernie said, patting Joan's hand.

Sydney raised her hands in boxing style. "I'll give her a face full of fist, if she tries."

I sighed and cut into my steak, chewing thoughtfully on the tender rib-eye. "So, what do each of you do for a living?" I asked, attempting to improve my social side.

Bernie swallowed a mouthful of food. "I own an outdoor pursuits center on the outskirts of Mainsel." She glanced at Joan. "Perhaps the four of you will visit one weekend. I could organize a couple of canoes, and we could paddle along the river."

Joan eagerly nodded her agreement.

"I'll see if I can find a spare weekend," I said casually.

"Sounds good to me," Sydney said, flexing her biceps. "Working out in my gymnasium means I've got the muscles to paddle us anywhere."

Ruby swooned and stroked Sydney's arms.

"Afterwards, you could all visit our yoga and well-being center," Joan said, nudging her sister. "We can relax and calm ourselves with a gong bath."

"Oh, yes," Ruby said. "Polly, you could attend. We can help ease your tension."

"I'm not tense," I said, my shoulders raising to my ears. Finishing my meal, I placed my cutlery across the plate and pushed it away. "I'm going to take a walk."

I followed the path to the harbor-side, darting across traffic filled roads, and walking through gardens of bright flowers.

When I reached the seafront, I discovered a historic boatyard. Fastened to the dock was a nineteenth century sailing ship, waiting patiently to be drawn. I sat on a wooden bench and sketched the vast boat, concentrating my lines on the mast, sails, and crisscrossing ropes. I added touches of color with my water paints.

When the sun sank into the sea, the light dimmed, making it impossible to finish my artwork. I took a photograph of my subject, aiming to complete the painting in my hotel room.

I closed my sketchbook and packed my equipment in my leather satchel. Standing, I looked along the seafront and spotted a woman wearing a bright red leather jacket. She was walking away from the dock-side carrying a conference goody bag.

"Meryl," I shouted. She didn't hear me, and turned around a corner, heading back to the hotel.

CHAPTER 3

Meryl

WHEN I LEFT THE HOTEL, Polly joined me in the lift and I had to give her a fake room number. I jumped out on my supposed floor and hurried to the stairs, rushing down to the foyer. Then I discreetly escaped through the hotel's side door.

There had been a positive attraction between me and Polly in the elevator. But she was one of those butch power lesbians and only interested in herself. For me, this was a good thing, because I didn't want anyone, especially her, taking an interest in me.

Thankfully, the rain had stopped. I wandered to the seafront and leaned on the metal rails, staring into the waves. I loved the open ocean; it led to other worlds, where crap didn't happen. A seagull flew toward me, landing by my side, his orange eyes staring at me. "What?" I asked. "Has the sea run out of fish?"

The gull's head tilted to one side, and he tucked back his wings. I took a sandwich from my bag and threw him a piece of crust. The bird squawked, winking at me before flying away. In this place, Polly wasn't the only one who felt the need to share opinions.

I studied the map on my phone. My route took me along the shoreline to a path leading away from the sea. I crossed the road, detoured around building sites and overflowing dustbins, wandering around one corner, then another.

The clean, decorative tourist laden seashore withered away. Tall glazed constructions disappeared, replaced by old, dilapidated buildings. Years ago, this would have been a busy metropolis. Today, the alleyways which lay between run-down terraces were dingy and soiled.

Along a disheveled street, a basketball court stood opposite graffiti covered buildings. Kids had torn away the diamond metal side netting from the uprights. Unclean people huddled in back doorways, smoking, drinking, and cursing.

A man sat in the weeds, leaning on a post. When I walked past, he held out his gnarled hand, his toothless mouth curving into a pleading smile. I stopped and rummaged in my goody bag, handing him an egg sandwich. Instantly, unkempt bodies appeared from the shadows. One grabbed my bag.

"Stop right there," I said, sharpness in my voice. The man jumped back. "Sort yourselves out and stand in line." Mouths grunted, and the group shuffled into a surly queue. I hummed with approval. "I don't have much, so be grateful for what you're given." Each person received either a sandwich or a pastry.

I wandered away. The only snacks I'd kept were a packet of crisps and a Scotch egg. When I turned the last corner, the wheel of my suitcase caught on a flagstone. There was a crack, and the wheel fell from its metal fixing, ending up lying forlornly on the ground. I swore, knowing that a fake Gucci wasn't sturdy like the real thing. I kicked the useless wheel into the road. Pushing down the handle, I lifted my over-packed case and continued my walk to the Youth Hostel.

The hostel stood amidst a terrace of three-story buildings,

opposite a white stoned basilica. A set of steps led down to a cellar room. I looked through the rails, gaping through the dirt covered windows into a small, sparsely decorated living room. An elderly lady pulled the curtains closed. She smiled at me. I waved, then climbed the stairs to the hostel's front door.

Standing beneath a coarsely painted porch, I attempted to open the door. It was locked. I pushed the bell and sensed an eye staring at me through the peep-hole. The door opened and a young man ushered me inside.

"Sorry," the man said, his head studying the road. "We have to stop people sneaking in and disturbing the residents." He scurried to a worn desk and shoved a register toward me.

"It's sad to see how many people struggle to survive," I said, writing out my name.

The man's face reddened as he checked my details. "We only have one room free, on the third floor at the rear. It's twenty-two dollars per night, so that'll be sixty-six dollars for three nights."

I counted out the cash in low dollar bills. He passed me a key, directing me along the corridor to the stairs. I clambered upward, my awkward case tugging me backward on each step. By the time I reached the third floor, I was sweating and my knees ached.

There were a dozen rooms along the dusty corridor. I discovered mine at the far end.

My stomach sank with dismay when I pushed the dull mahogany door open. The cream painted room was dour. The only brightness came from a bunch of yellow plastic daisies in a dusty vase on the windowsill.

I threw my case onto the bed and sat by its side, my backside squeezing the thin lumpy bedding. I imagined the brown stained mattress beneath me. Luckily, the hostel had covered it with a clean white sheet and a faded blue quilt.

I sighed and looked upwards. When I saw damp green patches creeping around the edges of the ceiling, I gagged.

In the corner was a small sink. I went to it, turning on the cold-water tap, splashing my face, startling my skin back to life. I stared into the cracked mirror above the sink, seeing my exhausted face, bags hanging from my eyes. The day had been draining, and I wanted to sleep, but I needed to get my blog written and published.

I removed my leather jacket, hanging it on a Victorian bronze hook on the back of the door. The hook was vintage. I could easily sell it to a collector on eBay. If only I'd brought my screwdriver.

Across the room, a table and wooden chair sat beneath the metal barred window. Wanting to clear the moldy air, I tried to pry the window open; but a screw fastened it shut. I gasped a mouthful of stale air in dismay and sat.

I opened my iPad and leaned back, staring through the window bars. Rears of bedraggled buildings, torn curtains, broken glass, rusted verandas, clothes pegged out on washing lines, filled my eyes. I sighed, forcing myself to ignore how I'd ended up in this mess.

My fingers twitched over the keypad, contemplating what to write. I'd met and observed many people today, and from their attitude and dress, I'd seen a lot of money waltzing around the conference.

I made a list and wrote notes on each person, deciding who was interesting enough to investigate further. Any of these divas could become my big story. But I had to be careful. After a recent incident, I'd been ordered by the court not to write intimate thoughts and details about individuals. Since then, the number of my blog followers had gone downhill, and I needed a great story to win them back.

I highlighted people of interest. Perhaps there was a story in the lives of Joan and her twin sister, Ruby. I needed to get their surnames and investigate them further. Bernie, the handsome outdoor type, might convince a few hikers and campers to follow my site. Not to mention Sydney. One picture of her could gain me thousands more followers. And I mustn't forget Polly. There could be something hiding in her background. I circled her name, needing to find out more about her.

To produce a document I could publish immediately, I'd write about the gorgeously attractive inventor of the International Leadership Institute for Women, Julia Baker-Zucchero. I scanned the Internet, discovering the woman with gray spiky hair was quite illustrious. Julia was married to Suzanna, a former employee, and they had a dog. I loved women with pets; they were outgoing yet sensitive.

I wrote the article, double checking my text with the spell checker, and having my iPad read my work back to me. I'd focused on the ideals of Julia's course and the benefits it brought women who could afford to attend. I pressed period, saving my work, and shut down the tablet.

Maybe my story could prompt Julia to publicize her institute on my blog site. If I could get additional advertising, my income would increase and I'd be able to do more for those who needed my help. Perhaps changing my name to 'Meryla' would help gain Julia's interest.

My stomach rumbled; it was time for food. I wandered to the ground floor and entered the shared kitchen. Using the hostel's offerings, I brewed a cup of insipid tea. Then arranged my miniature picnic on a cracked hostel plate.

A guy entered, carrying a bag of fries. He stared at me and my pathetic meal. Grabbing a fistful of fries in his grubby hand, he placed them on my plate. "Here, you look like you need a good meal," he said.

"Thanks." I winced with gratitude. I didn't appreciate people helping me.

"It's good to share. We've got to look out for each other. I'll see you at breakfast."

I stared at my food. He was right. Compared to those souls on the street, I was in an excellent position. It was the rich people who annoyed me with their private incomes and fancy houses. I often saw them walk past those who cried out for help, watching them turn their chin. At the conference, these people surrounded me.

On the way back to my *suite*, I used the communal bathroom. Then hurried passed rooms where cannabis smoke seeped under the woodwork. Safe in my abode, even though I trusted most people, I closed and bolted my door.

I arranged my creased dress on a coat hanger and hung it in the mothball smelling antique wardrobe. With the light turned off, I slid into bed, pushing away thoughts of what lurked beneath the sheet below me.

Sleep was tricky to come by. Lying on the bed, each time I took a breath, the pungent smell of bleached bedding infiltrated my nose. I stared at the ceiling, watching the lightbulb vibrate when someone stomped across the floor of the attic. A burst of loud music blared from below. The hostel commissioner yelled. In an instant, the music stopped. I tossed and turned, molding my hips between the springs until I drifted into an uncomfortable sleep.

* * *

A BIRD, perched on a metal window bar, woke me at six o'clock with its cheerful tweets. If I hurried, I'd be first in the bathroom, and might get the hot water. I jumped out of bed, grabbed my towel and wash-bag, and rushed across the hall. Securely locking the bathroom door, I took a lukewarm shower, feeling happy at being able to scrub myself clean.

I dressed in a modern copy of a 1970s denim dress, a thin waterproof jacket, and a comfortable pair of shoes.

Not being able to save any of my snacks for breakfast, I wandered to the Regal Duchess hotel. When I walked past a nearby coffee shop, a rich aroma emanated through the door and drew me inside. I scraped together enough cash to buy a small black coffee. With three sachets of sugar added, the drink gave me enough buzz to continue my long walk.

At the hotel, I skipped upstairs to the dining area and waited at the entrance desk. A sultry server appeared. "Yes," he asked.

"One for breakfast."

"Room number?"

"Eight zero four," I answered sincerely, tapping my pocket. "I'm sorry. I've forgotten my room card." I gave him a beaming smile and winked.

"No problem. Is it a table for one?"

I nodded, following him to a twin table with a view of the sea. Boats sailed across the sparkling water, catching oysters and shrimps to be served at the nearby fish bars.

"Tea or coffee?" the server asked, dark rings beneath his eyes.

"Coffee."

"Help yourself to the buffet," he said, pouring dark brown liquid into my cup.

I filled a bowl with cereal and added fresh fruit, then placed bread in the rotating mechanical toaster. The slices disappeared into a heated chamber and exited slightly browner than when they entered.

"I wouldn't put them through again. They'll burn next time."

I looked around, finding Bernie standing by my side. "Yeah, I think this will have to do." I lay the pale toast on my plate, beside two wedges of butter and several packets of jam. "Have you partnered yourself with anyone?" I asked with a wink.

"Maybe." Bernie grinned. "What about you? Seen anyone you fancy?"

"Not really. I'm keeping my eyes open. Catch you later," I said, heading for my table.

I munched the under cooked toast and studied my research notes. I wrote further questions to be answered to my list. When I finished my coffee, I headed for the lecture hall, taking a seat at the rear, where I could view everyone inconspicuously.

CHAPTER 4

Polly

EATING BREAKFAST IN MY SUITE, I considered today's activity; *'Networking and Building Pathways.'* Developing networks was one of my fortes. I'd created many in my legal department, using them to get tasks done efficiently.

I suppose my relationship with Verona was a sexual network, but it didn't follow a strongly built pathway. Apart from having great sex, we didn't really know each other, and she cost me a lot of money. And we lacked romance. Being romantic was hard work, and I didn't have time for such buncombe.

Perhaps I could learn how to build a pathway with Meryl, learn how to work with a person I disliked. There was a connection between us, though I wasn't sure what it was, apart from the fact she irritated me.

My first step would be to visit her room and invite her for coffee. Paying attention to a woman was always a good starting point and might tick some of my mentor's boxes.

The lift descended to the eighth floor, and I stood outside room eight zero four. I rolled back my shoulders and stood tall, then knocked on the door, not completely convinced I should be the one making the first move. There was no answer. Had she seen me through the spy hole? I knocked again; this had become a challenge I intended to win. The door swung open.

"What?" a gruff, hairy chested man asked, naked apart from the towel wrapped around his waist.

Startled at the unexpected form in front of me, I jumped backwards. "What are you doing in this room?"

"None of your business," he grunted, slamming the door closed.

My knuckles rapped on the woodwork, and the door wrenched open. "I want to speak to Meryl."

The man leaned into my face. "Don't know her, now go away," he spat.

I wiped his spittle from my face, turned, and marched along the corridor. What game was Meryl playing?

When I entered the lecture hall, I found Meryl sitting alone, staring at her tablet. I took a seat by her side. "Which room did you say you were staying in?" I asked, my tone sounding like a police interrogation.

She glared at me. "What's it got to do with you?"

"I called at your room this morning. An unsavory man answered. Is he a relation of yours?"

Meryl stared. "Why were you calling for me? Are you a detective? My dyslexia must have confused me, and I got the number wrong. Anyway, you wouldn't have found me. I was out taking a jog."

I studied her; she didn't look the type to go jogging. I settled back in my seat. "Have you written your speech?" I asked, changing the subject.

She nodded and smugly tapped the side of her forehead. "Yeah, no problem. It's all in here."

When Arabella appeared, I stood and informed her of my medical condition. She agreed to my suggestion that I spoke first. This meant I could leave the room if I felt an oncoming aura. I took my printed sheets and USB stick and went to the front of the room.

With the stick inserted in the laptop and the first image showing on the screen, I arranged my notes on the desk and smoothed my suit, ready to begin. Meryl's deep brown eyes glared at me. Her pouting mouth making her distractingly attractive. I looked away and began my talk.

I had given many talks at company meetings, and always followed my mother's advice, speaking on an outward breath. It meant my amplified voice filled the room, and when I rolled my hands in the air, my speech became invigorating. The words were supported by Matisse's images exhibited on the screen behind me, helping me create an impressive production.

When the alarm on Arabella's phone buzzed, the audience applauded, and I left the stage.

"I think my speech went well," I said, returning to Meryl's side.

"You were inspiring, but mundane," Meryl said.

"What do you mean?" I asked, disgusted by her harsh words.

"Your presentation was interesting, but your voice was monotone and dull."

I crossed my legs and turned away from the discourteous woman. To take my mind off her insults, I took my sketchbook from my satchel and drew each presenter while I listened to their words.

Using my artistic skills, I designed each of them an appropriate outfit. The spirit and confidence of each woman affecting the clothing I created. Sydney in a stylish sports kit, Bernie wearing practical climbing gear, and Ruby in a red dress, dancing a fandango.

Joan muttered through her speech; fighting her way to the

end, her hand clinging to Bernie's. I drew her in a lacy white frock, a veil covering her face. Bernie wore a knight's outfit and waved a sword in the air.

"Well done, Joan. Finally, we have Meryl," Arabella said, waving a hand at my neighbor.

"I wonder what you're going to dress me in," Meryl whispered, standing and walking empty-handed to the front of the room, giving everyone a charming smile. "Today, I want to discuss the use of social media in befriending people and sharing information. If you want to discover more details, please follow any of the sites I mention."

She discussed creating accounts on social media and security. The information she provided was interesting, and I made several notes to pass on to my legal team and share with mother.

Meryl bowed to an exorbitant round of applause. "Was I any good?" she asked when she returned to her seat.

I raised my shoulders, resting my hand on my sketchbook. "You were okay."

Meryl glanced at my sketch of her wearing a floor-length black frock. A diamond encrusted mask covered her eyes, long black silk gloves embraced her arms.

"Hm, what a lovely outfit. It suits me. Makes me a woman of mystery," she said with a smirk.

"Well done," Arabella said. "I appreciate your hard work. Go get yourself a coffee before your next session."

* * *

I STOOD by the atrium window with my latte, entranced by the pattern created by the waves flowing in the distant sea. A shadow appeared beside me.

"I'd like to see the Matisse work in the gallery," Meryl said, her face reflecting in the window.

Was she hinting at me taking her on an outing to the art

gallery? I doubted it. "Glad I inspired you," I replied, placing my cup on the table. "It's time for our next seminar."

Walking side by side, we followed the group into the lecture hall. Bernie and Joan were linking arms, giving each other tender smiles. Ruby was sitting on Sydney's lap, tracing a finger over her tattoos.

I shook my head and took a seat. "I thought this was supposed to be a conference, not a dating agency." I gazed at the other attendees, watching a twitchy woman sitting at the front, drinking from a water bottle. She gave a woman sitting in the back row an evil glance and sneered. I reared my eyebrows and shook my head.

"Good morning," the presenter said. "I'm Clara Glidden. I'll be the facilitator for this session, and be the mentor for some of you," she said, checking her register. "Now, the Institute likes to call this seminar 'Networking and Building Pathways,' but I prefer to think of it as making friends and playing nice with others."

Meryl snorted, and someone behind me laughed loudly. Clara raised her hands for quiet. "What comes to mind when we think of networking?"

"Err, making valuable business connections," Bernie said, glancing at a smiling Joan.

"For whom?" Clara asked.

Bernie rubbed the back of her neck. "Um, well for myself, and hopefully for them, too."

Clara held out a hand to Bernie. "What could be the outcome?"

"Well, maybe they can help me sometime or I can help them."

"How many of you have been to a so-called networking event?" Clara asked, observing the room. Myself and most of the group raised their hands.

"I've always found networking an interesting activity. My mother and I attend fashion events all the time, and they're excellent for making business connections," I said.

"I've only been to one event, and it was boring," Sydney said, her muscles flexing under her Lycra shirt.

"The ones I've attended were full of people telling tales and bullying," Ruby said, her eyes blazing at Meryl.

"Well, I hate networking with bumptious well-monied people who have no interest in the real world," Meryl said, slumping in her seat and waving her arm around. "It's a bit like being here and having to make friends with these miserable people."

Meryl's rude statements were unacceptable in the business world. But the despicable stares she received in response to her remarks made me smirk.

"Now then, ladies, let's try to remain courteous to each other," Clara said. "It's best if you make friends with those who share your interests, your passions, and even your field. The first requirement is to make a friend, and then to be a friend."

Clara continued to discuss the difficulty adults face in forging acquaintances. I wasn't listening closely and started doodling on the back of a worksheet.

"Who here is comfortable going to a friend's party and striking up a conversation with a total stranger?" Clara asked.

All hands, apart from mine and Meryl's, shot into the air. I admired the fact that me and Meryl hated parties and aimless conversation.

"Does everyone have a piece of paper and a pen?" Clara asked, looking around.

I tore a sheet of paper from my notepad. Meryl stared at it. "Here," I said, handing it to her and tearing out another piece.

"I want each of you to write four things you want to know about a potential friend. And," she waved a hand, "don't ask the basics, what they do for a living, are they partnered… we're not looking for their potential income level or making dates."

"Shame," Meryl said, observing some of the prettier members of the group. "Some of these women are beddable."

"Shut up, I'm concentrating," I said, listening to Clara explaining the activity.

"I'm going to give everyone a few minutes," Clara said. "Dig deep. Be unique."

Meryl scribbled an indecipherable question on her page, followed by another. She tapped the pen on her forehead. "Aha," she said, writing her last two questions. "Don't you want to know anything about this crew?" she asked, staring at my empty page.

"I'm still thinking," I said, contemplating the effects dyslexia must have on Meryl's work.

"Time's up," Clara called out.

"Shit," I muttered, jotting four questions on my sheet of paper.

"Now we're going to have some fun." Clara pointed at the front rows of seats. "Front row, turn your chairs around to face the folks behind you."

Chairs scraped as they were rotated. Clara gave more directions, asking the row in front of us to turn.

I was facing Joan, and Meryl chatted to Sydney, receiving an evil glare from Ruby.

Clara smiled. "You've heard of speed dating? Welcome to speed friending. Those questions you wrote are now going to be used on each other as best you can in our given situation. Not ideal, I know."

Clara explained the activity and Meryl rubbed the back of her head. "I don't get what she's going on about?"

I sighed. Why couldn't this woman pay attention? "You've got two minutes to ask Sydney your questions, then Sydney will ask hers if Ruby doesn't kill you first. After four minutes, Sydney will move to the left, and you repeat the activity with Joan," I said. "And you're not to judge anyone."

"Oh, right? I have dyslexia and attention deficit disorder," Meryl said, blushing. "But I think I'm going to enjoy this. I can work out who I'd like to chat up later. Know what I mean?" Meryl nudged me.

"Tart," I hissed, staring at Joan, who was waiting for my question. "What are your hobbies?" I asked. I had a few interests of my own and thought it would be nice to hear those of others.

"Well," Joan said, drumming her chin with her fingers. "My favorite thing to do is read. I love books."

"Me too," I said with a nod. "I enjoy reading Thomas Hardy. Have you read Tess of the D'Urbervilles?"

"No, but I enjoyed The Hobbit," Joan said, then stared at me expectantly.

"Is Tolkien your favorite author?" I asked.

"Yes, I've read all the middle earth stories." Joan gave long descriptions of her favorite sections of each of Tolkien's novels.

"Two minutes," Clara called. "If you haven't switched who is asking and who is answering, please switch now."

I pointed to Joan. "It's your turn to ask questions."

"Oh, yes, err. What do you enjoy eating?"

"Pizza, with ham and pineapple," I answered, "and anything with pasta. My favorite dish is my mother's lasagna with garlic bread."

We continued our question-and-answer session until Clara blew a whistle. "Time," Clara called out. "First and third rows, shift a seat, please. Last person, move to the first seat."

The group eagerly rotated, like Pavlov's dogs.

"Bye," Joan said, moving to the next seat and glaring menacingly at Meryl.

I was now sitting opposite Bernie, who turned out to be an excellent conversationalist.

The room echoed with the constant natter of chattering women. But at the next turnaround, the rotation system failed. Sitting side by side, Bernie and Joan fell into an in-depth conversation. Sydney and Ruby disappeared from the hall. Other women changed position completely and began talking to the girls they fancied.

I turned to Meryl. "I don't think Clara's plan is working."

"Doesn't worry me," Meryl said, moving around to sit opposite me. "I'm not fancying any of these women. Some are quite intimidating."

"Is finding a woman all you think about?"

"There's nothing wrong with admiring the fairer sex. I noticed your appreciation of a shapely pair of hips in the elevator yesterday." She outlined the female form with her hands. I felt my face redden and Meryl grinned.

I should have walked away at that point, but I didn't want to draw attention to myself, so I stayed. "Thankfully, I shouldn't have to talk to you for long. I've asked one question, only three more to go."

"You should join me for a drink later," Meryl said, leaning back in her seat.

"Why?"

"Aha, question two." Meryl ticked the air. "So, I can find out even more about you."

"I see you're the inquisitive type."

"I like to get an idea of who I'm dealing with," Meryl said.

"You should be careful with the questions you ask. I'm a lawyer."

Meryl clicked her fingers. "That's why you're wearing the power dyke suit. But the rest of you doesn't look right." She waved a hand around my head.

"What do you mean?"

"Having lank shoulder length hair makes you look old-fashioned, and those over-size glasses hide the twinkle in your eyes."

"What gives you the right to make personal comments?" I ran my hands through my hair. "My girlfriend cuts my hair and these glasses reflect my determined nature." I ran a hand down my thigh.

"Your girlfriend obviously doesn't want you meeting anyone else. Keeping you away from the competition."

My mouth dropped open as I glared at her, then my phone pinged.

Meryl sighed. "And it's irritating hearing your phone beeping when she constantly messages you."

"How do you know the message is from her?" I asked, glancing at my phone screen.

"I'm sorry. I'm unable to answer your question. You've reached your limit."

I crossed my arms and legs, leaning back and staring at her. "You really are something else."

"Okay, ladies," Clara said. "Let's have a five-minute toilet break."

I stood and stretched, bending from side to side. Meryl remained in her seat, watching me.

* * *

"WELCOME BACK," Clara said. "Now, if you've ever done speed dating, not asking for a show of hands here, you know you present a list of people you'd be interested in connecting with, and the organizers' link the matches. I'm going to match you with a person you met in the first part of the class for an extended assignment to get to know each other."

Joan shuffled closer to Bernie, clinging to her arm. Clara winked at them. "Don't worry, Joan, I'll allow you and Bernie to be together." Smiles beamed from both their faces.

Meryl poked two fingers in her mouth and gagged. I snorted, covering my mouth with my hand, trying to turn the sound into a cough.

"After that, you'll have a contact that shares at least some things in common with you, and maybe you'll even have a new friend. I'm giving you a half hour after I pair you. You can stay in here, go to the lobby, whatever you want to do." Clara passed out some paperwork and began pairing people together.

Unsurprisingly, Clara paired me with my nemesis.

"I'd rather get out of here. I've got lots of work to complete," Meryl said, watching the other couples discussing ideas, some leaving the venue. She shrugged. "But I suppose we'll have to follow the itinerary."

"Let's have a coffee in the lounge," I said. "We'll fill in these sheets and hand them back to Clara. Then we can do our own thing."

"Fair enough, but you're buying." Meryl trotted to a table in the window, waving to a waiter and ordering a cafetiere. "I told him to charge it to your room," she said, signing into her tablet and reading the messages which pinged through.

I gave the table a loud rap, making Meryl look at me. "Is your work more important than making friends?" I asked. "We're supposed to be completing our worksheets."

"I like to keep up to date with my emails. You know how important it is to keep track of events." Meryl pushed down the plunger on the coffee pot.

I read the instructions on the worksheet and clicked my gold Montblanc pen. "Okay, here's my first question. Why are you here?"

"Why do I have to answer first?"

"Because I asked," I said.

There was no response. Meryl just rested back and sipped her drink.

"At this rate, we'll get nowhere," I said, answering my ringing phone. "Polly Tulipano, how can I help you?"

"Is that your girlfriend?" Meryl whispered.

I glared at Meryl and spoke to the caller in Italian.

"I'm impressed," Meryl said when I hung up. "I love your accent; you seem to speak the language perfectly. It's quite a turn on." Meryl waggled her eyebrows.

"The language of love," I said. "I guess it's wasted on you."

Meryl typed some words into her tablet and checked her watch. "Fancy another coffee, or something stronger?"

"Why not? I'll have a red wine."

Meryl ordered, then disappeared to the toilet, clinging to her tablet. While she was away, the waiter brought a bottle of wine and two glasses.

"Hello, Polly, don't tell me Meryl's abandoned you so early in the session," Clara said, winding her way to our table.

"She's gone for a toilet break," I said, pouring myself a wine. "Would you like a drink?"

"I'm tempted, but no thanks, I need to keep a clear head." Clara picked up my empty page. "How are you doing filling in the forms?"

"We're getting there."

"This is terrible." Clara waved the sheet of paper under my nose. "Most people have already completed the task." She made notes in her folder and looked around. "Meryl is taking her time. I need to catch the rest of our gang. Tell her I was here and get this activity completed. By the way, I'm yours and Meryl's mentor, so I'll be watching the pair of you." She threw the page back at me. "I'll see you later." Clara stood and searched for her next couple.

Once she'd departed, Meryl appeared from around a corner. "Did I miss Clara?" she asked, filling her wineglass.

I nodded, pointing to our worksheet. "Your refusal to answer these questions disappointed her."

"I haven't heard you give any answers either," Meryl said, tapping my glass with hers.

"Hmm. By the way, this wine was a good choice."

"My ex-girlfriend ran her own vineyard. I learned a little from our wine tasting sessions."

"Impressive. How long were you together?" I asked, surprised Meryl could hold down a relationship.

Meryl sat back. "Long enough. Are you a helpful lawyer or one of those nasty ones who enjoys destroying people?"

"If people get on the wrong side of me, destruction is a good way to progress. But in the fashion industry, I prefer to reach a satisfactory conclusion for both sides."

"Fashion?"

"Yes," I said with a nod. "My mother is a fashion designer and runs her own fashion house."

"Did she make you come here?" Meryl waved around the room.

I drank a mouthful of wine and fiddled with the drinks mat. "She suggested the conference might improve my communication skills. Apparently, I'm too forceful when I talk to my junior staff."

"You should have written yourself a get-out clause," Meryl said with a snort. "Do you know your problem? Your mother and girlfriend have taken charge of your life." Meryl took another mouthful of wine and topped up her glass. "You should follow my example and tell them to stop controlling you."

"I presume these thoughts come from a woman with problems in her own family," I said, crossing my legs and leaning an elbow on my knee.

"No way. I stay in control of all my interactions," Meryl said with a shrug. "Is it always your mother who interferes, or is your father also involved?"

"My father died a long time ago."

"Oh, I'm sorry, was he ill?"

I stared out of the window and sat back. "He died in a motorcycle race."

"Was he famous?"

"To me, he was the most famous person in the world. Marco Tulipano, have you heard of him?"

Meryl shook her head. "Racing's not my thing," She typed more words, her eyes scanning her screen.

"I can see you're not interested in my life. You're far more focused on your business." I shifted my body. "I presume, since you like to be in control, you work for yourself?"

"Yes, I'm chief executive," Meryl said, smiling professionally. "Have a business card." She handed me a glitzy card advertising an internet blog page.

I burst into a peel of laughter. "You're a blogger."

"What's wrong with blogging? You should let me write about you and show your company's designs on my blog page. I have lots of viewers. I could make you famous. Check out my site and let me know what you think."

"I will investigate your blog site, *MeeMeeShush*, with great interest."

A receptionist arrived at our table. "Excuse me."

Meryl stared at her. "Yes."

"Could you come to the reception desk, please?" The receptionist leaned toward Meryl. "The resident of room eight hundred and four has complained about an imposter abusing his account. It appears you used his room number to order breakfast this morning."

Flustered, Meryl jumped from the chair and hurried to the desk, closely followed by the receptionist.

The cursor of Meryl's iPad sat blinking, waiting for her to add more notes. I stared at the screen and scanned the pages. The lines of misspelt words appeared to be about me and my family. I sat back in shock and clicked the Internet link. It revealed pages about my father, his accident, and my mother and her business. Then there were photos of me attending business events.

"Give me back my iPad," Meryl yelled on her return, trying to grab her tablet.

I waved it in front of her. "Why are you investigating me? Do you work in a government department?"

"No, give it here."

I deleted the internet pages, then highlighted and removed

her notes. It wouldn't make much difference. Meryl probably had a photographic memory, but it made me feel better. "Here." I threw her stupid tablet on the ground. "You are a nosy bitch."

Meryl dived onto the carpet to save her precious iPad.

I turned and attempted to stand. A pulse throbbed in my side. "No," I gasped. My hands clutched my abdomen, trying to force the trembling to stop. My head emptied and knees weakened. The throbbing enveloped my body, and I plummeted to the ground, convulsing around the floor.

I stared at the glistening chandelier swaying above my flickering eyes. The lights twinkled, the sparkles tormenting my brain.

I silently prayed for my body to pass out.

The light extinguished.

I disappeared into the darkness.

CHAPTER 5

Meryl

I GRITTED MY TEETH, seething, and collected my tablet from the floor, checking it for damage. Polly will have to pay for anything she's broken. I glanced at the woman, mesmerized by her swaying body. Suddenly, she dropped to the ground, her body juddering.

"Don't try to get out of this by throwing yourself on the floor," I shouted. "Causing a distraction with your hissy fit." I stared at Polly's vibrating body, foam frothing from her mouth. "Oh, shit." I kneeled by her side, my eyes gaping at her.

A woman rushed over, leaving her friend gawping in the background. "Hold her head; make sure she doesn't bump into anything," the woman said.

I placed a hand on the side of Polly's head. Polly's tongue lolled between her lips. I moved my other hand toward her mouth.

The woman grasped my arm, pulling it away, and kneeled by my side. "Don't put your fingers near her mouth. She might bite."

"But she's chewing her tongue," I said, attempting to hold Polly's head in one position.

"She'll be fine. You can clean the blood from her face later... uh. Sorry. I didn't get your name."

"I'm Meryl and she's Polly."

"Abigail," the woman said, introducing herself as she held Polly's hand. "I'm a doctor."

"Great, thanks for helping, Abby," I said.

"Abigail," she stated with a glare.

When Polly stopped shaking. I watched her body slip into an unconscious state. Abigail leaned closer to her face and tapped her cheek. "Hello, Polly, come back to us."

Polly's eyelids quivered, and her eyes opened a smidgen. She flicked her pupils from side to side, assessing the number of people standing around her, then tried to sit.

"Stay there, get yourself together," Abigail said. "Are you a diagnosed epileptic?"

Polly gave her head a slight nod.

"Did you take your medication today?"

"Yes," Polly mumbled, a dribble of bloodied spittle seeping from the side of her mouth.

"Good, I think you need to go to your room and sleep this off." Abigail studied Polly's body and glanced at me. "And she'll need to wash and change; uncontrolled urination is an unfortunate and unavoidable side effect."

I scowled. "She's nothing to do with me. I was just paired with her in our friendship session."

"Well, this is a good time to act as a friend," Abigail said. "Come on, let's go."

Abigail's friend Tonya appeared. She helped us get Polly to her feet and took most of Polly's weight as the four of us moved toward the elevator.

"I can walk by myself," Polly whispered in my ear, swaying on her legs.

I gave her a stern frown. "Just accept our help. It'll make life easier."

Polly groaned as her body leaned on Tonya's arms.

"What's your room number?" Abigail asked.

"Ten, twenty," Polly slurred, as the four of us traveled upwards.

On the tenth floor, Polly waved her door card in front of the key panel, and Tonya virtually carried her into the room, sitting her on the bed. "There we are."

"Thank you," Polly said to Abigail and Tonya.

"We'll leave you to it. Give me a shout if you need me," Abigail said, leaving the room.

I scanned the drooping body of my patient and sighed. "Get yourself undressed. I'll run the shower."

I went into the bathroom. The shower was wide with a folding seat. There were hand bars on the wall and an emergency pull switch. "Good job you booked a disabled room," I shouted, standing on the shower mat, ensuring it was secure. I turned on the water, then went to fetch my patient. "You've still got your clothes on."

"I'm not taking my clothes off in front of you. Anyway, you can go. I don't need your help," Polly said, staring at the floor.

"Your wish is my command. I can't see why I'm bothering to help you anyway, Miss Independent." I grabbed my handbag and walked toward the door. "The shower's running."

Polly's wailing sobs forced me to turn around.

"For crying out loud, Polly, have a shower, then get into bed," I said, returning my bag to the floor.

Polly removed her jacket and unbuttoned her shirt, shrugging it off her shoulders and revealing her bra. Her hands failed to unclip the straps. I leaned over and unfastened them for her; and she tugged the bra away, dropping it on the floor. Her perfectly formed breasts and pert pink nipples stirred my loins. If she changed those glasses for a more modern pair and allowed a professional to cut her hair, the woman would look overwhelmingly attractive. I shook my head, forcing myself to pay attention.

Polly loosened her trousers and stood, allowing them to slip to the floor. She pushed down her soaked pants, staggered into the bathroom, and sat safely on the shower seat. I rubbed her body with a soapy flannel, then rinsed her with warm water.

Turning off the shower, I handed Polly an Egyptian cotton towel. She held it limply in her hand, aimlessly staring.

"You need to dry yourself," I said.

She rubbed her skin. After constantly rubbing the same patch for a minute, I realized she was getting nowhere and took the towel from her. I dried her hair, then swept the towel around her body, delicately and professionally drying her breasts.

"Wait here," I said, when I'd finished. "I'll fetch your nightshirt. I won't shut the door in case I need to run in and save you again."

Polly smirked in response.

When I returned, Polly stood. I covered her naked body with the shirt, then guided her to the bed. She lay on the soft mattress, and I pulled the bed-covers over the long, shapely legs which protruded from the dressing gown.

"Thanks for staying. I feel a lot better now," she said, putting on her glasses.

"Good, you should be grateful I had the time to stick around." I placed a sachet into the coffee machine filter and a cup under the spout. Waiting for the water to boil, I dropped into a seat by the window and looked around. The room was a million percent grander than mine. It had a huge TV, a massive king-size bed, and a stunning view of the harbor. This is the life I wished for, if only things were the same for everybody. "Do you have many fits?" I asked.

"Not really. This was the first for a couple of years. My medication is usually good at controlling them."

"Is this why your mother makes you work in the legal team? Keeping the family freak in the background, out of the way?"

Polly's face paled, and her mouth dropped. "I'll have to phone her and tell her about this attack."

"Here, give me your phone." I held out my hand. "I'll call her."

"Really? You'd do that for me?"

"Sure, I'll pretend you're asleep."

Polly pressed her mother's number and handed me the phone. "Hello, Mrs. Tulipano, this is Meryl, a friend of Polly," I said when an Italian sounding woman answered. "I'm afraid she's had a fit. No, she's fine now, in bed, sleeping. Yes, she's seen a doctor and I've taken care of her. Okay, I'll ask Anton to drive her home. Yes, I'll look out for her. Goodbye."

"What did she say?"

"She wants Anton to drive you home straight away. Who's Anton?"

"My chauffer. He's supposed to have driven me here and be on hand in case there's a problem."

"How do I get hold of him?"

"You can't. He went to visit his boyfriend after I paid him to let me drive here alone. My plan was to collect him from the airport on my way home."

I kicked off my shoes and lounged in the chair. "So, what are you going to do?"

"I'll feel fine after I've had a good rest. So, I'll drive myself home tomorrow."

"That means you'll be breaking the law, and your vehicle insurance will be defunct. Sounds dodgy to me."

Polly's head fell back. "You're right."

"Why don't you ask Anton to change his flight to tomorrow, and I'll drive you to the airport," I said, reaching to the coffee machine and taking my cup.

"But the airport could be miles away from your house."

"No, if it's Mainsel airport, it's right next door to Salton, where I live."

"How the hell do you know I live in Mainsel?"

"Ah," I said, interlocking my fingers.

Polly rubbed her forehead. "Of course, before my fit, you were doing research about me on the Internet."

"Well, yes, but my research has been useful. So, what do you think?"

Polly shuffled upright. "I'm not sure I'm happy about you driving my car."

"I'll have you know; my driving skills are exceptional."

"I suppose it means mother won't find out about my deal with Anton. But what do you get out of it?" Polly asked, crossing her arms.

"I get out of this conference a day early; I won't have to hang around waiting for my train to depart; and we both gain extra friendship points with our mentor."

"Hmm, okay, I'll think about it." Polly sank into her pillows. "Go to your room and come and see me in the morning, then I'll tell you my decision. I'll phone you if I feel ill. What was your room number?"

I sipped my Italian coffee. "I don't have one."

"What?"

"I'm not staying in this hotel."

"But you said you were staying on the eighth floor." Polly shook her head, confused. "I know this isn't the best hotel in the area, but you could have told me it wasn't good enough for you instead of leading me on. I suppose you're staying in the Kilton Towers?"

"Hmm," I said, noncommittal with my answer. "Look, I'm happy to sleep in this chair and watch over you. You'll be quite safe."

Polly yawned and closed her eyes. "Whatever," she said, drifting into a fit induced sleep.

*　*　*

WHILE POLLY SLEPT, I found an Institute administrator and updated her on Polly's condition. Then I walked to the hostel. Since I'd only brought two interchangeable outfits, it didn't take me long to pack my belongings into the hold-all I'd borrowed from Polly's room.

In the alleyway, I gave my broken Gucci suitcase to an elderly lady whose eyes pleaded to own something special, and a young boy took my trashed suede boots. After saying farewell to my new buddies, I wandered back to the Regal Duchess.

I opened the door with Polly's key card to find her sitting in bed giggling at an episode of Mrs. Maisel. "Are you feeling better?" I asked.

"Yes, thanks. The sleep helped, though my heads still woozy. Abigail called while you were away to check me over. She says I'm fine."

"I hope I satisfied her with my caring abilities."

"She didn't say," Polly said, shrugging. "I phoned Anton. He's catching a flight tomorrow morning, and we can pick him up at the airport."

I dropped the hold-all on the floor. "Good, you've made the right decision."

"What are you doing with that?" Polly asked, glaring at the bag.

"Oh, I hope you don't mind. My suitcase broke, and I needed to collect my gear."

Polly's eyes scanned the room.

"Hey, I haven't taken anything else, I'm not a bloody thief," I said, picking up the room service menu. "Do you want any food? The hotel has an excellent selection." I studied the pictures on a shiny sheet of paper. "How about a hamburger? They're a tasty pick-me-up for anyone feeling lousy."

"Let me see?" Polly took the menu. "Why not? Get them to add cheese and bacon."

"No problem." I called reception and ordered two burgers with fries. "Should be with us in thirty minutes." I turned the chair to face the TV screen, sitting and adjusting the cushions to make myself comfortable.

"Did you watch the episode where a guy hypnotized Mrs. Maisel's mum and she mimicked her daughter's comedy routine? It was hilarious," Polly said, giggling.

"Oh, sure, that one was real funny." Not having a TV of my own, I'd never seen the program. A knock at the door saved me from having to discuss the episode further. "Aha, the food has arrived."

"Great, I'm starved." Polly grabbed the plate I handed her and tucked into her burger, eating with gusto.

I sat at the desk to eat mine. "What time do you take your next lot of medication?" I asked.

Polly checked the clock. "Better have my tablets now. They make me sleepy, so I'll probably nod off again."

"No worries, I'm here and I've got the phone number of the hotel medic if you have another of those shaky-shakes."

"I'm convinced I'm in terrible hands."

"I'll have you know; I spend half my life looking after people."

"Really? I wouldn't think you'd be the type. Who have you taken care of?"

"Family mainly, mine are extremely needy."

Fortunately, Polly didn't ask any further questions. She finished her burger, yawned, and closed her eyes. She was soon fast asleep.

I turned off the TV, collected Polly's plate, and left the tray of dirty dishes outside the bedroom door. Then I tucked the quilt around Polly's lumbering form and ran a bath.

Leaving the bathroom door ajar, I lay gloriously in the soapy suds. Reflecting how Polly's illness had improved my luck. I was spending a night in a superb room, TV to watch, decent food, and I got to sleep with a woman. Not physically, of course, because Polly wasn't my type. She was a rich, brazen hussy, with no care for other people.

I dried myself, smothering my body in the super soft towels, and wrapped myself in the hotel's thick, soft dressing gown. Jiggling in the chair, I tried to find a comfortable position. It was impossible.

Studying the bed, I saw Polly was lying on the far edge, leaving lots of space on the king-size mattress. There was more than enough room for two. And if I slept by her side, I'd easily notice if she had another fit.

I discarded the dressing gown, crept to the bed, and lowered myself onto the mattress.

CHAPTER 6

Polly

I WOKE with a feather quilt snuggled around me. A woman's hair swathed my face and lavender perfume engulfed my pillow. Comforted not to be alone, my arm pulled the body nearer. I kissed the back of the woman's neck. In response, she gave a soft murmur. It didn't take me long to realize I wasn't dreaming. "Meryl," I said, stroking her body, my fingers roaming around her breasts.

"Mmm."

"Why are you in my bed?"

The body rolled over. "Oh shit," Meryl said, sitting upright, knocking my fingers away.

"Hey," I said, rubbing her back. "It's okay, kinda nice." I kissed the bottom of her spine.

Meryl pulled herself away. "I'm sorry. I know I promised to stay in the chair, but your bed looked so comfortable."

"Look, today is our last day together. After you've driven me home, you'll never have to see me again. So, why don't we make the most of this opportunity?"

"No, thank you. Getting close to you doesn't meet my moral standards." Meryl stumbled out of bed and sat in the chair.

I flopped back on the pillows. "What's the problem with me? Is it the epilepsy that worries you?"

"No," I said, trying to sound sincere. "It's just that we're totally unmatched. There's no way I'm going to sleep with an arrogant woman like you. You've been given everything in your life. I've had to work to get myself where I am."

"Your very forward with your opinions," I said.

"I'm going to take a shower and get dressed while you satisfy yourself."

"Don't be disgusting. I'm going to find Clara and end this foolish situation."

"Why Clara?" Meryl asked.

"Oh, I forgot to tell you, Clara is our mentor."

"No way, she's awful. Her session yesterday was ridiculous."

"I don't think we've got a choice," I said, watching Meryl amble naked around the room, gathering her clothes, before disappearing into the bathroom.

While she was out of the room, I switched on my laptop and searched out Meryl's *MeeMeeShush* blog page. In some of her write-ups, she was condescending, but in her most recent blog, about Julia Baker-Zucchero, her words were positive. The pieces had received a thumbs up response from her thousands of followers. She was obviously good at her job.

I slapped the laptop lid closed, jumped out of bed, and pulled my clothes from the wardrobe. I dressed in a clean business suit and threw the rest of my clothes into a suitcase.

After phoning reception and requesting a porter collected my luggage, I hovered around the room. I needed to use the bathroom and freshen up. But Meryl was taking forever. How could anyone take so long to get themselves ready?

While I was waiting, I checked out the hold-all Meryl had borrowed. I examined her clothes, checking the maker's labels. There were none. When I packed Meryl's clothes back into the hold-all, her Prada wallet fell onto the floor. I picked it up and studied it, sighing as I placed it in the bag.

Eventually, Meryl emerged. "The water is lovely and hot. I used some of your products. They smell delicious. I was sure you wouldn't mind," Meryl said, rubbing her hair with vigor. "Oh, and don't forget to take your medication, don't want you having another incident."

* * *

MERYL ATE A FULL ENGLISH BREAKFAST, and a fruit waffle drenched in yoghurt. I watched her plow through the feast. "Have you eaten enough?" I asked.

"I like to drive on a full stomach," she said, waving her fork at me. "You should eat more; this is really tasty."

"I'm trying to keep my weight down; toast and coffee is fine for me."

"Is that a fashion thing?" Meryl asked, biting through the last piece of delicious looking waffle.

"Even though my body failed to turn you on, I've still got to look the part." I checked my watch. "Come on, let's catch Clara before the seminar starts, then we can leave." I grabbed my jacket and traveled to the conference floor.

Meryl grabbed her hold-all and trailed behind.

On the third floor, she stuck her head into each of the lecture rooms. "She's in here," she said, wandering into the room.

I turned and followed, finding Bernie and Joan sitting in their seats, waiting for the seminar to begin. "Excuse me," I said, "could you wait outside? We need to talk to Clara."

Bernie nodded. "No problem. Come on, sweetheart. I'll treat you to a morning mocktail." Joan smiled sweetly while Bernie led her away.

"Polly, how are you feeling?" Clara asked, clasping her hands together.

"Exhausted," I said, flopping childishly onto a seat.

"Polly's mother asked me to take her home today," Meryl said, standing by my side, her hand resting on my shoulder.

Clara glanced at me and Meryl. "In that case, we have a problem. To complete the course, you need to work with a partner and establish you can meet the standards we expect." Clara opened a folder and found our individual files. "The easiest thing to do is pair you together."

"You can't do that," I said, staring into Clara's eyes. "Meryl is a two faced, sardonic bitch. And she led me on." I could sense Meryl's eyes glaring into me.

"How did she do that?" Clara asked, not impressed with my complaining attitude.

"She got into my bed and then decided I wasn't good enough for her."

"I made a mistake," Meryl said, crossing her arms.

"Ladies!" Clara said in her professional voice. "We did not set this conference up to allow you to end up in bed together."

Meryl nodded. "That's what I told her."

"You liar, you said I didn't meet your standards."

There was a thud as Clara slammed her hands on the table. "Polly and Meryl, stop this ranting."

Meryl sat and crossed her legs. She leaned forward. "Since Polly has such strong views, I don't believe I'll benefit from being in her company much longer than I need to be."

Clara tapped the table with her pen. "From what I can see, you are both in need of essential help. Polly, you're tense and uptight. And Meryl striving to achieve success has destroyed all your relationships. Neither of you will get anywhere until you discover your proper focus. Therefore, you will work together and help each other improve."

In my slouched position, I pointed a finger at Meryl. "But she's been investigating my life, and no doubt she's planning to write disreputable things about me on her blog," I said with a huff.

"Meryl, is this true?"

"Sharing gossip is the best way of making my blog successful," Meryl said, rubbing the arm of her chair.

"To work well with Polly, you need to find another way of earning money. You've got brains. Use them," Clara said, rubbing her forehead. "Polly, the fact is, Meryl witnessed your illness and showed she could cope. Therefore, she's a perfect fit for you."

Meryl sat back and pointed at me. "Look, I'll go along with the idea if she makes some changes."

"Change what? There's nothing wrong with me."

"You look totally wrong, dressed for a specific role. You need to stop being the uppity woman you've become."

I glared at her. "Fair enough, if you promise to stop researching me and my family, and don't put my life on your stupid blog." I wanted to ensure she didn't drag me into her sleazy gutter. "Besides, if you do, I'll sue the hell out of you."

Meryl scowled, finally nodding. "Whatever."

"Good." Clara clapped her hands in her pathetic, supportive way. "Now, each of you needs to organize an activity where you can spend time together and share your interests." She looked at me and then at Meryl. "Any ideas?"

"I suppose we could go camping. Bernie invited me to her campsite," I said, certain Meryl would hate the idea. I glanced at her, seeing her shoulders tighten with tension.

Clara wrote my suggestion in her notebook. "And Meryl, what's your plan?"

"Maybe I can take Polly shopping, encourage her to improve

her style. We could even visit charity shops and I can bring her down to earth."

I waved a finger at her outfit. "Out of interest, did you buy your dress in a charity shop?" I asked, attempting to deduce where Meryl bought the clothes she was wearing.

"I did, and isn't it wonderful? It's sewn with perfection and has elegant styling."

"I agree, but you should be more careful when you buy cheap items."

"How do you mean?"

"Your Prada purse is a fake."

Her face fell at the shocking news.

Clara pushed her chair back. "Sorry to interrupt your chat. It's good that we have our activities planned. Please send me the dates you arrange, so I can attend and check on your progress. Now, I need to get this morning's seminar under way, so I'll say farewell. Have fun and I'll catch you soon."

I leaned on Clara's desk. "I'm not happy about this," I hissed. "Be ready to find yourself a new job." I pushed the door open and stormed out.

In reception, I collected my luggage, and, with Meryl in tow, descended to the car park.

"Which car is yours?" Meryl asked, eying up a red sports car.

"This one," I said, pressing the button on my key, unlocking my golden Range Rover, and placing my suitcase in the trunk.

When she threw her hold-all onto the rear seat, Meryl noticed my yellow pallor. "Are you sure you're well enough to travel?"

"I'm fine. Let's just get on with this."

Meryl clambered behind the steering wheel while I typed the address of the airport where we were meeting Anton into the Satnav. She twiddled the knobs surrounding the leather seat, adjusting the lumber support.

"Wow, this is something else," she said, gazing around the interior. "Your car is bigger than my flat."

I looked at her in surprise, considering the penthouse flat she must live in would be larger than a car interior. "Really?"

"I bet there's a kitchen sink somewhere in here?" Meryl giggled and gripped the leather steering wheel. "Have you got the key?"

"There isn't one. This car has an automatic start. Press that when you're ready." I pointed to a switch, my finger meeting Meryl's when she eagerly pushed the button. "Sorry," I said as the engine roared into life.

Meryl was a good driver. She stuck to the speed limits and carefully followed the directed route.

"If we see a roadside diner, do you want to pull over and have a coffee, see a bit of the view?" I asked, relaxing.

"Okay, but remember, I told your mother we'd be home promptly?"

"She won't notice. She never knows what the time is and won't be home until late tonight." I opened the sunroof, breathing in a lungful of fresh air.

"This car must have cost a lot of money," Meryl said, unable to stop her inquisitive nature.

"Probably, I don't deal with vehicles. I chose this car because it allows me to carry all my painting gear and get out of the city."

"It's the perfect vehicle to impress a girl. Though I suppose Anton hanging around might put them off."

"Meryl, about Anton, please don't say anything to mother about mine and his arrangement. She doesn't know anything about our deal." I gave her a pleading look and saw her nod. "Thanks," I said, grateful for Meryl's show of empathy. "What vehicle do you drive?"

"I don't own a car. I use public transport."

"Oh, right, that's why you traveled to the conference on the train. I suppose first class is a relaxing way to travel. Hey, there's a coffee stop."

Meryl pulled neatly into a parking spot. "I'll have a latte."

"You want me to fetch the coffee?"

"You offered." She slapped her forehead. "Oh, I forgot, you have people who do these things for you," Meryl said, sneering.

"No, I don't," I said, refusing to confirm she was telling the truth.

"And I'll have one of those brownies."

"Is there a flavor you prefer?" I asked, a hint of sarcasm in my voice.

"No, I don't mind, you choose."

I glared at Meryl and grabbed my wallet, venturing into the coffee stall.

Ordering the drinks and snacks was straightforward, and I wondered why I'd never attempted the activity before. There always seemed to be somebody around who could do things for me.

"Here," I said, handing Meryl a milky coffee and a chocolate brownie. "Do you want to take a walk?"

"Why not? It'll clear my head. This is a long drive."

We wandered along a short pathway, sitting ourselves on a bench and staring at the distant mountains. "You've done a good job," I said.

"At what?"

"Driving, and not asking your intrusive questions."

"It's been difficult. Your story is a gem. It could get my blog a lot of interest."

"I bet you'd love to write the tale of a sickly girl whose mummy gives her everything she wants?"

"It would be a dream, especially when I add the hair-cutting girlfriend who enjoys spending your money," Meryl said, chewing her cake.

"Thank goodness we made our agreement, and Clara was there as a witness."

"Too right. The threat of a lawyer loaded with money, my perfect nightmare."

"It wasn't a threat," I said, glaring at her.

"What was it then?"

"Protection from unwanted exposure."

"From what? Being rich, spoiled, or gay?"

"You don't give two hoots about anybody's feelings, do you? The only thing swimming around your head is earning cash. You fill your bank with filthy money." I stood and walked away from the uncouth woman. "Let's go. I can't wait to get you out of my life."

* * *

WE DROVE in silence to the airport, where we found Anton waiting outside the airport's main doors. Meryl sighed, jumped out of the driver's seat, flung the keys at Anton, and sat in the rear.

I pulled three cans of cola from the on-board cool-box and dished them out. I received a quiet whistle from Meryl. She emptied her can in one enormous gulp and rested back, slipping into an animated sleep. Me and Anton giggled as we watched her waving her arms around, muttering incoherent phrases.

My house wasn't far from the airport. The gates swung open, and Anton drove along the treelined drive.

Meryl glowered at the fake Tudor building. "Wow," she said, gawping at the vintage architecture.

"I know. The place looks awful," I said. "It's a dated look. But mother likes the style. Do you want to eat or need a drink?"

"No, I've got to go. Best get home and unpack."

"Anton will give you a lift." I waved to him. "Oh, and this is the equipment you'll need for camp." I handed her the list I'd made during the journey.

Meryl took the piece of paper and stared at the words.

"Great," she said, lifting the hold-all. "Can I give you this back when we meet next weekend?"

"You may as well keep it," I said, watching Meryl get into the front passenger seat, and Anton drive the car away.

I wandered into the house. As I'd predicted, mother wasn't home.

CHAPTER 7

Meryl

ANTON DROPPED ME IN SALTON, outside a fancy block of flats. I waved him away. When the car was out of sight, I wandered to a nearby bus stop and caught a bus to town.

Seated on the back seat, I reflected on the fiasco the Institute had drawn me and Polly into. Somehow, I'd become the unpaid helper of a spoiled, posh bird, who lived the life of Riley in a luxuriant house.

I found Polly's story frustrating. There were so many articles I could write based on her life. She could be an inspirational story. A talented woman with natural artistic flair, who, because of her illness, hid in her mother's legal department, shrouding her creativity.

But the story wasn't going to happen. I'd already destroyed a relationship by writing secretly about my ex-partner's life. When she found out, she went ballistic, kicking me out of my house and instigating solicitors. I'd lost everything and didn't want to go through the same scenario.

Jumping off the bus, I crossed the road and walked into the charity shop. "Morning Edith, how's it going?"

An elderly lady poked her head from beneath the counter. "Oh, Meryl, thank goodness you're back. I've dropped a tray of coins. They're all over the floor."

"No worries, make us both a drink while I pick them up." I ushered her into the rear kitchen and collected a fist full of cents. "How much am I looking for?" I asked, sorting the loose change into the till.

"I don't know. I'll be in terrible trouble when the manager finds out what I've done." Edith's face was red, and the teacups trembled in her hands.

"No need to mention anything. It was an accident, and, fingers crossed, I've found all the coins." I took the tea Edith passed me.

"Thank you, you're such a dear." Edith held up a carrier bag, pulling out dresses and blouses. "I've gathered you a fresh bag of clothes, all decorated with bright flowers."

"Oh, thanks. They're pretty. I'll take them to my mom and she can sew them to fit." I took a list from my pocket. "Have we got any of this stuff in the stores?"

Edith adjusted her glasses. "You're going traveling. How exciting."

"Yeah, an outcome of the conference is to make a trusted friend and get to know them. So, my would-be friend is taking me camping."

"Is she nice?" Edith asked with a wink.

"Who?"

"This friend, the one you're going camping with."

I shrugged. "Not really. We didn't click. But to pass the course, we've got to complete tasks together, and I hate to fail at anything."

"Well, let's make sure you make a good impression. We don't want you to let yourself down." Edith reviewed the listed items. "You handle the shop, and I'll search the boxes in the storeroom."

It took a while, and I made a few sales, but eventually Edith emerged, dragging a huge cardboard box.

"I think I've found everything," she said. "Here's your backpack." Edith handed me an orange canvas rucksack attached to a metal frame. "And a sleeping bag." She pulled a long, moldy smelling tube of padded material from a pouch. "And look at this tent."

I heaved a green canvas sack from the box. Loosening the strings, I peered inside. There was a small bag filled with tent pegs, a scruffily rolled piece of green fabric, a sheet of off-white cotton, and metal poles, which rattled when I retied the fastenings. "Seems okay," I muttered.

"I also found a stove." Edith held a tarnished brass campstove. "You'll need to buy some paraffin."

I placed the stove into the rucksack, fastened the tent on the bottom loops, and attached the sleeping bag to the top. Lifting the rucksack, I swung it onto my shoulders. The weight of the equipment was heavier than I expected and unbalanced me. Edith chortled with laughter when me and the rucksack fell to the ground. "I think this is going to take some getting used to," I said, joining in with her laughter.

* * *

A WEEK LATER, I stood outside the block of flats where Anton had dropped me earlier in the week, looking quite the part. I'd scoured the charity shop and found a beige walking blouse and blue cargo shorts. On my feet, I wore green Crocs atop a thick pair of red wooly socks. My rucksack contained a thin waterproof jacket, T-shirt, hiking trousers and a warm sweatshirt. I'd tied a pair of yellow Doc Martens to the side. I ditched the cooker; it looked far too dangerous.

Polly's golden Range Rover stopped at the curb. Anton leaped out of the driver's seat. "Make sure you look after my girl," he said, pointing a slim finger at me. He pecked Polly's cheek and swanked down the road.

I stood gawking after him.

Polly leaned out of the window. "Throw your bag in the trunk."

I opened the rear door and chucked my bag on top of her ton of equipment. "How long are we going for?" I asked.

"I like to be prepared."

Climbing into the driver's seat, I studied Polly, blinking at the sight before me. She'd been to the hairdressers; her golden hair was now short and layered in a pixie style. On her face sat a modern pair of glasses framed in fine bronze. When the light hit them, the glass morphed into a darker shade. The work suit had gone, and she wore a plaid short-sleeved shirt, cream jeans, and a sturdy pair of brown leather walking boots.

"What do you think of the new look?" she asked, turning her head from side to side. "Got to admit I feel so much like the real me now."

I ran my hands around the steering wheel. "You look good." If she cultivated a different attitude toward life, she'd be my ideal date. "What do mother and the girlfriend think?"

"They don't know. I only got myself kitted out this morning."

"Wish I could be a fly on the wall when they see you," I snorted. "Do you know where we're going?"

"Yes, the Satnav has plotted the directions. Your camping equipment looks vintage," Polly said, pressing the Satnav play button.

"Yeah, I like to go retro." I winced at my remark and started the engine.

"You'll find modern equipment is much sturdier and lightweight," Polly said, sniffing the aged stench permeating from my rucksack and lowering the window.

"Maybe, but my apparatus has seen the world."

"It looks like it's explored the shadow lands of a necropolis," Polly said with a snort.

In response to her rudeness, I braked sharply at a junction. Polly jarred forward, her seatbelt saving her from crashing into the windscreen.

"Shit Meryl, be careful."

"Sorry," I said. "Just getting used to the brakes."

Polly settled herself in her seat and drew a hand through her short hair, regaining her composure. "When we get to camp and have erected the tents, I'll light a fire and we can have a barbecue. I've brought home made burgers."

"Oh no, I've just started a meat-free diet," I said, glancing at her exasperated face.

"But I thought you loved burgers." She rubbed the back of her head. "I suppose we'll have to stop on the way and find you something vegetarian."

I laughed and patted her thigh. "I'm joking. I still love a burger, preferably with mayo and ketchup."

Polly winced. "I'd forgotten about your weird sense of humor."

"You need to learn how to laugh and have a go at being a tease yourself. You might make a few more friends."

"I've got enough friends, thank you."

"Then why were you on the making friends' course?" I asked, glancing at her. "I suppose Verona is your closest pal."

"Not really," Polly said, rubbing the spot on her thigh where my hand had been. "Anton is my bestie. He looks out for me."

"But he's an employee; your mother pays him wages."

"That's not the point. We're extremely close, and I can talk to him about anything. What about you?"

"I've got an endless number of friends."

"Rubbish. If you did, you wouldn't have been doing the course either."

"I'm telling the truth. Thousands of people read my blog every day."

"You don't even know who they are; they're just strangers reading your idle gossip!"

I shrugged. "No, they're people who want to indulge in and support my knowledge and thoughts."

"But they're not real friends. I'm talking about someone you can share your intimate thoughts with," Polly said, studying my profile.

I pointed to a narrow lane. "We're here," I stated, uncomfortable with the conversation.

* * *

I UNLOADED MY EQUIPMENT, spreading the old-fashioned gear on the grass. In fifteen minutes, Polly had erected her tent, and was inflating an air mattress with an electric pump. I stared at the instructions on how to construct my tent, but they made no sense. Picking up a metal tent pole, I studied the guy ropes and canvas sheeting.

Polly walked over and stood by my side. "Do you need any help?"

"No, I'm fine." I bent and connected three sets of poles, holding the two short sections aloft, trying to work out how to join the top pole.

"Let me hold them while you fit the cross bar and sheeting," Polly said, taking the uprights from me.

Not happy at having to accept her help, I grumpily connected the cross bar and threw over the canvas sheet. Polly continued to hold everything steady while I pushed metal pegs through the holes around the bottom edge of the canvas.

"There's a mallet in the car, if you want to hammer them down securely."

"No, they'll be fine," I said, confidently jiggling the tent and deciding it was quite secure.

"Are you going to fix the guy-ropes?"

"No, the weather's mild, and this tent can take anything thrown at it." I pulled the cotton inner lining from the tent bag.

"It clips inside," Polly said, answering the query which had blatantly appeared on my confused face. "It would have been better to connect it before putting on the outer canvas."

Bloody know it all, why didn't she tell me that before? I glared at her. "It's not a problem. I always put my tent up this way."

"I'll light a fire while you finish." Polly wandered to a small circle of stones, collecting an armful of sticks on her way.

I reached under my canvas and awkwardly clipped the inner tent in place. Content with my camp, I joined Polly. "Where are the toilets?" I asked, my eyes scanning the surroundings.

"You squat," Polly said, "behind a suitable bush."

My face paled in horror.

"I'm only teasing, just proving I can have a joke." A giggle burst from Polly's lips. "The toilets and shower are in the next field."

I threw her a scowl and hurried away, bursting for a pee.

When I returned, Bernie had joined Polly and was filling glasses with wine. She held the bottle aloft. "Hi Meryl, do you fancy a glass of Merlot?"

"Just a small one," I said, watching Polly tossing the burgers and sipping her wine. "This is a great campsite." I'd never stayed at any campsite in my life, but this one seemed to have everything a camper needed.

Bernie's eyes filled with mournful tears. "I inherited it from my parents when they died."

"That's sad news. But at least their bad luck was good for you.

There's always a silver lining." I slapped her on the shoulder. "Have Joan, Ruby, and Sydney arrived yet?"

"Joan will be here tomorrow morning; Ruby and Sydney are joining us when you've gone home."

"Charming," I said with a grin.

Bernie pulled a bobble hat onto her head and stood. "You'd better make sure your gear is secure. There's a storm due in later. I've arranged the canoes and a picnic for our trip tomorrow. Will nine o'clock suit you both?"

Polly nodded. "That's fine by me. I always wake early when I'm camping."

"Great. Enjoy your meal." Bernie waved and headed for her cabin.

Polly waggled her spatula at me. "The burgers are ready. Can you slice the buns?"

I ripped the bread rolls apart with my hands.

"There's a knife on the table," Polly said, giving me another spatula wiggle.

"It's faster by hand. They're clean. I washed them in the bathroom. If we're supposed to be friends, you'll have to trust me."

"I'm working on it." Polly placed a burger on each of our rolls and held up her glass in a toast. "To our attempt at friendship."

"Oh, right, cheers?" I tapped my glass on hers and emptied it in one gulp. "Tasty."

"Bernie left the wine over there, top me up," Polly said, handing me her glass.

"I'm not your servant."

Polly stopped eating and stared. "And I'm not treating you like one. I'd just appreciate another drink, and you're sitting beside the bottle. But if my request upsets you, I'll fill the glass." She reached over, grabbing the bottle. "Would you like more wine?"

I shook my head. I didn't want to drink too much alcohol. The stuff made me lose control of my inhibitions, creating turbulent relationship troubles.

While I ate my burger, the wind became brisk. The flames of the fire billowed and the temperature chilled. I wrapped my arms around myself. "Bernie was right about the weather," I said, studying the darkening sky.

"Yes, we'd better wash these dishes and get everything put away." Polly placed the dirty pots into the folding plastic wash bowl.

"I'll let you get on with that task." There was no way I was prepared to help Polly with menial activities. I stood and rubbed my forehead. "I'm going to my tent. I've got a headache coming on."

"And there was me thinking we could work together," Polly said, stomping to the wash block.

I crawled into my tent, the security of which was being challenged by the incoming storm. Sliding into my thin nylon sleeping bag, I adjusted my backside, trying to find a comfortable position, then I opened my book and attempted to read. After each word, I glanced at the surrounding canvas. It forced itself toward me with every gust of wind.

I heard Polly return and open the door of the Range Rover. She threw the cooking gear into the trunk, disturbing me with her exaggerated clanking sounds. "Silly cow," I said with a shrug. In a fatalistic response, the light of my torch flickered and went out. "Blast." I slapped it on my palm, trying to turn it on. But it refused to respond, and I remained in darkness.

I sunk into my sleeping bag and listened to drops of rain tapping on the outer cover of the tent. It was a soft gentle sound, and I drifted into a doze. Suddenly, the light raindrops became a torrent, the wind billowed, and in the distance, thunder rumbled in the sky. The bottom edge of the canvas flapped with each gust of wind, and water ran down the sides, easing its way through the seams.

"Meryl," Polly shouted. "Are you okay?"

"Yeah, I'm fine. I'm trying to sleep," I grunted, resting my head uncomfortably on the ground, wishing I'd brought a pillow.

"Okay, goodnight."

Coldness emanated from the lumpy ground beneath me. I shivered and clasped the sleeping bag tight around my body. Water dripped onto my forehead. I wiped it away and rolled over, soaking my face in a puddle of rainwater. Shuffling to the other side of the tent, I accidentally touched the canvas. This was my downfall. Water poured through, soaking my sleeping bag, and turning the puddle into a lake.

This was ridiculous. There was no point staying in here. Sitting in the truck seemed a better idea. I grabbed towels and warm clothes, and with shivering hands, unzipped the wafting door of the tent.

I headed for the Rover, splashing through deep puddles. Water soaked through the holes of my Crocs, and I reached the vehicle wearing drenched wooly socks. I pulled on the car's door handle, but it refused to open. Polly, *the bitch*, had locked the darned thing. I looked around, blinking water from my eyes.

Desperation wasn't my thing, and I hated the idea, but perhaps Polly would allow me to stay in her tent. I wandered over and was about to shout her name when I glanced through the blustering trees and saw the light of the toilet block. Taking shelter in there was a much safer and sensible idea.

CHAPTER 8

Polly

I STUDIED the storm damaged campsite. Meryl's saturated tent was on the verge of collapse. When I'd watched her putting the thing together, I knew it wouldn't survive a drizzly shower, never mind a tempest. But she'd ignored my suggestions, refusing to listen to my words of advice.

Wading through the muddy puddles, I called her name. There was no reply, and when I peered inside, the tent was empty. Where had she got to?

I found Meryl huddled in the corner of the toilet block, sleeping on the stone floor. I nudged her shoulder, waking her. "Hey," I said, gaping at her pathetic state. "I brought you a cup of tea."

With shaking hands, Meryl took hold of the mug I offered her, holding it under her frozen nose, the warmth reddening her colorless face.

"It's stopped raining, and I'm making porridge."

Meryl pulled her face in disapproval.

"It's good for you. It'll keep you going all day. Bernie and Joan are joining us in half an hour, if you still want to go canoeing?"

"Of course," Meryl said, standing, groaning, when her knees creaked. "It was only my tent which couldn't cope with the weather. I'm feeling great." She followed me out of the block and sat herself by the freshly lit fire, steam rising from her clothes.

I dished out a bowl of porridge, covering the soft oats with maple syrup and passed it to Meryl. She stared at the bubbling mixture and took a spoonful. "Mm, not bad," she said, tucking in.

Bernie arrived and assessed Meryl's tent. "It'll dry out. The forecast says it'll be sunny all day."

"I think her tent's had it," I said. "I've brought a spare."

"Who would need two tents?" Meryl asked, looking up from her breakfast.

"Somebody who's prepared for disaster," I replied.

Joan stuck her head inside the old tent, pulling out Meryl's wet sleeping bag and rucksack, hanging them on a tree branch to dry. Bernie and I scooped the tattered canvas and poles from the ground, and threw up the quick erect tent.

"That should see you safely through tonight," Bernie said, slapping Meryl's shoulder, when we joined her around the firepit.

She grunted in response.

Bernie took a notebook from her pocket. "Now, before we set off, I need to go through some safety instructions."

Meryl rubbed her head. "Just what I need, a health and safety lecture."

Ignoring her, Bernie continued with her talk. "When you get in your canoe," she said, "the stronger paddler should sit in the stern, at the rear. They need to steer around obstacles and keep the boat moving. The front paddler concentrates on spotting hazards."

Meryl raised her hand. "I thought we were in single canoes."

"What's the fun of being on your own?" Joan asked, rubbing Bernie's thigh.

"In that case, I suppose I'll sit in the back. I'm obviously the strongest between us," Meryl stated, a loud sneeze bursting from her mouth, pursued by another.

I sneered. "I don't think so. Look at the state of you. You spend one night in the great outdoors and catch a cold."

"Only because you brought me to this stupid camp and got me soaking wet."

"How great am I, having the power to control the weather?" I raised my arms to the sky. "You can sit in the front. I don't want to be infected by your sneezes. Anyway, with my height and body mass, I'd say I was the strongest."

Unfortunately, Meryl couldn't find the ability to agree with me. "I disagree. I must be stronger. I do a lot more physical work than you've ever done in your life."

"Perhaps we should arm wrestle and prove the point," I suggested.

"Okay, ladies," Bernie said, stopping our bickering. "You need to be a team. You're going to be in fast flowing water. Not working together will make things dangerous. As group leader, I'd say Polly should sit at the back."

Meryl wiped her nose on her sleeve. "Fair enough. I'm probably better at spotting signs of danger."

I snorted a laugh. "Oh yes, you prepared so well for last night's storm."

She stuck two fingers up at me.

"Charming," I said, throwing a damp tea towel and hitting Meryl in the face. "Help me wash the dishes, danger-woman. I've heard it's a hazardous experience."

"We'll do it," Joan piped, "give you time to change, and for the flu ridden to rest. Grab the dirty pots, Bernie." She stood and skipped to the washhouse, closely followed by her girlfriend.

I sniggered.

"What's so funny?" Meryl asked, desperately holding back another sneeze.

"They're so sweet together. I wish I could find someone who'd care for me."

A sneeze exploded from Meryl's face.

I tsked and threw a pack of tablets at her. "Take two of these. They should help."

Meryl popped out the tablets, swallowing them with a mouthful of coffee.

"I expect at some point you may learn to say thank you," I muttered, walking into my tent.

* * *

When Bernie and Joan returned, I came out of my tent dressed in a pair of knee-length, tight fitting neoprene shorts, a waterproof kayak top, and a pair of aqua-shoes.

"Hey," Bernie said, checking me out, "you're looking the part."

Meryl emerged in loose cotton shorts, a Spice Girls T-shirt, sports socks, and her plastic Crocs.

Bernie contemplated Meryl's clothing. "It can get chilly on the water, and when you get wet, cotton takes ages to dry. I could lend you some of my spare gear."

"I'll be fine. I don't intend to get wet again," Meryl said, pulling back her shoulders.

Bernie gave a huge grin. "If you don't fall in the water at some point, me and Joan will throw you in."

Meryl pointed a finger at them, stopping Joan's giggles. "Don't even try!"

"Only joking buddy. Follow me." Bernie led Joan and Meryl along a path to the riverside. I followed behind, strangely taken in by the hypnotic waddle of Meryl's backside.

Bernie showed us how to fit our lifejackets. I pulled the straps tight and blew on the whistle, checking it worked. Joan handed each of us a paddle, and we copied Bernie's air demonstration of how to stroke the paddle through the water.

Joan grabbed Bernie's arm, squeaking, and pointing to the floor. Bernie looked at the small green frog sitting on the grass. "Oh, hello little froggy." She bent and gathered the frog in her hand. "Here you go, sweetie."

"She's so cute," Joan said, the end of her finger stroking the frog's head. "If I kiss her, will she turn into my special princess?"

"Oh, now you're making me jealous." Bernie returned the frog to the ground and snaked an arm around Joan's waist. "You don't need a princess with me around."

I choked on their gushiness and walked into the river, gasping when my feet stood in the ice-cold water. I cocked a leg over the side of the canoe, climbed aboard, and held onto a nearby rock. "Meryl, you'd better get in, or I'll go without you."

Bernie held Joan's arm, helping her climb into their canoe and sit herself in the front seat. "Try to stay in the middle of the river," she said. "It can get shallow toward the side and you don't want to be grounded. When you hit a rapid, paddle fast and follow the line of the water."

Meryl clambered into her seat and sat facing me, waving her paddle in the air.

I whirled my finger. "You need to turn around; this isn't a pleasure cruise."

Meryl rotated on the plastic seat and faced the river. "Did I say I hated water?" she muttered as we drifted away from the bank.

"Why the fuck didn't you tell me that earlier?" I said, shocked by her announcement.

"Try to follow us," Bernie shouted, pushing her and Joan's canoe toward the middle of the river.

I stuck my paddle into the pebbles of the riverbed and copied Bernie's actions. Drenching Meryl with a splash of my blade as the rapid flow of water washed us down the river. "It would help if we both paddled."

Meryl plunged her paddle into the river, pulling a stroke, making the canoe turn in a circle.

"We need to co-ordinate," I said, trying to turn us back in line.

"In that case, you'll have to copy me. I can't see you through the back of my head," Meryl mumbled.

"What?" I asked, straining to hear Meryl over the rush of the water.

Meryl turned her head to face me. "Copy me." Turning back to the front, she shrieked as we approached a huge rock.

I stopped my paddling motion, dug one blade into the water, and somehow steered us around the boulder. Then I paddled hard, getting the boat back on track.

Meryl's shoulders tensed. One hand gripped her blade, the other clenched the side of the canoe. "Have you done this before?" she asked.

"Several times, when I was in the Guides."

"Why doesn't that come as a surprise? Someone of your caliber was bound to have been a girl guide," Meryl said with a shrug. "How did you deal with your epilepsy when you were camping out with the girls?"

"I took an assistant with me."

"Don't tell me your mother employed her?"

"Yes, and she was also my private tutor."

"So, we've got something in common. I never went to school either. I skipped lessons most days." Meryl was so busy reminiscing she missed the log which was drifting toward us. The canoe rammed into it, jarring me forward.

"*Puttana!*" I yelled, "I've lost my paddle." Leaning over the side, I tried to reach the paddle as it glided away. The canoe lurched, and I tumbled into the river, creating a huge splash. I sloshed my arms, treading water, glaring at Meryl. "You made me fall in."

Meryl failed to stifle a giggle. "Why was it my fault? You were the one leaning out of the boat!"

Swimming to a shallow area, I grabbed the side of the canoe and tried to climb aboard. The boat rocked and Meryl tumbled overboard.

"You bitch," she spluttered. "I can't swim."

The current took hold of her body, and she drifted away from me and the canoe. Meryl flailed her arms in some sort of stroke and kicked out her legs. It was no use. She continued to float away. I swam after her. Within moments, my arm was around her waist, and I was guiding the pair of us to the riverside.

"You should have told me you couldn't swim," I gasped, dragging Meryl onto the pebbly beach, attempting not to ogle the bountiful breasts beneath her wet T-shirt. "Bernie," I yelled, distracting myself by trying to catch the attention of the other canoe.

Meryl coughed frothy water out of her lungs and sneezed foam from her nose. "Sorry," was all she could say.

Bernie and Joan paddled to us, towing our upside-down canoe. "Are you two alright?" Bernie asked.

"I'm fine," I said. "I don't know about her." Water dripped from my fingertips when I pointed them at Meryl.

"A slight accident," Meryl said, her body quivering from the intensity of the event.

"Slight!" I hissed, glaring at her, my face millimeters from her nose. "We're soaked, and we've lost both paddles. You've basically ruined our day on the water."

"It's not ruined. Don't you think it was exciting?" Her hands held my cheeks, and she kissed my lips. "Thank you for saving me."

I stared at her, touching my lower lip, startled by her action.

"Polly, can you help me empty the water from your canoe?" Bernie shouted.

"Yes, I'm on my way." I looked away from Meryl's eyes. "Got to go," I mumbled.

CHAPTER 9

Meryl

Having lost both paddles, me and Polly sat in the canoe being towed back to camp. I sat at the rear this time, trying to gain Polly's attention with my aimless chatter. But she constantly stared ahead, avoiding conversation.

At one moment Polly turned her head and glanced at me. I spied a look of confusion in her eyes. I'd gone too far and shouldn't have kissed her. Now I had to find a way of diffusing the situation.

Polly held the canoe steady while I clambered out. "Thanks," I said, holding her arm to keep me steady.

"It's okay," Polly said, the muscles in her arm clenching, startled by my touch. She wandered away, helping Bernie carry the boats to the storage area.

* * *

SHOWERED AND CHANGED, I sat in a folding seat outside my newly improved tent. I closed my eyes and listened to the birds singing. Polly had gone for a walk along the hillside, her paintbox and sketchpad in her hands. She'd muttered that she'd see me later.

In order to impress her, I tidied the campsite and stacked a bunch of sticks on the fire pit. It took a while, and I almost emptied the box of matches, but eventually tiny flames flickered from my fire.

Bernie arrived carrying two bottles of wine. Joan followed clutching a gong, tapping it with a felt ended wooden stick, creating a sharp ringing sound which echoed around the atmosphere.

"Hope you enjoyed the day," Bernie said, placing chopped firewood around my feeble effort, making the fire roar.

Joan walked around me, tapping, filling my ears with noise. "I brought my gong to bathe the area and create a peaceful solstice."

"I need some calm. Today was exhilarating," I said, glancing up when I saw Polly returning. She wandered to the fire and took a seat opposite me.

Joan giggled and nudged me when she made her next clang. "Your face was a hoot when you sat drenched on the beach."

"Glad I entertained you." I selected a piece of wood from Bernie's stack to throw on the fire. "Ouch!" I yelled.

"What now?" Polly asked. "Can't you do anything without turning it into a drama?"

I grimaced. "It's nothing."

Bernie leaned over and reached for my hand. "Just a splinter. Soon get that out." She pulled a first aid kit from her pocket and fixed my injury with a pair of tweezers.

"Thanks," I said as she stuck a plaster over the tiny wound.

"Do you fancy a glass of wine? Celebrate you surviving the dangers you've met today?" Joan asked, pouring four glasses, holding one out to me.

Sometimes, the buzz of life overtakes sobriety, and I took

the glass. "Great idea, cheers." I swirled a mouthful of wine around my tongue. "Nice flavor, tastes of berries, squash, and hot red earth. It's got to be a South African, Stellenbosch Merlot."

Bernie grabbed the bottle and read the label, showing it to the others. "She's right."

"You're so clever," Joan gushed.

Challenging my intelligence, Polly sneered. "Her ex owned a vineyard, so she should know something."

* * *

AFTER TWO GLASSES OF WINE, Bernie and Joan said their goodnights and wandered to Bernie's cabin. Their urgency to escape me and Polly and have an early night suggested their relationship had reached a physical level.

Without them, the atmosphere around the fire became uncomfortable. "It's been a long, tiring day. Are you feeling alright?" I asked, being empathetic about Polly's epilepsy.

"Yes, my fits are deciding to control themselves, unlike you."

I ignored her comment and opened the last bottle of wine. "Californian this time."

"Thanks," Polly said, "what's your review of this one?"

"Bright, refreshing, and full of fun, a bit like me."

She curled her lip. "More like brash, forward and slightly bitter."

I raised my brows at her harsh words and gazed at Polly in contemplation. She needed to lighten up. I moved my chair to her side. "Tell me about your girlfriend?"

"Why do you want to know about her?"

"I'm interested."

"Haven't you already found the information on your worldwide web?"

"Hey, I promised to leave you and your life alone. I'm just

trying to have a conversation and get to know you better. Isn't that what friends do?"

Polly tilted her head and looked into my eyes, clearly unsure whether to discuss her life with me. "Verona's a model."

"Really? How did you get together?" I asked, surprised by her response.

"What do you mean? Don't you think I can pull a model?"

I stared at the stars in the sky. The problem with me and alcohol is my mouth runs uncontrollably away with me. "No, not really. I mean, a model doesn't seem to be the type of woman you'd go for."

"Oh, now you're an expert on my type."

"Don't get me wrong, but I'd say a model girlfriend is only with you to work with your company, get free clothes and enjoy spending your money."

Polly considered my words. "Maybe," she said, shrugging and drinking a mouthful of wine.

"Aha, you see I'm onto something. Does she get on with your mother?"

Polly nodded and rubbed her forehead. "Mother actually got us together."

I rested my hand on Polly's. "Poor you, your mother totally controls your life. You're a drip of water, not allowed to drop into the pool of life."

"Such poetic words, what should I do, oh faithful guider?" Polly asked, unable to mask her sarcasm.

I ignored her attitude and continued my drink laden speech. "It's not for me to tell you what to do. You're surrounded by people who will do that for you. Controlling the lives of others isn't my style. You're the one who needs to work out how to break free." I squeezed her hand in support.

Polly puffed out her chest. "I don't know what you're talking about? My life is great. I'm educated, employed, have a home and a girlfriend. What more could I want?"

I took a sip of wine and glanced at the portentous woman. "But your job hides you in an office in a back room, and your girlfriend doesn't seem to be around. I'd prefer to be with someone who loves to hang out with me, and have a job I enjoy."

"Hmm. What an interesting response."

"You must have passion and talent for something other than law."

Polly sat back, gazing at me. "I'd love to be an artist and travel the world, studying painting techniques."

"There, I was right. What would you draw on your grand tour?"

"Landscapes, buildings, people."

"Let's start now," I said, reclining in my seat. "Fetch your sketchbook and draw me."

Polly put down her glass. "You actually want me to draw right now."

"Why not?"

She stood and went to her tent, returning with a sketchbook, pencil, and paints. Sitting, she enthusiastically scrawled graphite around the page, drawing a faint outline of my body and filling areas with shade.

I watched, impressed with her ability.

"It's dark out here, luckily the light of the fire is creating highlights," she said, erasing parts of the drawing. Opening her paint pot, she washed a brush of sienna over the paper. "There," she said, holding the picture aloft, awaiting my response.

"Amazing," I said, truly in awe.

"I'll do another. Stay still." On the next page, she began a new drawing. This time, she focused on my face. "Stop smirking," she muttered.

"I can't, I'm enjoying being the center of your study."

Polly's hand swished around the page, this time with a stub of charcoal. She rubbed parts with her fingers, dirtying her hands. Then she stared at my eye sockets. "Meryl?"

"Yeah."

"Why did you kiss me earlier?" she asked as her charcoal created the lines around my eyes.

"I was excited, overwhelmed by the incident, and wanted to thank you for saving my life. I guess I was over-awed with adrenaline." My face flushed. The kiss had been an impulse. We'd been standing close, and even though Polly had been scolding me for causing the canoe incident, heat flew around my body, and I had a sudden urge to press my lips to hers. I'd hoped she'd decide to ignore my indiscretion.

"There was no other reason?" Polly asked, her head tilted in anticipation as she made some final strokes across the paper.

"No," I said with a shrug.

Polly's smile dropped. "There." She passed me the sketchbook.

I stared at the tired, vulnerable woman in the drawing. I wanted to tell Polly this wasn't me. But she'd only argue that she'd drawn what she saw.

Polly placed the charcoal into her pencil case and took my hand when I returned the sketchbook. "How's your finger?"

"Better, stinging a little."

"Nothing worse than an injured finger." She kissed the plaster, then her lips approached mine, her hand holding my cheek. "Is that better?"

"Much improved," I said, leaning toward her. "Are you going to be one of those artists who sleeps with her models?"

Polly winked. "Why not, if the model gives me a chance?" She pressed her lips on mine. They were tender to start, becoming firmer when the kiss intensified. Her tongue teased my lips, then drew away. "We could finish our wine in my tent." She pulled me upward and led me away from the fire.

Not thinking clearly, I pulled my hand from hers and pushed her away. "It's time for bed."

Polly glanced between the tents. "I know. That's what I'm suggesting."

"You in yours and me in mine," I said, heading for my tent.

"Oh, *merda*!" Polly's face dropped with disappointment, and she waggled her finger between us. "I thought you were coming on to me. My mistake, apologies." She leaned toward me, her shoulders tense, and kissed my cheek. "Sleep well."

I stood, gawking, watching Polly disappear into her tent, pulling the zipper closed. I slapped the middle of my forehead with my palm and opened the door to my new bijou tent. Inside, someone had placed an inflated bed, covered with a quilt and pillow. To the other side, my dry clothes sat folded in a tidy pile. A bottle of drinking water and a box of chocolates lay beside my pajamas. This was amazing; I must remember to thank Bernie and Joan tomorrow.

Wanting to avoid Polly, I grabbed my wash bag and hurried to the toilet block. She approached me as I was jogging back. "Hi," I said, panting from my run.

"I heard it was better to exercise in the morning, rather than before bed," she said, her voice terse.

"I know, but I can't wait to get back and settle myself into my fresh bed."

"Hopefully, you'll be more comfortable than last night. Enjoy the chocolates. See you in the morning."

CHAPTER 10

*P*olly

A DREAM FILLED MY SLEEP. It involved Meryl, Verona, and mother. They were arguing. I forced myself awake before one of them killed the other. Annoyed at Meryl infiltrating my dreams, the early morning dawn chorus calmed my mind.

I'd been attracted to Meryl last night; the intimacy of our situation took me by surprise. Being sexually close to anyone wasn't my forte, but after Meryl's earlier kiss, I thought she might take things further. She didn't, so I made a move on her, in the hope she would respond. I felt a fool when she pushed me away.

I'd been an idiot. Meryl was arrogant. She'd given me a meaningful kiss, then said it was only a means of saying thanks. I shook my head; kissing meant a lot more to me than it did to her.

I heard the breakfast pots rattling. When I roamed out of the tent, wrapped in my quilt, Meryl poured me a coffee from the pot she'd brewed.

"Are you feeling okay to join me on the walk I've planned?" I asked, wondering if, after the chaos of yesterday, I was going to be strolling solo.

"Of course, we've got to show Clara we can be friends. What time is she arriving?"

"She's meeting us here at one o'clock and is bringing lunch." I poured cereal into a bowl, added milk, and munched through the flakes. "Probably burgers."

"Great." Meryl hummed into her mug. "By the way, thank you for the bed. I had a wonderful night."

"No problem, but it could have been better."

Meryl blushed, unable to meet my eyes. "I'll get prepared for the day."

"Okay, give me a shout when you're ready."

* * *

I WAS PACKING my day bag with snacks and a flask of coffee when Meryl joined me. "Are you taking any food with you?" I asked. "Sometimes I need an energy boost to help me climb the hills."

Meryl rustled her coat pockets. "I've got a bag of sweets and a can of cola."

When I bent to tie my boots, I studied Meryl's yellow Doc Martens. I was concerned they weren't adequate footwear to tramp along the rugged trails.

"Are those comfortable?" I asked. "They look on the small side."

"Of course, otherwise I wouldn't be wearing them."

"Good," I said, throwing my bag onto my shoulder. "Follow me."

The beginning of the walk was pleasant. "It's great to be in the outdoors," I said, gazing into the blue sky as we wandered along a grassy path. Purple and white flowers decorated the verge, and birds twittered their songs from the shady trees.

"Usually, I only walk around the city, so this feels odd."

"In that case, you need to get out more."

"So do you." Meryl kicked a small stone and winced. "You should get away from the women surrounding you. They're making your life hell."

I glared at her. "Tell me about it."

"I'm only being honest with you. Your relationship with Verona is false and not working, and if you consider the outstanding paintings you produced last night, you need to discuss your career with your mother."

Why did Meryl have to be so open with her frank opinions? And, irritatingly, why was she always right? Mother, Verona, and now Meryl, were making my life hell.

The path became rockier, and we clambered upward toward the peak of the hill. While I waited for Meryl to catch me, I took in the views and pulled my camera from my day bag to shoot a few photos.

Meryl staggered to my side and slumped to the floor. Tugging off her boots, she waggled her toes and groaned. "My feet are killing me." She pulled away her socks, revealing bright red blisters on each of her heels and big toes.

"I think you should have bought the next size up," I said, lifting a boot from the floor and studying its construction.

"They're just a snug fit. I bought them because soldiers wear them, and they'll last forever."

"That's a total myth. These boots are okay for life in the city, but not out here in the hills. Look, the soles are wearing thin already. And, I don't think yellow is a fashionable hiker look."

"They looked good in the shop." Meryl rubbed her aching feet. "I don't think I can walk any further."

"We'll have a rest, then we can walk back."

"I've just told you I can't walk. I'm in agony."

"You don't have a choice. I can't carry you and I don't believe emergency rescue will pander to your whims." I rooted through my bag and removed my first aid kit. "Here." I handed Meryl a handful of blister plasters. "Put these on your wounds and loosen the ties on your boots."

I left Meryl covering her feet in plasters and went to a nearby thicket. I rummaged through the briars and brambles and pulled out a long, sturdy stick.

"If you use this, and we walk slowly, we should make it back," I said, handing Meryl the makeshift crutch.

Meryl examined the implement, then put a hand to her head. "No, the pain in my feet is excruciating. Go back without me and fetch help."

"I can't leave you here. There might be bears. I don't think Clara will give me a certificate if I allow my friend to be eaten by a wild animal."

Meryl giggled.

"Take my hand," I said, reaching out to her.

Clenching my arm and clinging to the stick, Meryl and I hobbled back to camp.

* * *

WHEN CLARA ARRIVED, Meryl was soaking her feet in a bowl of icy river water, easing her burning blisters.

"Hello both," Clara said. "Bernie and Joan are on the way." She handed Meryl a brown paper bag.

Meryl sniffed the mouth-watering aroma of a giant burger. "Just what I need after our awful morning."

"It wasn't too bad. Apart from your blisters, the walk was inspirational." I took my lunch from Clara and sat beside Meryl, nudging her in jest.

"Hi." Joan took a seat around the fire-pit. "How was your night?" she asked with a wink.

"We came by for a nightcap, but you were busy, so we went back to our cabin," Bernie said, snickering.

Meryl shrugged. I glanced at her and said nothing.

Clara smiled in surprise. "You all seem to be enjoying each other's company."

"Oh, definitely. Me and Bernie are dating," Joan said, squeezing Bernie's arm.

"From what I've seen, you could skip dating, move in together and marry," Meryl scoffed.

Bernie waggled a finger between me and Meryl. "I thought you'd be doing the same thing."

"I can assure you nothing happened between us." Meryl bit into her burger, sauce running down her cheek.

"Too right, there's absolutely no way we're getting together," I said, devouring my chips.

Clara pointed a finger. "Hmm, you two need to talk more. I suggest you create a list of questions for your next meeting, perhaps discuss themes which caused tension this weekend."

Meryl raised her shoulders. "Maybe."

"I don't believe Meryl wants any sort of friendship with me, so I suggest we don't bother meeting again," I said, irritated by Meryl's annoying behavior.

Clara shook her head. "Not yet. The program isn't finished. You need to complete the shopping experience Meryl has planned, and we'll take things from there."

I shrugged with indifference. "Whatever. I don't generally have a problem hanging out with people. It's the lingering idiots I can't stand."

Meryl choked on her food. "Are you calling me stupid?" she yelled, spluttering pieces of burger from her mouth.

"If the cap fits."

"You'd better find yourself a new driver to get you home. I'm getting a lift from Clara."

"Now, now," Clara gasped. "Let's not fall out. Polly, you need to apologize, and Meryl, fulfill your role and drive Polly home."

Meryl stared at me.

"*Spiacente*, sorry," I muttered.

"Hmph," Meryl replied.

Bernie grasped Joan's hand. "We're off to meet Ruby and Sydney."

"Clara, we'll see you next week. Bye." Joan followed Bernie to the cabin.

"It's also time for me to leave," Clara said, glancing at me and Meryl. "Don't forget to talk to each other. Goodbye."

With everyone gone, I stared at the ground. "Let's pack our things and get out of here. Stop dragging this disaster out any longer." I stood and headed for my tent.

"Polly, wait," Meryl said, her fingers intertwining.

"Yes."

"I'm not an idiot."

"If you say so." I yanked out my tent pegs, screwed the tent into a ball, forced it into its carry bag, and threw it into the trunk. Then I climbed into the passenger seat and waited for my juvenile delinquent so-called friend to drive me home.

Meryl carefully packed the gear I'd provided for her and stashed it in the trunk beside my equipment. Chuntering to herself, she sat in the driver's seat and started the engine.

I strapped on my seat belt and sat in silence all the way back to Meryl's flat.

When she pulled to the side, I was pleased to see Anton waiting. "Did you have a good time?" he asked, opening the door for Meryl.

"Don't ask," I said. "Meryl, do you want me to help you carry your gear inside?"

"No, I'm fine. I'll see you next weekend, bye." Meryl took her rucksack and walked to the block of flats, tapping numbers into the keypad.

"*Cagna ignorante*," I huffed.

* * *

"Hello, darling," mother said, raising her head from her laptop when I wandered into the lounge. "Did you have fun?"

I sank onto the sofa. "No, having to hang around with that unsavory woman from the conference was horrible."

"Do you mean Meryl? I thought she was supposed to be your friend."

"She deliberately wobbled the canoe, and I fell in the river. Then she spoiled the walk I'd planned by wearing a stupid pair of boots. I mean, everyone knows, Doc Marten's aren't hiking boots." I didn't want to go into too much detail, knowing me being dumped by Meryl wouldn't impress mother, and she would be sure to tell Verona.

"At least you tried."

"Besides, Meryl would be a rubbish friend. Not only is she a drama queen, she refused to share any information about herself. I came back, knowing nothing about her. She spent the whole weekend sticking her beaky nose into my business."

"Sounds mercenary. She must run a hard-core business?"

I wandered to my mother's side and opened the Internet. I found Meryl's web page, headed by her cartoon character. "Not really. She writes this blog."

Intrigued, mother studied the site, listening to several blog recordings. "Quite impressive. Does she want a job? We could do with someone to run our social media campaign."

"I've no idea, and if I ask, she wouldn't tell me." I jutted out my bottom lip.

"Polly, sulking doesn't look good."

"Sorry," I said. "Mother, I've been thinking."

Mother scrolled through an on-line document. "What about?"

"I want to leave the legal department and become an artist."

Her eyes glanced up from the laptop, and she gave me her patronizing smile. "Darling, you need to have creative talents to be successful in the art world. And that's an area where you're severely lacking."

Mother shunning my ideas made my shoulders sag. "They have a fantastic art course at the university. If I can get an interview, I can show them the portfolio I've created."

"Baby, your artwork is naïve and not up to professional standards." She patted my arm. "When you've accomplished the skills from Julia Baker Zucchero's seminars, you'll be happier in your legal role. Now, go check your emails. I've sent you an article that *Vogue* magazine plans to publish about our new designs. Let me know what you think." She returned to her typing, ending the conversation.

CHAPTER 11

Meryl

I watched Polly's sunset gold Rover drive off, then I walked away from the building. I tramped along the roads toward my actual residence, well away from the city's middle-class area.

When I reached my block, I met Charlie rooting through the dustbins. "Found anything useful?" I asked.

"Hey, bud, look at this." Charlie waved a picture in the air, gold peeling from the frame, a crack across the glass.

I studied the watercolor of roses, which brightened Charlie's face. "It's lovely. It'll liven up your squat."

"Exactly what I thought." He placed it carefully on the ground before diving back into the bin.

I gave a chuckle and opened the front door of the run-down block of bedsits. There was a brown envelope in my pigeon-hole, *important* stamped across it in red. It was from the bank. This wasn't good, especially since I thought they'd extended my credit limit. I stuffed the letter into my pocket and entered my room.

Exhausted, I dropped the rucksack on the floor and edged around the pull-down bed to the kitchen worktop. Desperate for a drink, I switched on the kettle, and stood staring through the window, waiting for the water to boil.

After several minutes of studying the rusty window bars and smears on the glass, I realized the kettle had died. I flicked the light switch. The room remained in its dullness. My electric meter was empty.

At least water ran from the tap, and I drank a glass of liquid, pulling my nose at its rancid taste.

My phone pinged. It was Polly, wanting to know where we were meeting on Saturday so she could add the details to her diary. I sent a return text, telling her to meet me at the Yellow Fever coffee bar on Old Town Lane, Salton, at nine in the morning.

"Interesting, I've never been to Salton," she replied with a smiling emoji.

I lay on the bed, gazing at the yellow stained ceiling, recalling mine and Polly's potential night of passion. Polly was difficult to refuse, especially with her fresh hair style and lithe body. I'd sensed she wanted me to make a move, but I forced myself to hold back. I didn't want her to discover my meagre, pathetic life. I had to keep her distant; she was way out of my league.

I opened my iPad. and, eager to kill off mine and Polly's relationship, wrote about our camping date. When she read this, she'd be shoving me away with a barge pole.

* * *

I WAS LATE ARRIVING at the Yellow Fever. Polly was sitting at a twin table drinking a black coffee, her fingers strumming her thigh. When she saw me, she glanced at the Rolex embracing her wrist.

"Well done, only twenty minutes late," she said, pulling a small bunch of flowers from beneath the table. "I wanted to say sorry for dragging you on a camping trip you totally hated."

Surprised, I took the flowers and sat in a chair, guilt from the blog I'd recently published pressing down on my shoulders. "Thanks."

A server brought me a cappuccino, the foam topping dusted with two chocolate hearts.

"Do you want a Danish or croissant?" Polly asked, as the server hovered awaiting my reply.

"Apple Danish would be lovely," I said, admiring the glint of cleavage appearing from Polly's pressed white shirt. Fitted denim jeans dressed her legs, torn in all the right places, and black biker boots covered her feet. A distressed, black leather jacket hung on the rear of her seat. She was so hot; a shimmer of sweat glistened on my neck.

Polly studied my multicolored striped dress and sipped her coffee. "You have an elegant taste in clothes."

"So have you." I circled my hand around her body. "I prefer this look to your pinstripes, though the plaid hiker look was quite fetching."

"My mother tries to make me look more girly, but the clothes she keeps providing don't suit me."

"Do you have a matching motorbike?" I joked, savoring the sweet pastry.

"Yes, a red Yamaha Tracer. I would have ridden here; but I can only ride around the grounds of the house. You know, because of the fit."

I drank my cappuccino and swallowed the last of my food; the wind blown out of my sails by Polly's honesty.

Polly was watching, intrigue on her face. "You like your food," she said, tipping her head to one side.

"I didn't have time for breakfast." I bit my bottom lip, hating having to lie. The loaf of bread in my cupboard had gone moldy, and the fridge was empty. Which in foresight was fortunate since I still had no electric.

"Oh," she said. "Do you want me to get you something else to eat?"

I shook my head. "No, we can get a bacon roll at the market."

"Market? I thought we were going to the shopping plaza."

"No, that's boring. My date is a journey to the flea market."

"A what?"

"It's a market where people sell a myriad of things: antiques, bric-à-brac, old clothes, collectables."

"You mean trash."

"It may be rubbish to you, but to other people, it's treasure. This way." I led Polly out of the café to a nearby bus stop. The computerized display told us a bus would be along in five minutes.

"You're taking me on a bus?"

"Do you have a problem with buses?"

Polly shrugged. "No, I pay my taxes to support facilities, so I suppose there's no harm in experiencing public transport."

"I don't suppose you have a travel pass," I said, waving mine at her. "So, you'll need a couple of dollars to pay for your ticket?"

"I only carry credit cards." Polly's hand entered the inside pocket of her jacket, removing a small wallet.

"There's an ATM on the wall over there." I pointed to a nearby banking facility.

Polly stared at the contraption, confusion on her face.

"You use it to get money out of the bank," I explained, stumped to have come across a woman who'd never used an automated teller. "Come on, I'll show you."

Polly walked up to the cash machine and followed my instructions. I almost passed out when I saw the contents of her account. "Maybe you should get some extra cash; in case you find yourself a bargain." My eyes grew wide when she agreed and withdrew five hundred dollars.

We returned to the stop just as the bus arrived and I showed Polly how to use the farebox, then directed her to a couple of seats. "You sit by the window. You can view the outside world better from there."

"I'm not an alien," Polly said. "I know what happens in the world."

"Maybe, but you need to experience it." I nudged her. She tsked and stared out of the window, watching people hurry along the pavements.

When the bus filled, I could feel Polly's body stiffen. "Only a couple more stops, and we'll be at the Free Trades Hall," I said. "They hold a market there every two months."

"What do you buy at these markets?"

"I try to find antiques to sell on-line and make myself a profit. Do you collect anything? We might find you a bargain."

Polly shrugged. "I guess I could look for stuff about motorcycling."

"There you go, rubbish to me, treasure for you." I pulled the yellow chord, making the stop bell ring, and tugged Polly's jacket, pulling her from her seat and off the bus. Taking her hand, I led her to the hall.

It was early in the day, but people packed the flea market. Polly followed me, watching me wander from stall to stall, scouring each table, then rummaging through the boxes on the floor, searching for hidden artifacts.

After the third stall, I noticed Polly wasn't with me. I looked around; she'd stopped at a stall filled with sporting memorabilia. Glad she'd found something interesting; I rooted through a box of pottery. I selected a few pieces and bartered with the seller.

When I approached Polly, she was flicking through a folder of press photos, chatting in Italian with the stallholder. She filled a carrier bag with magazines, photographs, and a jersey. She paid, hugged the seller, and came to my side.

"This is amazing." Polly grasped me in a hug and kissed my

cheek. "Hold this bag and wait here." She disappeared into the toilet block.

When she returned, Polly had replaced her white shirt with a motorcycle jersey. She twirled the green, white, and orange shirt, merging the colors. On the front, a black horse reared inside a yellow shield; on the back it said number forty-seven. "What do you think?"

"Looks great," I said, puzzled by how happy the shirt had made this woman.

Polly stroked the fabric, raising the front to her nose, inhaling deeply. "This was my father's," she said, tears gathering in her eyes.

"Oh wow, what a lucky find." I opened the bag and spotted a stash of racing leaflets. Images of the motorcyclist, Marco Tulipani, covered the front pages.

"I didn't know what happened to my father's things after he died. It seems my mother auctioned everything. The man at the stall bought most of the items and stored them for years in his garage. Look, he gave me his address, so I can see the rest of his collection. This is one of the best days of my life." She grabbed me once more, kissing my other cheek. "Grazi, grazi," she gushed.

I enjoyed the attraction of her touch, smile, and laughter.

"Let's eat." Polly led me out of the hall to a nearby diner.

"We don't need to go anywhere fancy," I said. "There's a sandwich stall in the hall."

"I'm treating you for providing me with this." Her hand stroked the shirt once more, her bosoms raising when her hand glided across them.

I felt perspiration trickle across my brow and casually attempted to wipe it away.

Polly grinned and winked. "After you." She held open the diner door. "What shall we eat?"

"Well, since we're in a burger joint, maybe we should go for the Double Whammy."

"And to drink?"

"Cola," I said, watching Polly go up to the counter and place the order. When she returned, a grin was still covering her face. "Is this the first time you've been in a McDougall's burger bar?" I asked.

She blushed when she nodded.

"Number forty-six," a boy shouted, a forced smile on his face.

Polly jumped out of her seat and fetched the tray. She handed me a bag of food and a plastic topped paper cup. "Cheers," she said, supping cola through her straw.

"You're behaving like a small child," I said, chewing a bunch of fries.

Polly unwrapped her packets of food and peeled the lid from a pot of mayonnaise. The edges of her mouth drooped. "I'm just enjoying having an exciting day out." Polly bit into her burger. "So delicious," she murmured.

I looked around the room filled with smiling people, tucking into food, engrossed in conversation. Most people appeared to enjoy eating out with family and friends. Maybe I needed to relax.

Polly dipped a fry into her sauce. "I read about our camping trip on your blog."

"Ah," I said, staring at my bun, guilt burning my innards. "So, I guess you're disgusted by my actions and won't want to see me again."

"What? No, you didn't mention my name, so I wasn't affected. The only thing is, why do you have to exploit people and create gossip when you write?"

"It gets me readers, and more readers means I get more advertising and I make more money. My followers would ditch me if they had to read about people buying over-priced designer clothes made by underpaid workers in distant foreign factories; and the ridiculous profits made by companies like the one your mother runs. Besides, I thought the tale of a couple capsizing in the river, then ending up sleeping together, was entertaining."

"I suppose you have a point. Pity we didn't get as far as the girls in your tale." Polly chewed her food while she considered my words. Her phone rang. "Sorry," Polly said when she answered. *"Ciao Verona, ti lascio,* I'm leaving you. *Io so, sono sorpreso,* I'm surprised at my decision as well, but things haven't been going well between us. I'll pay the rent for another month, give you time to organize yourself." Polly's face paled when a stream of loud foreign words poured from her phone. *"Okay, ciao."*

I stared at Polly while she spoke, mesmerized by the words and her sultry Italian accent. It generated feelings in my lower body. How could the way someone spoke create such urges?

"There," Polly said, ending the call, "I've finished with Verona."

"That was a callous way to be dumped, and, from what I heard, Verona sounded upset."

"I'm sorry you heard her swearing. She has a mouth like a fish-wife. But it's like you said, I was someone who got her modeling jobs and handed her money." She wiped her lips with a serviette. "Why are you staring at me?"

I blinked my eyes away from her. "We need to go," I said, piling my waste into the bag and depositing it in the diner's recycling bin.

Polly copied my actions and bounced out of the front door into the lane of shops. As we walked along, Polly stopped and looked in the windows of every store. I couldn't believe how new this was to her. "Are we going to the charity store now?" she asked. "See if you can dress me fashionably."

"Oh, yeah, we're almost there."

After passing a couple of clothing stores and discussing the fashions, we stared through the window of a grimy antique store.

"Wow, there are some stunning treasures in here. Is the shop open?" Polly asked, peering into the dark interior.

"No, Alf's emporium is closed on a Saturday. Come and look around the charity store instead." I walked to the adjacent shop.

"What charity do they support?"

"People who are destitute. You know, the ones we've walked past on the way here."

Polly stared at me in surprise, then looked up and down the road. Her eyes spotted bodies sitting on the ground, holding out their hands, greeting passers-by and being ignored. An intense blush crossed her face.

Pushing on the door of the charity shop, I held it open for Polly, and she hurried inside.

Edith was sitting behind the counter. She gave me a beaming smile. "Meryl," she said, standing and approaching me, giving me a friendly hug. "How are you, my darling? How was your camping trip?"

"Oh, it was fine. This is Polly, my camping companion."

"Polly, it's nice to meet you. Meryl has mentioned you a few times."

"Hello," Polly said, gently shaking Edith's frail hand. "This is a lovely shop, so well laid out."

"Yes, Meryl does all the arranging of clothes and artifacts. She's so creative."

Polly wandered around the rails of clothes. "I didn't realize you worked here." She studied some fashionable dresses and glanced at me. Then she clicked her fingers. "Now it makes sense."

"What are you talking about?" I asked.

"This is the reason you're wearing my clothes?"

"What?" I said in shock, looking at myself in the mirror, then at Polly and Edith. "

"I pass the clothes my mother gives me to Anton, and he must donate them to this shop."

"Oh, yes, Anton, he's always popping in," Edith said, walking around me. "I cut out the labels and give the clothes to you, because on your body, they look gorgeous."

My face paled, and I backed toward the door. I had no words, only complete embarrassment. I turned and rushed outside. I had to get away.

CHAPTER 12

Polly

I WAS SURPRISED by Meryl's behavior. Being given decent clothes for free should have made her happy, yet she ran away. "What's wrong with her?" I asked Edith, who was standing at the door, watching Meryl's escape.

"You embarrassed her," Edith said, staring at me, her eyes burning into my brain.

"How did I do that?"

"By telling her about the clothes." Edith grabbed my shoulder and marched me into the back room.

"I don't understand why you're angry with me," I said, perching my backside on a stool. "And I don't get why you give Meryl clothes? She runs her own company and has thousands of followers. She must make a fortune."

Edith made two cups of instant coffee, handing me one and sitting on the opposite stool. "Meryl only earns enough for the basics in life. She can't afford to buy anything for herself."

My face dropped. "In that case, how could she afford to attend the conference?"

"She won the ticket in our charity lottery. The poor dear scraped together enough money to stay at the youth hostel."

I rubbed the side of my head. "No, you're wrong. Meryl had a suite at the top-class Kilton Towers on the other side of town?"

Edith shook her head. "She's an expert at fooling people."

I drank a mouthful of coffee, wincing and trying not to pull my face at the vile flavor. "So, everything Meryl owns comes from here?" I waved my hand around the shop.

"Yes, even the camping gear. It had been hanging around in the storeroom for years."

"That equipment was rubbish. The tent leaked, her rucksack must have broken her spine, and the boots wrecked her feet."

"Oh dear, I'll have to apologize when I see her."

I gazed around the shop interior. "Why does she work in here? Raising money for down and outs, when she can hardly support herself?" I found it unbelievable that Meryl would help others without getting something out of it for herself.

"Because she's a good person and helping people makes her feel useful." Edith blew the steam from her coffee.

"I guess I should apologize. Will she come back here today?"

Edith put down her cup and waved her hands from side to side. "Maybe she will. Maybe she won't. Who knows?"

"I'll go to her flat, talk to her."

"Good idea. It'll be good for you to learn how to deal with a vulnerable person."

"I'm a fully trained legal professional. I work with vulnerable people all the time."

"Get real. I bet you work in a room filling in forms, talking gobbledy-gook on the phone."

I hung my head, shamed by Edith's accuracy. "What's Meryl's address?" I asked, pouting my upper lip.

"No idea."

"How can you not know where she lives? She works with you?"

"Meryl's a volunteer. I only know what she wants to tell me and what I see with my eyes." Edith tapped the edge of her glasses.

I emptied my cup. "I think I've got a vague idea she lives on the East Side. When we went camping, I collected her from a block in that area."

Edith patted my arm. "Find her and be nice. She's surrounded by pain."

* * *

STANDING ON THE PAVEMENT, I phoned Anton. The Rover appeared from around the corner and stopped outside the charity shop.

"Are you following me?" I asked, getting into the car.

"You know I must follow your mother's orders; got to do what I'm told. Where's your girlfriend?"

"She's not my girlfriend, and I presume she's gone home. I need to find her and apologize."

"What? I've never heard you apologize to anybody. Even when you broke your grandmother's favorite vase, you blamed the table and not yourself." He looked me up and down, shaking his head in disbelief. "Do you even know how to apologize?"

"Shut your mouth and drive to the block where we collected Meryl the other weekend."

"Okay, boss." Anton grinned and drove across the city to a modern block of flats.

On the way, I telephoned Clara to cancel our next appointment. I told her Meryl had been feeling ill and had gone home. Clara sounded disappointed by mine and Meryl's lack of progress. She agreed to re-arrange the meeting and give us one more chance to prove our friendship.

"This is the spot," Anton said, parking outside the Lister Building. "This is a pretty smart area."

"Yes, I was right all along. She's doing better for herself than most people think. Hopefully, this apology thing won't take long," I said, stepping out of the car.

I studied the doorway, searching the flat numbers; Meryl's name didn't appear on any labels. I rang a button on the ground floor.

"What do you want?" asked the voice of an aged man.

"Oh, good afternoon," I said in my politest voice.

"We don't want any." The man switched off the intercom.

Not to be defeated, I pressed another call button.

"Yes?" a woman asked, a child screeching in the background.

I tried to sound more informal. "Hi, I'm looking for Meryl McGuire. I believe she lives in these flats?"

"I've never heard of her. Perhaps you've got the wrong block. Tommy, get back in front of the TV, and don't bloody move again," she yelled. "I'm only a babysitter, and I don't really know who lives around here."

"Could you let me in so I can check the other flats?"

"Whatever! I've got to go. Tommy, leave the cat alone!"

The door buzzed, and I pushed it open. In the hallway, I studied the residents' names on the postal box fixed to the wall. But found no Meryl McGuire. I rubbed my head, confused.

I wandered back to the car and slipped into the passenger seat. "She doesn't live here," I said.

Anton gazed at my disturbed face. "Weird, maybe she moved, or we got the wrong apartment block. I'll drive around."

Hoping to spot Meryl on her walk home, we toured the streets. Anton drove along roads lined with distressed houses. People sat on the steps, talking, smoking, watching our posh vehicle drive past.

"I'm not sure this is a good idea," I said, growing nervous about my Range Rover trundling through the area. I peered at the newspaper covered windows, pressing the lock button on the door.

"It's not a problem. In a car like this, they'll think we're drug dealers," Anton said, laughing and throwing back his head.

"Not funny. Let's get out of here. Take me to the office. I need to carry out some investigatory work."

* * *

SITTING AT MY DESK, I phoned an associate who had the facilities to search out people. I gave him the details I'd gathered during my time with Meryl, which wasn't much. He told me he'd get back to me when he had any information.

I tapped my fingers on the mahogany. What to do now? I hated waiting. I flicked through my emails, boring messages, all of which could wait. Subconsciously, I searched for art courses. There were thousands. They held some in colleges and universities, and I'd have to apply to get myself a place. Others were online and led by real artists. Following a variety of these courses might be a better option for me.

My email pinged with a message from my detective. He'd gathered a lot of information in a short amount of time. I thanked him and downloaded the attached documents. This was the part of the legal world I loved. Deciphering the information, people prefer to hide.

Studying the first document, I found Meryl's actual address and date of birth. Then there were confidential social service files dating from Meryl's childhood. They told me she'd hardly ever attended school, and there were possible problems at home. It was apparent the education and Department of Social Services did nothing to address Meryl's needs, and the case had been closed.

A newspaper article told me about Meryl being sued by a woman she'd degraded on her blog. According to the story, the woman was Meryl's wine growing girlfriend. "Wow," I gasped. No wonder Meryl was terrified to write about me after my legal threats.

A search on my map's app led me to a rundown area of Salton. It appeared Anton and I hadn't been far from her flat when we drove through those dirty streets.

What to do now? I'd discuss the situation with Anton. He seemed to understand Meryl's thinking better than I did.

CHAPTER 13

Meryl

I SAT on the end of the bed, staring at the rail of clothes. I loved each of the designer dresses, the perfectly cut jeans, flower patterned blouses, and the beautiful red leather jacket. They made me feel confident and appear more successful than I was. But none of them were mine. Every single piece belonged to Polly. I had to return the clothes to the charity shop. There was no way I could wear them without feeling shame and humility.

Grabbing Polly's hold-all, I stuffed each item inside, filling the bag to the top. I tugged open the bottom drawer of my dresser and donned a faded T-shirt and tracksuit bottoms. I covered my drab clothes with the soccer hoodie hanging on the back of my door. On my trip to mom and pop's, I'd deliver Polly's clothes to the charity shop.

Downhearted, I stood on the crowded bus. Right now, my life was crap. But I had to remember there were millions of people whose lives were worse than mine. My life would improve. I just had to keep working on my blog. Gossip about Polly and her family was the best way to advance my situation. She owed me that.

Before depositing Polly's clothing, I popped into Alf's antique store. I'd brought the China crockery purchased at the flea market, hoping I could make some profit. Alf was a decent bloke. I'd known him for years, always calling into his shop when I skived off school. He'd taught me what to look out for and what he'd prefer to buy from me.

"Meryl, my darling," he said, a modern-day Fagin rubbing his hands together. "What have you brought me today?"

"You're going to love the vases I found. The colors are so cheerful." I rummaged through my box, unwrapping each of the bubble wrapped pottery items.

"Lovely. You've done a wonderful job; these are all by Clarice Cliff." He rubbed his stubbly chin and grumbled. "I hope you bought them at a good price."

"I'm no fool. The seller knew nothing about the designer. They were the bargain of the year."

"You got anything for me in the hold-all?" Alf asked, peering at the large green bag.

"No, only old clothes for charity."

He unlocked his safe and nodded, removing a bundle of notes. Licking the end of his thumb, one note at a time, he placed them on the table. He stopped and stared at me with his hooded eyes, seeing a look that told him to carry on doling out the cash. He gathered the notes he'd dealt, holding them in his wrinkled hand. "This should give you some profit."

"A little more wouldn't hurt," I said. "You're going to make loads of money from my finds."

"Hmm," Alf grunted, holding and rotating one of the colorful bowls. "I suppose you're right." He handed me two more notes and studied my attire. "Where are your pretty clothes?"

"On their way back to their owner," I said, stuffing the money into my jacket pocket.

"How'd you mean?"

"They weren't mine, so I'm giving them back."

"I thought they suited you, made you look distinguished."

"Alf, I'm nothing. I dragged myself from the gutter and I'll probably end up in the same place."

"I'll make us some tea. We need to talk." He lit his ancient gas stove, placing a rusting kettle on the burner. The water hissed to a boil, and he filled two chipped mugs with steaming water. Stirring the tea bag with a silver spoon, he removed it and placed it in the next cup. "Waste not wants not. No milk, no sugar, is better for you," he announced, passing me my cup and peering into my eyes. "So, tell me why you're feeling down?"

I told Alf about the conference and having to force myself to make friends with this horrid woman. Then finding out the clothes I'd been wearing were her cast offs. I was ashamed.

Alf sat back, tapping a gnarled nail on his mug. "When I escaped from Poland, I had nothing," he said. "The Nazis had taken my belongings and my family. As I traveled, people gave me simple things: a pen, a book, a coat to keep me warm. To me, each item was precious. When your life is grim," he waved his aged hand between us, "it helps to take what's offered."

"I don't want her stuff," I said, sticking out my chin.

"But you liked the clothes, and they made you look assured."

"I love them." I shuffled my feet on the floor. "But I don't want anything from her." I picked up the bag and stormed to the door. "Got to go. See you soon."

Being a key-holder, I let myself into the charity shop. I unloaded Polly's hold-all, throwing the empty bag into the corner of the room. With a heavy heart, I dressed a mannequin in a flower print dress and the red leather jacket, creating a fashionable display. Then I placed the other clothes onto hangers and hung them in the relevant sections. I checked my watch; I'd have to hurry, or I'd miss the bus to my parent's place.

***

THE BUS TRAVELED HALTINGLY through the busy traffic. When it reached the trailer park, I alighted. Alf had given me enough money to visit the nearby supermarket, and I bought plenty of food, intent on making me and my parents a decent breakfast.

When I arrived at the trailer carrying two plastic shopping bags, my mom was sitting outside on a plastic seat, a cup of tea in her hand. Her red eyes showed her weariness.

"Hi, mom," I said, setting down the bags and kissing her damp cheek. "Did pop keep you awake all night?"

She nodded, sniffed, and wiped her nose. "He's doing the usual, parading around the trailer, mumbling and wailing."

"Mom, I'll try to talk to him. He needs to see a doctor."

Mom sniveled. "He won't. He says he'd prefer to die than continue suffering in this life."

"Has he been drinking?"

"Yeah, he says it eases his pain." Mom rubbed my arm, peering into the bags. "I've adjusted those clothes you left last week. I'll fetch them and you can try them on, make sure they fit."

Blast, I'd forgotten about those dresses. Now I had more of Polly's designer wear to dispose of. I sighed and climbed the metal steps. "Let's make some food first," I said. "It'll cheer pop having something good to start his day, but no doubt he'll wash it down with a can of beer."

I found my father sitting in his sagging armchair, empty beer cans surrounding his disheveled body. "Morning, baby," he said, dragging an arm across the bottom of his snotty nosed face. "What've you brought us today?"

"A good healthy breakfast."

"Lovely." He took a can of warm beer, popped the top, and swallowed a mouthful.

I helped mom unpack the bags, then ripped open a packet of bacon, tossing the slices into a frying pan. I broke eggs into another pan and placed bread in the toaster. Pushing aside the unopened pile of letters on the dining table, I set down three plates.

"I'll eat mine here," pop said, setting down his can and pulling himself upright. Mom placed his plate on his lap. "Thank you, darling."

I joined my mom at the table in front of a plate of freshly cooked food.

"Have you got any spare cash?" pop asked, chewing a piece of bacon.

I tapped the bottom of the sauce bottle, encouraging ketchup to cover my eggs. "None for you to waste on booze,"

"Beer is the only medicine that takes away my nightmares. The terrible things I've seen keep haunting me."

"Pop, since you won't tell us what happened, and what you saw was so traumatic, why don't you go visit the doctor, tell him what's upsetting you," I said, stacking my fork with beans and egg.

"No!" pop yelled, horror surrounding his eyes as they glared from his face. "I can't find words to describe the hysteria in my brain." Tears poured down his cheeks, and he covered his face with his hands. "Beer is the only thing that helps."

Mom kneeled in front of him, rubbing his knees. "Darling, the booze is going to kill you. We can find you a better way of dealing with the pain."

Pop leaned forward, his plate slipping to the floor, egg yolk splattering across the linoleum. He wrapped his arms around mom, sobbing on her shoulder.

"Why don't you have a sleep?" mom asked.

"No, I need a drink." Pop stood and pushed mom to the rear of the trailer. He headed toward me. "Please, give me some money." One of his hands grasped the neck of my shirt, the other searched my pockets.

"Pop, drink isn't the answer." I tried to remain calm, even

though my innards were shaking. His hands wrapped themselves around my neck, the pressure on my throat tightening. When I tried to push him away, his grip hardened. "Pop," I gasped. "You're choking me."

Pop's eyes widened when he realized what he was doing. He threw his hands apart. "Oh, no, what's wrong with me?" He slumped to his knees.

I stroked his thin gray hair. "It's okay, pop, no harm done," I croaked, rubbing my painful neck.

My mom moved toward us. She clutched pop's shoulder. He attempted to stand, but his weak legs couldn't hold his weight. He tumbled backwards, falling into my body, pushing me to the window. My head crashed into the glass; shards flew outwards. A cry of pain howled from my mouth. I touched my skin, feeling fragments of glass protruding from my face. When I looked at my hands, I found them covered in blood.

Pop and mom stared at me, horror covering their faces. Mom approached me, and Pop wailed.

"I've got to go," I mumbled.

"Baby, you're hurt." Mom handed me a tea towel, which I pressed to the side of my face.

"I'm fine, I'll see you soon." Turning away, I staggered out of the door and down the steps. My head spinning as I wandered away from the trailer and approached the road. I saw a bus at the stop and waved an arm manically. My shoulders slumped when the engine roared and the bus pulled away.

Clenching the tea towel over my wounds, I began my long walk home. At one point, I stopped for a rest, sitting on the edge of a low wall. When I noticed the amount of blood covering the tea towel, bile rose in my throat. My body dropped to the paving stones. I puked and closed my eyes. I just needed a boost of energy to get myself home.

CHAPTER 14

Polly

After a meaningful discussion with Anton, we decided I should give Meryl space. However, Edith's words and the need to apologize rang in my ears. Also, I missed her being around. I phoned several times; she ignored my calls. So, I left messages, hoping at some point she'd call me back.

I spent the morning studying the clothing we planned to release in the fall. I had to check we weren't copying other designs, and the work remained unique to Tulipano. There was an issue with one fabric, and a potential battle with another clothing company using the same material. I emailed the manufacturer, arranging a meeting with their representative. I'd attempt to get them on our side with a few bottles of wine.

Anton arrived at my office at the time we'd arranged. I'd been invited to attend an exhibition at a contemporary art studio in the newly developed cultural center of the city. The chance to meet the artists and curator was exciting. I'd get some tips on how to progress my art career.

While Anton drove at his usual steady pace, I tapped my fingers on my chin. "Anton, when I give you my unwanted clothes, where do you take them?" I wanted to confirm why my clothes were in Meryl's charity shop.

"They go to a charity store in Salton, the one which supports down and out local people." Anton nudged my arm and pointed to a figure sprawled on the pavement. "People like her. Those who are desperate and live on the streets."

I looked at the wall of the building where Anton was pointing. A bedraggled woman was kneeling on the paving stones. She leaned on the wall and tried to stand. I grasped Anton's shoulder. "Stop the car."

"Why?"

"The woman on the ground is Meryl."

"Really?" Anton pulled into a parking space and stared at the ailing girl. "She's bleeding," he said, leaping out of the car and hurrying to her.

I followed. "Meryl," I said, bending and putting my arm around her shoulders, noticing her blood drenched hair, and the purple lump growing on her forehead. "What happened to you?"

"I'm fine," she mumbled, juddering, trying to hide her injured face.

"Let's get her to the hospital." I helped Anton hoist Meryl upward and carry her to the car.

"I just want to go home," Meryl slurred, slumping on the leather seat, leaning on the car door, looking as if she were about to vomit.

I sat by her side, holding the bloodied cloth on her injury. "We'll drive you home when the hospital has examined you."

Reaching the hospital car park, Anton rushed inside and fetched a wheelchair. We pushed an almost unconscious Meryl into the emergency department. I completed a form with Meryl's information, my knowledge of which had increased since my investigations. I now knew her full name, telephone number, age, and the address of the building where she lived.

"What's her medical history?" the receptionist asked when I handed back the form.

"I've no idea," I replied with a shrug. The woman tsked and fixed the form to a clipboard, placing it on top of a pile of others. "She needs to be seen urgently," I said. "She has a head injury."

"Look around you. There's a host of people with injuries." The woman waved her arm around the waiting area.

I slammed my hands on the counter. The receptionist ignored me. Turning, I walked to Anton, who was pressing a wad of paper towels on Meryl's wound.

"Wait here. I'll try to speed things along," I whispered, sneaking through a door into the treatment area and standing at the nursing station. "Is there a doctor available?" I shouted.

A woman in a long white coat peered from her files. "You're not allowed in here. Please leave and wait your turn."

"But my friend's been in an accident. She's bleeding badly and they're making her wait. Could you see her?"

The doctor looked at the rows of beds filled with people. "I shouldn't, really. There's a system."

"I could make a substantial donation to the hospital fund if you could look at her." I removed a gold credit card from my jacket pocket.

She studied me, her eyes flicking at the card. "Okay, bring her through. There's a private side-room at the end. Take her in there."

"Thanks." I ran to the door and waved to Anton, urging him toward me.

He pushed Meryl around the chairs, ignoring the scowls and comments he was receiving from other patients.

"Take her in there," I said, pointing to the side-room.

When the doctor saw the state of Meryl, she summonsed a nurse and helped us lift Meryl onto the bed.

"You've made a mess of yourself, young lady. My name's Doctor Jones. Can I look at your injuries?" she asked, studying the cuts covering Meryl's face.

Meryl swung her head in a nodding motion.

Doctor Jones pulled over a trolley of implements. She snipped Meryl's hair around the wound and removed fine slices of glass with a pair of narrow tweezers. "We'll send her for an x-ray, to check I've found all the glass and ensure she hasn't fractured her skull." The doctor grabbed a porter and requested he take Meryl to radiography.

On Meryl's return, the doctor checked the images. Content her skull was still in one piece, and the wounds were clean and glass free, she stitched the deepest cut and covered the smaller lacerations with iodine.

Meryl couldn't form any sensible words; she constantly giggled and grasped my hand. "Is Meryl a close friend?" the doctor asked, smirking.

"No," I said, aghast. "We're just building a friendship pathway."

"I'd say your pathway is sound," she said when Meryl pulled me close. "Meryl will have to stay here overnight; I'm concerned the blow might have caused a concussion. Was she hit by a car?"

"I don't know, we found her collapsed in the street."

"Hopefully, she'll come around in a few hours and tell us what happened. Go home; I'll phone you when we know more."

"It's okay, I'll stay. I'm supposed to be looking out for her. Anton, go back to the house. Come and fetch us in the morning."

Anton nodded and obediently left, whistling the tune to *Love is in the Air*, when he left the room.

* * *

When I opened my eyes the next morning, I saw Meryl sitting in bed, staring around the room.

"Where am I?" she asked.

"Hospital," I said, "you appear to have been in an accident." Taking me by surprise, tears dripped from Meryl's eyes. "Are you okay?" I asked, going to her side.

"Not really." She wiped her eyes, grimacing when her hand touched the side of her face. "Fetch me a mirror."

"I don't think you should look. Your face is quite gruesome."

"I need a mirror right now."

I went to the nursing desk and borrowed a tiny examination mirror. "This is all I could find," I said on my return to Meryl's room.

Meryl took the implement, blinking when she focused on the dressing covering the side of her forehead, bruising emerging from beneath. Smaller cuts checkered her face. She frowned and handed the mirror back. "Thanks," she muttered.

Seeing her awake, a nurse entered the room. Lifting the dressing, she checked the wound. "It's looking fine. Did you fall?"

"No," Meryl said, "I just became embroiled in a minor incident."

The nurse looked concerned. "Do you want to report what happened? I can call the police for you."

"No need. It was a family thing. I'll deal with it." Meryl's face was determined. There was no way she was going to involve outsiders. "Just fetch my painkillers, and I'll leave," she said, looking around the room. "Where are my clothes?"

"Anton took them home," I said. "They were blood soaked and needed washing. He'll bring you a new outfit when he returns."

Meryl's bottom lip jutted out. "I refuse to wear any more of your clothes."

"Then you'll have to travel in your blood-stained gown," I said, sitting back.

"Phone me a cab?"

"Unfortunately, I can't. You're only allowed home under my care, so we're going back to my house."

"Rubbish, I'll go where I want." Meryl pushed back her sheet and swung her legs off the bed. When she stood, her face paled and her knees gave way. She grabbed the bed rail.

I held her. "You're too ill. There's still a possibility of concussion. So, you either come with me or stay here."

"I can't afford to stay in this place," Meryl said, studying her private room.

"Then I win."

Anton barged into the room carrying a large bag of clothes. "Now what do you fancy wearing today?" he asked, pulling out a variety of garments. Meryl's eyes studied the designer wear. She picked through the items, selecting a skirt and matching blouse.

"I'll help you dress," I said.

Meryl raised her eyebrows.

"*Porca miseria*, you've seen me naked. It's my turn now."

Anton's bushy eyebrows rose higher than Meryl's.

I waved my finger at him. "Don't tell mother."

"I heard nothing," he said, giggling and making a cross over his heart. "Shout me when you want me to return."

I helped Meryl to the en-suite bathroom, directing her to the disability seat. I unfastened the hospital robe, and Meryl allowed it to drop around her waist, revealing her ample breasts.

Filling the sink with warm water, I rubbed soap onto a flannel, seduced by the aroma of rose perfume. "Here, give yourself a wash. I'll fetch your clothes." I wandered out of the bathroom, perspiring from the hot flush caused by Meryl's nakedness.

When I returned, Meryl was drying herself. "They're well out of your price range," she said, noticing me ogling her bare breasts.

I tore my eyes from her body and handed her each item of clothing. Meryl needed my help to fasten her bra and button her blouse. My fingers trembled when I touched her soft skin.

"That feels better," Meryl said. "Thank you for helping."

"No problem. Let me find the doctor and get permission for us to leave." Outside the room, I leaned on the wall, a stupid grin on my face.

"What's wrong?" Anton asked, holding my elbow.

"I'm not sure. Helping Meryl got me a little flustered."

"Oh, the delightful sprinklings of love."

"Don't be silly. I was only helping her out. Once our mentor, Clara, ticks the *'perfect friends'* box, we never need to see each other again."

"I think when Meryl's gone, you'll miss her. She's got you out of the house, given you an interest, and even your mother approves of her."

"Mother is only interested in Meryl's computer skills, and there's no relationship happening, so forget it," I said, wandering to the nursing station in search of Doctor Jones.

* * *

WHEN WE ARRIVED at the house, I showed Meryl to the downstairs guest room. She stared around, her mouth dropping open.

"I hope this room is good enough for you. You only need to stay for a couple of days until you feel better. I've invited Clara to visit us tomorrow. She can see we're getting on fine, sign our forms, and we'll have completed the project. Then you can get on with being a snide internet bitch."

Meryl groaned and sat on the side of the bed, attempting to bend and take off her shoes.

"Let me." I kneeled, holding Meryl's smooth calves while I removed her pumps.

"Thanks." Meryl raised her legs and leaned into the feather pillows.

"I wish you'd stop thanking me. I'm only doing the decent thing." I handed Meryl the tablets she'd been prescribed and studied her relaxed face. "I think the bump on the head was more damaging than we thought."

"How do you mean?" Meryl asked, swallowing her tablets.

"You're accepting my help without complaining."

"I know, and it's giving me a happy feeling." Meryl closed her eyes, a pleasant smile on her face. "I'm sleepy," she said, yawning.

I stared at Meryl's injuries, tenderly touching the cut on the side of her attractive mouth. The mouth I'd enjoyed kissing. Even though she hadn't appreciated my attentions, and she'd forced me away, I sensed a need to protect Meryl. Something bad happened to her yesterday, making her vulnerable, and I wanted to look out for her. It may be a sign of friendship, or, since I was lusting after her body, maybe it was more.

CHAPTER 15

Meryl

When I opened my eyes, I was in the middle of a delightful dream: lying on a soft bed, in a silk night-gown, my head resting on a cloud of feather pillows. A fragrance of lavender filled the air, and birds sang joyously in the background. A door handle clicked, and someone approached the bed. Blinking my weary eyes, I saw it was Polly.

"How are you feeling?" she asked, perching herself on the edge of the bed.

"Like I've spent ten rounds in a boxing match, and came out worst off," I said, pulling my swollen lip into a grin.

Polly's hand rested on my arm. "What happened to you?"

I shrugged. "It was just an incident at my parent's house, nothing for you to worry about."

Polly sat back. The concern in her eyes was moving, but I couldn't tell her too much about the confrontation with my pop. Her interference might get him into trouble. I'd sort things out when I visited my parents next week with their rent money. My face sank as I tried to work out how I could earn some extra cash.

"Do you feel able to join me and mother for some food?" Polly asked, her head tilted at an angle.

My stomach rumbled with hunger. "What time is it?"

"Two o'clock. You've been asleep for a while."

"You're right, food would be great." I swayed my legs out of bed. "That's if I'm able to stand," I said with a chuckle.

"Let me help." Polly stood by my side, holding my arm while I pulled on a dressing gown and staggered along a hall decorated with Ruskin wallpaper.

"We usually eat in the kitchen," Polly said. "It's more casual."

"Wow, our physical lives are so different," I said, patting puzzled Polly's hand and walking into a huge kitchen cum diner.

A tall, smartly dressed woman greeted me, ushering me to a chair. "Hello, you must be Meryl. Come and sit down."

Polly pulled two stools from under the table, ushering me to one. The woman pushed a dish of salad, a plate covered with various continental cheeses, and a bowl of pasta, dressed with a delicious smelling sauce, toward me. "I'm Sarah, mother of Polly. Help yourself to food."

"Thank you," I said, trying not to drool. "I hope you don't expect me to eat all of this."

Sarah smirked. "Polly, you're right. Meryl has a witty sense of humor."

I glanced at Polly, surprised she'd been discussing me with her mother. I leaned toward Sarah. "Hope she hasn't been telling you all my secrets."

When Sarah laughed, Polly's face shone bright red.

"Polly dear, did you put our proposition to Meryl?" Sarah asked.

"Not yet. Meryl has only just woken, and I didn't feel she was ready for a conversation."

I cocked my head to one side, intrigued by what Sarah was going to say.

"Meryl, I've studied your on-line presence, and I'm impressed. My company is way behind in the social media side of life, and I want to ask you to join us."

I choked on a piece of lettuce. "Sorry, I don't understand."

Sarah glanced at her daughter.

"Mother's offering you a job," Polly said, pouring me a glass of water.

"Yes, social media manager. What are your salary expectations?" Sarah asked with a business-like smile. "Hopefully, since the job is a downward step from your own high-profile post, we can afford you."

"A job," I stammered, drinking the water, before my choking got out of hand.

Sarah gave me a long wink. "Why don't you think about my offer and let me know? I must be off, business calls, yet another fashion show. Bye dear, see you later." She kissed Polly's cheek and considered kissing mine. She resisted and patted my shoulder. "Bye Meryl, and thank you for looking out for my little girl."

Polly blushed once more, making me smile.

"Strange you didn't mention the job," I said, when Sarah had left me and Polly alone.

"How could I? When I found you yesterday, you were virtually unconscious, and you've been out of your head for the rest of the time."

I tapped my fingers on my chin. "Hang on, if you found me, that means you were looking for me. Why?"

"Because I've been phoning you for days, and you've ignored me. And I wanted to apologize for upsetting you with what I said. You know, about the clothes."

I sliced a piece of cheese, placing it on a thin cracker. "No need for any apology. The clothes are back in the shop. I didn't need them; I just didn't want to upset Edith by saying no after she'd offered them to me."

Polly frowned and pulled a grape from the bunch in the fruit bowl. "So, what do you think about my mother's job offer?" she asked, biting into the soft flesh, grape juice glazing her lips. "Meryl?"

"What?" I said, blinking away the rapturous sight. "I don't know. I'd have to decide if the company's principals match mine."

"If it helps you decide, I've been investigating our working methods and have made some adjustments, which will help the company produce clothes more ethically and support the workers who rely on us. I've put together a folder of evidence I can go through with you. And if you're on board, you can use the information on our social media."

"That's good, but taking the job would mean us working together," I said, biting into the cheese cracker.

"Not a problem. The company offices are large enough for us never to see each other."

"Perhaps when we're at work, you could speak in Italian, and I wouldn't know what you were saying. Your words could be full of insults, and I'd never be upset by them."

"*Posso dire qualcosa?*" Polly said, smiling at my inability to understand.

I hummed at Polly's words, gazing at her lips. "It's such a sexy language," I murmured.

"*Desidero tenerti stretto e baciare le tue morbide labbra.*" Polly spoke her tender words and took my hand.

I melted, unable to make any response.

"You're right," Polly said. "I can say absolutely anything and turn you to mush. I love having that power over you."

"I can handle it." I shook my body straight, looking Polly in the eye. "What about my issue with dyslexia?"

"What helps you at the moment?" Polly asked, squeezing my fingers.

"I've loaded my iPad with software to support my reading and writing. And sometimes I ask my mom to check what I've written."

"Well, we can get you a ready prepared laptop, and explore what new software is available. And we can train a member of clerical staff to assist you," Polly said with a wink. "I might even help you out myself."

I blushed at the thought and finished my food.

Polly checked the wall clock. "Clara's visiting in a couple of hours. Do you want to rest until then?"

After having a good sleep and filled with tasty food, I didn't feel like sleeping. "No, maybe we could take a walk around the grounds."

"Oh, right, okay? But let's get you dressed first."

Polly helped me back to the bedroom. I was less wobbly on my legs, but I appreciated her help. She slid open the wardrobe doors. "You can choose anything in here. And, before you ask, none of it is mine. It's where mother keeps her past design ideas."

"Wow, your mom's personal museum?"

Polly laughed. "I'm sure you'll find something which suits your taste."

Staring at Polly, a heartfelt sense of taste invaded my mind. The woman standing beside me, in slashed jeans and a t-shirt, met my taste perfectly. The look in her eyes was endearing, tempting me to touch her cheeks and kiss her lips.

Polly gazed at me. "I'll meet you in the lounge," she said, backing out of the door.

I chose a pair of sleek black leather trousers and a cream silk blouse, throwing a fine woolen wrap across my shoulders. Once dressed, I ventured into the lounge, where Polly was lying on the sofa, reading.

She sat upright when she heard me approach; her face studied the clothes I'd chosen. "Hi," she said, lost for words.

"The grounds," I said, reminding her of our planned walk.

"Oh yes, this way." She walked through the lounge, pulled open the patio doors, and led me into the garden.

The smell of roses invaded my nose. Bees buzzed in and out of the petals, busily searching for nectar. Paths ran in and out of raised beds planted with different types and colors of flowers. "This is fantastic," I said, sniffing a white lily.

"Mother loves to work in the garden, and I spend ages out here drawing and painting the flowers." She fluttered a hand through a star jasmine growing around a trellis. "Do you want to see my motorbike?" Polly asked, a bright light in her eyes.

"Sure," I said, following her across the garden to a huge double garage. We entered through a side door. When she flicked on the light, I stood gawping at a vintage campervan. "That is so cool."

Polly lifted her eyes, glancing at the vehicle I was ogling. "Oh, that's our old campervan." She wandered to it, pulling open the side door and gazing inside. "When he wasn't famous, we used to go to father's races in this van. It was great fun, all huddled together inside. The poor old thing doesn't run anymore." Polly's shoulders slumped when she patted the bonnet and wandered to her red and chrome motorbike. "Would you like to take a ride?" she asked, touching the leather seat.

"I don't know. I've never been on a motorbike," I said, stroking my hand through my hair.

"You'll be fine. I'll only drive around the grounds, no high speeds involved." Polly handed me a helmet.

The headgear was a tight fit, and my hands struggled with the strap and buckles. Polly's hands joined mine. They were warm and delicate. Expertly adjusting the connections, they made the chin strap a comfortable fit.

Polly pushed a button on the side wall, and the door of the garage rolled upwards. She pushed the bike outside and sat on the seat. "All aboard," she said, patting the seat behind her. "Put your foot there, swing your leg over and slide yourself into place."

I did as Polly directed and sat behind her. I was so close I could feel the heat of her body emanating from her shirt.

"You can hold the side of the seat, or wrap your arms around me if you want to feel safer."

Hold her! I don't think so. There was no way I was going to get that close to Polly. "I think I'll be fine holding the seat," I said, grasping the side, clinging tight.

Polly gave me a thumbs up and started the engine. A roar vibrated through the machine, trembling my sex like an out-of-control vibrator. I gave a pleasant hum as we moved lazily across the tarmac. Arriving at a longer stretch of drive, Polly upped the pace, shocking me out of my reverie. I yelped and threw my arms around her body. Burying my helmeted head in the middle of her back as she swooshed along the lane.

When she slowed the bike, Polly's head rotated slightly. She couldn't see me. Buried behind her, my eyes screwed shut, wishing I'd never agreed to this. My only comfort came from my hands, which felt the warmth of Polly's body and the calm throb of her heart.

The bike turned, and Polly raced back up the drive. Squealing to a halt outside the garage door, she kicked down the foot stand. There was an instant silence when the engine turned off. The only movement was the shaking of my body.

"Oh shit," Polly said, removing her helmet, helping me climb off the bike. She held me close. "I didn't mean to scare you."

"I'm fine," I said, my arms wrapped around Polly's neck.

When she unbuckled the strap of the helmet and lifted it from my head, I gave Polly another of those adrenaline-fueled kisses.

"*Porca puttana*, I love it when you get exhilarated," Polly murmured, relaxing into my kiss, which grew stronger when I heard her Italian words.

"Coo-eee," a high-pitched voice said from a car window. "It's so nice to see you two getting along." Clara opened her car door and clambered out.

Polly's hold slackened. "Hello Clara, we've just been for a ride on my bike."

I released my arms. "It was lovely," I said, a satisfied grin on my lips.

Clara studied my face. "Your injury looks dreadful. It was lucky Polly was around to take care of you."

"Absolutely, we've become adept at dealing with each other's medical needs, and I've learned how to accept the help which is offered."

"I'm pleased you've discovered working in partnership helps in different situations." Clara opened a folder and made notes on a sheet of paper.

"Come inside," Polly said. "Let me fetch some drinks."

"I'll help." I stormed after Polly. "What the hell was that? You said you'd go slow. But no, you raced around like a lunatic. I... I..."

"Hey, I'm sorry, I forgot you were a newbie. I thought you might enjoy the thrill."

"I did," I said, my body still quivering from the excitement. I grasped Polly's shoulders, leaned into her, and kissed her lips. Her hands rolled through my hair when she responded with enthusiasm. Panting for breath, we parted.

"I'll check on Clara," I said, hurrying out of the kitchen door.

When Polly came into the lounge carrying a jug of orange juice and three empty glasses, me and Clara were having a conversation about my potential new job.

"I think it's wonderful," Clara said, filling a glass. "You must concentrate on the role and remember to ask for help when needed."

I nodded in agreement and took the glass Polly offered me as she sat by my side.

"So, Polly? What positive outcome have you discovered from this project?"

Polly stared at the shagpile carpet. "I was concerned at the beginning. Meryl made me feel vulnerable. I worried she would publicly out my life on her blog and humiliate me. But when I read Meryl's words, I see honesty and humor."

Sweat beaded on my neck, and I twitched my fingers, embarrassed by Polly's thoughtful words.

"Anyway, since I've got to know her better, I've overcome my fear, and accept that exposure is part of Meryl's job. Besides, she's shown me the lives of others and how they suffer. And I guess I've realized not everyone is as fortunate as me."

"Excellent, you've helped each other resolve individual weaknesses. What a perfect conclusion to the project." Clara clapped her hands in her annoying, childish way. She pulled two certificates from her briefcase and handed us one each. "Wonderful, so what happens now?"

Polly juggled her certificate. "How do you mean?"

"How are you going to ensure your pathway, or relationship, continues to grow?"

"We... err... perhaps..."

I placed my arm around Polly's shoulder, giving her a reassuring hug. "First, we're going to have a celebratory meal."

Clara smiled and clapped her hands. "Looking at the two of you, I think I made the perfect pairing. Could I take a photograph for the conference website?"

Polly glanced at me. "Err, I don't know... we've only just..."

"A photo will be fine," I said, butting into Polly's sentence. "Where do you want us?"

"In the garden would be perfect."

I took Polly's hand and led her through the open patio doors into her mother's rose garden.

"Perhaps Polly could present you with one of those gorgeous pink roses," Clara said, readying her camera.

"This is ridiculous," Polly muttered, "we haven't talked about…"

"Here you are dear." I snapped a sweet-smelling rose from a bush and handed it to Polly. She stood with the bloom in her hand, gaping at me. I grinned as Clara snapped the photo.

"Wonderful," Clara gasped. "You look so in love."

Polly coughed.

"She has hay-fever," I said, leading Polly and Clara back into the house. "It's been lovely to see you again and thank you for bringing us together." I took Clara's hand, giving it a firm shake.

"Yes, thank you," Polly said through gritted teeth, glaring at me when she escorted Clara from the house. The frightening stare remained when Polly returned. "What's going on in your weird mind? We've managed a few kisses, but we haven't got near to talking about any kind of relationship, and Clara has us virtually married."

"But can't you see Clara loves how close we've become? We're a success."

"How can we be close? You only kiss me when you're hyped up after an exciting activity. At any other time, you clearly have an aversion to me."

"Hang on a minute," I said, my jaw slackening. "Why do you think I don't like you?"

Polly slumped into the easy chair, tapping each of her fingers. "Number one, you don't tell me the truth. You even lied about where you live. Two, you hate that I have money and a fancy job in an industry you despise. Three, the words you say upset people. At camp you even made Bernie cry. Four, you tell the world nasty things about people. Five…"

"Okay, don't go on. I get the message." I sat on the arm of her chair, staring through the window. "Do you like anything about me?"

"I suppose you have some attractive traits." Polly rubbed her forehead, creating a visible red mark. "You're caring, thoughtful, and even though you're stupid with what you say, you make me laugh. And your infrequent kisses are adorable."

"So, there's some hope," I said, leaning down and giving Polly an infrequent kiss on the cheek. "Could you ask Anton to take me home? I need to show you the truth."

* * *

I DIRECTED Anton to my flat, telling him to park in a nearby council car park. It would be safer than on the street. Anton waited with the car while Polly followed me to my flat. I could see she was hesitant, overwhelmed by the despondent location. I took her hand and led her forward.

Charlie was sitting on the bottom step of my building, his limp body resting on the rails. "Hi Charlie," I said, releasing Polly and kneeling by his side. "Are you okay?"

His bleared eyes stared at me. A light of recognition appeared, and he nodded.

"Hold on there and I'll bring you some food." I stood and walked to the front door. Polly scurried close behind me.

I crept along the hallway, but my landlady had the ears of a bat, and her door swung open. "Oy, when are you going to pay your rent?" she screeched.

"I'll get it to you tomorrow," I muttered.

"You said you'd pay today."

"I got mugged. They stole all my money." I showed her the cut on the side of my face.

"You're always full of bullshit. Pay tomorrow or you're out this time. No excuses." She slammed her door closed.

"How much do you owe?" Polly asked while we climbed the stairs.

"Only a couple of months. Hopefully, I'll get some advertising payments later this week. That should take care of it."

"I could give you the money."

I stopped and stared at her. "Why would you do that?"

"Because I can."

"That's the problem. You take me in when I'm injured and pay my health care bills, and now you offer to pay my rent, all because you're loaded."

Polly went red with embarrassment. "I can't help that I have money. It's just the way I was born."

I opened my door and walked into my musty smelling room. I watched her looking around, dismay etched on her face. "Here is my life, which, as you have clearly pointed out, I can't afford." I slumped onto the edge of the bed. "Look, it's just that I don't want to rely on other people. They always want something in return."

Polly walked around my twelve-foot square abode. Finally, she stopped and stared through the grimy windows, picking at the paint flaking from the sill. "Well, why don't I give you part of your first month's wages, then I'll get payroll to deduct what you owe me?" She walked to me and sat by my side. She took my hand, rubbing my palm with her thumb. "Edith told me how hard you work in the charity shop, raising money to support others. The only difference is, now you are the one in need."

I shook my head and sighed. "Okay, your idea sounds fair enough. At least it'll get Mrs. O'Brien off my back. But I want you to know if we develop any kind of relationship, it's not because of your money."

Polly squeezed my hand and massaged the stained carpet with her foot. She raised her head and stared into my agitated eyes. "I'm glad about that, because, for some unexpected reason, I'm infatuated."

"Who with?" I asked defiantly.

Polly held my cheeks in her hands. "You, stupid."

CHAPTER 16

Polly

AFTER THE WORDS blurted from my mouth, I leaned forward and kissed Meryl. She gave no response, sitting frigid and staring at me with brooding eyes. I smirked. "I don't suppose kissing works when you're not in an excitable mood. We'd better get going." I pushed myself from the bed and walked toward the door.

Meryl stood and grasped my arm, pulling me back to her body. She held me close. I could hear her heart pounding beneath her blouse. Then I felt her tears dampening my neck.

"Meryl, what's wrong?" I asked.

"No-one's ever considered me infatuating before," she said, sniffing and loosening her hold.

"Surely your ex adored you, and your parents must have given you a ton of loving attention."

"My ex destroyed me, and my parents are something else."

I rubbed her back. "Not loving you is their loss." My mouth hovered in front of Meryl's lips. "Can I try that kiss again?"

She clenched the back of my neck, pulling herself closer, her body relaxing when our lips met. The kiss deepened my passion, and when we parted, Meryl was blushing. "I can't expect you to want to be with me until I've shown you everything," she said, going to the desk and opening a folder. "I wrote about you and your family."

I took the papers she handed me, flicking through the pages, dumbfounded by the amount of information she'd sourced.

"But I felt guilty about hurting you and didn't have the nerve to press the enter button." She opened her laptop and deleted the files labeled with my name. Meryl picked her fingernails. "I'd appreciate it if Anton could take us to visit my parents?"

"Of course, it'll be good to meet them."

"Be prepared to change your mind," Meryl said with a frown.

I threw the folder on the floor and pulled Meryl onto her lumpy mattress. "Before we leave, I think we should try out your bed." My hands loosened the silk blouse from the waistband of her skirt, and stroked the soft skin of her back. Our lips met with a passionate intensity.

Meryl pushed me away again. "What about Anton?"

"He'll wait. He's always having to wait for me."

"Do you mean you do this all the time?"

"No," I smirked, my hands stroking her breasts. "Usually, I'm stuck in a never-ending meeting. This is the first time I want to be delayed. *Il tuo seno e delizioso.*"

In response to my Italian words, Meryl removed her blouse and rolled on top of me. I mumbled more Italian phrases, receiving increased passion as I spoke each word.

* * *

A COUPLE OF HOURS LATER, Anton pulled into the trailer park, Meryl directed him to the disheveled static vans toward the rear.

A woman sat in front of a paint-chipped van, peeling carrots. She smiled when she saw Meryl getting out of the car.

"Hi mom." Meryl took the woman in her arms. "Where's pop?"

Meryl's mother jerked her head to the doorway. "Watching the TV. Who's this?" She pointed a sharp knife at me.

"This is Polly," Meryl said with a smile. "Polly, my mom."

"Hello," I said, afraid of approaching the woman and her deadly weapon.

She studied my racing shirt and boots. "Do you ride motorbikes?"

I nodded. "My father was a bike racer, Marco Tulipani."

"Who knows, Marco?" yelled a man from inside the trailer. A chair groaned, and a head appeared in the doorway. He stared at me, recognition emerging in his groggy mind. "Paulina?"

I raised a hand, giving the man a small wave. "Uncle Mac," I said, astounded to meet my father's mechanical engineer after so many years.

"It's been a long time," he said, pulling me into a huge hug. "You want a drink?"

"No, I'm fine, thanks. By the way, everyone calls me Polly now."

Confounded, Meryl stared at me. "You know my pop?"

I gave her a nod. "But I haven't seen him for years, since my father's funeral."

Uncle Mac gave a beaming smile. "Polly was such a cute kid, always following me around in her red boiler suit, helping me fix the engines. But what are you doing hanging around with my little girl?" Mac clenched Meryl's shoulder and tugged her to him, wrapping his arm around her.

"Actually, pop," Meryl said, rubbing her forehead. "I asked Polly to visit and convince you to seek help."

I glanced at Meryl in surprise.

She shrugged. "Pop drinks too much and finds it difficult to control his temper. He needs to talk to a doctor or a therapist."

Uncle Mac stepped back, staring at his wife, tears appearing in his eyes. "Polly, I don't want to act the way I do. It's just that alcohol numbs the pain of watching your daddy burning in that horrific accident. I etched the image in my mind and the guilt is unbearable. I should have checked the seal on the engine gasket before he drove away. The fire was my fault."

Meryl and her mother stood back, astounded at hearing Mac's story for the first time.

I retracted my shoulders, making myself appear more in control of a situation I wasn't prepared for. "Mac, I had to deal with the trauma too, but I gained help by speaking to a professional. They'll support you in sorting yourself out. You need to do that and stop hurting the people who love you. If you truly cared for my father, you would do this in his memory. He would be ashamed to see you like you are now. A shadow of the man he had great respect for."

Mac looked from me to Meryl, visibly shocked by my rant. "I'll think about it." Defeated, he sank into the plastic seat beside his wife and stared at the wounds decorating Meryl's face. Tears filled his eyes. Meryl kneeled beside him, and he stroked her hair. "I'm so sorry," he mumbled.

"It's okay, pop, no harm done, just a sexy scar. Anyway, I've got some good news," she said with confidence. "I've been offered a real job."

A smile lit her mother's face. "Oh, that's wonderful. It's good to see you've dug your way out of the hole that bitch of a woman dropped you in." She glared at me, giving a wary wave of her knife.

"I'll be able to pay your rent and have food delivered every week," Meryl said with excitement.

"You'll still visit, though?" her pop asked.

"Of course, and I'll earn enough money to buy a car and take you out on day trips."

Meryl's mother stroked her face. "My perfect baby." She glanced up at me. "Will you stay for dinner?"

I nodded. "I'd love to stay. Tell you what? I'll ask Anton to buy a couple of cooked chickens and some extra vegetables?"

"Anton is here?" Mac jumped from his seat and looked around. When he saw my driver, he threw his hand in front of his mouth. "My old friend," he exclaimed, walking with purpose toward Anton and falling into his arms, quivering with emotion.

* * *

WE HAD AN AWESOME AFTERNOON. Meryl's dad and Anton talked about the old times, discussing motorbikes and father's races. I sat beside Meryl's mum, listening to the pair chatting about places they could visit together. It seemed to be a perfect family gathering.

"I can't believe you brought me and my family back together," Meryl said, when we walked away from the trailer and climbed into the rear of the Rover.

"Not a problem. It was lovely to meet Mac again. I just can't believe you're his daughter. Why did we never meet before?"

"Pop left home when I was a toddler. Me and mom didn't know where he'd gone and had to get through life without him. He always sent money, but mom still had to work three jobs to keep us housed, and ensure there was food on the table. The kids at school always teased me, telling me my pop was in prison." Meryl sighed. "When he came home, it took a while to get used to him being there. He never told us where he'd been, and we didn't ask because of his mental health issues."

I rubbed Meryl's thigh. "The important thing is you love each other."

"I'd give them my last dime to keep them safe." Meryl snuggled into my side as Anton drove us back to the house.

"I saw a sewing machine in the trailer. Is it your mum's?"

"Yeah, she makes her own clothes," Meryl said, blushing. "And she adjusted all the clothes I got from the charity store, so they fitted me better."

"She did a good job; I didn't notice any changes to my outfits. Do you think she'd accept a job if I offered her one?" I asked, not wanting to be too forceful and step on Meryl's toes.

"Doing what?"

"The company needs another machinist to sew mother's current designs, ready for the fashion shows."

Meryl tapped a finger on her chin. "I'll ask her, but she'll probably say no. She has agoraphobia and finds it difficult to travel."

"Oh, that's a shame. I suppose she could work from home. It'll be no problem dropping off the patterns and materials and collecting the dresses when they're sewn."

"Hmm, I think she'll appreciate the opportunity to earn her own money again. Leave it with me." Meryl rested a hand on my thigh and squeezed, sending a shiver through my core. "Can Anton drop me at your mother's office on the way home? I need to negotiate my pay."

"Sure," I said. "Do you want to eat out tonight?"

Meryl placed a gentle kiss on my cheek. "To be honest, I think it would be perfect to stay at home. I want to see if your bed is more comfortable than mine."

Her lips moved to mine. I saw Anton watching us in the mirror and gave him a wink. He pressed a button. Soft music played in the rear and a screen raised, blanking us off while we made out on the back seat.

* * *

THE FRONT DOOR SLAMMED CLOSED. "POLLY!" mother shouted from the hallway.

Sinking into the patio wicker seat, I tried to hide my head with my book.

"There you are." Mother sat on the edge of the table.

I peered across the top of my book. "Hi."

"I've had a good chat with Meryl, and she's joining us next week. I'm excited about developing our social media." Mother paused. "Polly, darling, I've got something for you."

Sighing loudly, I snapped my book closed.

"Follow me." Mother grabbed my hand and pulled me out of the seat, dragging me to her office. "Now, sit down there." She pointed to a chair and busied herself in a walk-in cupboard. When she emerged, she was carrying a large box and a folio. "These are for you. I've been selfish, trying to take care of you and keep you safe, making you work in a role you dislike."

I gaped at her, not fully convinced by her words. "Do you think I'm not good at my job?" I asked, rummaging through the box, finding paints, brushes, pencils.

"You're a fantastic legal advisor; however, I think your heart is elsewhere. And I don't want you to blame me for holding you back. If you want to be an artist, you can make a start with my old equipment."

I sat back. "I won't need to paint full time; I just want to follow some on-line courses and improve my technique."

"In that case, perhaps you could work in the legal department part-time while you train."

The door opened. "Can I join you?" Meryl asked, sliding into the room.

I slapped my forehead and wagged a finger between the two of them as the conspiracy plot dawned on me. "You've been talking?"

Mother's face reddened, and she gave a slight grin. "This woman is persuasive," she said, putting an arm around Meryl. "Now, I've got to rush to a meeting. Are you happy?"

"Sort of!" I said, chewing my lower lip.

"Let's talk later and investigate what courses are available." She leaned on Meryl. "I hope I've done the right thing. I'll see you both later."

Meryl looked concerned, kneeling by my side. "What's wrong?"

"I think I'm in shock. Look at all this stuff." I waved my hand over the art equipment sprawled in front of me.

"Why don't you try them out? Grab your paints. There's a life model waiting in your bed." She dashed out of the room, discarding her clothes as she ran to my bedroom.

EPILOGUE

Three Months Later

MERYL SHUFFLED CLOSER TO POLLY, kissing her neck, her hands roaming across Polly's hips. Polly murmured and rolled over, slipping her leg between Meryl's. "Good morning," she said, as their lips met.

A vehicle beeped in the drive.

"*Ardarsene!*" Polly shouted, panting when her body vibrated to the touch of Meryl's tongue.

The beeping continued.

Working her way down Polly's body, Meryl sucked each nipple and kissed her stomach, making Polly arch her back.

"What the hell?" Meryl said, reaching Polly's sex and lifting her head at the sound of another beep.

Polly trembled and attempted to push Meryl back into position. "Don't stop."

"I'll have to see what's going on. There might have been an accident." Meryl rose from the bed, pulled on her silk dressing gown, and went to the window of their new apartment. "Oh my God," she said, her hand covering her mouth.

"What's happened," Polly said, hurrying to Meryl's side.

Meryl's dad, Mac, and Polly's mum, Sarah, stood outside, beside a campervan. Sarah waved a set of keys. "What do you think of this?" she shouted.

Polly and Meryl pulled on some clothes, tore down the stairs and out of the front door.

"I don't understand," Polly said, examining the newly painted van.

Mac put his arm around her shoulders. "I've been renovating her. She's all tickety-boo. Try the engine."

While she jumped into the driver's seat, Meryl opened the side door and looked around the inside.

"Your mum covered the seats and bed with designer fabric, and made curtains for the windows," Sarah said, pointing out the decorative features. "We've fitted a new cooker and sink." She opened a cupboard. "And look in here, a miniature refrigerator."

"This is fantastic," Meryl said, pecking Sarah's cheek.

Polly turned the key, and the engine purred to life.

"I had to do a load of welding, and the exhaust was shit," Mac said. "I rebuilt the engine, fitted new brakes, and upgraded the gears. And look at that dashboard, brand new music player and Satnav. She's ready to go."

"Where's she going?" Polly asked.

"Anywhere you want to take her," Sarah said. "For the next six months, you can work from a distance. We can talk via phone, email, and video messenger. I want you to travel, paint, and blog to your heart's content. When you return, you can decide if you want to continue working for my company or do your own thing."

"Really?" Meryl and Polly said in unison.

* * *

Polly threw a stack of t-shirts, shorts, and outdoor trousers into a rucksack. It took Meryl a lot longer to determine which clothes to take. While she decided, Polly loaded the van with food, water, and wine.

"Are you ready yet?" Polly yelled.

Meryl emerged with two suitcases filled with her designer gear.

Polly sighed. "We don't have room for all those clothes. We're in a VW campervan, not a RV motorhome."

"I'll make room," Meryl said, lugging her bags to the camper, squeezing them inside and taking the driver's seat.

Polly climbed into the passenger side and opened the travel atlas. "Okay, which way shall we go?"

"We don't need that old thing." Meryl tore the map from Polly's hands and chucked it out of the window. "We're gonna create our own route and pave it with ecstatic kisses. In fact, let's start right now."

ABOUT THE AUTHOR

Alysia D Evans is a sapphic literature author. She enjoys writing contemporary sapphic romance, dystopian adventure, and historical fiction. She began writing in 2019, to fill time during the Covid lockdown. This culminated in books one, two and three of The Life of Lucy. *Red Bush and Lemon; Red Wine and Mint Cake;* and *Red Mist and Solace.* In her books, readers will find deep, flawed women, with problems which need to be solved to allow them to move on. Alysia is a member of the self-published author collective iReadIndies. You can also find her books on the https://iheartsapphfic.com/bookfinder/ website under the archetype Librarian / Bookseller.

Facebook: https://www.facebook.com/alysiad.evans
iReadIndies: https://ireadindies.com/index.html

Red Bush and Lemon – The Life of Lucy: Part 1

Approaching fifty, Lucy's life is unsettled and disturbing. Venturing to Botswana, she determinedly immerses herself in the country's inspirational culture. Bumping into an irresistible young woman, Lucy discovers a new side to herself, her holiday becoming life-changing. Jae says, 'Twist and turns, interesting characters and beautiful descriptions of South Africa.'

Red Wine and Mint Cake - The Life of Lucy: Part 2

From Jaz, Lucy discovered true love. Slowly, she was overcoming the negativity instilled in her by an abusive ex-husband. However, living rurally, away from her hometown, makes Lucy insecure. She needs Jaz's help to navigate a way through her new life. Busy working and helping her family, Jaz doesn't realise Lucy is finding her new life challenging. Jaz's workaholic actions disappoint Lucy, causing their relationship to fall from wonder to despair. Will the two of them be able to reconcile and re-align their lives to take on the challenges the future may bring?

Red Mist and Solace – The Life of Lucy: Part 3

Lucy fell in love and survived a potential break-up with Jaz. Now she is on the verge of marrying the woman who invited her into her family and freed her from a vindictive husband. The only event which could improve Lucy's life is locating her daughter, adopted from her at birth. If she could apologise, and ensure her daughter had a safe, content life, Lucy could move on and live her own life in peace.

VOLUME THREE

TURNING TWO

ANNE HAGAN

TURNING TWO

Anne Hagan

Dedicated to SFC Dodge

PUBLISHED BY:
Jug Run Press, USA
Copyright © 2023

https://annehaganauthor.com/

All rights reserved: No part of this publication may be replicated, redistributed or given away in any form or by any electronic or mechanical means including information storage and retrieval systems without prior written consent of the author or the publisher except by a reviewer, who may quote brief passages for review.

This is a work of fiction. Names, characters, places and incidents are products of the author's imagination or are actual places used entirely fictitiously and are not to be construed as real. Any resemblance to actual events, organizations, or persons, living or deceased, is entirely coincidental.

CHAPTER 1–TONYA

Saturday Afternoon
Donohue Field
Fort Hays

Tonya flung her ball glove into her bag with enough force to draw her assistant team manager's attention to her as she walked into the dugout.

"You okay?" Atlee asked. "It was a good scrimmage, and we pulled out a win, so—"

"Just annoyed." She flashed her phone at the only woman she really considered to be a friend. "I just got a message from the CO. My orders are in for some damn training he signed me up to go to starting Monday. It really puts a dent in our time to get ready for the season opener."

"Training for what?"

Tonya spread her hands. "Beats the hell out of me. It's being put on by some outfit called the International Leadership Institute for Women. He says it will be good for me if I want to make

Master Sergeant and be a First Sergeant before I retire." She made a scoffing sound.

"What about your day job?"

"I put in for a five-day military leave of absence. Oh, the Guard is going to pay me for this! If I have to go, they're eating all the cost of it."

"Where do you have to go?"

"Some hotel over in Queensborough."

Atlee shrugged. "That's only an hour away. Maybe you could still make it to practices."

"I have no idea what I'm getting into, and I have to stay on site according to the CO. I'll keep you posted."

"If you can't be here, don't worry. I'll make sure things get taken care of. Baines will help me."

Tonya seethed. *I don't want Lynn Baines messing with the setup of the team. We're finally firing on all cylinders.*

* * *

*Sunday afternoon
Tonya's Apartment
Severn*

Tonya inspected her closet for the third time. Department uniforms. Military uniforms. Softball uniforms. *Not a damn thing in here I can wear to a civilian conference. A women's conference.* She ran a hand over the top of her head, feeling the shortened length of her coarse, black hair. *At least I got a decent cut last week. Won't have to mess with it.*

She dug in the back of the closet and pulled out a few polos she kept for more dressy occasions. They looked new. She grabbed a pair of jeans and a couple pairs of her work khaki's and tossed them in her duffle, then added the polos. Underwear, sports bras, boxers, Nike socks, and a couple of doo rags went in next. *Done. No wait.*

She reached up onto the closet shelf and pulled down the toiletry bag she always took along when she went on training missions with the National Guard. Peeking inside, she saw her travel toothbrush, most of a travel sized tube of toothpaste, and a stick of her favorite deodorant. She dipped into the bathroom and grabbed a bottle of hair product, just in case, and put that in the bag too. *Good enough. The hotel should have soap.* She zipped it closed and threw it in her duffle too.

This thing better not be a meat market. I don't have time for that.

CHAPTER 2-ABIGAIL

Saturday Evening
Abigail's Apartment
Oaklee

*E*xhaustion. Sheer exhaustion. Abigail Ross collapsed onto her sofa. She was too tired to eat. Too tired to do anything.

When she realized several minutes later she was drifting off, she hauled herself up, went into the bathroom and started the shower. She stripped off her scrubs and stepped under the warm spray. *I don't need an eye opener. I need to get clean and relax.*

SHE WOKE up naked on top of her still made bed. She didn't remember going to bed or even getting out of the shower. Her bedside clock told her it was 7:42 AM Sunday morning. Her stomach told her it had been many hours since she'd eaten anything. She rose, pulled on panties, sweatpants, and a t-shirt and padded to the kitchen.

The fridge yielded little that was suitable for breakfast. She grabbed the last apple in a bag, rinsed it, and munched on it while she contemplated the pile of frozen entrees and meals in her freezer. Lunches for a month, which were often tossed away because they thawed after a day in the unit fridge, but then never got eaten. There just wasn't time.

She reached in, grabbed a random box, and pulled it out. Santa Fe rice and beans. *Eh, could do worse for breakfast.*

She set the microwave, then went to the hall closet. She fished out her rolling case, suit bag, toiletries case, and her extra briefcase. *Don't feel like switching out all my work stuff for...well, for anything.* By the time she'd piled all of that on the sofa, the microwave dinged.

She carried the bags to the bedroom, then fetched her food and carried that in there, too. She had a bite and then resigned herself to inspecting her closet for suitable clothes that were not scrubs.

Maybe a week away from the hospital will at least be restful. More restful than packing for it, anyway.

*5:00 AM M*ONDAY *morning*
  St. Agnes Ascension Hospital

"WHY ARE YOU HERE?" Doctor Silbeth asked Abigail as he took the empty seat next to her. "Don't you have a conference to get to?"

"Morning education and rounds," she told the attending orthopedic surgeon. "Check in for the conference doesn't even start until 10:00 AM."

"In Queensborough?"

"Yes. It's less than an hour's drive."

"I don't want you cutting it too close."

She lowered her voice as the speaker from the cardiac unit began his presentation. "I'm not sure what you expect me to get out of it to begin with. My time is much better spent here."

"Doctor Ross, we've talked about this."

She drew in a deep breath. *Don't say something you'll regret.* "I'll be here for rounds in the morning," she whispered. "I've looked at the sessions. There's nothing that applies to me before 10:00 AM." *Or even before noon.*

"Whatever for?"

"Mrs. Peterson gets discharged tomorrow morning."

He waved her off. "One of the other residents and a PT can handle that. You need to focus on the conference."

"But she's my patient. One thing you've been..." she tried to choose an appropriate word, "telling me is to see things all the way through."

"Doctor Ross, this isn't the time. Come to my office right after education and we'll discuss it." He stood and moved away from her before she could respond.

Dr. Silbeth leaned across his desk as he spoke in a firm tone. "Abigail, you're one of, if not the most promising future surgeon we have. You have the most talent in the OR. That said, you're the lowest rated on patient surveys. You come in at ratings of six and seven consistently on a scale of ten. Patients say you're abrupt and you don't seem to want to take the time to explain things fully."

"There's only so much time," she said.

He held up his hand. "That's not all. They say you don't give them a lot of emotional support or encouragement, either. Those things are as important to patients facing major orthopedic issues as the surgeries they'll undergo."

She stared at him, unsure of what to say.

"You need to find empathy. You'll go far if you do. Get any fellowship you want. Get invited into a top orthopedic practice."

"What if I can't?"

"You'll still have a career, Abigail. No one denies your talent. But your patients and, dare I say, your co-workers liking you, being able to relate to you, will take you a lot further."

CHAPTER 3–CONFERENCE TIME

*Late Monday Morning
The Regal Duchess Hotel and Conference Center
Queensborough*

Tonya checked her watch again. *This damn line is taking forever. Just like the Army. Hurry up and wait.* She glared at the back of the woman in front of her. *Hang up and move up two feet already.*

"Next." A woman at the check-in table waved at the woman just in front of the woman absorbed with her cell phone. When the first woman moved off, but the one staring at her phone didn't budge, Tonya tapped her on the shoulder.

The woman whirled and almost smacked her in the stomach with the hand holding the phone. "Why are you so close to me?"

Tonya pointed. "You're next. Just letting you know."

"I could see that," the obviously younger woman said. "I'm giving everyone their space. Covid protocols."

"Yet, you're not masked."

"I've had multiple vaccines, and I carry this everywhere." She took a small bottle of hand sanitizer out of her blazer pocket. "I also keep my distance from other people in public settings."

"Next," another woman at the check-in table called out.

The woman in front of Tonya tilted her head and gave her a tight-lipped grin. "That's me." With that, she whirled back around and marched forward.

. . .

"Hi there. I'm Clara. I'll be leading some of the sessions. And you are?"

"Tonya Trube."

"Nice to meet you, Tonya." Clara rifled through a bin of hanging folders placed between herself and the other staffer.

"Here we are." She held out an overstuffed envelope. "This is your seminar packet. You'll find a program with a schedule of sessions in there, so if you haven't already picked out a track to focus on, you'll want to do that before the lunch opening. We'll get started right after lunch."

"Track?"

The younger woman that had been in front of her in line turned toward her and held up her phone. "Tracks." She tapped the screen. "There's a leadership track. A collaboration track. A—"

Tonya turned back to Clara. "Probably the leadership track."

Clara smiled. "Have you checked into the hotel?"

"Did that first. Early check-in."

"Why don't you go back to your room, think about why you're here, look at the sessions in the tracks, then decide?"

"How hard could it be?"

Clara just smiled.

. . .

Tonya scowled at the note in her packet from her CO as she read his brief scrawl again.

Follow the collaboration track, please. Be sure to include sessions on making friends and building trust, key skills in your quest to advance your military career.

CPT Clark

She crumpled the note and pitched it toward the wastebasket, but she missed. She got up and stomped the few steps to the can to pick up the offending ball of paper.

As she tossed it in, she muttered to herself. "Friends? It's the damn Army! And trust? He doesn't know what he's talking about. People trust me."

She sat back down, but she thought better of it and retrieved the commander's note. After smoothing it out, she slid it into the back of her portfolio, then with a sigh turned her attention to the rest of the contents of the packet.

'Constructive Collaboration: Driving Performance for Teams,' she read in the conference program. *Seriously? I already hate this.*

Reluctantly, she turned to the indicated page to look at the individual collaboration track sessions.

"Encouraging Creative Conflict?" she read aloud. *Really? It's the military, not an artist colony!* She shook her head. *Not doing that session.*

She scanned through the rest of the collaboration track session descriptions. *Nothing here interests me in the least.*

Tonya flipped to the scheduling grid and looked at the schedule for the afternoon. "Humph." *The only thing that interests me today is lunch.*

Resigned, she glanced through the grid again at the rest of the day's schedule and tapped a finger on the heading 'Designing Collaboration: Building Teamwork, Trust, and Communication,' a two-hour session starting right after the lunch session. *Looks like that's got to be it.* There were other sessions after that one, but she closed the program. *That will probably be more than enough fun for one day.*

TONYA GRIMACED as she filled her plate. *Chicken, fish, and rabbit food. No potatoes. No pasta. Dark Brown bread. What the hell did the CO get me into?* She looked ahead at the drink station. *At least there's coffee.*

Tonya avoided all the nearly full tables. Instead, she weaved her way through the room toward an empty table well away from the buffet spread. She didn't even look up a couple minutes later when someone asked if a seat was taken. She waved the women to a chair.

"I'm Beth," the woman said.

"Tonya," she answered, as she gave Beth a quick glance and a nod before turning her concentration back to her plate.

She glanced around moments later and watched as a woman in a medical mask wove through the room right toward them. She stopped at their table and chose a seat apart from her and Beth without a word.

Recognizing her as the woman from the registration line, Tonya couldn't help herself. "That seat is saved."

The first woman who had joined Tonya shot her a look.

It did not sway the masked woman. "There are five empty seats. She can choose one on either side of you since you don't seem to mind people sharing your space."

"Am I missing something?" Beth asked.

"Just a joke," Tonya said.

The newcomer made a brief show of removing her mask. "I figured it would be fairly crowded at mealtimes."

"I'm Elizabeth," the other woman offered, "but everyone calls me Beth. I take it you two know each other?" She pointed at Tonya.

"Abigail. And, no. We were just at registration at the same time."

"A pretty name. What do you go by? Abby?"

"Abigail."

"Ah," Beth said. "What brings you here then, Abigail? I mean, if I can ask? I guess that was pretty forward of me."

Tonya grimaced. *How do I even answer that sort of question when someone asks me?*

"I'm here for my job," Abigail answered.

Bethany said, "Me too."

"Me too," Tonya volunteered. She was saved from further small talk when a woman grabbed a microphone and began welcoming them all to the conference.

TONYA PURPOSEFULLY CHOSE a seat at the back of the room, near one of the exit doors for the 'Designing Collaboration' session. *If this gets dull, or heaven forbid, rah-rah like those lunch speakers, I'm ducking out.* She remembered the short video greeting from Julia something or other. *Pure sugar. Insane.*

Tonya watched a stream of women wander into the meeting room in ones and twos. Most ignored the back rows, opting for seats in the front.

Suckers. They really think this is going to be worth their time.

A speaker took the stage and fiddled with a laptop to set up her slides. Tonya dutifully opened her paper notebook and jotted down the session title and speaker's name from the first slide.

Someone slid into the seat next to her. When she glanced that way, she did a double take. "Seriously? Are you stalking me?"

A masked Abigail held a hand out and waved it about. "I took the only open seat that's not in the middle of the room, in the middle of a row."

"So, I take it you're on the collaboration track?"

Abigail shot her a look. "And I take it that's what you threw a dart at and hit when Clara sent you off to your room?"

"Ha, ha. No. It's the only class today that didn't seem physically repulsive."

"None of them are going to be 'physically' repulsive," Abigail said as she made air quotes.

"Says you."

"How old are you? Two?"

"Okay folks," the presenter called out from the podium. "Let's get started."

Tonya thought about sticking her tongue out at Abigail, but she restrained herself.

* * *

Monday Evening
Tonya's Room
The Regal Duchess Hotel and Conference Center

WHERE THE HELL IS ATLEE? Tonya paced the floor as her call rolled over to Atlee's voicemail. "Hey. Call me. It's important," she said, leaving a message.

She laid the phone down on the bed and stared at it, willing it to ring. When the screen lit up with a text from Atlee a couple of minutes later, she read it and frowned.

"What's up?" it said.

She typed back. "Can you call me?"

The phone rang moments later. Instead of saying hello, she

just launched in. "I need you to make sure some things get done at practice tomorrow."

"Hello to you too."

"Atlee, come on. This is important."

"It's practice."

That makes it not important? "Listen, I'd much rather be there to handle things myself, but I'm stuck here in this hellhole, captain's orders."

"It can't be that bad. Is the hotel nice?"

"It's okay, I guess. It's not my place."

"So it's nice is what I hear you saying."

"My place is nice."

Atlee scoffed.

"Anyway, I want you to make sure all the infield drills get run, but give lots of attention to grounders and line drives to short, and turning two. I'm worried we're a little slow and we won't get double plays we should get."

"Gotcha. Lotta women there?"

"Atlee, focus."

"I am focused. Work on turning two. Got it. Now, about the women?"

"It's a conference for women."

"And?"

"And what?"

"Meet anyone?"

"That's not what I'm here for."

"Your point is what?"

"No. I haven't met anyone."

"But?"

"There's one woman who hit on me after a session this afternoon, but I'm just not interested in a relationship right now. And," she said, contempt entering her tone, "one woman called me sir and thought I was part of the hotel staff."

"Ouch."

"Yeah. I mean, I have a goofy conference badge I have to wear and everything. Some people are clueless. What's bad is, she's not the only one."

"Sounds like the staff there needs some training."

"Sorry. That's not what I meant. I was talking about one of the other attendees. She just rubs me the wrong way. Very uppity and annoying."

"A match made in heaven."

"What?"

"Nothing," Atlee said.

Tonya figured out what she had muttered. "I can't stand her. She's far too full of herself. And, for the record, she's got to be at least ten or fifteen years younger than me, if not more. I'm 46 and likely the oldest one here, period, except for a couple presenters."

CHAPTER 4—RESIGNED

Monday Evening
Abigail's Room
The Regal Duchess Hotel and Conference Center

"Doctor Silbeth, it's Doctor Ross. Just checking in."

"Are you at the conference?"

"Yes. I just came up from a session and thought I ought to check up on things."

"Everything is fine here. No major changes since this morning."

"And Mrs. Peterson?"

"I appreciate your…concern, but she's not due to be discharged until morning. That's still on track. No complications."

"Oh. Okay."

"How's it going there, Abigail?"

"Fine." *It's not medical. A waste of my time. Not going to make me into every patient's buddy and get me the fellowship I want. Get me out of St. Agnes and into University, Sanai, or Hopkins.*

"Are you still there?"

"Yes. Sorry doctor."

"Focus on the conference, Abigail. Get everything you can out of it."

"Yes." With that, she hung up. *He calls me Abigail instead of Dr. Ross when he's not seeing me as an equal.*

"Damn conference. What am I going to do for three more days of this nonsense?" *And now I'm talking to myself. Get a grip, Abigail!*

An image of Tonya flitted through her head. She tried to shake it away. *One of two attendees I've met–her and Beth. I'm pitiful. I'm a doctor. Graduated second in my class. I'm an orthopedic surgery resident. I shouldn't have to be here, but I am. I certainly should be able to command a room better than I have been.*

She debated going out to get dinner or calling for room service. Tonya distracted her thoughts again as she scanned the room service menu for something healthy and appealing. "She's insufferable. Worse than any patient. So full of herself." *And there I go again, talking to myself. Patients have reason to be distraught or demanding or flippant. What's Tonya's excuse?*

She tossed the menu down and grabbed a mask and a jacket. As she headed out the door, she continued to think about the gruff older woman.

Why is she here? What could she be getting out of this? She said 'work.' She chuckled. *They think I have trouble relating to people. They ought to meet her.*

As she walked down the block toward the hubbub of the inner harbor area, she pushed thoughts of everything away, but how she could return to the hospital on Friday and show she was a different person, the type of person people wanted to be around. *I have to figure out how to model better behavior when I'm* with patients and my coworkers if I want to get what I want. I'm smart. I can play the game.

* * *

Tuesday Morning

REFRESHED after a half hour each on a stationary bike and the treadmill in the hotel's tiny gym, and then a cool shower, Abigail headed back downstairs, taking the stairs, to catch an early session. She thought she saw Tonya going into a conference room as she went into a different room and wondered what session Tonya was doing, but then she tried to shake all thoughts of the brash woman off. *Why do I care?*

Quickly bored with the speaker at the session she'd chosen, she plotted the things she would need to do to show the attending medical staff at St. Agnes she was prepared to move out of year three of her residency and into a fellowship that would lead her to a long and lucrative surgical career.

The session ended and people were walking out of the room before she realized what was happening. Hustling, she gathered her things, then checked the conference app for the location of the next session, one on networking and building pathways. *I can use it later, when I've got my fellowship to help me make the connections to move into a practice.*

The room was surprisingly small. She hurried forward to grab a seat at the front. When Clara, the worker from the registration line the day before, stepped up to the podium on a slightly raised platform, she was surprised.

Clara didn't open a laptop or put up any slides on the screen that stood a couple of paces behind her. She didn't even spread out any notes. She just looked around the room, smiling as women entered and chose seats. At one point, she even stepped to the edge of the dais to wave several attendees closer.

"Good morning!" she called out without using the microphone. "If this is your first session of the day, go back out and grab a cup of coffee. You're going to need it. You've got some work to do."

Laughter rose in the room. Clara walked over to the mic and leaned in. "I'm serious, and I'll wait."

Abigail grabbed her water bottle and took a sip as she turned and watched people get up and leave the room. *There's no time for coffee breaks on the floor. Glad I broke my college habit.*

Her gaze found Tonya in a back corner. Quickly, she spun back around. *Why is she here?*

She didn't have time to ponder it for long. Clara moved back over to the microphone and called the coffee goers back to their seats.

"Again, good morning. Many of you met me in the registration line yesterday. If you didn't, I'm Clara Glidden. I'll be your facilitator for this session, which the Institute likes to call networking and building pathways. I like to call it Making Friends and Playing Nice with Others."

There were chuckles around the room and one loud guffaw from the back. Abigail had a gut feeling the guffaw came from Tonya.

Clara raised her hands for quiet. "What do we think of, when we think of networking?"

A woman in Abigail's row called out, "Making valuable business connections."

"For whom?" Clara asked her.

"Um, well for myself, and hopefully for them, too."

Clara held out a hand to the woman. "So what can happen?"

"Well, so maybe they can help me sometime or I can help them."

Changing tactics, Clara raised a hand in the air and asked, "How many of you have been to a so-called networking event?"

Abigail didn't raise her hand, but when she glanced around, she saw several hands were up.

Clara pointed at a woman. "What was that like, Joanie?"

To Abigail, the woman at first seemed surprised Clara remembered her name. She responded, "Boring, really."

"People walking around with a drink, giving an elevator pitch about what they do, and handing out business cards?"

Joanie shook her head. "I wish there had been drinks! That might have made it better." Several people laughed and Clara smiled.

Clara looked around. "I didn't see many of you in here at the mixer last night. Trust me when I say, you'll make better contacts here than you ever will at a stuffy networking event. I encourage you to come this evening to see what I mean."

Continuing, as she stepped down from the dais and took a position between the first two tables, she said, "The problem with traditional networking, especially at a networking event or a specialty conference, is there are not a variety of connections to be made. You're usually talking to people who do what you do."

"Why is that bad?" Abigail couldn't help but ask.

Clara gave her a nod. "Let's say you're a financial analyst and your networking efforts have gotten you dozens of connections in banking and finance, that would be good if you were looking for a new position in the industry or looking to connect someone you know with a network contact, but what if you were looking for, say, a highly recommended orthopedic surgeon to do a delicate operation on your young daughter's foot? Would you ask a financial analyst for a recommendation? No. Right?" She looked at the woman to her immediate right. "Paula?"

"Heaven's no."

"In the interest of full disclosure," Clara pointed at Paula as she talked, "Paula is a financial analyst."

"And you've got an incredible memory," Paula said. "Did you ever work in finance?"

"Heaven's no," Clara repeated the expression. "I've no head for facts and figures."

Abigail marveled. *She didn't check me in, but she had to know what my field is when she chose her example.*

"I'm not saying networking with your peers is bad. I'm saying we need diversity in our connections, and we rarely find that by staying within our comfort zones."

Clara looked at the woman at the end of the aisle on her left. "Susan, is your best friend a personal chef and caterer like you?"

"No." The woman laughed. "She can barely cook. She owns a dog grooming business."

"Has she ever referred business to you?"

Susan nodded. "And I take my dog to her, and I've referred other people to her."

"See?" Clara glanced around the room, then returned to Susan. "Are any of your other friends chefs or caterers?"

"One is the pastry chef for a restaurant. We met in culinary school, but no one does what I do."

"And your other friends, have they sent business your way?"

"Sometimes, yes. And, I've helped others when and where I could."

"Have I made my point?" Clara asked.

Heads nodded around the room.

"I'm not saying make friends to use them. I'm saying make friends who share your interests, your passions, and even your field and help each other if you can. The first requirement is to make a friend and then to be a friend."

"It's not that easy," said a voice from the back of the room, which Abigail instantly recognized as Tonya's.

"You're right. We're not six anymore. It's harder for adults, but it's not impossible. Think about this; maybe you're approaching things all wrong. You go to work. You go home. When you venture out, you're going mostly to industry only conferences, seminars, and industry only networking events. When you venture outside your bubble, it's for entertainment with your current tribe. A movie. Drinks. A meal. You're usually not trying to meet anyone new."

Clara raised her hand again. "Who here is comfortable going to a friend's party and striking up a conversation with a total stranger?"

A few hands went up.

"Why do you suppose there are so few of you? Are the rest of you shy? Introverted, maybe? Feel you're not as interesting as the other people there?"

Abigail suppressed a shudder.

"But, you went to the party. You put yourself out there. Why not take the next step? Why not approach someone and strike up a genuine conversation that isn't about the party or the weather?"

Abigail blew off the idea. *Who has time for parties? I'm too busy for that.*

"Maybe you don't go to parties," Clara said. "Not your thing? How about the dog park, the art gallery, the modern science museum, a baseball game, the shop where you get your morning coffee? I could go on and on, but I think you get the idea."

A woman in the center of the room asked, "How?"

Clara held up a finger. "That's the big question and one we're about to tackle. Does everyone have a piece of paper and a pen?"

Abigail opened her portfolio notebook for the first time and sat with her pen poised for the wisdom she hoped Clara was about to pour forth.

"I want each of you to write four things you'd want to know about a potential friend. And," she waved a hand, "Don't write what they do for a living, are they partnered…we're not looking for their potential income level or for dates."

"Like hobbies?" Susan asked.

"You could go that way, yes, but in context. If you're in the floss section of a craft store, you could ask someone about needlepoint, but you wouldn't ask needlepoint questions to someone at a dog park. Instead, you might ask them how they taught their dog to play frisbee and maybe if they could give you some pointers with your dog."

"So," Susan said, "instead of asking a general question, ask a specific one?"

"Exactly."

Abigail shook her head. "So, how does that work for this exercise? Do we just write ask a specific question in the situation's context?"

Clara gave her a smile. "So analytical, doctor.

When Abigail frowned, Clara gave in. "Yes, you can write that, but it won't serve your purposes in our next exercise. Dig a little deeper. Do you and your friends enjoy wine? Maybe you'd like to add to your tasting circle. Or, maybe none of your current friends like it but you do. Maybe you hope to find a kindred soul. You might ask someone in the wine section of your favorite place to buy the wine you already like what else they recommend and why."

"So, in context again."

"True. But you could do it at a ball game too. Say, you're next to someone who also seems to eschew beer and is wishing for wine."

No help. Maybe this session is a waste of my time too.

"I'm going to give everyone a few minutes. Dig deep. Be unique."

Abigail laid her pen down and just stared at her paper. *Total waste of time, after all.* She spun the pen around on the paper a couple times but stopped when the woman to her right glanced her way. She picked it up, thought for a few seconds, and put it down again.

When a shadow crossed her blank paper a minute later, she

looked up. She hadn't seen Clara approach, but now the facilitator was standing right in front of her.

"Let's chat," Clara said. She stepped back and signaled to Abigail to join her at the front of the room.

"WHY ARE YOU HERE?" Clara asked.

"Pardon?"

"Work? Personal interest? You've got some reason for being here."

"Work."

"And what are you hoping to get out of this for work?"

Abigail let out a small sigh, then lied. "I'm an orthopedic surgery resident. I'm competing against mostly men for a fellowship, and I need help to boost my resume and my profile."

"Hmm. Okay. And why do you think you need help? You strike me as very put together and very competent."

She ignored the compliment. "I guess...I don't know." She gave in and laid some of the truth on Clara. "I come from a family of successes. Careers, athletics, relationships. I've always felt second best in everything compared to any of them."

"How did you do, just as yourself?"

Abigail shrugged.

"Are you a success?"

"Sure. I guess."

"You graduated from medical school."

"Second in my class."

"Congratulations. That's quite an accomplishment."

"I suppose."

"Oh, so you don't think you were successful because you weren't first?"

Yes. She couldn't say it out loud. She looked away.

Clara called her out. "You're too hard on yourself. It's tougher to graduate from medical school than anything most of us will ever do. You didn't wash out and you finished in the top one or two percent of your class."

"At a tier two school...State."

"There you go again. Do you know what they call the student who graduates last in his class at a 'tier two' state school?"

"The goat?"

"Doctor."

"Time's up," Clara called out. She pointed toward the front rows on both sides of the aisle. "Now we're going to have some fun. Front row, turn your chairs around to face the folks at the table behind you."

The seat at the far end of the second row on Abigail's side of the aisle was empty. Clara looked toward the back of the room. "Tonya, please move up and take that seat for this next exercise," she commanded her as she pointed to the end seat.

Abigail watched Tonya gather her things and do as she was told without comment. *There's a surprise.*

Clara commanded the third row to turn around and face the fourth row, then pulled from the fifth row again to fill empty seats until there was no one left in the fifth row.

The facilitator rubbed her hands together and smiled. "You've heard of speed dating? Welcome to speed friending. Those questions you wrote you are now going to use on each other as best you can in our given situation. Not ideal, I know."

Abigail gave the woman across the table a nervous look. The woman smiled back.

"We're going to do this for a half hour, four minutes a round. You each have two minutes to ask your questions and try to connect. At four minutes, rows one and three will move one seat to the left. The last person in the row will move to the center aisle seat.

Abigail swallowed hard. *Two women and then Tonya.*

"One rule," Clara cautioned. "No judgements."

"What are your views on climate change?"

Leading with a political football. Okay. "I believe it exists," Abigail said. "I don't believe we're doing enough to stop it or slow it, if it can, in fact, be stopped or slowed. I have no idea what will work."

"Do you care?"

Wow. Okay. No judgements, huh? "Yes. I care."

"What do you do personally to combat climate change?"

Does this woman even have friends? Is this how she treats them? "I...I do what I can within...within what is feasible for me to do. We do lots of things at work." She flailed for specific examples and finally blurted, "We recycle what we can. Paper, plastic, cans."

"What about personally?"

Annoyed, Abigail fired back, "Do you have any other questions you'd like to ask, or are they all on the one topic?"

The woman gave her a half shrug. "This is what's important to me. I want to associate with people who share my passion."

Let it go, Abigail. She's not someone you'll ever see again. She gave in and said, "Fair enough."

"You're not passionate about it?"

"It's not a specific focus for me. I do things, sure. I'm mindful most of the time, but my work consumes my life and most of what I do revolves around work."

"Two minutes," Clara called from the end of the fourth row. "If you haven't switched who is asking and who is answering, please switch."

Oops. I'd almost rather she kept asking. Almost. She didn't have to look at her paper. There was only one question there. "Um, if there was a sport you could be one of the best at, what sport would it be and why?"

"Oh, I'm not interested in sports."

"Um, okay. Uh, honestly, I didn't come up with many questions."

"I like to read," the woman volunteered. "You?"

Paper or electronic? Better not ask. "When I have time. Most of my reading is for work. And, I'm really sorry I didn't ask before, but I never got your name."

"Lorelei. People call me Lori and I already know you're Abigail. So, you never read for pleasure?"

This woman is just taking everything over. "I don't have a lot of time."

"We make time for the things that are important to us like reading, and reducing our carbon footprint."

No, not judgmental at all. She thought about throwing out what she did for a living just in case dear Lori hadn't caught Clara's hint.

"Time," Clara called out. "First and third rows, shift a seat, please. Last person, move to the first seat."

Abigail barely heard the next woman in the row as she introduced herself. One seat from being across from Tonya had her perched on the edge of her chair. Her mouth was dry.

The woman across the narrow table was talking. All Abigail could think was she should have masked prior to the exercise. *Would this woman take offense? Tonya will call me out, for sure.*

It got quiet and Abigail realized her new sparring partner was waiting for a response. She turned away, excusing herself, and feigned a cough. When she turned back around, she apologized and asked the woman to repeat the question.

ABIGAIL GAVE TONYA A TIGHT SMILE.

"I'm surprised you didn't mask for this."

"And here we go."

"What did I say? You're two feet from each person."

Abigail looked up to see Clara watching them closely. "Shh. You're going to get us in trouble."

"Did you really just shush me?"

"Is that your first question for me?"

"No. That was, 'What did I say?'"

"Pardon?"

"Never mind. Over your head."

"Over my head?"

"Oh, is the surgeon offended?"

"You got that, did you? Would have thought that went over *your* head."

"Shh!" Clara bent in and said, "Ladies, play nice."

Abigail folded her arms and eyed the butch woman across the table, taking in her tightly clipped hair, her flawless medium brown skin devoid of any hint of make-up, the deep brown eyes, and the polo buttoned up far enough to conceal any hint of cleavage. *Sports bra, probably.* She couldn't be sure, but she thought she probably had khaki pants on, too.

Tonya was tall for a woman; taller than she was by a few inches and she wasn't considered short, but the butch had a bigger, broader build.

"Like what you see?" Tonya said in a near whisper.

Caught, Abigail felt guilt burn the back of her neck. *Don't know why I was staring. She's definitely not interested in me. Who could be?* She tried to cover by asking, "Are we doing this little exercise or not?"

"I thought we were."

"You're insufferable."

"No judgements, remember?"

"Enough. That's been several questions for you now."

"Who died and made you the boss?"

"Ha ha." That came out a little louder than she'd intended it. The pair to their right were looking on with interest.

"Why don't you just ask me your questions," Tonya said. "We've already used up at least a minute."

"Or, you could ask me yours."

"You were just complaining I'd already asked too many questions."

Insufferable! "Fine," she huffed. "If there was a sport you could be one of the best at, what sport would it be and why?"

"Easy one. Although I'm already superb, just too old to play in the semi-pro or pro leagues now that they actually exist. Softball."

"Softball?" *Not rugby?*

"Yes. Have you ever played? Wait, I'd guess probably not. You don't strike me as the sports type."

Abigail jabbed a finger into the tabletop. "I have played. Throughout high school, actually. Not only that, I went to college on a track scholarship. I was going back and forth between both sports, every spring."

"I had you pegged for an academic scholarship. You're such a smart ass."

"Pot. Kettle!" She glared at Tonya, unblinking. Tonya glared back at her.

The stare down ended several seconds later when Clara called, "Time. Switch, please."

CHAPTER 5–STUCK LIKE GLUE?

Clara gave the entire group a five-minute break after the speed friending session. As participants left the room chatting amicably, she stopped Tonya, calling to her to hold off for a minute.

"I'm not going to pull punches with you. What's your beef with Abigail Ross?"

Tonya tried to shrug the question off.

Clara gave her a smile. "Come on now. It's between us."

"She rubs me the wrong way, is all."

"Do you two know each other?"

"No. We met yesterday."

"And you've formed a full picture of her in less than 24 hours and what, maybe a couple of hours in the same rooms together?"

Ouch. It does make me sound bad. "I guess I'm being a little judgmental."

Clara raised an eyebrow, but she said nothing.

"I'll try to steer clear and mind my manners."

"Why don't you approach her as being a potential valuable network contact, or dare a say even a potential new friend with a different perspective?"

"We have *nothing* in common."
"You have more in common than you think."
Doubtful.

"Welcome back," Clara said. "Now then, if you've ever done speed dating–not asking for a show of hands here–you know you present a list of people you'd be interested in connecting with to the organizers and they link matches. I'm going to match you up with one of the six people you met in the first part of the class for an extended assignment to get to know each other."

Tonya felt a case of heartburn coming on.

"Who knows," Clara went on. "After that, you'll have a contact that shares at least some things in common with you, and maybe you'll even have a new friend."

Yep. I need an antacid. Tonya looked at Abigail who sat in the front row, unmoving. *She knows it too.*

"I'm giving you a half hour after I pair you. You can stay in here, go to the lobby, whatever you want to do. Be back here at 10:30." She passed out some paperwork and then began pairing people together.

The lobby was full when they reached it. Tonya glanced over at the lounge and noticed it was open, but empty given the time of the morning. She pointed. "Let's go in there."

Abigail shot her down. "I don't drink."

"And I don't drink at 10:00 AM. I'll buy you a coffee, if they're serving anything at all right now."

"I don't drink coffee either. Sorry."

"Listen, I'm trying here." She waved her papers at Abigail. "I don't want to do this anymore than you do, so let's just get it over with." She turned and walked into the lounge without waiting to see if the younger woman followed.

Tonya chose a small table near the door, sat and waited while Abigail situated herself across from her. She looked down at the paper when Abigail took time to look at hers.

"It seems pretty straightforward," Abigail said. "Almost like an interview."

"Do you want to trade papers, fill them out, then trade back?" Tonya asked.

Two other women from the class walked into the lounge and took a table a couple of tables over.

"Better not," Abigail said. "Why don't you start?"

Tonya sighed. "Name?"

"Abigail."

"All of it."

"Abigail Ross."

"Where are you from?"

"Laurel."

"Here, in state?"

Abigail nodded.

That's near me. "Do you still live there?"

After glancing at her paper, Abigail argued, "That's not on mine."

"Just wondering."

"Oh. My parents are still in Laurel. I live in Oaklee, about a half hour from there."

Also close. Very close. "Do you like where you live?"

"I suppose. It's close to work."

Tonya marked her paper.

A server interrupted and took Tonya's order for a coffee and Abigail's request for unsweetened iced tea with lemon.

When the server left, Abigail suggested, "Why don't we just go back and forth? It will be faster."

Tonya nodded in agreement. "Tonya Trube. T-R-U-B-E. I grew up in the Atlanta area. I live in Cherry Hill because it's close to downtown and close to where I work, too. It's okay, I guess."

She gave Abigail time to write her answers down, then she began again. "The next few questions are about friendship. Do you want to go first?"

"Asking or answering?"

"Answering."

"Not really," Abigail said, "but we both have to do it, so I guess it doesn't matter."

"What attracted you to your closest friend?"

"Um, well, I...That's a hard question to answer."

"You have friends, don't you?"

Abigail sat back hard in her chair and crossed her arms. "Yes, smartass. I have friends."

"Okay, so pick one."

"You pick one."

"Easy," Tonya said. "I met my best friend at...work, and it turns out she shares my interest in softball."

"That's it?"

"What?"

"You were attracted to her because of softball?"

"Work and softball, and either is as good a reason as any."

"I suppose. Most of my friends are from college track or from medical school."

"Was that so hard?" Tonya asked.

"Let's move on, shall we?"

"Why? It only gets more asinine from here."

When Abigail looked down at the list of questions, Tonya took a few seconds to study her. She had to admit, despite the obvious stress and tension evident in the woman's face, she found her attractive.

Abigail cleared her throat, snapping her out of her reverie. She said, "This has us talk about our hobbies, and passions."

"I told you. It's asinine."

"I don't see it like that, but I don't have a lot to contribute to that sort of discussion right now. I'm a third-year resident in orthopedic surgery. I work 12 to 16-hour days, six or seven days a week."

"No time for a life? I get that."

"Do you really? You have time for softball."

"It's sort of aligned with my job."

"Seriously? Sort of?"

"Yes, seriously," Tonya answered.

"And where do you work?"

"A, um, police department."

"You're a cop? I should have seen that."

"What's that supposed to mean?"

"Your entire demeanor."

"Actually, I'm not a cop, for your information. I'm a mechanic for the College Park Police Department. I work on all their cruisers and other vehicles."

Tonya bristled when Abigail went off script asking, "You said 'work' sent you here. Why?"

"How is that relevant to this…this assignment we're working on?"

"I don't know that to answer it."

"It's not important." *Just tell her about the guard already!*

"My employer sent me here, too. Do you want to know why?"

"Why?"

"You first."

Tonya sneered. "Pass. Like I said, not important."

"There's something you don't want me to know."

"No. It just isn't relevant to this assignment. And, it's nothing you could help with, anyway."

Abigail groaned. "Then I guess we're done." She gathered her things, but a thud from a couple of tables away got her attention. One of their classmates had fallen from her chair and was on the floor, convulsing. She dropped the papers and her notebook back on the table and rushed to the woman's aid.

. . .

"Hold her head, make sure she doesn't bang into anything," Abigail instructed the woman paired with her. "No, don't put your fingers near her mouth. She might bite."

"But she's chewing her tongue," the woman said while she attempted to hold the stricken woman's head still.

"She'll be fine. You can clean up any blood later...uh. Sorry. I didn't get your name."

"I'm Meryl and she's Polly."

"Abigail," she said by way of introduction as she kneeled, holding Polly's hand.

The shaking stopped and Polly's body went limp. Abigail kept watch. When she spotted movement, she leaned over and tapped a cheek. "Hello, Polly, come back to us."

Polly blinked open her eyes and took in the group of people gathered around her. She tried to sit up.

"Stay there and get yourself together," Abigail said. "Are you a diagnosed epileptic?"

Polly gave her head a slight nod.

"Did you take your medication today?"

"I think so," Polly said. She drooled, a dribble of fluid seeping from the side of her mouth.

"Good, I think you need to go to your room and sleep this off."

Abigail looked up at the now standing Meryl. "And she'll need to wash and change. Uncontrolled urination is an unfortunate side effect."

Meryl shot Abigail a look. "She's nothing to do with me. I was just paired up with her in our friendship session.

"Well, this is a good time to act as a friend. Come on, let's go."

Tonya jumped in to help get Polly up and did most of the work of supporting her as the four of them moved toward the elevators to take her to her room.

. . .

Tonya did what she could to help Abigail get Polly cleaned up and settled in her room, but they left most of the job to Meryl. As the two of them walked back to the elevator bank, Abigail surprised her.

"Thanks for your help to get her up here and, well, everything."

"Sure." She couldn't help staring at the younger woman as they waited for the elevator.

"What?"

Tonya said, "You really are a doctor."

"What was your first clue?"

"Ah. Sarcasm, eh?"

"Let me guess?" Abigail asked. "You can dish it out, but you can't take it?"

The elevator arrived, empty. Once they were inside and the doors closed, Tonya turned to Abigail and stuck out a hand. "Truce?"

Abigail seemed to hesitate, but then took the offered hand. "Truce."

"If we think about it, we only have to occupy the same space for a couple of days," Tonya said.

"Right. We're adults. We can handle that."

"Right."

"Can I have my hand back?"

Tonya let go. "Sorry." She missed the feeling immediately, but she didn't dare let on. As the doors opened on the ground floor and they stepped out, she checked the time on her phone. "We're too late to go back and finish the session. It's almost over."

"It's probably just as well."

"Maybe not. What do you say we go back to the lounge and finish the exercise, anyway? I'll buy you a Coke."

"We can go back, if you like, but I don't drink soda either," Abigail said. "Doctor, remember?"

. . .

The lounge was busier than it had been an hour before. A hostess seated them and handed them lunch menus.

"How about I buy you lunch instead?" Tonya asked. "We're missing the conference spread."

"I can get my own."

"I insist. It's the least I can do for a first responder."

"That wasn't life or death."

"But if you weren't there, who knows how Meryl might have handled things."

"Hopefully, she would have called for help."

"And Polly would have likely been embarrassed even more than she was, and they would have had her hauled off to a hospital to boot. You were exactly what she needed."

"I just did what I've been trained to do."

"Train as you fight."

"What?"

"Nothing. We can talk about it later."

When a server came to the table to take their orders, Abigail surprised Tonya with hers. When the server left, she couldn't help commenting. "A grilled chicken sandwich on whole wheat? Are you sure about that?"

"A girl's gotta eat."

They finished the assignment and had nearly finished eating when Clara found them. "There you are!" she said. "I've just talked with Meryl, Abigail. I can't thank you enough for what you did for Polly. You too, Tonya. You two jumped right in there, from what I hear."

Abigail ignored the platitudes and asked instead, "Did Meryl say what Polly is doing right now?"

"Sleeping," Clara reported. "Meryl was down to check in with me and get some food for the two of them and she was going back to sit with her." Clara's tone changed. "Will she be okay?"

Abigail nodded. "She's fine now, just sleepy. That's fairly normal, and it might take a while to wear off. It may exhaust her for a day or more."

"Oh. I hadn't realized that would happen. Perhaps I should speak with her about rescheduling her conference experience with us? When she's feeling up to it, that is."

"I'd wait until tomorrow," Abigail said.

Tonya held up her worksheet. "We've actually just finished the assignment. Care to look?"

"I would like to see what you two came up with, yes. I'm sorry you missed the rest of the session, so let me look at these and then get back to you."

"SHOULD you have said all that to Clara?" Tonya asked when Clara left.

"Pardon?"

"Isn't Polly entitled to her privacy?"

"Damned if I do. Damned if I don't."

"Now I beg your pardon."

"Nothing. Never mind."

"Don't look now."

Abigail turned in her seat and followed Tonya's gaze. "Meryl?"

"I said not to look."

"I don't take orders from you."

CHAPTER 6 – CLARA'S PLOT

Abigail stood up and gathered her things.
Tonya rose as well.
"What are you doing?" Abigail asked her.
"I'm not letting you walk out on me. We're finally getting somewhere here."
Abigail took a step toward the exit. "Go ahead, try to stop me," she challenged.
"Oh dear," Meryl said.
Both women froze.
Meryl approached them slowly.
"I think we need to have a discussion," she said.

"Why did you just leave me with Polly?" Meryl asked Abigail after they all sat down. "Because you don't care what happens to your patients? Or maybe you do care, but you don't know any better? Or—and I have to admit this is a possibility—maybe you don't feel any responsibility toward your patients? I mean, you are an intern, right? They aren't really *your* patients."
"I'm a resident, specializing in orthopedic surgery."

"Do you have children, Abigail?"

"No. And what's that got to do with anything? With Polly?"

"Do you think you could raise a child, teach him or her to be responsible and caring, and then send them off into the world without worrying about whether he or she would make smart choices? Would you want to, knowing how many people there are who never learned those lessons? Who are constantly making the wrong decisions? Some of them are good kids, Abigail, and they still make poor decisions. But most of the ones who cause the problems aren't. They're selfish and irresponsible and they'll keep doing it until someone stops them. And then they'll do it again somewhere else."

Abigail snarked, "Sounds like you're speaking from experience."

"Do you know where Polly is right now? If she's okay, that is? I'm sure you do. Don't you care about her? You were here with her when her seizure started. Didn't you feel anything for her? Did you do all you could for her? Wouldn't it bother you to find out that she died because you were careless? Wouldn't you wish that something had gone differently? Could you live with yourself if one of your patients suffered permanent injury or even death because you made mistakes?"

"She's alive, Meryl! She's...she's an epileptic. She admitted that. She said she took her medication today. She had an epileptic seizure--"

"Can you be sure she took her medication? *She* wasn't sure."

Tonya joined in. "That's true. She said she 'thought' she took it."

Meryl stabbed a finger into the table. "Maybe sometimes, she lies to herself, just like you lie to others and to yourself, Doctor. Maybe that's why she does it. To protect herself from being hurt by anyone, especially herself. Can you blame her? Isn't that what we all do?"

"No!" Abigail's body shook. She swallowed hard to fight the bile rising in her throat.

Tonya stood and leaned across the table, getting into Meryl's personal space. "Back off! You're way out of line. What Abigail did for Polly was above and beyond."

Abigail put a hand on Tonya's arm and applied pressure. "It's okay."

Meryl scrambled away.

"It was uncalled for," Tonya went on loud enough for the retreating woman to hear.

Abigail whispered, "And all true."

"What are you saying?"

"Nothing. I have to go." When she gathered her things again, Tonya didn't stop her.

ABIGAIL WANDERED through the lobby intending to step outside and get some air, but the rain battering the windows that ran the length of the front of the hotel's main floor changed her mind. She wheeled around and headed back toward the conference rooms.

She chose an empty session room and took a seat in a back corner. Tipping her head back against the back of the chair, she closed her eyes and breathed deeply for several minutes.

She didn't know how long she sat there. Eventually, women started to come in for a session, but she had no idea what for. She didn't care. When notebooks and laptops started coming out, she pulled hers out too.

What could it hurt? Maybe I'll learn something useful outside of the collaboration track.

When the speaker seemed to pick up in the middle of some sort of case analysis, Abigail tuned in and tried to follow the conversation.

The presenter made some valid points, and the group debated the best course of action.

As the conversation grew more heated, Abigail found her own view forming in her mind and after a few moments of listening, she spoke up. Everyone in the room stopped and looked at her.

"I think..." she started, her voice shaky. She cleared her throat and swallowed. "I think that the best approach here might be to be creative. Instead of focusing on the same solutions that have been tried previously, let's look for original ideas and pathways."

The speaker smiled and nodded her head. "That's exactly right. I think that's a great suggestion, and I'd love to hear what some of the other people in the room think."

The debate continued on, with everyone in the room contributing their own opinion. Abigail was surprised to find that she had more ideas to offer, and the others respected her input.

By the time the session was over, Abigail was excited and brimming with ideas for her own work, well apart from the sample case the women had been discussing. *Who knew actually taking a session seriously and taking part in it could be so rewarding?* She made her way back to the lobby, the sound of excited conversation still buzzing in her head.

Her eyes darted around as she searched for Tonya, but then she stopped herself. *Why do I care?* She kicked herself mentally. *It's a three-day conference. You'll never see her again after this and you don't have time for that, anyway.*

"You look pensive," Clara noted as she stepped out of the session room and spotted her.

"Pensive good, or pensive bad?"

"Good, I'd say."

"I was just in a session that gave me quite a lot to think about. Some good ideas, really."

"Oh? Which session?"

Abigail looked sheepish. "Actually, I don't even know."

Clara gave her a look.

"I wandered into an empty room to take a breather. It didn't stay empty long and I thought it would be rude to leave."

"Ah. Learning by accident is sometimes the best."

"I admit, I've never done anything by accident, like that."

"I would bet that's true."

"They were doing a SWOT Analysis. I'd never heard of it."

Clara asked, "So, I take it you're enjoying the seminar so far?"

Abigail told the truth. "Some. Yes, and no. Before that session, I have to admit there wasn't a lot here that I thought applied to me."

"Why did you feel that way? Or, a better question might be, why are you here? Really here?"

Abigail took a deep breath and came clean. "The orthopedic surgery chief who is my boss sent me here to try to get some insight into ways to become more patient focused."

"You're not considered patient focused as someone whose job it is to operate on patients?"

"Well, that's not exactly what they mean. I do focus on the needs of my patients but I...I guess I'm more interested in their records, their histories, and in doing the surgery itself and not so much about the personal side of it.

"Listening?"

"I listen."

"Empathizing?"

Abigail nodded. "That."

"Do you care about them?"

"I care. I do. It's just...it's so busy. Twelve-hour plus days, six days a week. Sometimes seven."

"It won't always be like that."

"Oh, I know."

"So, your goal is to become an orthopedic surgeon, and to reach that goal you need to do what besides become more empathetic?"

"I need to get good enough reviews at the end of this year to get taken on by an ortho physician group for the last two years of residency or choose a specific ortho specialty and try for a fellowship."

"Can I ask a personal question?"

"I...I guess."

"How do you get along with your colleagues? The other residents, the nursing staff, the rest of the support staff?"

"Fine." The look on Clara's face told Abigail she wasn't convinced. She admitted, "The attending's are all okay. Well, except that they're the ones who are giving me ratings on everything."

"But the other residents and staff?"

"The nurses are fine, too." She sighed, then conceded, "The other residents are all men. The ortho residents, anyway. It's...difficult."

"Woman in a man's world?"

"That's part of it."

"That," Clara declared as she held up a finger, "the institute can help with. And, that gives me an idea, too."

"What's that?"

"You just leave that to me, for now." Clara glanced at her watch. "The next round of sessions starts in five minutes. Might I suggest you go to the 'Empowering Women' session in the gold room? It's part of the leadership track, and I think you'll find it interesting. Look for me right here at the end of the hour."

* * *

Tonya

CLARA FOUND Tonya waiting in front of the bank of elevators to the upper floors of the hotel. "Got a minute?"

"Sure. There are no sessions I'm interested in right now. I was going upstairs to take a break."

"That sounds nice. How about you join me in the staff lounge for a coffee break instead? I promise I won't keep you long."

"Coffee sounds great." *I don't know what you're up to, but I will not turn down coffee that I don't have to make.*

ONCE THEY POURED coffee and sat down at a small table in the staff lounge room, Clara didn't mince words. "Tonya, I get you. I do. I know you're not being on the level with everyone here. I don't know for sure why, but I can make some educated guesses."

"Based on what intel?"

Clara's answer surprised her. "Military intel."

Tonya dipped her head. "How did you know?"

"My friend, I'm the one who dealt with your commanding officer to make conference arrangements for you. I put his note in your packet."

When Tonya didn't respond, Clara continued. "Don't you think it's time to make some decisions about your life? About what you want? Decide how important advancing in your military career is to you, and if it's important, what you need to do to make that happen?"

Tonya asked, "Why do you care?"

"You'll be a wonderful teacher and mentor to some young soldiers. And," she went on, "I know someone you could mentor right now. Get a little practice in, let's say."

Tonya's eyes narrowed. "Who?" *Don't say Abigail.*

"Abigail."

And she said it. Tonya scoffed.

At the shake of her head, Clara put out a hand, touching her arm. "I'm serious."

Tonya pulled away from the touch and picked up her coffee cup.

"Hear me out. You don't know the real reason Abigail is at the seminar any more than Abigail knows why you are. Neither of you has been honest with the other."

"Our backgrounds have nothing to do with each other. We're years apart in age, experience…you name it," Tonya argued.

"You fix engines. She fixes bodies. I see lots of parallels there."

Tonya cocked her head to the side and looked at Clara, her curiosity finally piqued.

"It's like this. You love the challenge of taking something that's broken and making it new. Making it look brand new, sound new, feel new. It's the same with Abigail. In her job, she helps people take something that's broken: a broken leg, an arm, a broken spirit, a broken life, and she takes that person in and helps them discover the potential that lies within their brokenness. She starts the process to breathe life back into areas of their life that had seemed dead. You both have the drive and passion to create and renew life."

Tonya looked up at her, amazed. "Maybe we have something in common after all."

Clara smiled. "Yes, you do. And maybe if you took the time to talk to each other, you would learn more about each other and understand why you're both here. All change, no matter how it's done, starts with honest and courageous conversations."

Tonya paused, realizing the truth of Clara's words. "So, what do we do now?"

"There are two ways we could go here. We have a formal mentorship program. But I think that might not be the right fit for the two of you. You don't need someone like me to hold your hands and lead you through exercises. What you need to do is to be honest and open with each other. Listen and respect each other without judgment. And, if you can, find ways to help each other out. No one has to do it alone."

Tonya nodded and smiled, feeling better. "Thanks, Clara. Maybe you're right. I think maybe we could help each other out."

Clara smiled back. "Exactly. I'm glad you see it. Give it some thought tonight and sit down with Abigail tomorrow before things wrap up. Promise me."

"I will."

* * *

"What did you think of the session?" Clara asked Abigail, when they met back up.

"Honestly?"

"Of course."

"I thought you covered a lot of it in the networking session."

"Practice makes perfect. The more you hear certain things, the more likely you are to integrate them into your approach to challenges. But frankly, I'm surprised you didn't pick up more from it. Many women who come to the institute benefit from the mentoring program they talk about in the session or from, shall we say, less formal mentorships."

"I have a mentor. Several, in fact."

"The attending physicians at the hospital?"

"Yes."

"How's that working for you both professionally and personally?"

"Fine. Professionally very well."

"But personally?"

"I don't have time for a personal life."

"That's not necessarily what I meant. I was thinking more about someone to help you sharpen your other skills like emphatic listening. Bedside manner. That sort of thing."

A thought occurred to Abigail. "Would you mentor me? Could you?"

"That's not exactly what I was thinking."

"Why not? You understand the situation I'm in. I trust you. I don't trust many people, but I trust you."

"Abigail, I'm flattered. Truly. Unfortunately, that's not something I think will be helpful in your case. If you really insist, I can though get you into our formal program that pairs you with someone local, or—"

When Clara didn't finish the thought, Abigail prompted, "Or?"

Clara gave her a nod. "Or, I could pair you with an attendee who could also use a mentor. I think you'd be of great help to each other."

"Here at the conference?"

"Yes."

"Not Tonya."

"No? Why not? You know her best of everyone else here."

"That's exactly why not. There's not a thing she could teach me about bedside manner, trust me." The blush came quickly as she realized how that must have sounded.

If Clara noticed her fluster, she didn't call it out. Instead, she asked, "Wouldn't it be nice for the two of you to have someone you could call to bounce your frustrations off of? Your exhaustion with your jobs? Talk about challenges? Talk about opportunities?"

"I have people I can do those things with."

"In your field?"

"She's not in my field. Nowhere near it."

"That's the point; having someone completely apart from medicine who can offer an outside, unbiased view."

Tonya, unbiased? Not likely. She held her tongue.

"You could be the same person for her."

"I don't even know why she's here. She wouldn't tell me."

"Why don't you try talking to her again? I think she's coming around."

CHAPTER 7–LAST DAY

Thursday Morning
Last day of the conference

Tonya

Clara caught up to Tonya's stride and walked alongside her toward the last session room in the conference hall. "Did you give some thought to what we talked about yesterday?"

"I did." She pre-empted anything further from Clara with, "I don't think it's going to work. In fact, I know it won't. Abigail won't be interested in any sort of mentorship. She thinks all of this is a waste of time." She waved a hand about.

"As did you, when you got here. When's the last time you talked to her?"

"You think she might want to try?"

"You don't know until you ask."

* * *

TONYA PULLED Abigail aside and quickly tried to paraphrase what Clara had said to her the day before about engines and bodies when she tracked her down at the snack station in between the first and second morning session times. It didn't all come out right, but Abigail seemed to understand.

They exchanged a long glance.

"Maybe we both have something to learn from each other," Abigail said slowly.

Tonya sighed. "Yeah, I guess so. I mean, I know I'd love to learn more about how to fix people - bodies, minds, souls - like you do. Especially, mind and soul. I'm a lot older than most of the...well, most of my coworkers."

Abigail smiled. "Me too. Fixing minds and souls, I mean. That's definitely not my area of expertise either, but maybe we really could help each other. So how about we try it and see where it takes us?"

"That sounds great," Tonya said, a grin spreading across her face. She glanced at her watch. "Do you have time to lay out some sort of plan with me right now?"

"I was on my way to the last collaboration track session. You're not going?"

Tonya shook her head. "I want to check out some of the leadership track stuff today. Mix and match a little."

"How about lunch? We could take the conference lunch to go, or—"

"Or we could step out and get some real food," Tonya suggested.

Abigail rolled her eyes. "We can, but I pick the restaurant."

Tonya gave in. "Just please, no strictly vegetarian stuff. I want beef. I need beef."

"You don't *need* beef."

"Oh, I need it."

* * *

"Does this work for you?" Abigail asked her. She waved a hand around the McCormick and Schmick steakhouse after the maître d seated them.

"So close to the hotel and to the harbor. It's pricey, I bet."

"I've got it."

"I can't let you do that," Tonya said. "We can split it."

"Please, I get reimbursed."

"I get per diem too. I can help."

Abigail let out an audible sigh. "We can't even work out the bill. How are we going to work together on anything else?"

A server glided over, turned over their water glasses and filled them.

Tonya opened her menu. "Have you ever eaten here? Wait. Let me rephrase that. Is there anything here you'll eat?"

"The beef is excellent, but so is the seafood. This is my father's favorite for birthdays and anniversaries. Mom indulges him."

"What's your father do?"

"He has a medical practice. Mom's a lawyer."

"Is he a surgeon?"

"You're really asking, am I following in his footsteps, aren't you?"

"Just making conversation." *And wondering exactly that.*

"No. He's actually a family doctor. Mom's a tax lawyer for a corporation."

Why couldn't she just say that?

"What about your folks?"

Tonya laid her menu down and a server walked over, taking her by surprise. He asked Abigail for her order first.

Tonya tried not to pull a face when her tablemate ordered salmon pesto. When he turned to her, she said, "I'll have the New York strip, medium rare."

"Very good. I'll be back with your salads."

When he left, Abigail said, "It's not good for you to eat it so bloody. You should go for medium or medium well."

"Shoe leather? No thanks."

"It's not shoe leather. It's just not raw."

"Medium rare isn't raw. Rare isn't even raw, when we're talking about cooked steak."

"Okay, so this is our last lunch date collaboration."

"So, this is a date?"

"No," Abigail seemed to sputter. "You know what I meant."

Tonya laughed.

"You avoided the question."

"What question?"

"I asked about your parents."

"Oh. There's not a lot to tell, there. I was raised mostly by my mom. She's a strong, God fearing, woman. She worked a lot of jobs. My father was never in my life."

"Sorry."

Tonya waved her off. "No big deal. My mom's parents were great. They're both long gone now. Have been for years, but I had them the whole time I was growing up."

"No siblings?"

"Nope. Mom almost died giving birth to me. She never tried for any others. And she was way overprotective of me. She didn't approve of me going into the army, but I was eighteen and she couldn't stop me. You have any brothers or sisters?"

"Two of each. I'm the baby." She made air quotes.

"Why the quotes?"

"That's what my dad always threw back at my siblings when they were being their usual competitive selves and tormenting me. 'Leave her alone. She's the baby,' he'd say."

"Five kids. That must have been fun."

Abigail gave a half shrug. "Not really. I was four years behind the next youngest, my brother Stephen. The oldest, my sister Catherine, was a freshman in high school when I was born. She was a basketball star and in the National Honor Society."

"Were they all like that?" Tonya asked.

"Yes. Very competitive. Very high achieving. Catherine set the pace and we all followed. I always felt like I was playing catch up to all of them, trying to measure up." She blew out a heavy breath. "What about you? How did you end up becoming a mechanic?"

"That was the army's doing," Tonya admitted but she didn't elaborate.

The server brought their salads. Tonya held back her disdain as he laid a plate of walnut mixed greens in front of Abigail, but she smiled broadly when her chopped salad with bacon and blue cheese touched down on the table.

"Now that's a salad!"

"No. That's a heart attack in a shallow bowl."

"Your salad has blue cheese on it, too."

"But not bacon and all that dressing."

"Can you just live a little?"

"How about we just don't talk about each other's eating habits anymore?" Abigail suggested.

"But then, what would we talk about?"

"Oh, I don't know. The reason we're here in the first place."

"Here? Lunch. Beef!"

Abigail speared a leafy green. "I meant at the conference."

Tonya took a bite of her salad and moaned as she chewed.

"You're insufferable," Abigail hissed.

"What? It's good."

"This isn't going to work."

"Okay. Okay! No more talk about food."

"And moaning."

"Right. About food, anyway."

"Insufferable."

"Now what?"

"You know what," Abigail said, "You can knock it off with the innuendo too."

"And you could live a little. Have a little fun. Stop being such an uptight, b...ice queen."

"Bitch? That's what you were going to call me? Pot. Kettle."

"I think that's your favorite expression."

Abigail ate the greens she'd been holding over the plate on her fork. When she finished the bite, she said to Tonya, "I'm starving or I'd leave. I was looking forward to this lunch. For the food. Even for the company."

Tonya lolled her head back and closed her eyes for a moment. When she opened them, she laid her fork down and gave Abigail a look she hoped was contrite. "I'm sorry. I...This is part of my problem, I guess you could say. I'm sarcastic. Always have been. People take it wrong...or at least they take it not in the fun I meant it."

"What did you do about your wisecracking when you were in the army?"

Tonya coughed involuntarily. "Excuse me."

"You okay?"

She nodded. "Sorry."

"The army?" Abigail asked again.

"That was different. I went along because I wanted to make it. Like I said, my mom wasn't supportive." *Still isn't.* "But my grandad was a soldier. I wanted him to be proud of me."

"So, how did you control it?"

"The army is a full-time, 24/7 thing, especially in training. You're running on fumes most of the time. There isn't time to be cute about stuff."

"Sounds like residency."

"I don't doubt that," Tonya said.

"What about now, with the police department?"

"What about them?"

"The sarcasm. The snark. Is that holding you back somehow?"

"Um, yeah. You could say that. I've had to adapt a lot over the years. The sarcasm is a way of coping."

"Adapt how?"

"Oh, you know. Woman working almost exclusively with men."

"Yes. I get that. It's the same for me. Well, with the attendings and the other residents in ortho. Most of the other staff, the nurses, the techs, they're women."

"But you do work mostly alongside men?"

"Yes, and in direct competition with many of them. All the third-year residents like me are looking for prestigious spots at better hospitals, fellowship—"

"Try being a black woman," Tonya interrupted.

"I can only imagine, in all seriousness. None of our third-year residents are people of color."

"Anyone else gay?"

"Besides me? No."

"Do they know there?"

"No. It's never come up. Look, there's no time for personal chats. There's no time for a partner, or *a life*. It's all about work, all the time."

"Just for you or for everyone?"

Their entrees arrived then, and Abigail didn't answer. When the server moved away, she asked Tonya, "Are you the only gay mechanic?"

"Yeah, but I'm out at work. Not that it matters. I don't have time for a life either. Not counting softball, before you say it."

They both cut into their food and were silent for a couple of minutes. Tonya was the first to speak. "How do we do this? I mean, I know zero about being a mentor."

Abigail asked, "*Do* we do this? First, you're how much older than me? Our fields are different. We've already established our lives are different…at least somewhat. I'm not sure that I can help you with anything other than to be a sounding board for you. I don't know that something like that helps either of us."

Tonya had to agree, Abigail was right. Then she thought about making master sergeant. *I really want that, before I retire.* "I was going to say I agree, but I've just changed my mind."

"Why?"

"Because I'm up for a promotion I really want. There's some competition for it. All men." *Two platoon sergeants, and a supply sergeant, but none of them with as much time in service as me.* "I need to clean up my act. Be less...abrasive and more...nurturing to my younger, um, coworkers."

"That was hard for you to admit, wasn't it?"

Tonya nodded and took another bite of her steak. She couldn't meet Abigail's eyes. She felt bad about not telling her the whole truth and even worse when the younger woman responded.

"And I'm younger, so I could potentially coach you–more gently than I have been–when you're overstepping with me?"

"Well, in a way, yes. You've still got a few years on several of them."

"These mechanics are pretty young." She sounded surprised.

"They're not all mechanics. Most of them aren't, actually. It's a long story." She changed the subject. "So, that's me. What about you? You said something at lunch yesterday after Meryl—"

"Right. It's the same thing for me. It's like Meryl has been reading my patient evals. I love my job. Really love my job inside the surgical suite. I'm just not good with the touchy-feely stuff the patients seem to want from me, too."

"Some patients."

"A lot of patients."

"I wouldn't want touchy-feely stuff. I hate to see a doctor, period."

"You're not everyone."

"True."

"And you would want to know exactly what I'm going to be doing for your surgery if you were having one, how long it would take—"

"No. Not really."

"Well, most people do, and apparently they want the information delivered in a comforting, unhurried way."

"What could I do to help with that?"

"I'm told the biggest part of that is being a more emphatic listener. Maybe I just need to learn to listen more."

"By listening to me?"

"Maybe we could role play or something. I don't know. I'm trying to be creative here, something I learned yesterday."

"We could try, but I'll tell you now, I'm not very good at playacting."

"Neither am I. I guess we'll learn together."

* * *

Thursday Afternoon
The Regal Duchess Hotel and Conference Center
Queensborough

Abigail

CLARA APPROACHED Abigail when she and Tonya split off from each other back at the hotel. "I saw you and Tonya come in. Did you two have a chance to talk?"

Abigail said, "We've agreed to help each other as much as possible. We've traded phone numbers and agreed to talk for sure on Sundays, the only day I usually have off. Beyond that, nothing is settled, and I'm not even sure if it's going to work."

"It will. You'll get out of it what you put into it." She drew closer.

Abigail self-consciously touched her mask and Clara stopped her advance. "Sorry. But I have to ask something, and I want you to be honest with me," Clara said. "Is there something else that I should know about?"

Abigail looked at her in surprise. "There's nothing else. Not from me. Why would you even think that?"

"How do you feel about Tonya?" Clara asked. "Personally?"

She didn't hesitate. "It bothers me she seems to keep things from me and she knows I know she is, but she doesn't seem to care either way. "

"Is that all?"

"No," she replied. "But I don't want to get into it right now. My primary focus is getting through this year of residency and moving on. Nothing else is important to me right now."

"I'm going to tell you something, but this is for your ears only."

Abigail nodded.

"Tonya was ordered here by her commander. She's made progress this week and he's going to be pleased. Anything at all you can help her with is only going to result in a more positive outcome for her and the people she serves with."

An odd way of putting it. She's not a police officer. It almost sounds like she's still in the Army. If she's serving, why wouldn't she just say that? Why hide it? She filed the strange reference away in her mind to be looked into later. To Clara, she simply nodded.

Tonya approached the two of them then and Abigail's mind wandered from trying to decipher the secret Tonya was keeping from her to grappling with her growing feelings of desire for the woman now in front of her. While she was aware any pairing between them would be fraught with conflict, she couldn't help but feel a strong pull towards Tonya. *No. I certainly don't want to talk to Clara about that. Or Tonya. Focus. Eyes on the prize.*

"Talking about me over here?" Tonya asked.

Abigail railed at her. "Everything isn't always about you!"

Clara made noises to excuse herself, leaving them squared off, facing each other.

They stared at each other, the air between them filled with electricity. To Abigail, there was a strange feeling of familiarity and yet, also the usual feeling of hostility between them. Neither one seemed willing to break the silence that had descended upon them.

Abigail finally did. "Are you going to the closing address?"

"I hadn't planned to. You?"

"I think so."

"I'll probably regret it, but maybe I will."

"Look at you, changing your mind on a dime. All because I'm going?"

"Everything isn't always about you, either," Tonya said.

T hey sat next to each other in the back row of the largest conference room.

"A mask, still?" Tonya asked.

"I've worn one several times this week."

"And you haven't several other times."

"Mostly with you or when I was eating, which seemed to also be mostly with you."

"So, you're assuming I'm germ free?"

"I assume nothing, but you seem very healthy." She regretted her choice of words as soon as she saw Tonya's smirk. She tried to play it off. "Does the department make you test pretty regularly?"

"Me? No. I'm a mechanic, remember? I've got my head under the hood or my whole body under a cruiser all day, every day."

Abigail thought about her chat with Clara. *There was no hesitation in Tonya's answer. Clara has something mixed up.*

"Good afternoon ladies!" the woman who was the director of the local conference called out as she took the stage in the front of the room.

A cheer went up from the crowd.

"Did everyone enjoy the conference?"

Another cheer.

"Too rah, rah already for me," Tonya said.

"Shh!"

She whispered back, "Don't start that again."

Abigail didn't take the bait.

"Most of you here are from in and around the local area," the woman was saying. "The Institute doesn't have an office here, but we're in most major cities, offering all sorts of training above and beyond the little taste you got this week. If you want to dive deeper, until we get an office here–and it's in the works—"

Several people clapped.

She waved her hands for quiet. "It's in the works, but Philly is only a quick ride away. That's the office I work out of, and I'm more than happy to connect you to your heart's desires." She thanked the attendees, Clara–the floater who was more than an ultra-capable right hand for multiple directors–the other presenters, and the hotel staff.

"Our managing director, Julia Baker-Zucchero, can't be everywhere, every week. She's somewhere every week, and this month she's touring conferences in Europe. She still always gets the last say." With those words, the house lights went low. "The video is brief. Only a few minutes. Enjoy! And, afterwards, please join us in the lounge for a last round of refreshments before you leave."

TONYA STOOD AS SOON as the video ended.

Abigail rose too. "I guess that's that. Are you going to the lounge?"

After looking at her watch, Tonya responded, "No. If I hurry, I can make it home to change and go to softball practice." She sketched a wave and left without another word.

I'll probably never hear from her again.

. . .

Her apartment smelled musty when she got home. She opened a couple of windows to let some of the fresh spring air in, then started unpacking. She stopped twice when thoughts of Tonya crossed her mind, but she pushed through them.

The third time images of the brash older woman entered her mind she shook them off for a few more moments as she started her washing machine, then she sat down hard on her sofa and gave some thought to the week and the women who dominated it for her, Clara, Polly, Meryl, and Tonya.

Abigail thought first of Clara. She marveled at the woman's ability to motivate, whether it was to do a job better, take on a new challenge, or even just enjoy life more. She then smiled fondly at the memory of Polly, strong and clever in the face of adversity.

Meryl was the more serious of the other pair of women. She was the one who made sure everyone was on the same page and she, like Clara, held everyone accountable, though she was far less diplomatically than Clara.

And then there was Tonya. *Tonya. Different from anyone I've ever known.* While they were often at odds, and she sometimes found the older woman sarcastic and obnoxious, there was something about her that Abigail found admirable. She was always direct and never gave up, no matter how rough the going got.

Tonya was a tough one, and she'd made an impression on Abigail. But for all of that, there was something endearing about her that was hard to ignore. She snuggled into her sofa, thinking about the women she'd spent the week with, and appreciating the unique qualities of each woman, but she came right back to Tonya. Tall and broad shouldered, muscular too, but also soft in all the right places. Her laugh was deep and throaty, often punctuating her own biting wit.

Abigail thought of her hands; how calloused they were. Certainly, the hands of a person who worked with them daily. And strong. She was so strong. Polly wasn't a large woman and certainly not overweight, but she wasn't slight either and Tonya had assisted her up and mostly carried her from the lounge to the elevator and from the elevator to her room with seeming ease.

She thought about all she'd learned during the week. Even before the session she had accidentally taken part in, she learned more than she had thought she would as she was going into the week. *I don't know how much of it is actually going to be useful to me for the purpose I attended this conference, but I have to admit, I have more insight into why I'm the way I am and how to channel some of it.*

The pairing with Tonya going forward weighed on her mind. She hated to admit she was developing feelings for the other woman despite herself. She didn't think pairing with her was a good idea for personal or professional reasons.

They had agreed Tonya would initiate their first Sunday check-in call. *We'll see what happens. She probably won't call, and this will all be over with. Out of sight, out of touch, out of mind.* She got off the couch and changed into her workout clothes. *First a run, since I didn't use the hotel gym this morning, then I'll call in and see what's on tap for tomorrow.*

CHAPTER 8–TURNING TWO

The Same Afternoon

Tonya

Tonya dropped her bag just inside her front door and hustled through the living room into her room. She stripped off the Khaki work pants she'd worn at the conference that day, gave them a quick sniff, then hurled them toward the laundry basket in the corner. *Can't wear those tomorrow.* Her polo shirt followed her pants into the basket.

She yanked on sliding shorts and baseball pants, pulled on a t-shirt, stepped into slides for the drive and hustled back to the front door.

She checked her trunk for her cleats and her equipment bag before she jumped into the driver's seat. The clock on the dash said 5:46 as she backed out of her parking space. Barring running into heavy traffic, she'd still be a couple of minutes late. *Should have taken practice clothes with me, just in case.*

. . .

SHE SAW ALL the usual cars there when she pulled in. The team gathered at one end of the dugout. Atlee, who was standing next to the fence on the first base line side turned when she heard Tonya's car door slam closed and waved.

As Tonya approached, she could hear Lynn Baines talking. She wrinkled her nose in distaste and strode forward.

Baines addressed her first. "You're late Trube. You know what that means."

"Back off, Lynn," Atlee cautioned the other woman. "She is the coach and she's been out of town. Right?" Atlee asked as she turned toward Tonya.

"Right. I'm just glad to be back in time for practice tonight, but I'll do those laps if it makes you feel any better, Baines." She knew calling Sergeant First Class George Baines' wife by her last name without calling her 'Mrs.' rankled her since Lynn wasn't military herself. She did it on purpose.

When the other woman didn't respond, Tonya said, "Let's stretch and get warmed up. Then I'll take the infield and do some grounder drills. Baines, you can take the outfield."

"I've been practicing at shortstop this week," Baines said.

"Whatever for?" Tonya shot a look at Sherry Carter, their usual shortstop. "Where have you been playing?"

"Center Field."

"Why?"

Carter shrugged.

"She's got a great arm," Baines said.

"And she's great at shortstop," Tonya said to Baines. She looked back at Carter. "You okay with the move?"

"It's okay, coach. I started in the outfield."

"And how long has it been since you've played out there?"

"Other than this week? Maybe ten years."

Tonya looked at Atlee. "You knew about this?" *And you didn't tell me?*

Atlee answered, "You told me to have them work on turning two this week. We've tried different things. Sherry's good there. Lynn is too. Lynn volunteered and Sherry didn't seem to mind..." Atlee trailed off with a shrug.

"All right," Tonya said, giving in. "I guess it doesn't hurt to have a backup, so let's try it. Atlee, you take the outfielders."

"That conference must have been something," Atlee said as they walked to their cars after practice.

"Oh, it was something, all right. A pain in my ass and time away from work and the team I didn't need."

"I think you got more out of it than you're admitting."

"What makes you say that?" Tonya popped her trunk and threw her ball bag and her cleats inside.

"We switched things up without clearing it with you, and you didn't blow up."

"Whose idea was it to switch those two, yours or Baines?"

Atlee toed some gravel. "Mostly mine."

"Mostly?"

"Sherry is great at shagging the ball, then making the throw to first or covering second. She's a little slow shagging, getting the out at second, and then getting the ball to first. She gets off balance and sometimes throws wild to first when she has to hurry."

Tonya had to admit, "She's better at second base, but we have an amazing second baseman this year with Larner."

"Exactly."

"But Baines? Really?"

"You saw her out there. She didn't let anything get by her today. And, she turns two pretty well."

"But, Baines? I just can't with her."

"Ugh," Atlee groaned. "What's your real beef with her?"

"For one, she hates me."

"She doesn't hate you."

"I'm her husband's competition for the next Master Sergeant opening."

"There are four of you that could take that slot. Do you think she hates the other two men, too?"

"Probably."

"You're insufferable."

As she walked over to the driver's side, Tonya said, "I've been hearing that a lot lately."

Atlee followed. "From whom?"

"Look at you, all formal."

"Was it that woman at the conference? The one you like?"

"There were no women at the conference that I liked."

Atlee grinned. "Right. Okay. Whatever you say."

"I'm not kidding. Everyone I had to deal with made me regret having to be there even more."

"So, you're trying to tell me you got nothing out of it?"

"Complete waste of time," she said as she slid behind the wheel.

Atlee didn't let her close the door. "So, it was no help to you in beating the guys out for master sergeant?"

"Not even close. Now, sorry but I have to go. I didn't even unpack. I need to get home and get ready to go back to my day job tomorrow."

When she got back to her apartment, she walked right past her bag from the conference as she carried the remnants of her fast-food dinner to the island that divided her kitchen and living room. She sat down on one of the two barstools and finished eating.

Her mind wandered back to practice while she ate. *Atlee betrayed me. Pure and simple. She knows I don't even want Baines on the team.* She sighed. With only three subs, she also knew her options were limited. If anything happened to their catcher or their first baseman, they were screwed. One of the other three women spelled her at pitcher and the other two were outfielders with no infield experience.

Her cell phone rang. *Atlee.* She answered it. "I was just thinking about you."

"Thinking about me, or cursing me?"

"You know me too well."

"Someone has to challenge you once in a while."

"No. Not really. But, I thought about it, and I get what you were trying to do with the team."

"There are only so many women in the unit who play, Tonya. Most of the women in the unit are on the team. She's the only wife who came out."

"I know, and I admit, she's a decent ball player."

"She's better than decent."

Tonya sighed. "Yes."

"And, she doesn't have any influence with the command over who gets that promotion when Blevins retires this fall, or when Top moves on, if that comes first. That's all on you."

"I wish you would let me get a look at their NCOERs, see their ratings."

"You know I can't do that. They'd take my job."

"Am I at least competitive?" she asked the unit's full-time administrator.

"Tonya, come on."

"You can't even tell me that?"

"Look, I'm surprised you haven't asked all this before, but no. I can't." Atlee paused, then asked, "Do you feel you are?"

"I have time in service over two of them, and I have time in grade over all three. My ratings are all highly qualified or most qualified, but my overall is usually just highly qualified."

"Highly qualified isn't a bad thing."

"It is if any of them are getting 'most qualified' ratings."

"So, fix it. Do what you need to do to step it up a notch in the areas where you're *only* coming up as highly qualified. I'm guessing sending you to that conference had something to do with that."

Grumbling, Tonya admitted, "It did."

"But you got nothing out of it?"

An image of Abigail passed through her mind. "Not a lot on site that I can use." She thought of Clara. "I got hooked up with a person I'm supposed to mentor, sort of. Actually, we're supposed to help each other."

"Oh?"

Tonya read into Atlee's tone. "It's not like that."

"All I said was, 'oh,' my friend. So, how is the person you're supposed to work with?"

"A pain."

"Is it—"

"Abigail, the pain in my ass, yes."

Atlee laughed. "Oh girl, that's rich!"

"I'm glad you find it so amusing."

GUESS *I better unpack my junk*. She grabbed her bottle of laundry detergent and headed toward the door, picking up the bag she'd dropped there as she went.

The laundry room was busy, but one washing machine was free. "Just great," she muttered. "I'll be coming down here half the night checking for an empty dryer."

"What's that you say?" an old man asked as he cupped his ear.

"Nothing."

"Eh?"

She finished filling the machine with clothes from her conference bag and left. *Some people need to mind their own business.*

. . .

8:30 PM, and not a free dryer to be had. Tonya trudged back to her apartment for the third time, this time hauling her wet laundry with her. Good thing I already showered, she thought, as she hung her things over the shower rod in the bathroom. She vowed, not for the first time, her next apartment would have hookups for a washer and dryer. *This is nuts. I have to work in the morning. I hate laundry.*

Abigail popped into her head for the second time that evening. *Bet she gets all those suit jackets dry cleaned. Hell, she probably didn't get a speck of anything on them. Probably hung them right back in her closet.*

Why did I agree to call her on Sunday? I'm betting we won't have a thing to talk about. Just as well. I've got no time for all that mess, anyway. Gotta stay away from her.

A stirring in her loins, something she hadn't felt in years, threatened her resolve. "Oh no, no, no!" she chided herself aloud. "Not hardly, and certainly not her."

She pushed Abigail out of her head and finished her task. Once done, she stripped down to her boxers, tied on a doo rag, and went to bed.

Sleep was slow to come. She blamed Abigail for that.

TONYA YAWNED her way through two brake jobs and the beginning of a cruiser engine overhaul before she could call it a day.

"You look beat," one of her co-workers said. "Need a vacation from your vacation?"

"It wasn't a vacation. Stuff for the Guard, but yeah. I should have taken today off."

"You don't have drill this weekend, do you?"

"No, thank goodness, but our season opener for the military league is Monday night. Is your son playing for the Navy team this year?"

"Yeah. He talks about the team more than about his job. We'll be there to watch his opener."

"Wish him luck for me." She wasn't worried about the Navy team. There were so many military players in the metro area, even in the slow pitch league, men and women played on separate teams.

"Will do. You should get rested up."

"No can do. We've got practice tonight."

* * *

TONYA FELT like Sunday came before she could even catch her breath. She was worried about Monday's game and worried about her afternoon call with Abigail. She rolled out of bed before 6:00 AM, still a time she considered sleeping in for her, and started a full pot of coffee.

None of those one cup at a time brewers were good enough for her. She wanted to smell good, strong coffee all day and pour cups until the pot was gone. She waited impatiently until the whole ten cup pot was done and she could pour her first cup.

6:10, she noted. *Just under ten hours until I have to think up something to talk about with Abigail. Where do I even go with that? I haven't had drill. The only people from the unit I've seen are on the softball team, and none of them are in the motor pool.*

She shrugged to herself. *Maybe she went back to the hospital on Friday and flubbed something we can talk about. Maybe she won't even answer her phone. I can only hope.*

She ran through her morning routine then, even though she'd been gone most of the week, she started her weekly quick cleaning ritual.

At 6:45, she poured her second cup and made her way down the hall to work on the bathroom. As she did so, she heard the buzzer for her door ring. She turned off the water and rushed over to the intercom. "Yes?"

"Hi Tonya," Abigail said.

Tonya's heart skipped a beat. *What the hell is this? Why is she here?* "How did you find me? I thought I was supposed to call you later."

Abigail laughed. "I called your cell, but it just went straight to voice mail. Don't worry, I'm not stalking you."

"It's really early."

"And we're both up. I always am, and I guessed you would be too. I was right."

"You still haven't answered my question."

"And I'm still standing here in the entryway. Are you decent? Can I come up?"

"I...I was just getting dressed." *I don't want her to see this place.* "Oh."

"If you give me a few minutes, I can come down."

"That's fine. Bring a jacket and decent walking shoes."

"Is that an order?"

"Not an order, no. You'll be more comfortable, especially if you decide to go with me."

Tired of playing intercom tag, Tonya said, "I'll be down in a couple of minutes, and we can talk about it then."

It took her less than a minute to lace on hikers, grab a jacket and her wallet, so she took another minute to fill a travel mug with coffee and turn the warmer off. *No sense wasting it, but the doc is on her own...non coffee drinking woman.*

"Ever been to Sandy Point?" Abigail asked.

"Many times. Love it there."

"It's really nice early on a spring Sunday morning. Not too hot, not too cold, and not at all crowded. I need the break. Thought I'd try you too."

Sounds nice, actually. "Sure. Sure."

"I'm not normally so impulsive. I mean, I go places a lot on Sunday, just to get outside and get away, but I usually go alone."

CHAPTER 9–SANDY POINT

Abigail

"J was back on the floor Friday morning," Abigail told Tonya as they walked along the beach toward the Bay Bridge. "Couldn't stay away."

"How did it go?"

"Not bad. Friday starts the same as Monday through Thursday, but they are a little easier overall. Less elective procedures and scheduled procedures. No one wants to be in the hospital on purpose over a weekend, I guess."

"No run-ins with anyone?"

She shook her head. "I had to sit down with Dr. Silbeth, the attending orthopedic surgeon who is my direct supervisor, and talk with him about the conference. That wasn't fun, but it was mercifully short. He had other things he needed to get to."

"Did you mention...mention mentoring?"

"I did. I didn't go into a lot of detail with him, but he seemed to think it was a good idea."

Tonya gave her a slight nod, then asked, "Did you work yesterday, too?"

"I did morning rounds and paperwork. Short day. Only about seven hours."

That's short? "How many patients do you have?"

"I don't have any right now; not since I was gone most of the week."

"So, why do rounds?"

"Everyone does them. Third year residents like me usually brief on specific patients while first year residents listen and learn. Since I was gone all week, I didn't have to brief, but I had to play catch up so I'd know what was going on with patients that were still held over on Monday."

They walked for a few minutes in silence, breathing in the salt air then Abigail asked, "What about you?"

"I, uh, I didn't go back to work yet."

"Not to work at all, or not to that particular job?" She shot Tonya a look, but she said nothing else. *Patience!*

Tonya stopped walking. "You know?"

"That you're full-time military, or you really do work for a police department and you're in the reserves, yes."

"Part-time military. The Guard. How did you know?"

"Lots of ways, actually. What I don't know is why it was such a secret."

Tonya took a couple of steps closer to the water and toed at the sand around a piece of half buried driftwood. Abigail watched and waited.

"It...It's embarrassing."

"And you think I wasn't embarrassed?"

"Everything I told you was true. I just omitted which job sent me and why. I'm a mechanic for the College Park Police Department and I'm a motor sergeant for an Army National Guard unit." She bent down and tried to pry the piece of wood out of the sand. It barely moved. "Must be a lot bigger than it looks on the surface."

"Isn't everything?"

"What's that supposed to mean?"

Abigail backtracked. "Please don't get defensive. I just mean there's always more to everything than just what's on the surface."

They started walking again. Abigail didn't feel bad for calling Tonya out and she broke their silence again to let her know it. "We're supposed to be helping each other. I can't be a sounding board for you if you can't be honest with me."

Tonya sucked in a deep breath and let it out slowly. "I know. I just...I've never really been able to talk about this stuff."

"You can start now. It's just between us. If you never talk about it, you'll never get past it."

They kept walking. To Abigail, the waves seemed in sync with their steps.

"I guess I just felt like no one at that conference would understand my experience as a woman in the National Guard, A black woman, at that," Tonya said. "It wasn't always easy. At times it's been damn hard, and I'd rather just forget about all of it."

Abigail looked out at the bridge and took in its size. "I've definitely been there."

Tonya nodded.

"It's just so hard to open up about something that you think no one will understand," Abigail said. "Trust me, I know. But that doesn't mean you don't deserve to be heard. You don't have to be alone with it."

"I can't talk to my mom. She thinks I should be married to some guy and...and or have a passel of kids by now. Guy or no guy. Kids have never even been in my thoughts."

"Mine either."

"I heard a long time ago that you can only do three things well. Only excel at three things. That really got to me."

"Do you have three things you've picked, then?"

"Funny you said 'picked,' because that's exactly what I did. I picked motors, the military, and fast pitch, which, as I've gotten older, evolved into slow pitch."

"That military one is kind of broad. You can't excel at everything in the military."

"Sure I can. That's the way the military is built. You find your MOS, and you become the best at that, and you do all the leadership schools all along the way so you can lead troops as you gain rank, or you gain rank so you can lead troops. It works either way."

"Except when it doesn't," Abigail reminded her. "Can we talk about that more?"

Tonya threw out a hand but kept walking. "Part of it comes back to all the things we've already talked about. Being a woman. Being a woman of color. A woman is in a man's world. A very competitive world." She sucked in a deep breath and looked out at the water. She said, "I accept the competitive nature of it all. I do. What's tough is the playing field is tilted against me."

"You're extremely competitive. Maybe too much so." Abigail grabbed Tonya's arm and stopped her. "So am I, I'm admitting, before you get upset. We both have to be competitive in our fields to get what we want. I can see why you've thrived in that environment, and I can also see how you're running into walls, not all of your own making. But, admit it; some of them are."

"And you have to admit that you see things in me you're not seeing in yourself."

Her tone was matter of fact to Abigail's ear and she accepted what she heard with a nod. "You're right. We think we're so opposite, but we're not at all."

"Now I didn't say all that!"

Abigail shook her head as she started walking again. "And the snark comes roaring back!"

"I'm not calling you this afternoon."

"I didn't figure you would."

"This has been enough soul baring for one lifetime."

CHAPTER 10–OPENING NIGHT

Monday Evening
Carroll Park

Tonya

Tonya looked in at the batter. She swallowed. *Keep it low, girl. Keep it low.* She let go of the pitch.

"Ball!" the umpire called out.

She glared at him.

"Watch your arc," he warned.

It had plenty of arc. The catcher gave her a slight shrug, then threw the ball back.

Don't want this one to hit it out again with the tying run standing there at first. She toed the rubber and threw the next pitch.

The batter hit a hard grounder toward Baines who was playing shortstop. Baines grabbed the ball on a bounce, jumped on the second base bag, and threw a rocket to first. The umpire between the bases called both runners out.

"Nice, Baines!" Tonya called out to her. She held two fingers in the air and yelled, "Two down! One more. Let's go."

The next hitter moved into the batter's box. She'd grounded out in her first at bat and hit a pop-up in her second. Tonya lobbed the ball to the plate without a lot of thought.

The woman hit a line drive straight back at her that hit her at the top of her right arm, her pitching arm, before she could even get her glove up. She fell on the mound after the ball hit her. It skittered toward Baines, who picked it up and held it as the runner crossed the first base bag.

Tonya winced at the pain and rubbed her shoulder.

"You okay?" Lynn Baines asked her. She held out a hand to help her up.

"Ahhh!" Tonya couldn't help yelling as Baines tugged her up.

Atlee ran in from the outfield yelling, "Time! Timeout!" When she got to Tonya, she asked, "How bad?"

Tonya stuck her arm out and tried to rotate her shoulder. She held back from saying anything, but her expression must have been all Atlee needed to see.

"Go ice it now. Roth can warm up."

She didn't argue. She went toward the dugout as Rochelle Roth trotted out. "Hold them!" she turned and called out to her teammates before ducking inside to dig some ice out of the water jug.

The medic on standby popped his head into the dugout. "Want me to take a look?"

Tonya waved him off. *Looks like he's twelve.* "It only hurts now because it just happened and there's going to be a nasty mark, but I'm sure it's not serious. I'm going to ice it now."

"Best thing for it, then."

* * *

TUESDAY EVENING

TONYA STEERED her motorcycle into the lot at their practice diamond and parked. *I babied the arm all day, but riding the bike tonight was a mistake.*

"Nice afternoon for a ride! How's the arm feel, coach?" Roth asked her as she approached the dugout. "Must not be too bad."

"It's okay. Tender."

Atlee wandered over. "Let's see it."

"See what?"

"You know what."

"I'm fine." She tried to suppress the wince that was threatening to give her away as a wave of pain came on.

"You're not," Atlee said.

"Sometimes it throbs a little."

Atlee got closer than Tonya liked anyone to be and pushed up the right sleeve of the oversized t-shirt she'd worn. "Um hum. Probably bruised. Definitely still swollen. When is the last time you iced?"

"For about ten minutes right after work," Tonya admitted.

"And you were probably lifting all day?"

"No. Well, I tried to take it easy."

"But you didn't."

"It's my job, Atlee."

"Maybe you better coach from the bench today."

"I'm fine."

"You're not. Get some ice on it."

"I outrank you, you know."

"We're not at the unit."

"I'm the coach."

"And I'm the assistant coach and your best friend. Probably your only friend. For once in your life, listen. There's a chem pack in the first aid kit. It'll have to do for now."

Tonya sulked her way over to the bench, found the ice pack,

and gave it a twist to break it, and activate the chemical compounds that made it cold. Even through the t-shirt, the chill stung when she laid the pack over her shoulder to hang down over the swollen, bruised area.

"I'M DRIVING YOU HOME."

Atlee's tone was no nonsense, but Tonya wasn't about to give in. "My bike—"

"Theo can drive me back here later to get it."

"Don't be silly. I'm way out of your way and you're going to do it twice?"

"You're five minutes further. You're just worried I'll mess up your precious bike."

Got me. "Yeah, she's my baby."

"She'll be fine. Now, get in the car." Atlee pointed at her Honda CR-V.

Tonya grimaced. "When are you going to get a truck?"

"Don't need a truck. You don't need one either."

"This is too small."

"Theo has a truck. Now, stop arguing and get in the car."

"You're not the boss of me," Tonya muttered.

"What was that?"

"Nothing."

"That's what I thought."

Tonya lowered herself into the seat as Atlee watched her closely.

"Maybe you call off work tomorrow and go see a doctor."

"And they tell me what? I've got a deep bruise? Ice and elevation?"

"Maybe it's broken."

"It's not broken."

"Now you're a medical expert?"

"I'm not going to the doctor, Atlee."

"Then the ER it is."

"You're not taking me to the ER."

"Watch me."

"Atlee, I said no."

"All I'm saying is, get an x-ray. Make sure it's not more serious."

"No."

"Not an option."

"I hate you."

Atlee chuckled. "Wouldn't be you if you didn't say that to me once a day or so."

"No, I really hate you."

"Yeah, yeah."

THE WAITING ROOM at Ascension Hospital was quiet. Tonya got checked in with little fuss and was taken to triage before she could even get herself seated.

The nurse who took her vitals and checked her arm over told her the doctor would be around once they assigned her to a bed in the unit.

"I don't need a bed. I just need an x-ray to appease my friend out there that there's nothing more serious than a nasty bruise going on here." She tapped her upper arm and regretted it instantly.

The nurse gave her a knowing look. "Well, the doctor will take a look and order the x-ray, so we need to get you assigned to a bed for that to happen. If you choose not to use the actual bed..." She shrugged. "Wait here. We'll get you taken care of shortly. Hang tight."

A while later, after being moved to a curtained exam room, before a doctor ever appeared, Tonya was escorted to the imaging suite for an x-ray. The technician was friendly and efficient, and within minutes the scan was done, and the images were sent to be read.

When she got back to her assigned bed, Atlee was waiting for her. "Your nurse let me back here. Said you were in x-ray."

"Yeah. I got one. Can we go now?" She picked her t-shirt up from the bed, intending to exchange it for the hospital gown the nurse made her put on.

"Seriously? There's a little more to it than just getting the x-ray."

"That's all you said I had to do."

"Don't be so damn hard-headed!"

Tonya stuck out her lip in a pout. Atlee couldn't see it anyway, since they were both masked. She refused to sit on the bed. Instead, she moved the side chair Atlee wasn't occupying a little away from the other woman and sat down.

Twenty minutes passed while the two women barely spoke. Atlee stared at her phone while Tonya watched the medical staff and patients walk back and forth past the open front curtain to her exam room.

"Do you want me to close that?" Atlee asked.

"I can close it myself if I want it closed—"

She bit back her tongue when Abigail walked through the opening followed by an older male who pulled the curtain shut behind them.

"Hello," Abigail said.

Tonya waited a few beats until recognition dawned in the resident's eyes. The only change in the other woman's demeanor was a slight dip of the head in some sort of acknowledgment.

"I'm doctor Ross, and this is doctor Silbeth," Abigail went on.

"Tonya." *Why is she here?*

"And who else do we have here today?" Abigail looked at Atlee.

"I'm Atlee, the one that makes this stubborn woman here do things she doesn't want to do, like come in here."

"Ah," was all Abigail said. She pointed at Tonya's right arm. "May I?"

"If you must." *Has she been here all day?*

"I must."

Abigail tugged gently at the gown fabric, pulling it down to expose Tonya's right shoulder and upper arm. "There's a lot of swelling. When did this happen?"

"Yesterday," Atlee volunteered.

"Line drive," Tonya said. "I didn't catch it."

"I would say not. Not with your glove, at least."

Tonya could hear the smile in Abigail's voice. She looked over at the man standing, watching. *Silbeth. Rings a bell. Must be the guy she answers to.*

In a different tone, Abigail cautioned her, "I have to palp it. It may hurt a little." She didn't wait for a response.

"Ow," Tonya said when the resident manipulated her arm despite her best effort to remain stoic.

"Sorry," Abigail said.

Tonya tried to play it off for the benefit of Dr. Silbeth. "You warned me, doc." She stiffened, but not because of the pain. Abigail's touch was leaving a trail of heat along her shoulder.

"What motion hurts the worst, Tonya?"

Get a hold of yourself. "Throwing a ball...overhand, anyway. Lobbing a pitch isn't too bad. Totally different motion."

"How about lifting?" Abigail asked.

Tonya admitted, "Anything more than a few pounds, and I feel it."

"And this?" She touched the strap of Tonya's sports bra. "Too much pressure?"

Tonya shrugged her shoulder twice. "No. Not really. It's up higher, so it doesn't really bother it."

Abigail moved her gown back into place, then went over to the computer in the room, turned it on and punched some keys.

Tonya missed her touch. She forgot about it though, when an x-ray popped up on the computer screen.

As she pointed along the upper arm, Abigail explained, "The x-ray doesn't tell us a lot because there's so much swelling. There's no obvious break. It might be just a sprain, but until we can get a better picture, we can't rule out a hairline fracture in the upper humerus–your upper arm–or the part of your shoulder blade–the scapula–closest to the point of the swelling."

"I have to come back?"

Abigail's face was unreadable behind her mask, but she nodded. "I'd advise it, yes. But first, keep icing it. No lifting anything over the weight of a half-gallon of milk and no throwing softballs for a few days."

"Even underhand? I'm a pitcher."

"Even underhand, champ," Atlee said before Abigail could respond.

Abigail stared at Atlee until Tonya prompted her. "That true, Doc?"

Abigail refocused on Tonya. "Don't you have to be able to field your position? Grab a grounder, let's say, and throw a runner out at first?"

"Yes," Atlee answered for her.

Tonya tried to give her friend her best threatening glare, but her mask hampered her attempt at looking fierce.

"Then I'd say no." Abigail said. She turned back to type something into the computer then shut it down. "Two things," she said when she was facing Tonya again. "Do you want to make an appointment with your primary care provider, or do you want to come back here for another x-ray and follow-up?"

"Would I see you if I came back here?"

"The appointment would be with me, yes."

"Let's do that, then." She tried to read Abigail's eyes, but Atlee's exclamation distracted her.

"Wow! Had to drag you here and now—"

"Shut up," Tonya growled.

"Right. Shutting up. Just glad you're doing it."

Tonya noticed Abigail staring at Atlee again. "You said there were two things, Doc?"

"Hmm? Oh, right. Also, do you need a work excuse? Or a note for your softball coach, maybe?"

"I am the coach."

"Of course you are," Abigail said.

"A note for light duty at work would be okay, though." *I really hate admitting that.*

"And what is it you do?"

She knows what I do. "I'm a mechanic."

"Can you do that without a lot of lifting?"

"I can try."

"The less you use your arm, the faster we're going to get answers."

"Yes, ma'am." Tonya refrained from giving her a mock salute.

"What about pain meds?"

"No meds."

"If you won't fill a prescription, you can alternate acetaminophen and ibuprofen."

"I can, yes." *But I won't.*

She knew Abigail was on to her when the doctor said, "Ibuprofen will help reduce the swelling faster."

Tonya simply nodded.

"Let me know if you experience any more pain or difficulty, okay?"

She shifted in her seat. "Sure." She had no intention of taking any pain medication, swelling or not. *I didn't agree with her stomach.*

"Can you come back in on Thursday?"

Tonya asked, "Can we make it after 4:00?"

Abigail nodded. "Sure. I'll set you up to go right to x-ray first." She glanced from Dr. Silbeth to Atlee and said, "Let's give her some privacy to get dressed, and I'll get the follow-up and the light duty written up."

"I'll help her. It isn't like I've never seen her naked," Atlee said.

Tonya started to elbow her friend but realized she'd be hitting her with her right arm, and she pulled back. "Thanks, Doc," she said instead.

When the pair of doctors left, Tonya hissed at Atlee, "That was her!"

"Her? Her who?"

"The woman from the conference. Abigail."

"No."

"Yeah."

"The one you like?"

"I don't—"

"Hard to tell with the mask and all, but she looks kind of cute."

"Atlee, focus."

"No wonder you were acting so weird."

"I wasn't acting weird."

Atlee stood. "Let's get that gown off you and get you dressed before she comes back with your discharge stuff."

Tonya stood, too. "She won't be back. She'll send a nurse in with everything. That's what these places do."

"Oh, she'll be back."

"What makes you think that?"

"The way she was shooting daggers at me. Couldn't figure it out. Now I know."

"Why...what..."

"Tonya, please. She sees me as competition."

"For what?"

"You, dummy. Oh, I have to set that record straight."

"There will be none of that."

Atlee ignored her as she went to the curtain and stuck her head out. "Can we get the nurse in here, please?"

"Who are you talking to?"

"Some guy out here in scrubs."

"Atlee!"

"What?"

"Why do we need the nurse?"

"We need to have her get Dr. Ross back in here."

"No, we do not!"

A female aide stuck her head in. "Did you need something in here?"

"No," Tonya said. "Everything is fine."

"Is Dr. Ross out there somewhere?" Atlee asked.

"At the desk. At least she was when I passed by there a minute ago."

"Be right back," Atlee tossed over her shoulder and stepped beyond the curtain.

"Atlee!" Tonya hissed as she yanked her sports bra over her head with her good arm, but the other woman was gone.

CHAPTER 11–BUT SHE'S MY PATIENT

Abigail

Abigail stared at the computer screen without really seeing it. *Tonya. Here. As my patient. And, she sure looks cozy with that cutesy Atlee woman.* She was a pixie in size, if not in spirit. She'd already shown enough spunk to handle Tonya. Her features were fair and tidy, almost angelic, though vaguely Asian, and framed by her hair, dark as a raven's wing and cut just above her slim shoulders. *Not the sort of woman I'd picture her with, but what do I know?*

"Doctor Ross?"

Abigail bristled at the voice. *Atlee.* She raised her mask and turned toward the counter. "I'll be just another minute and you'll be all set...er, Ms. Trube will be all set."

"That's fine, but that's not why I came up here." The other woman looked over her shoulder, then leaned into the high counter as though she were trying to get closer. She whispered, "I know who you are. Tonya told me."

At least she doesn't keep things from her partner. Abigail felt her defenses go up.

"It's not what you think," the other woman was saying.

"What am I thinking?"

Atlee lowered her voice when a nurse appeared behind the counter at the far end. "Tonya told me about the conference and about your, um, mentorship agreement. I think that's great. Might be just what she needs. I can only help her along so much. We're friends, but she doesn't always take me seriously."

"Friends?"

"Best friends, yes, and we're in the same National Guard unit. That's where we met."

"And you play softball together too?"

Atlee nodded several times. "Yeah. The unit sponsors both men's and women's teams. It's a military league."

"Ah."

"I'm no threat to you."

"Pardon?"

A cell phone ringtone interrupted their hushed conversation. Atlee held her phone up and glanced at the screen. "My husband, finally! I texted him an hour ago."

Husband. Abigail sat back down at the computer to finish her tasks while Atlee stepped away from the counter to take the call, but she couldn't help listening in on the other woman's side of the conversation.

ATLEE: "Sorry babe. I'm still at Ascension with Tonya."

There was a pause for a few beats.

Atlee: "Unfortunately, the dumbass rode her Harley to practice. I'm going to have to run her home. Can you meet me at her apartment, and run me down to our practice field so I can get her bike and ride it back to her place?"

Another pause.

Atlee: "I know, but if anything happens to that bike…"

ABIGAIL ROSE and waved at Atlee.
Atlee: "Hang on a second, babe. The doctor's waving at me."

ABIGAIL POINTED at the computer screen. "I know where she lives. It's close to me and I'll be off shift as soon as I finish up here. I can run her home if that helps you."

"Thanks! I'll take you up on that," Atlee said to Abigail.

ATLEE: "Change in plans, maybe. Can you get someone to come with you? I've got her a way home, but we'll need to get my vehicle to her place so I don't end up leaving it here at the hospital. I'll drive down to the field, grab the bike, take it there and whoever you bring if you can find someone can take my CR-V to her place?"

ABIGAIL TRIED TO INTERRUPT. "I didn't mean to make more work for you—"

Atlee waved her off, then moments later gave her a thumbs up. When she hung up the phone, she said, "He was sitting in the garage listening to a ball game with the neighbor. They're on the way already." She started to walk away from the desk area. "I'll go check in on Tonya, then I'll get going."

* * *

"YOU DIDN'T NEED to go to all this trouble," Tonya said.

"Happy to help," Abigail said without taking her eyes off the road.

"I'm betting you've had a really long day. Don't you want to get home?"

"Is my company that awful?"

"No," Tonya said. "That's not what I meant at all. I just know you go in really early and—"

"We each do one shift a month in the ER and look at all ortho injuries that come in. It's a seven-to-seven shift."

"That doctor with you—"

"Silbeth."

"He your boss?"

"Yes."

"Does he always do the ER shift with you?"

"Him or one of the other attending ortho doctors, but usually him. It's not just me though, if that's what you're asking." She swallowed. "I...I want to say thanks."

"For what?"

"For making me look good...half decent, at least, in front of him."

Tonya chuckled out loud. "He was hanging on every word you said."

"That's his job."

"Will there be a patient survey?"

"I don't know how all that works. They mail them, but I don't know if everyone gets one or if it's random."

Tonya turned slightly toward her in her seat. "If I get one, I'll give you good marks. Especially for the personal escort service."

"Maybe it's best you don't mention that."

AT TONYA'S APARTMENT, Abigail got out of the car and got out the ball bag Atlee had brought back into the hospital before she left. When she hefted it, she grimaced.

"I'll get that," Tonya said.

"You most certainly won't. Half a gallon of milk, remember? I just can't figure out how you got this to the ballpark on a motorcycle."

Tonya gave a half shrug and a sheepish grin. "It carries like a backpack."

Abigail looked at the straps and slung it on that way herself. "Oof. No wonder you're hurting and swelling. How many bats do you have in here?"

"Just four. And my cleats, a couple of gloves and a few practice balls. Atlee keeps a bucket of balls in her CR-V."

"Lead on," Abigail said as she both shook her head and pointed at the apartment building. "And, why two gloves?"

"One for when I'm pitching and one for fielding drills, of course."

"Of course."

When they got inside Tonya's apartment, Abigail detected a slight smell of mustiness in the air. She noted an old couch and a small table with a flat-screen TV in the living room. An end table beside the couch held a lamp, a laptop, and some books. Other than two bar stools at a counter dividing the kitchen and the empty dining area, those were the only pieces of furniture in the main room. The walls were mostly bare.

The only sound was an AC unit in a living room window, humming quietly.

"It's a nice night," Abigail said. "You might want to turn that off and open some windows. Let a breeze in."

Tonya looked around. "I guess. I know it isn't much to look at."

Abigail thought her tone sounded defensive. She was sure it was when Tonya said, "I'm not here much."

She touched the other woman's arm. "Don't worry about it. Frankly, this is how I live, too. My place is just a place to sleep between shifts, so this is nothing to be embarrassed about."

"Not embarrassed," Tonya muttered.

Abigail changed the subject. "Your ice pack is looking a little liquid there. Do you have ice in the freezer?"

Tonya nodded. "I'll get it."

Abigail pointed at the couch. "Sit. I think I can find your freezer." She took the hospital issued ice pack from the older woman and took it to the kitchen. She called out from there, "What about ibuprofen?"

When Tonya didn't answer, she prompted her again.

"Don't like meds," Tonya admitted.

"So, you don't have any, is what I hear you saying." She approached from the kitchen. As she laid the ice pack over Tonya's shoulder, she directed her, "Text Atlee and ask her to stop and get you some. I'll wait with you until she gets here, and you take a couple."

Tonya shot her a look, but when Abigail didn't waver, she sighed and picked up her phone.

Abigail took a seat at the other end of the sofa.

"You're pushy," Tonya said.

"I'm a doctor. You're now, like it or not, my patient."

"I could give you a critical review."

"Be my guest. It wouldn't be the first time. You know it would be all your own fault, though."

Tonya glared at her, but her glare gave way to a grin. "You really are good at what you do."

"I'm good in surgery. This stuff," she waved a hand at Tonya's arm, "any second-year medical student could do."

"I wouldn't let a second-year medical student touch me."

"You won't let anyone touch you. You flinched when I touched you medically just to move your gown, nowhere near your injury."

"That was different."

"Different how?"

Tonya looked away.

Abigail felt her face color when the implication of the other woman's words dawned on her. They sat for a few minutes in the quiet room, Abigail feeling slightly uncomfortable with the situation. She shifted in her seat and studied Tonya, but Tonya continued to look away, not seeming to want to make eye contact.

The silence became thick. Abigail struggled to find something mundane they could talk about without it feeling false.

Tonya looked her way and took a deep breath. "We should probably talk."

"About?" *I know, but she's my patient now. This can't go there.*

"Me seeing you medically. Let's not let it change anything between us."

"Change anything, how? You are my patient."

"No. You just happened to be on duty tonight. I'm Ascension's patient. I don't even have a doctor I go to. The military handles my physicals and shots."

Abigail staved off a shudder. "You really should take a little better care of yourself than that."

"I go to the dentist regularly."

"Well, that's something, I guess." *What am I going to do with this woman?*

"When's the last time you had a pap done, or a mammogram?"

Tonya's face split into a wide smile. "Thinking about my lady parts, are you?"

"Ugh! Incorrigible!"

"You were. You so were!"

"I'm a *doctor*."

"But not mine. We're just...we're just..."

"Enemies?" Abigail threw out. "Mentor/mentee? I mean, what are we?"

Tonya appeared to give it some thought. "How about, becoming friends?" She leaned forward and shifted position. The icepack slipped from her shoulder.

Abigail lunged for it and caught it just before it hit the floor.

She looked up at Tonya from a leaning position close to the other woman's right knee. As she slid toward her to reapply the ice pack, Tonya turned more toward her. "Maybe friends? Maybe more?"

Abigail drew in a deep breath and whispered, "More how?" She didn't even notice she still had a hand on Tonya's shoulder.

"I don't know how to describe what..." she trailed off.

"Describe what?" Tonya asked when several seconds went by. "Tell me."

"How I'm feeling. What I'm feeling. What I want."

Abigail felt heat spread through her loins. *No. No. We can't. She's my patient whether or not she admits to it.*

"I admit," Tonya was saying, "I'm no good at all at relationships. And, I haven't wanted what I feel when I'm around you for years. It was never a powerful pull for me."

"What wasn't?"

Tonya coughed. The word 'sex' came out in a croak.

Abigail was feeling the same, but she attempted to lighten the mood for the sake of their patient/doctor relationship. "You must be feeling better if you're thinking about sex."

"Only with you."

Whew! Okay... "What about your shoulder?" She knew she was grasping for an excuse she really didn't want.

"My shoulder wouldn't hinder anything I could do to you, for you, in the bedroom." Tonya reached across her own body with her left arm and put a hand inside Abigail's thigh. She leaned in at the same time and claimed her lips.

Unbridled desire surged through Abigail's veins, electrifying her body with an intensity she hadn't felt since her sophomore year of college. She ached with a raw, carnal hunger that begged to be sated. She returned the kiss with such passion, Tonya deepened it, probing her mouth with her tongue.

The heat from the kiss and the hand on her thigh had

Abigail's senses in overdrive. She wanted to touch Tonya, too. Vaguely conscious of the other woman's injury, she reached out with her right hand and laid it on the other woman's shoulder. When she couldn't pull her any closer, given their position on the couch, she instead ran the hand down to Tonya's breast.

Tonya stiffened and pulled slightly away.

"What?" Abigail whispered. "Did I hurt you?"

"No. No, it's not that. It's just—"

A bike roared up outside, interrupting her.

"Atlee," they both said.

Abigail rose and tried to compose herself as she said, "I'll buzz her in."

CHAPTER 12–FOLLOW-UP

Thursday Afternoon
Ascension Hospital

Tonya

Tonya showed up for her follow-up appointment in her work khakis and a work shirt over a white t-shirt.

"I need to send you for an x-ray," Abigail reminded her.

"No gown," Tonya pleaded. She closed the exam room door then took her work shirt off with Abigail watching, "This has grease on it, but my t-shirt should be clean. I didn't have time to go home and change."

"You can't use the department locker rooms?"

"We're not collocated with them. There's not enough property around the main station, so the garage is a half mile away."

She caught Abigail staring, lowered her mask, and smiled. "Like what you see?"

"Shh!" was all Abigail could manage.

. . .

An hour and a mostly clean bill of health later, Tonya asked Abigail, "When do you get off work?"

"Technically, at five, but usually more like six with all the paperwork to wrap up. Why?"

"Dinner? Unfinished business?" She watched Abigail lick her lips then purse them quickly.

"I...I could manage dinner. I'm back here at 5:00 AM tomorrow, and you, um, you still need to take it easy a while longer."

"Dinner it is, then."

"Can I pick the place? You have to admit, I didn't steer you wrong the last time."

Tonya waited while a nurse breezed in and out of the little exam room to drop off her discharge notes.

"Nope. I'm picking. Don't worry. You'll like it." She tapped her forehead. "I've got your dietary restrictions memorized."

"They're not restrictions. They're preferences. Healthy ones."

Tonya circled a finger in the air. "I got this. I'll text you where to meet me. See ya later, doc."

Violetville Park

"We're literally around the corner from my apartment complex," Abigail said as she got out of her car.

"Oh? I wasn't aware of that," Tonya said. *Yes, I was*. "Oaklee, I think you said at the conference?"

"You know what I said." She took a quick look around. "Ball games are going on. Is your team playing?"

"No, and we don't play here. I got us takeout, but I didn't want to eat in at the restaurant. Small place. We couldn't talk, so to speak. And this, isn't far from home for me, or for you either I guess."

Tonya thought Abigail looked suspicious. Her thinking was confirmed when the other woman asked, "So, what did you get us?" in a tentative tone.

"Thai from Thai Heaven."

Her entire demeanor changed. "Ooh! Good choice. I love that place."

Tonya led the way to a small, but mercifully empty picnic shelter carrying the bag of takeout dishes she'd chosen.

Abigail looped her legs over a table bench and waited as Tonya unpacked the bag.

"I hope you like at least something I picked. I've got tofu summer rolls for your appetizer." She pulled a face, but she masked it quickly. "And then for entrees I've got pad Thai both with and without chicken, and some of their red curry we can share, if you like it. Well, we can share all of it except those summer rolls. Those are all you."

"That's a lot of food."

"I was thinking about leftovers for lunch tomorrow, too," Tonya admitted. She took plates and chopsticks out of the bag. "Would you rather have a fork?"

Abigail pulled the chopsticks out of the paper package as she answered, "These are fine."

Tonya felt guilty as she took a fork out of the bag for herself. "I never mastered those."

"I'm not big on them, but they make me eat a little more slowly."

They made their plates and ate in silence for a couple of minutes before Abigail asked Tonya, "So, how was work?"

"At the shop? Fine. I have drill this weekend. Not looking forward to that. It's sad, because usually I am."

"First time back since the conference?"

"Yeah. I'll have to report to my CO."

"You can call me, you know, if you need to vent."

"Thanks." She took a deep breath. "Maybe we should still keep our mentoring appointments. I mean, what do you think about that?"

Abigail laid her chopsticks across her plate and looked Tonya in the eye. "I don't know where we are, but I think maybe we moved past that Monday night."

"I don't exactly have an answer, myself. One minute we're arguing and the next minute…" She looked away.

"I'll be honest. I wasn't looking for a relationship…of any kind," Abigail said. "My career comes first. There's little time for anything, as you've seen. And there's our age difference. And, admit it, I'm not what you would normally seek in a woman. I'm young. I'm opinionated. I'm—"

Tonya pushed her plate aside. "You're a hell of a lot more mature than 90% of the women I know, even Atlee, and that's saying something because she's one of the few women I tolerate around me at all. You're a professional. You know what you want and you're going after it. Clara was right. We're so much alike it's scary. But…"

When the pause lasted several seconds, Abigail prompted her, "But?"

"There's something you need to know about me. Something I don't talk about to anyone, even to Atlee."

"What?"

The question was simple, but so complex for Tonya. She drew in a deep breath. "It's been a long time since I've had a partner. Any sort of partner. Not because of my lifestyle, but because of me." She paused a beat, but Abigail said nothing. She just waited.

"Back in the day, and you've probably never heard the term, I would have been called a stone butch."

"I've heard it. I'm not sure what you're getting at. I mean, I can see you, and—"

"It's not about my appearance, it's about my…" She drew in another deep breath and let it out in a huff. "This is so hard."

"It's okay. We don't have to talk about it."

"Yeah, we do. I do. I just…I just need you to listen."

"Okay. I'll do my best, but you of all people know that's my weak point."

Tonya smiled and felt some of her tension slip away. "Let me put it to you this way. I have feelings for you. Romantic feelings. Certainly, sexual feelings. If I'm honest, that day you sat next to me in that first session, I could feel the tension ratchet up in my body and it wasn't…wasn't… Well, let's just say it was a different kind of energy."

"Okay."

Tonya held up a hand. "That's not everything."

At Abigail's answering nod, she went on. "I want to make love to you. Fuck your brains out."

Abigail shifted in her seat, but kept her eyes trained on Tonya's face and said nothing.

"I just…I don't want to be touched." *I said it*. She let out another big huff of air.

"At all?"

"No. Not…not sexually."

"So, you're asexual?"

"I guess that's the term they use now. I mean, I feel very attracted to you. But it's only you and…"

"And you don't want me to touch you in certain ways?"

"Yes." Tonya sighed. "I'm sorry." She stood. "Maybe I should go." All the confidence she'd mustered to tell Abigail her truth she felt slipping away.

Abigail stood too and met Tonya's eyes. "Let's finish dinner, and then let's take this somewhere a lot more private to talk about."

"You're…You're not upset?"

"No."

"I know it's a lot and—"

"Thank you for being honest with me. That means a lot, and I know that had to be really hard to admit to anyone."

"I never have, actually. It took a long time to come to terms with it myself."

"I could kiss you right now, but now I know that's probably not going to happen again."

Tonya waved her hands. "You are misunderstanding me to a point. I want you. I loved kissing you. It was the highlight of my week. Damn, Atlee anyway."

"If Atlee hadn't come along, where would we be?" Abigail asked. "Would you have told me all this, then?"

Tonya looked away.

"You wouldn't have, would you?"

"Actually, I was trying to, but I was relieved when she showed up. I wanted you. Wanted to bed you. But I was in no condition to do it, and I wasn't sure what you'd want to do to me…if anything. I mean, I think you were interested—"

"Oh, I was interested." Abigail shifted again. "And, we need to eat this food because I want you to take me somewhere. My place. Yours. Doesn't matter, but if you don't touch me soon, I'm going to have to do something I haven't done in years and take matters into my own hands."

Tonya snatched her fork back up and tucked into her plate with gusto.

* * *

Abigail's Apartment
Oaklee

Tonya sucked a nipple into her mouth and pulled hard on it until it stiffened into a tighter peak than it had already been.

Abigail gasped and writhed on her bed.

Tonya replaced her mouth with her fingers and pulled Abigail sideways to her. She claimed the younger woman's lips as she worked her nipple with her thumb and index finger.

Abigail bucked against her, trying to get closer.

She let go of the nipple and pushed her back a little. Before the other woman missed anything, she trailed a hand down her stomach, found her clit, and traced around it with her finger.

"Ahhhh," was all Abigail could manage.

Her clit was wet. Tonya stroked even lower and soaked her hand in Abigail's folds. "Tell me what you want."

"Fuck me. Fuck me hard."

Tonya met Abigail's lips in a kiss again as she plunged a couple of fingers inside. *Tight. So tight.*

Abigail groaned.

She tried to pull back and go a little easy.

Abigail wasn't having it. "Fuck. Me!"

Tonya did as she was told.

When Abigail came, Tonya came too for the first time in more time than she cared to remember. *Have I finally found a woman that will accept me for me?*

CHAPTER 13 - FRIDAY

Ascension Hospital
4:58 AM

Abigail

Abigail tried hard not to stagger onto the ortho floor at the hospital. She'd kicked Tonya out of her bed around 10:30 the night before after reminding her they both had an early morning coming up. Her body ached from the nipples down. She wasn't sure it was such a good thing now, though what made her ache the way she was had been thrilling at the time.

"You okay, Dr. Ross?" one of the other residents asked her. She looked over at Cameron Williams and smiled at the only married third-year resident in their cycle. "Fine. Fine. Thanks for asking. How are you?"

He raised an eyebrow and drew closer. "Okay, please don't take offense to me saying this, but now I know you're not fine.

You've never asked after me or anyone else that wasn't a patient, that I can recall. Just an observation. No hard feelings involved."

"Maybe I'm just turning over a new leaf."

"Right." He drew the word out.

Abigail gave him a smile and a pat on the arm. "Come on. We're going to be late for education."

He leaned toward her as they walked toward the little makeshift classroom they met in each morning and asked in a whisper, "What's her name?"

She stopped up short and mouthed, "You know?" to him.

He gave her a half shrug and whispered back, "Let's just say someone you dated briefly your first year of college or so was my next-door neighbor growing up and I remember seeing you over there a few times."

Okay, then.

During rounds, as she was daydreaming about the evening before, she almost missed a question from one of the attending surgeons about a patient's prognosis. *Snap out of it, Abigail. Be a professional, not a hormonal teenager.*

She couldn't help sneaking a peek at her phone when it buzzed with a message as they trooped to the next patient's room, though.

Tonya: I'm so tired.

Abigail ducked into a restroom and texted back quickly: On rounds, but me too, and sore.

Tonya texted back a devil emoji.

She did her best to wipe the smile from her face before she rejoined her colleagues in the next patient's room. Cameron shot her a look, but no one else took notice of her momentary absence. She did her best to avoid him and any more questions from him for the rest of morning.

CHAPTER 14 - DRILL

Saturday Morning
Fort Hayes
111th Water Purification Unit

Tonya

"The flooding is bad," the commander, Captain Clark, was telling his XO and his senior NCO staff. "Be prepared. We may come down on orders soon. I'll know within 24 hours. That info doesn't leave this room, though. Not until we have a definite answer."

Sergeant First Class George Baines, spoke up. "We can't even forewarn our civilian employers?"

"Not yet."

The XO asked, "Everyone? The entire unit if we go?"

"Probably," came the response from Clark, "but the reason we can't let it out yet is because we may be split and sent to two different locations. One platoon and their ROWPUs will go to Iowa. The other may go into Illinois if the rain there ever lets up."

"Where would the command element go?" the first Sergeant asked.

"Can't answer that either, Top. The platoon sergeants and the platoon leaders will go with their platoons, of course, but where you, the XO, and I go is currently undetermined, pending the decisions on everything else. They'll probably split us up, too."

A lot of to do with no real intel, Tonya thought. *Oh well. Not my first rodeo. I'll probably have to split the motor pool and send mechanics both ways if we end up in two places.* She thought about which of her troops she had enough confidence in to lead whichever team she wasn't on.

She sighed to herself as she walked out of the little office CPT Clark and the First Sergeant shared. *Might as well flip a coin on that one. They all have their strengths and weaknesses. I'm probably going to be driving back and forth, driving myself crazy. The only good that's come out of today so far is that I didn't have to chat with Clark about the conference. He's too worried about mobilizing to worry about that.*

She went through the rest of the day as a tough taskmaster, making sure her troops did a thorough preventative maintenance check on every vehicle and got all fluid levels full in everything, including fuel.

On the way home that evening, she mentally checked off the things she'd have to pack. She knew they'd be called up for flood duty. A rural state, Iowa didn't have a water purification unit. Illinois only had one. With such widespread flooding, she knew the Illinois unit couldn't handle all the needs.

She grabbed food on the way home and ate it at her apartment as she dug out her go bag, packed uniforms in a duffle, and went over all her tactical gear.

Abigail sent her a text message around 6:00. Feel like meeting up? No pressure.

Tonya texted back: Sorry. Long day. Tomorrow will be longer.

Abigail: Okay. Check in tomorrow after your drill? Phone is fine.

Tonya: I hope so.

She put the phone on the charger and went in search of her spare to throw in her go bag. She regretted putting Abigail off, but she knew she'd really be breaking protocol if she said anything, and she couldn't trust herself not to say anything.

Probably the worst time ever to get involved with someone. I shouldn't have done it. I should have left it all alone.

CHAPTER 15-SUNDAY FUNDAY

The call went out late Saturday night. The First Sergeant called her, then she called her motor pool troops. 'Report Sunday with all your gear for a mobilization of indeterminate length. Plan for at least a couple of weeks.'

She called her police motor pool boss and let him know she'd been called up for flood duty, then tried to get some sleep for probably the last time in a while in a proper bed.

She got to the armory far earlier than her usual hour early, but personnel from battalion headquarters were already manning the doors, checking in troops as they arrived with their gear.

She had only just been checked off a roster when the First Sergeant looked over the railing at the drill floor from the second floor and spotted her. "Trube, up here," he called out and waved an arm.

She staged her gear quickly in the area marked off for the motor pool, then took the stairs two at a time to the unit's small suite of offices.

"Morning," she addressed the four men already in the office, the CO, the XO, the First Sergeant and a platoon sergeant whom, like she and George Baines, was also interested in the next Master Sergeant opening in the unit, Sergeant First Class Stokes.

The XO was the only one in the room to verbally acknowledge her. "Good morning, Sergeant." He went on without waiting for a response from her. "You and I are going to Iowa with half your crew and the first platoon." He nodded toward the first platoon sergeant, SFC Stokes. "We'll locate in place, near Dubuque. CPT Clark, Top, and 2nd platoon are going to Illinois. They'll be more mobile, going where the needs are day to day."

She cut in. "Shouldn't it be the other way around, then? Shouldn't I go where our vehicles are going to be in constant motion?"

Clark answered. "Illinois has mobilized their entire state force and they're getting other outside support aside from us. There will be plenty of transport to move our troops around. Top and I will coordinate all of that. You'll be in charge in Iowa. You and the XO."

"In charge?"

The First Sergeant answered, "Noncommissioned Officer in Charge. NCOIC."

Tonya knew what he meant; she was just surprised. She shot a look at Stokes. He didn't look happy, but she had time in service and time in grade over him, and he was aware of that. Regardless, he wouldn't take her directing his platoon around well. He didn't have high regard for her or for the XO, a decent guy, but a fairly young one who had just made 1LT, who wasn't fully versed in running a command.

True to his nature, Stokes wasn't going down without a fight. "Wouldn't it make more sense for you to come with us, Top? Let Trube do her thing with the motor pool."

"Half a motor pool, and no," the CO answered. "There's going to be a lot of scheduling and movement in Illinois. Top needs to be there so we can divide and conquer."

So, no pressure. Ha! This sucks! Abigail flitted through her mind, but Tonya quickly pushed all thoughts of her aside. *That's done for a while. I'll text her when I get a minute to let her know what's up, but otherwise there's no time for all that business.*

THE DRILL DAY turned mobilization day seemed to grind on interminably to Tonya, right from the start. Troops used to arriving at the armory by 7:00 AM sharp for drill were still filtering in after 9:00 AM after having to pack and take care of last-minute needs at home.

After that first of what she knew would be several briefings during the day, Tonya had escaped to the motor pool and busied herself deciding which troops would go with which platoon. She spent a half hour creating a list and noting who would be responsible for what, before she headed back into the armory.

At 1000 hours, the 1SG called morning formation and took roll call. After that, the commander stepped forward, told the soldiers to take a seat on the floor, and briefed them for the next twenty minutes on what was going to happen.

While CPT Clark talked, Tonya looked over her squad sized element of troops. Short one who was recovering from Covid, there were seven. She'd take three with her and hope the other soldier recovered enough to join them shortly.

The other four soldiers would go to Illinois, led by a young sergeant who was not only Army trained on diesel vehicles but also tech school trained and had a job with a civilian trucking company. Though he was often cocky about his skills, she knew SGT Keplee knew his stuff. He'd get things done and get hands-on lessons in being a leader instead of only spouting the theory he'd learned in the PLDC course he'd taken the previous summer.

Top will be there to monitor him; not let him get on too much of a power trip or pick him up if he falters.

Once the commander finished speaking, they broke out into

platoons and sections. She quickly went through her list with her troops, gave Keplee his instructions, then had the soldiers take their gear to the staging areas of the platoons they'd be moving out with.

After lugging her own gear over to the first platoon area, she looked around for the commander. He was chatting up the battalion XO, who was in charge of the stations her unit's soldiers were already moving through for payroll, personnel needs, civilian employer contacts, and supply. She started toward the two men, but her own unit XO stopped her.

"Sergeant Trube, a word, please?"

"Sure, sir." It still felt weird after all her years of service to call an officer who was so much younger than she, sir or ma'am. It was especially odd with 1LT Rickard. He didn't have the sort of look of most military men. His military bearing and his STRAC uniform were as expected for an officer, but he was on the short side for a male, and he had always struck Tonya as more of a nerdy intellectual type than as a gung-ho warrior type with his wire-rim glasses, his sandy brown hair, and the formal way he spoke almost all the time.

He looked around and directed her to a corner of the drill floor away from the staging areas and the area where the folks from their battalion headquarters had set up their processing operation.

Dread filled her veins. *Whatever this is about, he wants it to be just between us.*

"We probably only have a minute," Rickard began. "I'm new to all of this. You know that. I'm going to have to rely on you to help me out a lot, keep me straight."

She suppressed a grin at his use of a common military phrase in relation to anything to do with her. Instead, she told him, "Stokes is good too, LT."

"I know that, but we tapped you to be the NCOIC, not him. It's your chance to shine, if you know what I mean."

She did. "I'll take care of you, lieutenant, if you run interference with him, for me. Deal?" She knew he knew exactly what she meant.

"Deal, Sergeant."

They didn't dare shake on it.

THE CONVOY for Iowa pulled out at 1500 hours.

Tonya didn't realize she dropped her cell phone as she climbed into the HMMWV one of her troops was driving for the first part of the movement west. The deuce and a half truck that rolled out behind them with half of the tools in the motor pool shop made quick work of the downed phone.

She did a radio check with the XO's vehicle ahead of them, then proceeded with the all the vehicles trailing them from the 1st platoon. After that, she settled in for a long evening. It would be five hours before they stopped to do more than rotate drivers.

THE ARMORY IN YOUNGSTOWN, Ohio where they were bedding down for the night was a newer one than many of the ones Tonya had been in back home. There were communal showers for males and females, and the troops all had to bed down on the drill floor, but there were a few small private rooms for the senior people.

After a check on the vehicles, and a chat with the two soldiers taking the first watch rotation, she took a quick shower then gratefully closed a door behind herself and sank down onto the twin sized bunk where she'd already spread out her sleeping bag.

She dug through her go bag for her cell phone. It wasn't there. She searched it again. Nothing. She looked at her duffle bag. *No way it's in there.* She'd only opened it when she was going through the mandatory supply shakedown that morning.

She opened the top, emptied it, and searched through everything anyway. Nothing. As she repacked it, she tried to remember the last time she'd seen the phone. She remembered grabbing it just after the safety and commo briefing before they pulled out. *It's got to be in the HMMWV.* Tired, she resigned herself to looking for it the next morning.

It's just as well, she thought. *The only person I'd call besides Atlee is Abigail, and I don't even know where I'd begin with her. I don't know how long this mobilization is going to last and I don't know if this will be the last one. Times are crazy. Getting involved with someone wasn't at all fair of me to do. Best not to let it go any further.*

CHAPTER 16-GHOSTED

Abigail

Six O'clock came and went. Abigail busied herself in her small apartment and tried not to stare at her phone. She'll call as soon as she gets home, she told herself. She couldn't imagine what a day of military drill must be like for Tonya.

After seven, she couldn't wait any longer. She picked up her phone and typed a text, then erased it and started over. She went for brief and as light as she could make it given that Tonya had told her about probably having to fill her commanding officer in on the women's conference.

ABIGAIL: Hey. How was your weekend?

SHE HELD the phone and tried to will a response from Tonya to appear. When none was forthcoming after several minutes, she attempted to justify things in her mind. *She worked her police mechanic job all week, then had her military training all weekend, and she starts all over again tomorrow. She's probably beyond exhausted.*

After yawning herself, she picked up her phone and sent a couple of final texts for the evening.

ABIGAIL: Have a great week. I hope we can catch up soon.

Abigail: I've got an early day tomorrow, so I'm off to bed. Goodnight.

THERE WERE SO many things she thought about saying, but she couldn't bring herself to say any of them. She wanted Tonya to know that she was there for her; she was thinking of her, and she was proud of her for facing up to her challenges, but it was hard to say those things out loud, at least through text. *I don't want to sound trite or condescending, and I certainly don't want to sound fake. I may be a hard case, but I'm no mentor.*

With a heavy heart, she put away the phone and settled into bed for the night.

* * *

NO TEXTS from Tonya arrived overnight. There were no missed calls, either. A bad feeling washed over her. *Please let her be okay.*

At training that morning, Abigail stood in a back corner of the room and barely listened. She avoided both Cameron and the attending doctors.

As the morning's speaker launched into his presentation, her thoughts were only on Tonya. *I pushed her too hard, too fast. I showed up at her apartment like a stalker, and I pursued her. Then, she divulges something so personal to me, something she's never shared with anyone, and I take advantage of her for my own sexual gratification.*

Professional. I should have kept it professional. Mentor only. We should never have gone any further.

She smacked a hand against her head before remembering where she was. She looked at her colleagues all standing around the small classroom. They were focused on the speaker.

I suck at reading cues. That's what got me into this whole mess to begin with. She shook her head but stopped herself when she realized the speaker was looking her way.

"Do you have a question, doctor?" he asked. Everyone turned and looked at her.

"No. I'm sorry. Please continue." She saw Cameron give her a look before he turned back to the speaker himself.

Way to go, Abigail! It's going to be a long day.

As the day went on, she caught herself peeking at her phone, hoping for a message from Tonya, then she would berate herself for doing it. *She's at work, and even if she wasn't, she won't answer. I knew better than to get involved with someone so much older and more experienced in...well, everything. I'm not good enough for her. I'm not good enough for here either.*

CHAPTER 17-IOWA

They pushed well into the evening Monday to make it to Dubuque before sundown. Tonya noted there were many streets still flooded with homes and businesses suffering water levels that reached nearly to the second story. Where the streets weren't flooded, she could see high water mark lines on nearly everything still standing. There was debris everywhere.

For at least the first couple of days, their base was going to be a high school where the Federal Emergency Management Agency had set up their disaster relief operations. Tonya was grateful for any time they got to be there because FEMA hired a contract company to operate the high school cafeteria around the clock saving them from having to eat MRE's for three meals a day since the mess section had gone to Illinois with most of the command element.

A few hours before, the XO had confirmation that the other half plus of the unit had reached Alton, Illinois, a town north of St. Louis, along a portion of the Mississippi River well south of them. They were already looking at locations to set up water purification operations.

She hadn't found her cell phone, so she had to rely on the LT to relay her information from his calls until they could get sat phones set up. She planned to avoid calling Top and the commander as much as possible outside of normal, daily reporting requirements.

FEMA also had several classrooms in the building set up like dorms with bunks and cots. Their allotment was two classrooms, one for males and one for females. It wasn't ideal for most of the troops, but to Tonya a building on high ground, with a solid roof, and a temperature controlled room with a cot to sleep on were far better accommodations than she had expected.

SFC Stokes wasn't happy about having to stay in the same room as the XO and all the lower ranking male troops they'd brought, especially since Tonya was only sharing with four other females, but 1LT Rickard stepped between him and Tonya and redirected him like a small child when she first relayed the information that was dispensed to them by FEMA representatives. *It's not like we'll be in the rooms more than to sleep anyway,* she'd thought when she saw his look of indignation.

After she stowed her gear and shoed her road weary troops toward the cafeteria, she went off to the briefing room to get the latest updates.

"DETACHMENT," she called out, "Attention!" She gave a side-eyed glance to the armband she now wore over her upper right arm, giving her the temporary rank and authority of a First Sergeant. It made her feel proud and self-conscious at the same time.

The troops fell into some semblance of order with 1st Platoon split off from everyone else in their usual platoon formation. She called the roll quickly to make sure they had everyone.

The XO joined her up front. "I'll be brief," 1LT Rickard told the assembly. "It's late and it's been a long day. Thank you, everyone, for your patience and your willingness to push through. Tomorrow is going to be longer."

"Much of the town is still underwater, especially just to this side of the levees, which could only hold back so much. There's little to no potable water for the residents that have not evacuated, or for those who did and who have returned. Pumps at the water treatment facility have been heavily damaged by all the flooding."

"FEMA is supplying this facility and most of the disaster relief force with bottled water and what they can truck in, but they can't meet every need. That's where all of you come in. They've identified a location just off the river bank that has drained off, mostly, for us to set up our ROWPUs tomorrow and begin purification operations. Those of you not part of those operations will assist in setup, distribution, crowd control, and anything else that is needed. There are a lot of other helping hands out there, but there is also a lot of need."

He looked at Tonya and gave her a nod. "Top."

She suppressed taking a deep breath and stepped forward. "The men's and women's locker rooms off the gymnasium are open for showers. Please clean up after yourself. Bunk down when you're finished. Wake up is at 0530. We'll meet right here for a quick headcount at 0550, and chow is at 0600. A quick chow. We roll to the set-up site at 0630. FEMA is providing security for the building and lots surrounding it, so there will be no watch duty assignments tonight."

There were smiles and nods all around.

"Thought you'd like that." She cracked a smile herself for the first time in hours. "When I release you, go get cleaned up and get some rest. We have a lot to do tomorrow. Questions?"

Her stomach clenched. *If there are, I hope I can answer them.* She pushed out of her mind how much she hated it when the 1SG or the CO asked for questions especially near the end of the final formation of Sunday afternoon drill. There was always someone who asked something inane or off the wall, it tied them all up for several more minutes.

. . .

AFTER SHE RELEASED the detachment to the showers and bed, she went to the command center where she could use a sat phone to give her final report to the commander.

Atlee got on the line. "Trube, any chance you can get a regular cell phone anytime soon?"

"FEMA may be able to issue me one tomorrow for use while we're located here. Their commo supply guy was out doing a set-up off site when we got in."

"You're going to need it. It will make it a lot easier for you. The commander said he'll sign off on and fax or email whatever you need, even if you have to go civilian to get it."

"Ha. If anything is even open anywhere near here. The FEMA folks are our best bet. We're well upriver from you and almost everything within a mile of the river is still under at least four feet of water, if not more. Further away from the bank is only slightly better. The power is out in a lot of areas too."

"Have you been in touch with—"

When she dropped her voice, Tonya felt like she knew what she was going to ask and she cut her off. "No. No phone. No time. No need." *And I don't have her number memorized anyway.*

CHAPTER 18-NEW PATIENT, OLD PAIN

Wednesday Morning
St. Agnes Ascension Hospital

Abigail

She finished scrubbing, gowned, gloved and entered the surgical suite. The patient, an elderly woman who'd been a front seat passenger in a car involved in a multi-car accident two days before was already on the operating table, still conscious, but barely.

The woman, Sarah, hadn't been very lucid when she'd seen her in pre-op either to describe the procedure to her which she and doctor Silbeth were going to perform to repair her right wrist and hand. The impact of another car had crushed them.

At least she survived, Abigail thought. A couple of people had perished at the scene, and another died in the hospital. Small comfort to her, though, probably. She knew the woman was in intense pain and her semi-conscious state resulted from the painkillers she was on for multiple injuries, many of which didn't require surgery but were still severe.

"How are you doing?" she asked from above the patient's face. She could see the confusion in her eyes.

"It's me again, Doctor Ross," she explained. "We're going to give you some anesthesia in just a moment. When you wake up, you'll see me again and we'll talk about your new hand, okay?"

Sarah's eyes blinked, but she didn't otherwise move.

Abigail looked at Dr. Silbeth, standing next to her. He gave her a nod. She signaled the anesthesiologist to start the gas.

FOUR HOURS LATER, she scrubbed out, used the restroom, scrubbed again, then went to see her patient's husband and daughter in the family waiting room.

The man got to his feet. "How's she doing? Can I see her?"

"She's in recovery, Mr. Hanes, and she'll probably be there for at least another hour. Let's talk in there." She pointed out a small room off the larger room, even though there were only a couple of other people waiting for loved one's because of ongoing Covid protocols limiting the number of visitors.

Inside the small consultation room, she laid out what she'd done to Sarah for them and finished by telling them, "She's going to be in a cast up to her elbow for about a month. We'll take more x-rays then."

"And see if you need to do anything else?" the daughter asked.

Abigail gave her a firm nod. "Yes. The damage was extensive. We fixed what we could, but—"

Sarah's husband interrupted. "Will she ever have full use of it, doctor? She's right-handed, you know. She likes to cook."

"We're going to do our best, Mr. Hanes." *But it's going to be a long road to recovery for her.* She held her tongue on that last part.

Their daughter gave her a knowing look. "We understand," she said. "Thank you, doctor."

She saw the sadness in Mr. Hanes' eyes, but also the determination to be strong for Sarah. She told him. "You'll get to see your wife soon. She'll need your comfort."

That Evening
Abigail's Apartment
Oaklee

Her cell phone rang. She looked at the screen but didn't pick it up since she didn't recognize the number with the odd area code. *Spammers, probably.*

When the message icon flashed a minute later, she was curious and listened to it.

"Abigail, *it's Tonya. I'm calling you from a government phone because I lost mine on Sunday. Long story. Then I had to have someone track down your number. Anyway, can you call me back? I promise to answer if I can, but I don't want to do this over voicemail."*

Government phone? Something with the military? She doesn't want to do what? All those thoughts and more ran through her mind.

Did she even get my texts? I tried to be positive, so she doesn't want to tell me we're done over voicemail? That's probably what it is. Why call her back to hear that?

She debated with herself for several minutes, then reluctantly called the number up and let it ring through. Might as well be an adult and hear what she has to say.

After the phone Tonya called from rang four times, her call went to voicemail, but no mailbox had been set up and it cut her off. *Figures. Just forget all about her. Sounds like she's going to write me off, anyway.*

After 11:00 PM, Abigail's phone rang again. She roused herself from sleep, saw the strange number, and answered.

Tonya said, "I'm sorry to call you so late."

"It's after 11:00."

"Oh. I'm really sorry. It's just after 10:00 here."

"What? Where? Where is here?" Abigail asked.

"I've been mobilized. We left on Sunday. I lost my phone in the process."

Mobilized?

Tonya asked, "Are you still there?"

Abigail shook herself more awake. "Yes. Yes. Mobilized to where? For how long?"

"I'm not sure that's something that should be public information, yet," Tonya said, "and I don't know."

"So, you can't tell me where you are, and you can't tell me how long you'll be there?"

"Right. Not how long in this place, and not how long the mobilization is going to be."

Abigail's temper reared up. "So, why are you calling me if you can't tell my anything, anyway?" When Tonya didn't answer right away, she prompted her, "Tonya? What are you trying to say?"

"Look, I didn't want to start a fight. I just…I guess I wanted to say that I feel bad about leaving you without a word, even though it wasn't directly my fault and…"

Abigail waited, but Tonya didn't elaborate further. "And what? You don't owe me anything, so 'and' what?"

"This could go on for a long time. This mobilization. It isn't really fair to you, so—"

"So, this is goodbye?"

"I…yes. I guess it is."

"Goodbye, Tonya. Lose my number...again." She slowly put her phone down, her heart heavy with sorrow. Her eyes welled with tears, yet a part of her wanted to stay awake and hold on to the hope that things could still turn around. With a deep exhale, she let her eyelids close, allowing her sobs to carry her back to sleep.

CHAPTER 19-SELF PITY

Tonya looked at the now black screen. *That didn't go well.* She mentally kicked herself. *As if you really thought it would.*

She crept back into the classroom turned bunkhouse and got on her cot but not into her sleeping bag. She knew sleep wouldn't come easily, if at all, for her.

You can't have everything Trube. Three things. Remember your own damn rule! Motors, the military, and softball. You're finally getting a chance to do what you wanted with your military career. You can't screw this up.

She thought about Abigail. *It wasn't fair to her to lead her on, anyway.*

The last thought brought a picture into her mind of them in Abigail's bed, the younger woman writhing under her touch. She quickly pushed that thought away. *This isn't the time or place for that.*

She thought about the conference and her promise to Clara to work with Abigail, to be a mentor and to be mentored. She couldn't suppress a smile to herself. *That damn Clara was probably playing both sides. Who knows what she said to Abigail to get her to work with my sorry ass.*

I tried to tell them both I wasn't mentor material. I didn't need one either. What I needed got dealt to me by force of nature and now I have to make it all work.

Across the room, one of the female soldiers she was sharing the room with called out in her sleep. Tonya waited and listened, but the young woman settled back down.

She thought about the situation she was in. *We had a good day. Processed and loaded thousands of gallons of water for distribution.* They weren't running two shifts, not because they couldn't–the machines didn't need that much downtime for maintenance–but because there were only so many containers to be had for them to fill. There were shortages of jugs and lidded buckets and other approved containers for potable water across a nine-state area bordering the Mississippi River.

Another soldier shifted around on her cot, sat up, then laid back down. Larner, Tonya thought. *Good ball player and, turns out, a good soldier too. She worked hard the past two days as the primary operator of her squad's ROWPU. She keeps this up, she's getting recommended for an award when we get back.*

She gave some thought to that. *There are several that are deserving. There are a few who need a little more encouragement to step up their game. And, there are a couple who are only serving to get a free college tuition ride. No amount of encouragement or mentoring from me or anyone else is going to change them, make them work harder.*

She chuckled, then suppressed it. *Mentoring. Me. Who would have thought it, but here we are.*

The LT, true to his word had run interference for her for the first full day of operations with SFC Stokes. Once the water purification operations were up and running, Stokes had his hands full, and things eased a bit. She admitted to herself that the man was professional, and he knew what he was doing. His troops all seemed to like and respect him, too. That sort of respect was something she needed to build if she hoped to succeed on this mission without too many hiccups.

She did her best to help Rickard out, too. Although Stokes offered his opinion on things often, the LT was judicious in how he went about accepting the advice given from each of them leaving her feeling she wasn't missing important things from her lack of experience with the line platoons and their water purification operations.

Sleep finally claimed her about two hours before the alarm on her watch buzzed her arm enough to wake her. She crept out of bed and headed to the locker room so she could get a shower before the rest of the women bedded down in the facility were awake and moving about.

Early Thursday Morning

Rough night, she thought to herself as she donned her shower cap, then stepped into the spray. *Gotta put it behind you Trube. There's a job to do. You need to make sure it gets done.*

She thought about the mission. With the limited resources they had, every drop of water had to count in order to help the affected citizens in the area.

The ROWPU machines hadn't been running the twenty hours a day they were designed to run, but she was well aware they weren't new units either. The platoons each had people, counting the platoon sergeants, who could do basic maintenance on them, and the platoon sergeants were supposed to be able to do minor plumbing repairs. If anything major went wrong with them during training missions, they were usually shipped to a depot for repair.

Tonya knew it had been a long time since they'd run a live

mission that wasn't just annual training where clean water could be had otherwise in the event of a full equipment failure.

The FEMA folks, while happy to have their support, had no one on staff trained to take care of major equipment failures of their own equipment, let alone her unit's equipment.

I don't know a lot about plumbing. I'll have to rely on Stokes for that, but an engine is an engine. A diesel engine is a diesel engine. In her mind, she ran through the motor pool gear they had on hand that she could use to work on small diesel engines. She'd have a couple of her folks put a separate toolbox together first thing that morning.

AFTER THE MORNING ACCOUNTABILITY FORMATION, she pulled SGT Comella Reyes aside.

"Reyes, a quick word, please."

The young buck sergeant waved one of the other women from 1st Platoon, SPC Larner, on to chow. "Yes, First Sergeant?"

"Top, or Sergeant Trube are fine, Reyes."

"It's an honor to call you first sergeant. Everybody says you should be our next one. This just proves it."

"Uh, thank you, Reyes. I appreciate that." She suppressed a smile at the unexpected, and she felt, unwarranted, compliment. Instead, she turned things around as she motioned for them to move toward the cafeteria, as well. "I just want to say I appreciate how you've stepped up for your squad and your platoon and taken over. You got your stripes and kind of got thrown right into the fire having to come out here. You're doing a great job."

"Thank you, First...Top."

"That's not my only reason for stopping you, but it's the main one."

"What else?"

"Did the platoon bring any extra operations manuals along

for the ROWPUs besides the ones I see you using while you're doing your PM checks and adjusting settings?"

Reyes nodded. "There should be several. One is always with each piece of equipment, but every operator is supposed to have one too. I have one. I know at least a couple of my squad members have one. Larner does, for sure."

"STRAC troops that you are," Tonya said.

Reyes grinned.

"Could I trouble you to borrow yours? I want to familiarize myself in case I have to do some engine repairs."

"Sure Top. Good thinking. See what I mean? You're the right person for this job."

I'm glad she has so much confidence in me. If only I could be sure the commander does.

* * *

WHEN A FEMA TRUCK pulled up to the pump site at lunch time to deliver the sack lunches the contract caterer made, a surprise followed. The commander's unit vehicle followed FEMA's.

Tonya trained her eyes on the passenger side and watched CPT Clark as he got out. She missed Atlee getting out of the driver's side completely until her friend reached the commander's side and walked with him toward the water purification site.

"Sir." Tonya acknowledged him. "This is a surprise."

"Just checking on the troops. The XO didn't tell you I was coming, I take it?"

She shot 1LT Rickard a look as he strode toward them. "No, he did not."

"Good. I told him not to. I didn't want you to worry unnecessarily."

I'm going to kill Atlee. She gave the other woman a quick look she hoped conveyed her displeasure at being left in the dark.

"It's an informal, health and welfare visit," Clark said.

"It's a long way to drive for that, sir."

"About four and a half hours," Atlee answered. "We left after breakfast. Mess made pancakes. What did you all have?"

Atlee mentioning what they had for breakfast was a dig. The mess sergeant was a short-order cook in a well-known restaurant back home. He made killer pancakes.

Tonya decided two could play the game. "Pancakes. Eggs. Omelets. Waffles. Cereal. Whatever we wanted, really," she shot back.

"FEMA's got a contractor running the kitchen at the high school where we're staying," 1LT Rickard said. He got in on the clap back, too. "Did I forget to mention that? In fact," he looked past them and pointed as two young men walked toward them with cardboard boxes and a spouted cooler full of the bug juice all the troops liked, "here comes lunch."

They all watched as the two men set the cooler and a stack of cups on a table then made their way to the soldiers tending to the line of ROWPUs along the riverbank.

"I'm going to follow behind them," CPT Clark said. "Say hello to everyone."

"I'll go with you sir and show you how they've got everything set up so they can eat," Rickard told him.

When the two men were out of earshot, Tonya let Atlee have it. "You could have warned me!"

"Oh no I couldn't. First, I didn't know we were doing this today until this morning. He talked about coming up here yesterday morning if it looked like you were going to be here a while. Looks like you are."

Tonya wasn't ready to give in yet, but she was curious to know what Atlee knew. "Are you hearing anything?"

Atlee shrugged. "Most of Western Illinois is still in terrible shape. It looks only slightly better here since you're not standing up to your waist in water, but looks aren't all of it. Plus, downstream from where we are in Illinois, it's still flooded pretty bad in a lot of places. At least up here, most of the water is receding."

"And," Tonya told her, "It hasn't rained for a couple of days. Not more than a light sprinkle for a few minutes. That helps, but the forecast doesn't look good."

"Yeah," Atlee said, "We're worried about that too." She looked around and tilted her chin toward the lineup of ROWPUs. "How's it going, here, really?"

"Good. As well as can be expected. We've only had minor issues so far, easily resolved."

"What about Stokes over there?"

Tonya rolled her eyes in response.

"That bad?"

"He's had his moments, but he's busy here all day and the XO keeps him in check when we're in garrison...well, back at the high school."

She made a come-on motion. "We should probably get over there."

"Walk slow," Atlee said. "I wanted to ask you something."

"Uh, oh. Now what?" Tonya stopped walking.

Atlee gave her a little shrug. "Something a little more personal. When you got a phone, did you get a hold of the good doctor Ross after I tracked down her number?"

Tonya averted her gaze.

"No," Atlee said in a low voice.

She faced her again. "No, what?"

"You messed it up, didn't you?"

Tonya scrambled to defend herself. "What? No."

"Don't lie to me. I've known you too long."

She tried to justify what she'd done. "First, I lost my phone. Then, this is a military mission, and I didn't know how much I should tell her—"

"Really? You're using that? We're on the national news! It's a nine-state disaster, Tonya, not a secret mission to Timbuktu."

When she puts it like that...

"Aren't you supposed to be mentoring her and vice versa?"

"There's not a lot I can do for her." *Not professionally.*

"But she could be a sounding board for you while you're out here, doing what you're doing."

"So can you."

"Uh, uh. I get about five hours of shut eye away from Top and the commander. You don't want to be bouncing things off me when they're around."

They started walking toward the line of ROWPUs and the troops again, as Tonya said, "Everything's fine, so far. I've got this."

CHAPTER 20 - NEW BLOOD

Also Thursday Morning
St. Agnes Ascension Hospital

Abigail

"Um, Doctor Ross, could I talk to you?"

The question came from behind her as she did some quick charting after rounds. She spun to see a first-year resident standing on the other side of the nurse's station countertop. She couldn't for the life of her remember the young woman's name. The resident was so short; Abigail couldn't see the name stitched on her lab coat over the high counter, either.

"Sure. What can I help you with?" The words felt funny coming out of her mouth, but she was making a conscious effort to be more amenable to her co-workers. "Something about rounds, this morning?" It wasn't unusual for first years to ask questions about what they saw and heard. It was unusual for any of them to approach her, though.

A nurse moved behind the desk and sat down to do some paperwork. The other woman looked around.

Abigail got the hint, got up, and moved toward her. "Let's take a walk, Dr. Stewart." She was relieved she caught the name tag but also annoyed with herself that she'd never taken enough interest in knowing the woman's name in the first place.

As they started down the hall, the other woman said, "I'm Maddie."

"Abigail."

"I know."

And now I really feel bad. "What's going on Maddie?"

"I guess I should have asked if you have a procedure you need to get to."

"No," Abigail told her as she shook her head. "The hospital has some disaster preparedness training going on today." *And you should well know that.* "They didn't want us to schedule anything that wasn't an emergency."

"Oh. That's right. There's always so much going on. Sometimes it feels overwhelming."

"It does, or you just adjust to the pace of it all." *That's probably more accurate.*

"That's just it. I...I need some advice."

"From me?" I said that out loud.

"You're the only female third year. There are two second years and I'm the only first year. We're a pretty small group, us women."

Abigail mentally chastised herself for not having noticed that beyond her own situation.

"How do you...manage it? How do you stand out from them? You're so good. I mean, medical school was competitive. This doesn't feel a lot different. They're always talking over me, jumping in. I feel like they all see me as inferior. I can't find my place."

Abigail pulled Maddie aside as a team in full Hazmat gear

pushed a gurney with a role-playing patient on it rapidly down the hallway. She didn't miss a beat as she told the other woman, "Orthopedic surgery is one of the harder disciplines, but they chose you to be here. To be honest, I tried for a couple of bigger, better-known hospitals in the area, and I felt sorry for myself for a while that I didn't get one of those spots." *Felt sorry for myself until a couple of weeks ago, actually.* "But, you know what? I'm better off here."

"Why do you say that?"

"Listen, the guys were jerks my first year here, too, always trying to prove something. I admit, I let it get to me. I thought I had to compete with them. Be better than them. I imagine that whole scenario would have been even worse in a larger hospital. The men pretty much all settled down and settled in by the middle of our second year, but I didn't. That was my mistake. I wanted to be the best in the surgical suite and I wanted everyone to know I was. I kept pushing like they all had the first year."

"But I hear you are the best in surgery. That's one reason I came to you. I was thinking I should do the same as you did."

"Maybe, but probably not," she quickly clarified. "My point is, I drove for that and let everything else go. Getting to know my patients and taking care of all their needs, not just the surgical ones, for example." She left it at that, feeling the heat of embarrassment creeping up her neck from admitting that much.

She turned to go back the way they came and motioned for Maddie to follow. "Forget about the men. My advice now, and it was hard coming to this, is to focus on a niche that interests you, whether that's arms, hands, knees, hips…what have you. Pick the one for you and learn all you can. Try to get into a viewing spot for those surgeries every time you can if you're not actually assisting. Aside from that, focus on the patients you're assigned to and all of their needs."

"And if what I want to do, one of the guys wants to do? Especially a third year?"

"Don't worry about third year residents. We're not competition. We're more like...think of us more like...mentors." She surprised herself with the word.

"Are you planning to specialize, Abigail?"

"Yes. On hands."

"Oh. I guess you wouldn't be able to mentor me, then."

She tried not to sound incredulous. "You would want me to mentor you?"

"It would be great, but it probably won't work. I'm more interested in the back, the spine."

"That's a good one."

"There's a second year interested in that and already focused on it, Crandall."

"Watch him. Learn from him. Ask him questions. Do the same with the attending doctors. If you think Doctor Crandall might be open to it, ask him to be your mentor. He's only a year ahead of you, not two, so he'll be here longer than I will. To go further with hands, I hope to get a fellowship or into a group with hand specialists. I may not be here."

She noted the look on Maddie's face and added, "But, for as long as I am here, we can always talk and maybe even after. I just won't be able to help you much with back surgeries." They were nearly back to the desk, so she lowered her voice. "I guess, if you're open to the idea and Crandall agrees, you could have two mentors."

"Or a mentor and a friend?"

Abigail smiled. "Or a mentor and a friend," she agreed. *Because I really do need more friends.*

CHAPTER 21-TEN O'CLOCK NEWS

Friday Morning

Tonya had her head in the engine compartment of the number two ROWPU when a local TV news showed up on site. They'd been warned the reporter and her film crew had asked about visiting the site now that most of the Dubuque areas along the banks of the Mississippi had been deemed safe for non-emergency personnel.

The motor pool soldier handing her wrenches noticed them first. "Hey Top, you probably better go check them out."

She asked, "What?" as she stepped back, wrench still in hand.

He pointed.

"Great." *Why couldn't they show up when Rickard and Stokes were here?* The ROWPU got some diesel she thought might have gotten some water in it. The engine had sputtered and surged, blowing a fitting in a line. Water had sprayed everywhere before Stokes and the second squad could get the system shut down.

Stokes and 1LT Rickard had spent several minutes

rummaging around, looking for another appropriate fitting to no avail. They'd gone to a Lowe's store further inland to see what they could find.

She grabbed a rag and wiped her hands down as she approached the camera crew. "How can I help you folks?"

* * *

"I HOPE I didn't just screw up," Tonya said to Atlee. "It was literally a two-minute interview."

"I've got you on speaker and CPT Clark is here, hearing this. He says you're probably fine."

She could have told me that. "Oh, okay. Still wish the XO had been here, or they had done this yesterday when you were here."

Clark's voice came across. "Have you heard from Rickard and Stokes? Did they find a fitting that will work?"

"They think so. They're on their way back, but they're probably another 45 minutes out."

"Good, good," he said. "When's your interview going to air?"

"They said the 10:00 news out of Des Moines."

"So local," he said. "I was hoping to see it."

And I hope no one does. I don't even want to see it.

"What network?" Atlee asked.

"Uh, NBC, I think."

Clark said, "Maybe it will stream too. Regardless, keep us posted."

"Yes, sir."

She heard Atlee say something to him, but she couldn't make out what. She was about to hang up when Atlee said, "I took you off speaker. He's on another call now."

"That's all I had to tell you right now, anyway."

"Have you talked to Abigail?"

"No. Why?"

"Tonya, come on. Call her."

Tonya was suspicious. "Have *you* talked to her?"

"No. I just tracked down the number for you. Didn't know you were going to do something dumb with it."

"You haven't left her any messages or sent her a text or anything?"

"Trust me. I'm busy here doing a little of everything and, even if I weren't, that's your mess to clean up."

* * *

HER TWO-MINUTE INTERVIEW was cut to a thirty-second clip for the 10:00 news that they watched on one of the school televisions set up in a media room. The clip was mostly a voiceover from her while the camera panned from a distance far enough to capture the lineup of four ROWPU systems and the soldiers moving around, tending to them and filling containers with clean water.

She was relieved to see she appeared on camera for only a few seconds each at the beginning and at the end of the clip. She felt even more relief that most of the troops were in bed and didn't see it. They were all hoping the camera zoomed in on them and they got closeups so they could tell friends and family they were on TV.

1LT Rickard gave her a light elbow tap. "Good job, Top. You did us proud."

"Thanks sir, I think. Just promise me you'll be here the next time they show up. This face was not made for television." *Nor was my stomach.* It was still doing flip-flops even though the station had moved on to the weather forecast.

She turned away, not interested in watching. FEMA kept them apprised of the weather.

* * *

SATURDAY MORNING

. . .

THEY WERE MOUNTING up to head to the pump site when the voice of the FEMA area operations manager came over her radio. "First Sergeant Trube, you've got a call in here on the sat phone you should probably take."

She answered back, "We're getting ready to pull out. Can you patch it through?"

She thought she detected a chuckle as he replied, "I don't think you want me to do that."

Now what? Trouble? That damn news report? "Go on ahead," she told 1LT Rickard. "Those night duty guards need relief. I'll hold the maintenance deuce and ride out with them."

She waved the deuce and a half out of line and the rest of the small convoy forward, asked the deuce driver to wait, then went back inside.

THE FEMA COMMAND center was in the throes of its usual bustle of morning activity. Whatever was happening on the other end of the phone, she would not get any privacy to face.

She took a deep breath and picked the phone up. "Sergeant First Class Trube. How can I help you sir or ma'am?"

"Isn't it supposed to be First Sergeant? And, whoo boy, are you a tough one to track down!"

Mama?

"Tonya, are you there?"

"Yes, ma'am." A guy running a computer simulation of flood water dissipation in the downtown area a few feet away gave her a grin before refocusing on his task. "Is there something wrong? Everyone okay?" She tried to recall the last time they had talked on the phone. *Christmas? No, Thanksgiving.*

"Everything is fine here. No flooding in Georgia. Not here in Atlanta, anyway. I'm calling to check up on you, see how you're doing. See if everything's okay."

"I'm fine, Mama."

"You should have called me; told me you were being mobilized. You know I worry."

No, I didn't know that. "I...I lost my cell phone, all my numbers—"

"Girl," she got loud, "Don't tell me that! The number hasn't changed here since you were a little child. You're a grown woman."

She tried to put her hand over the speaker portion of the phone. The guy running the simulation made a show of staring at his screen.

"I'm fine, Mama, and I'm sorry for not calling. If you'll excuse me, I really have to get back to my troops."

"Ah, baby, you sound just like your granddaddy. 'My troops.' He would have been so proud. I wish he could see you now."

Okay.

"I'm so proud of you."

What? Where is that coming from? She'd never expressed pride in Tonya's military career before.

"I'm praying for you and all those young people with you out there."

A feeling of dread washed over her. Her throat constricted and her mouth went dry. She coughed and choked out, "Mama, how did you know I was mobilized and I'm with a bunch of young people?"

"Why, I saw you all on the 11:00 news. The floods are all over the national news and last night, so were you."

SHE DIDN'T TALK about her mother with Atlee. She didn't talk to her mother much at all, let alone talk about her. *The only one I've talked to her about recently was Abigail...*

She sighed as she climbed up into the deuce and a half. *Atlee is right. I really messed that up.*

Tonya told the driver, "Let's get going and always remember

this. Never admit to Atlee that she's right about anything."

* * *

SHE STOOD outside the building in the parking lot that night so she could have some privacy. She thought about calling Abigail, but she didn't think she would answer. Instead, she called Atlee.

"Go someplace we can talk," she commanded her friend.

"Girl, we don't have cush like you. I'm in a tent city, here."

"I'd hardly call a cot in a high school classroom cushy."

Atlee wasn't in the mood to argue. "Just tell me what's up."

She considered leading in with the call from her mother, but she knew that would be procrastinating over what she really wanted to talk about. She chose the honest route. "I need some help with Abigail. I mean, I have no clue what to do."

"Help, how?"

"You know how."

"So, you admit you have feelings for her?"

"Yes."

"Romantic feelings?"

"Is there any other kind?"

"There're all kinds, and you've been in total denial up to this point so, even though I knew it was more than a mentor thing, I didn't know if it was some sort of lust, or fling, or I don't know. You haven't dated much in the time I've known you."

"It's not lust or a fling, trust me."

"You're attracted to her, though."

"Yes, but it's more than that. She...she exasperates me, contradicts me, confounds me."

"So, you're just alike."

"No...okay, yes. We have our differences too, though."

"Uh, huh. Name one."

"Different ages. Different jobs. Totally different."

"That's not what I mean. Your way of walking through life

sounds the same, Tonya. I admit, I've barely met her, but I've got a couple of doctors in my family. It takes a certain sort of person to want to be an orthopedic surgeon. They're not meek, mousy types."

"Oh, she's not."

"It sounds like you've finally met your match, in more ways than one."

"How do I get her back? I mean, I'm not sure I ever really had her, but…"

"Do you love her?"

Tonya contemplated that for several seconds. "I don't know that, not yet. I mean, we knew each other maybe two weeks when I got mobilized and I've been gone almost a week now."

"If you don't know, then maybe this is just lust or—"

"It's not lust. I know I miss her and I feel awful about dumping her. I know I…" she closed her eyes and took a few breaths. "I know I want to be with her. I don't know if I love her because I… I've never loved anyone before. What does love even feel like?"

"Everything you just described, my friend."

"Really?"

"Yeah, really."

"That fast?"

"Sometimes, for some people, yes."

"So, what do I do now? How do I make this right?"

"We'll work on that, but I suggest you wait and do it in person. No more over the phone stuff."

CHAPTER 22-SARAH'S SONG

Late Saturday Morning
St. Agnes Ascension Hospital

Abigail

"Dr. Ross, Mrs. Hanes is ready for her release instructions."

"Thank you, nurse."

Abigail went straight to the patient's room, expecting to see at least the woman's daughter with her and possibly her husband too, but Sarah was alone, sitting, dressed in street clothes on the edge of her bed. She was staring at the television mounted high on the wall, watching a commercial for a local restaurant.

"I hear you're ready to leave us, Mrs. Hanes."

"Sarah, please. Yes, I am, but I have a feeling we're going to be seeing a lot of each other over the next several months."

"We will as long as you continue to follow your plan and allow your hand to heal."

"And, if it doesn't heal correctly?"

"Then you're probably going to need to be referred out to a hand specialist." *Who isn't me. Not yet.*

Sarah ran her left hand over the bottom part of the cast that extended from the fingertips of her right hand up to her elbow. Her sling prevented her from going past the wrist. "You've done a fine job, dear. I'm sure it will heal well."

"Do you have someone to drive you home?"

"My daughter went to get the car to pull it up front. She said she had to park in the south lot today."

Abigail gave her a knowing nod. "Saturday. Lots of visitors today, even though we typically have fewer patients on the weekend."

"It will be one fewer as soon as you let me go."

"Then let's get to it, shall we?" Abigail really wished Sarah's daughter was there. The older woman seemed lucid, but she wasn't sure how much she could remember, and she was still taking powerful pain killers for her collection of injuries from the accident.

She held up the release paperwork and started to go over it, when the noon news flashed onto the television, drawing Sarah's attention back to the screen.

"I'm sorry, Doctor," she apologized. "My daughter's husband, George, is in a local National Guard Unit that was mobilized for the floods in Illinois. They're on the news."

Local unit that's mobilized? Tonya's unit? Abigail stared at the screen along with her patient.

REPORTER: "A local water purification unit of the Army National Guard that was split in two and mobilized to provide clean drinking water to residents of Iowa and Illinois towns along the Mississippi River last week is coming back together and coming home soon."

. . .

THE CAMERA CUT AWAY from the local reporter to a shot of some water purification systems sitting along the bank of a river. Another reporter appeared on the screen.

REPORTER: Myrna Manning with NBC News, Dubuque. I'm here with Sergeant First Class, Tonya Trube, the acting First Sergeant for the platoon of Army National Guard soldiers who have been providing the residents of our city with tens of thousands of gallons of clean drinking water each day for the past five days. Sergeant Trube, can you walk us through how all of this works?

THE CAMERA CUT to Tonya and then back to the lineup of water purification units as she sketched how the soldiers pumped and purified water.

"I thought she was a motor sergeant," Abigail said out loud, when Tonya finished speaking.

"Pardon, dear? Do you know her?"

"Yes ma'am. We, uh, we met at a conference a few weeks ago."

The coverage switched back to the reporter with their local affiliate.

REPORTER: "Operations in both Iowa and Illinois will wrap up over the next few days and both elements of the unit will be headed home. Stay tuned right here for all the welcome home information and coverage."

"WELCOME HOME INFORMATION?" Abigail asked.

"Yes. Whenever they go somewhere, like when they went to

Honduras for a month a couple of years ago, there's a welcome home like what you see on TV for units that go to war. I was really hoping to go, but…" She raised her arm in a sling slightly."

"Where would it be?"

"Usually right there at their armory."

Abigail didn't know where that was, but she was determined to find out.

CHAPTER 23-WELCOME HOME

Abigail had never taken a personal day from the hospital before, but she felt compelled to do it five days later when Tonya's water purification unit was due home after a two-day convoy from Iowa that included meeting up with the portion of the unit that had been working a similar mission in Illinois. She had to prove to Tonya that she still cared, no matter what she'd said on the phone in her anger and dismay.

She took a deep breath, buttoned up her blazer and marched confidently into the armory, onto the crowded drill floor, prepared for the surprise she knew Tonya was about to receive.

The armory was filled with families of younger soldiers and members of the media, all eager to reunite with the returning soldiers.

Someone made an announcement over a PA system about the imminent arrival of the members of the unit. Moments later, the crowd outside the armory cheered as the sounds of military vehicles approached the building. Inside, everyone quieted down, waiting in nervous anticipation.

Abigail wasn't sure she should be in the building with the immediate families of the returning soldiers. She thought about moving outside, but she was too late. The inside crowd surged forward slightly when a big bay door at one end of the drill floor opened, and the entire unit marched inside, in formation.

Everyone present clapped and cheered as the soldiers entered the building.

A man moved to the front of the group and introduced himself as the commander. He commended his soldiers for completing their missions to provide humanitarian aid and disaster relief. He remarked briefly on the specific contributions of a few of the senior people in the unit, including Tonya, who was standing to one side of the formation with her motor pool troops rather than with the first platoon, and then he thanked the families present at the welcome home ceremony for their support.

After only a couple of minutes, he told everyone the soldiers needed to return the next day to wrap things up, then he called out, "Company, attention! Dismissed!"

Another cheer went up. The crowd surged toward the rapidly deteriorating formation. Soldiers were swallowed up by their loved ones.

Abigail lost sight of Tonya for a couple of minutes. When her eyes finally tracked her down, she saw she was being mobbed by parents, many of whom were thanking her for taking such good care of their sons and daughters.

Abigail watched from a distance as well-wishers surrounded Tonya. She caught her eye for a brief second, just long enough for Tonya to nod in acknowledgment before the crowd swallowed her up again.

Abigail turned to leave after that, but a hand on her arm stopped her. Atlee was there at her side. She hadn't noticed her before.

"Thanks for being here, Abigail. Tonya appreciates it, even if she doesn't show it. She's pretty hardheaded," Atlee added, with a knowing smile.

Abigail nodded, more than aware of Tonya's stubbornness.

Atlee reached into her pocket and pulled out her phone. "It'd be nice to catch up," she said. "Can I call you? My friend over there might need another friend right now, even if she doesn't know it yet."

"Sure," Abigail said. "That would be nice." They exchanged numbers, then she watched as Atlee walked away.

She felt a wave of sadness. She was determined to make things right with Tonya, with or without Atlee's help, no matter how long it took.

* * *

THE COMMANDER HAD DISMISSED his soldiers, but Abigail doubted Tonya would just leave and leave everything for the next day. *That's not her style. Not at all!*

She went home to her apartment, resigned to wait for Atlee's call, whenever it came. *And she probably has a lot of work to catch up on there, too.*

She cleaned her little apartment from top-to-bottom that afternoon, even emptied the garbage and recycling bins before she sat down on her couch to wait and wonder what to do with herself until it was time to go to work the next morning. She knew getting sleep was a lost cause, so she decided to go for a run to try to at least clear her head for a while. Before she could lace on her shoes, her cell phone rang. It surprised her to find it was Tonya on the other end.

"Hey, I just thought I'd call and see how you are," Tonya said. "I appreciate you coming today, and I wanted to thank you for that."

Abigail was speechless at first, unable to respond. She'd been so eager to make things right, and so sure it wouldn't be this simple. It wasn't until Tonya laughed at her silence that she found her voice again.

"That's all right," she said with a nervous laugh. "I'm glad you called. I was a little anxious about showing up there today and how you'd take that."

Tonya chuckled again, her voice light. "Don't worry, I understand you wanted to show support. I appreciate it, really."

"You must be exhausted, though."

"Oh, I can't even begin to tell you."

"Then I'll let you go. Rest. I know you have to go back there tomorrow and do heaven knows what all. Try to take it easy on yourself tonight."

With her voice growing sober, "We should really talk" Tonya said.

"We can, and we will, but you do what you need to do first, and then you take care of you."

"It may be a few days or more. There's a lot to wrap up, and my job and—"

"It's okay. I'm not going anywhere but to work."

CHAPTER 24 - SERGEANT'S MAJOR

The Following Tuesday Evening
Abigail's Apartment
Oaklee

Abigail was cleaning up after a late, light supper and contemplating bed when her phone rang. She glanced at the screen. 'Atlee.'

"Hey there," she said as she answered. "How in the world are you?" She moved over to her sofa and took a seat.

"Exhausted. It's been a long few weeks. Maybe more. I lost count."

"I bet. Is everything all wrapped up, finally?"

"If you mean from the mobilization, then yes. Everything is cleaned up, put away, the payroll is done, all that good stuff. All the things we dropped to go west are still undone though, and we're all bone tired."

"It's sweet of you to call, but there was no obligation. I won't keep you."

"I wanted to call you Abigail. There are some things I want to tell you I think you should know, and honestly, I think we really should get to know each other. I think we'll be seeing a lot more of each other. At least, I hope so."

I hope so too. "Tonya called me, Atlee. That evening you got in."

"She told me she did. She didn't say what you talked about, though. She's been pretty tight-lipped about the call, and she hasn't said anything else at all, which is why I thought we should talk. Are you okay?"

Abigail stood and went to the window. "I'm fine. She said she had to go back there and do some wrap up stuff, and then go back to work. She…she was pretty worn out, too. We agreed we'd talk at some point, but I didn't push her for a time."

"I don't know how much I should tell you, but there are a lot of new things going on. Tonya…Well, she's going to be even busier than normal for a long time."

Abigail worried about her. "Is that bad?" she asked, as she paced the small piece of floor between the back of the couch and the window.

"Not bad for her, but maybe for the two of you and any relationship you're trying to have, knowing Tonya. Has she ever told you about her three things philosophy?"

Abigail mentally rolled her eyes. "Yes. Motors, the military, and softball. Well, fast pitch that has evolved into slow pitch."

"That's the one."

"So, let me guess, one of those is even more intense than it was previously?" She stopped pacing and sat back down.

"Yes," Atlee answered. "Well, two are, actually. For one, we had just started our softball season when we got mobilized. We missed three games and, if we don't play tonight, it will be four."

"So, you had to forfeit those games?" *I'll bet that's eating at Tonya.*

"No, but we forfeit them if we don't make them up by the end of the season. It's a military league, so there is some understanding and flexibility there, but not much!"

"So, you've got to squeeze in some additional games."

"If we can, yes. Everyone on the team has a regular job or is in school, though it's summer and most guard college students don't take classes over the summer so they can do their annual training and such. Two weeks of annual training are still coming up for us, which we already had to make up two games for. We had a bye for one weeknight series of games because of AT, but we had one that weekend and the following week that were already rescheduled."

"And Tonya...all of you, have to do this annual training besides."

"You got it. And here's the part I should probably leave up to her to tell you, but who knows when she's going to get time—"

"Don't tell me anything that would be something she might want to keep private, Atlee."

"Oh, it's not private. At least, it won't be for long."

Abigail leaned forward, listening intently.

"She's getting promoted before AT. She was told today. Actually, I kind of knew before she did, but I couldn't say anything. All orders that come down, come across my desk."

"Promoted. That's what she's been wanting."

"Our First Sergeant is being promoted to Sergeant Major and he's leaving the unit after our next drill, which is in two weeks. It's our prep drill for AT. We leave for those two weeks of training the following weekend."

Atlee went on. "Tonya is being promoted to Master Sergeant and will be the acting First Sergeant until she completes what's called the pre-command course. Then she'll get her First Sergeant diamond added to her rank insignia." Atlee laughed on her end. "And I know I'm talking to a civilian who is used to lots of hospital acronyms and jargon, but not military ones," she said. "Sorry."

"It's okay. I sort of followed. My oldest brother was a Master Sergeant in the Air Force before he became a warrant officer, but I believe for them, that's the rank Tonya holds now."

"E7, yes."

"Well, good for Tonya. She really is getting what she wanted."

"Yes, but she's sort of getting thrown right into the fire and it doesn't leave a lot of time for you, doc. We've got drill, prep for AT, AT, her doing the course, her day job, soft—"

"That's just it. I never had a lot of time for her either. I'm not a full-fledged orthopedic surgeon yet. I'm a third-year resident looking at another two years of either fellowship or putting my time in at a hospital before I can become board certified in a specialty."

We're so alike in so many ways. "Tonya was built for that kind of pressure, Atlee. I may not know her well, but I know that because I know her type. And, when she gets two minutes, we'll talk, and we'll figure out where we go from there." *And if she doesn't call me in the next week or so, I'll track her down. Nothing I haven't done before.*

CHAPTER 25-1SG TRUBE

Tonya strode into the outer office to find Atlee seated at her desk that faced the door.

The younger soldier jumped up. "Good afternoon, First Sergeant!"

She shook her head. "Don't call me that. Not yet."

"Your orders start Monday."

"And today is only Friday."

"And you're here this evening to do what he does every Friday night before drill to get ready for the weekend."

"Is he here?"

"Not yet. On the way. What, did you race here from work?"

Tonya held up a neatly pressed uniform on a hanger. "Should I change before he gets here?"

"You're paid for tonight, but you can be casual. Top will be, and so will the Commander, if he makes it in at all. He's been out of town the last couple of days."

"Just before AT?"

"He has a civilian employer, too. There are only two of us here full-time, remember?"

Tonya looked around the office with fresh eyes. It wasn't big by most standards. There was the room Atlee sat in right off the balcony over the drill floor. Two doors opened off either side of her office. The one to the right led into the small office shared by the commander and the first sergeant, both part-time positions. The one to the left led to an office that was a little larger than Atlee's. Tonya knew that before the military drawdown in the early 2000s, the full-time NCOs responsible for training and readiness shared it. Now part-time soldiers like she was held those positions, with Atlee handling most of the day-to-day needs that had to be met outside of weekend drills.

The only other full-time person left was the Staff Sergeant who ran the unit's supply operation. No easy task, she knew, when the unit's supply inventory included things to keep all the ROWPUs in operation. She wondered aloud where he was, but Atlee waved her off.

"He rarely hangs around for this. His long day is always the Monday after drill when he's got to figure out if everything he issued was returned or signed for. Then he has to order re-supply and such."

Tonya tapped her forehead. "Good to know. Making a mental note." She sighed. "It's shocking how much I'm already learning that I never realized."

"You'll be fine," Atlee said.

They both looked toward the office door when one of the heavy doors into the building closed with a thud downstairs.

"That will be Top," Atlee said. "He has a key. We'll probably be reassigning his key to you once he goes."

Moments later, the First Sergeant appeared in the doorway, with an "Evening," and a dip of the head by way of greeting. He was carrying an armload of stuff and hustled into the office he shared with CPT Clark to relieve himself of it.

. . .

OUTSIDE, after they had finished running through the prep for the weekend, Tonya and Atlee went outside, leaned against their cars, and talked.

Atlee said, "I want to be straight up with you. You can be mad at me all you want, but I called Abigail and told her about your promotion. I told you when you were in Iowa I wouldn't mess in it, but after what you called me and told me later and a lot of thinking about it since we've been back, I did."

Tonya crossed her arms over her chest to match her crossed ankles. She wasn't mad, but a thousand thoughts seemed to crowd her head all at once. She pushed them aside and asked, "Did she say anything when you told her?"

"She's happy for you. She knows this is what you wanted and she seemed genuine about that. She also seems to understand what a drag this is going to be on your personal life, at least for a while, and she seems genuinely okay with that, too."

"So it sounds to me like she's not interested in hearing any more from me."

"That's what you got out of that?"

"Yeah."

"With all due respect, you're an idiot."

"Hey!"

"Just call her, Tonya. Talk to her yourself."

"Do you honestly think she wants me to?"

"I know she does."

Tonya pushed off the car and stood up to her full height, but hung her head. "Now, if I only knew what to say."

"How about, I love you?"

Tonya looked Atlee in the eye. "Don't you think it's still too soon for that?"

"Not if that's how you feel."

"What if she doesn't feel that way about me?"

"I don't think you need to worry about that."

Tonya wasn't so sure. "Regardless, I'm not doing it this weekend. I need my head to be clear for that conversation."

"When, then?"

"Maybe Monday night, after practice?"

"Are you asking me or telling me?"

"Monday. After practice."

"Why don't we cancel practice on Monday? We have drill this weekend."

"Look, I'm tired too, but we have a game on Tuesday. Maybe we can shorten it a little."

Atlee went right back to her original line of questioning. "So Monday, then, you'll call her?"

"Yes."

"Promise?"

"Yes, but don't you call her and tell her that."

"So, what I hear you saying is you may not keep your promise?"

"I'm going to keep it. You've got my word."

"Okay then. Tell her I said hi."

"Tell her yourself when you call her."

"I told you I wouldn't. You've got *my* word."

CHAPTER 26-RHS

Another Saturday Morning
at
St. Agnes Ascension Hospital

Abigail

It was quiet on the med/surge ward. It was quieter still for the orthopedic residents. Abigail only had one in-patient. They had skipped education that morning, and they had completed rounds quickly given the summer lull in people who wanted to be laid up in a hospital over the weekend.

The two attending surgeons had been closeted in an office since rounds ended.

Abigail finished her charting and stood staring out a window. Outside, it was a gorgeous, sunny day for late June. Shorts weather, she thought, but without the oppressive heat of mid-July to mid-August. She was thinking about calling it a day a little early when Cameron approached her.

"Dr. Ross, can I talk to you for a few minutes?"

She turned to him. Her head said, be leery, but he was smiling and appeared to have no ulterior motive, so she relaxed and agreed.

He looked out the window. "Nice out there. How about in the courtyard? I'm sure we won't be missed for a few minutes."

"Sure, I guess," she said. *What's so private? Does he really want to talk to me about his neighbor?* She remembered her freshman year fling with another young woman on the track team, a business major. It had lasted a few months and then her lover had transferred schools, taking a scholarship offer for her sophomore year to a bigger Division One school with a nationally ranked track and field program. She had Olympic dreams, and Abigail was an inconvenience.

Abigail swore off women after that. She even quit following the Olympics, something her family had always watched hours of on television as if they were right in the thick of things themselves. She threw herself into her schooling instead.

She was an All-American sprinter her senior year and heavily recruited by club programs, but getting into and starting medical school was her only focus, much to the dismay of her family who thought she had Team USA chances for sure.

They were getting off the elevator on the ground floor when Abigail realized she had zoned out on Cameron and hadn't said a word. "What did you want to talk about?" she asked him as they walked down a short hallway to doors leading out to a courtyard the ambulatory patients could use, if they chose.

He pointed to an empty bench along a walking pathway that ringed the space.

Once they were seated, he jumped right in. "We're both on the same path, you know?"

"Come again?"

"Specialties."

"Hands?" she asked.

Cameron nodded.

Her heart sank. He was good in the OR, and the attending surgeons liked him. If he was looking for a fellowship too, he was more likely to get it than she. *And he would be deserving.*

"I wanted to run an idea by you," he was saying. "Something to give some thought to."

She swallowed. "What's that?"

"My mother is Helena Galatas. She reverted to her maiden name after my father died."

"It sounds familiar, but I'm at a loss. I'm sorry."

"She's a principal of the private hospital group, RHS."

Abigail's eyes grew wide. "The RHS that was in the news a couple of years ago?"

"Yes," he admitted. "The one and only. That was one person who stirred up all the trouble and she's gone. Plead guilty to a slew of heinous things and she's in prison. A very nice, cushy place, for people who can afford it, but prison all the same."

"The company survived it?"

"Not only survived, but thrived. RHS is doing some of the foremost work in hand and finger reattachments and replacements in the country. In the world, even. There are branches now in several major US cities–something that was in the works before Sherri pulled her crap–and we're looking at expanding around the globe."

"We're? So, you're joining the family business?"

"Yes, as a surgical fellow, in the fall at our newest facility right here under the direction of Dr. Ludwig Von Strassmann."

"Any relation to the father of forensic medicine, Von Strassmann?"

"Direct descendent and a renowned hand specialist in Germany before he immigrated here twenty years ago. He's been in private practice until now."

"That's quite a coup, then." She marveled at it all. "Wow. Congratulations, Cameron!"

He smiled. "Thanks. We're recruiting top talent. Do you care to join me?"

She was taken aback. Gathering herself quickly, she asked him if he was serious.

He held up his right hand, two fingers extended. "Scout's honor."

"I…I don't know what to say."

"You don't have to give me an answer, yet…or ever. Not to me. You can talk to Ludwig. You can talk to my mom. She works out of the headquarters in New York, but we can arrange something. She does a lot of the recruiting these days since Sherri went to jail." He shrugged. "I know that's a stain on the entire organization, but it's a legitimate fellowship with real pay, and benefits, and everything, and all the surgery you can handle."

"Cutting edge, too."

"Yes." He nodded again. "We do traditional stuff too like you did for Mrs. Hanes, but the replacements, the reattachments–reanimations if you will–that's where we shine."

"You're sure you want me?"

"You're the best. We want the best."

She leaned back against the bench and gave him a long look. "Why aren't you at Hopkins or somewhere like that? I know you graduated from Penn, so why are you here at St. Agnes?"

"What's wrong with here?"

She backtracked. "Nothing, but this isn't exactly the best place for you to learn to join RHS and it's not the most fertile recruiting ground either. No offense meant to any of our colleagues."

"Most people who do their residency at a place like Hopkins, stay at Hopkins and they specialize in neurology or neurosurgery. We get more trauma patients here than they get there for stuff like we do."

He has me there.

"It's better training than you think. Now then, questions?"

"Millions. My mind is going crazy. This isn't something I ever would have thought of. I was hoping to compete against everyone else in the world for a spot at a place like University Hospital, or Sanai, or…I don't even know."

"Would you like to talk to Ludwig?"

She only had to consider it a second before nodding. "Yes. Yes, I think I would."

He stood and offered her a hand up. When they were face to face, he told her, "I hope you join us. I think you'll find the work fascinating. And, bonus, you'll actually have time for a life. We don't do 14-16-hour days, six days a week. Sometimes we only run four days a week. There's a full medical staff to take care of inpatient needs beyond surgeries."

"Well, there's something to think about." As they started walking back toward the building, a thought occurred to her.

She asked him, "How do you do it? I mean, I know you're married. How do you balance all of this with a wife? Do you ever see her?"

He laughed. "It's tough, especially on our son, but she stays at home with him, so that helps."

"You have a child too?"

"He turned one in November, and we have a little girl on the way. She's due in late September."

"Wow!" *Go you.* "I'm exhausted all the time. I can only imagine."

"Me too. My wife is very understanding."

Hmm. Imagine that.

CHAPTER 27 - RECONNECT

Monday Evening

Tonya

"Hi there," Tonya said when Abigail answered the phone.

"Hello yourself. How are you?"

"Good…well, not good. Tired. I'm lying flat out on my bed and can't move because I've been running myself ragged, and I feel guilty because I've been blowing you off for a week and a half now. I want to apologize for being so out of touch."

"Tonya, it's okay. I get it. Life is crazy, but I understand congratulations are in order on your promotion."

"Thanks. I think. I'm not so sure this is the right thing for me, after all."

"That's your exhaustion talking. You went from your job, to drill, to mobilization for a couple weeks, back to your job, and now to First Sergeant getting ready for your AT, and you haven't had a break."

"And you really have been talking to Atlee."

"True, but I'm also trying overall to pay better attention to what's going on all around me. I've missed a lot."

And I miss you. "How...how are things going for you?"

"Okay. Things actually slow down a little in the summer. At least they do until people have stupid accidents. It'll be crazy again soon. I did get an interesting proposition over the weekend, though."

"Excuse me?" Her blood started to boil.

"I got a fellowship offer out of the blue."

Tonya blew out the breath she hadn't realized she was holding. "When you said 'proposition,' I thought you meant you met someone."

"No, Tonya. There's no room in my life for anyone else. Anyone but you, that is."

Tonya sighed. "I want you in my life, but I don't know how much I can offer you."

"Do you agree that life is busy for me too?"

"Yes. Of course."

"Well, the guy that offered me a chance at a fellowship today is our only married third-year resident. And he has a toddler and a baby on the way."

"What's your point?"

"He's crazy busy here like me, and he's getting ready to jump into the family business aside from that, but he also takes care of family business, if you know what I mean."

"Sex with his wife, at least twice?"

"You got it!" Abigail couldn't help but laugh. "I can always count on you, even when you're tired, to pick up on innuendo."

"His wife, is she as hot as you?"

"And there's the Tonya I know."

"Is she?"

"I don't know. I've never met her. I knew he was married, but nothing else. I didn't know about the kids…well kid and a baby on the way."

"If he has time for sex, and even more if she does with a toddler, I guess we could make time for a little us time."

"Us time, or sex?" Abigail asked. *I'd be happy with either, but I really want both.*

"Both, but here's the thing. I leave for AT Saturday morning. Gotta be at the armory Friday night."

"I know."

"I'll be gone two weeks and come home to another full-scale cleanup operation."

"Sure."

"I don't know if I can see you before then."

"It's okay."

"I want to. I want you."

"I want you too."

There was a long pause.

"Abigail?"

"Hmm?"

"I'm getting really sleepy, but I want you to know it's not just fucking to me, when I touch you."

"I know."

"You do?"

"I love you too, Tonya."

"Good night, Abigail. I love you."

CHAPTER 28-WOMAN DOWN

Monday Evening

Abigail

It was the top of the fifth inning and Tonya's team was on the field by the time Abigail made it to the ballpark from the hospital. The score was tied, one to one. No one was on base, and there were two outs.

Atlee was playing centerfield. Abigail caught her eye as she took a seat in the stands behind the team's dugout and gave her a thumbs up.

Atlee returned the signal.

Tonya was intent on her pitching and didn't notice her. It was just as well. She was just trying to be there for her, not to distract her.

The batter connected with the pitch, sending a bouncing grounder toward the third baseman. As Abigail watched, the young woman playing the bag charged it, scooped it up, and threw a rocket to first base.

"Out!" the umpire called.

Abigail clapped along with the handful of fans in the stands and called out, "Nice play," as the National Guard team came off the field.

Tonya looked up at the sound of her voice and dropped her glove. After she picked it up, she looked Abigail's way again.

Abigail waved.

"Damn it, Atlee," Tonya hissed when she got into the dugout. "You could have told me!"

"And spoil the surprise? Uh, uh."

At the sound of a moan, they both whirled. Lynn Baines sat on the end of the bench, head against the ice water jug, her face ash white. She was sweating even though it was a cool evening.

Atlee reacted first. "What's up Lynn? Are you okay?"

"Side." She pointed. "Feels like…I can't even describe it."

Tonya stuck her head out of the dugout and called to a man behind the backstop. "Medic!"

Abigail heard her and clambered down out of her seat.

Tonya called, "Injury time out," to the Umpire behind the plate and then stepped out of the way as Abigail entered the dugout well ahead of the medic.

"What's the problem?" she asked.

Atlee pointed at Lynn Baines.

She strode the length of the dugout in a few steps. "Doctor Abigail Ross," she said to Lynn. She gave her a quick once over and asked, "Where's your pain?"

"Side. It hurts so bad. I was trying to hang on. We don't have any subs tonight."

"Pardon me, ma'am," the young military medic said to Abigail. "Step aside, please."

She turned and gave him a sweet smile as she held Lynn's wrist and checked her pulse. "I've got it. I'm a doctor."

"Oh. Sorry, ma'am."

She asked Lynn, "Is there anyone here with you?"

"Me," a male voice said from behind her and the medic who was still standing there, watching. "I'm her husband. I was in the porta-pot. What's going on?"

"I can't be sure without checking her out and maybe having an x-ray done, but I'm thinking appendicitis. She needs to go to the hospital."

The young medic asked, "Should I call a squad?"

Abigail looked at George Baines. "She's in a lot of pain, but you're five minutes from University Hospital walking. By the time they scramble a squad." She held up a hand. "Are you able to take her there?"

He nodded.

"We'll help get her to the car," Atlee said from behind all the extra people in the dugout.

"I'll help him, the young man volunteered."

Tonya collected Lynn's things and followed the two men as they carried a sobbing Lynn to the car. Once she was settled inside, sprawled across the back seat, she returned to the field and told the plate umpire, "Unless you'll let us play with eight, we'll have to forfeit. We were already shorthanded today."

Abigail was standing on the field by the dugout with Atlee and the rest of the team. "I can play," she volunteered, "if that's allowed, that is."

The umpire started to say something, but Atlee jumped in. "Military members, spouses, and partners is what it says in the rules. She's a partner."

All the other women on the team looked around at each other.

"She's with me," Tonya said to the umpire.

More looks were exchanged, but none of the women said a word.

"Give her name to the scorer," the umpire said, "and then get a batter up here."

"I DON'T SUPPOSE you have cleats?" Tonya asked Abigail as she dug her spare glove out of her ball bag and handed it to her.

Abigail looked down at her cross trainers. "No. These will have to do." She pulled the glove onto her left hand and pounded her right fist into the pocket. It felt good on her hand.

Everyone in the dugout was hanging on every word, ignoring the batter at the plate.

"I'm sorry. I remember you telling me you played all through high school, but not the position," Tonya said.

"Anywhere, but mostly outfield."

Tonya made a quick decision. "Sherry, you'll go back to shortstop. Abigail, you'll go to right field."

"All right, Top," Sherry said.

"Got it," Abigail said.

Tonya sighed. "Our number two batter is up. We'll put you at the end of the order. You may have to bat next inning."

"Or this inning, if we go on a tear," Atlee said with vigor. "Let's go, ladies!"

They went three up and three down to end the inning.

The top of the sixth passed with no balls flying Abigail's way. Nothing made it out of the infield.

The game entered the bottom of the sixth inning still tied at one. The inning ended that way too.

Tonya tried to rally the team as they took the field again for the last inning. "Let's hold them! I know we're all tired, but we've got this!"

The first batter hit a hard, bouncing grounder to Sherry at shortstop. She fielded it cleanly and threw the runner out at first base.

Tonya held up a finger on the mound. "One down!"

The next batter hit a line drive to left field that cut between the shortstop and the woman covering third base. The left fielder caught it on a bounce and threw it back to Tonya as the batter crossed first.

"Play's at second!" Atlee yelled from centerfield.

Tonya lobbed a pitch in. The batter got a piece of it but fouled it off far down the left field side.

From right field, Abigail thought, watch pitching this one low and inside.

Tonya lobbed another pitch in. It was on the outside corner and slightly higher.

The batter turned on it and hit a line drive her way.

Abigail got the glove Tonya lent her up, caught the ball cleanly, and fired it back to first base to catch the runner leaning off too far. The first baseman tagged her to be sure.

"Out!" the umpire called. "That's three."

Tonya pumped a fist in the air. "Way to turn two!"

As Abigail entered the dugout, Tonya gave her a fist bump. "No rust on you."

"It's amazing how fast it all comes back."

"Well, hopefully hitting does too."

Atlee called out from inside the dugout, "Sherry, you're up. Abigail, you're on deck, then we're back to the top of the order with Larner."

Sherry took a couple of cuts and went to the plate. Three pitches later she was standing on second base after the center fielder misjudged her hard pop-up and got just enough of the ball on a diving attempt to catch it that it went skittering toward the right fielder.

The right fielder was playing shallow enough to grab it, but not before Sherry slid into the bag.

Abigail walked to the plate with a bat on her shoulder she'd never swung. *Try to bunt to first maybe and advance her to third?*

She took up a position on the left side of the plate from the pitcher's view.

"Time!" Tonya called.

Everyone looked her way.

She held her hands up as she walked toward Abigail, but Abigail waved her off. "I've got this, coach."

The first pitch hit in front of the plate for a ball, but she'd already shown bunt. The infielders moved in, ready for it now.

She held her position on her switch-hitting side. *Connect, Abigail. Just get a piece of it.*

The pitch came in waist high, down the middle of the plate. In her high school years, she would have put a hurt on it. Not having played more than a pick-up game here and there in ten years, she was a little slow, but the ball tinged off the bat and flew past the pitcher and the leaping second baseman.

She ran. She ran as fast as she could because running was something she could still do. She was on second base when she heard the cheers from the dugout. Sherry had scored. They won!

She hustled back to the dugout and got a fist bump from the first woman out. "That was awesome, doc!"

"Thanks! Glad I got a piece of it."

Sherry gave her a high five.

Atlee pushed Tonya forward but gave Abigail a thumbs up over Tonya's shoulder.

"Well done, Abigail. Thanks," Tonya said. "You saved our three-games so far perfect season."

Atlee elbowed Tonya.

"Thanks for, uh, coming out tonight too. I appreciate it. We all do." She swung an arm back before Atlee could elbow her again. "I really do, and I love you."

"Love you too."

"Aww, isn't that nice," Atlee said. She pushed past them to join the line to shake hands with the Air Force team that had been their opponent. "Come on," she told the two of them.

Tonya tapped Abigail's shoulder. "Let's go. Get moving."
Abigail smiled. "Yes, ma'am."
"That's, 'Yes First Sergeant,' not ma'am."
"Don't push your luck. I don't take orders from you."

EPILOGUE

Six Months Later
McCormick and Schmick

"Are we celebrating something special tonight, ladies?" the server asked.

Abigail nodded toward Tonya. "She just finished the Army Pre-Command course."

"Wonderful," the man said. If he didn't know what they were talking about, he didn't let on.

"She said I could have whatever I want," Tonya told him.

"And what will you have?" he asked.

"Porterhouse. Medium. Baked potato with the works. A Cobb salad to start with plenty of bacon and bleu cheese. Oh, and a tall glass of whatever is on draft."

"Ale, Pilsner, Stout—"

"Ale."

"Very good." He turned to Abigail who was doing her best not to make a face. "I'll have a mixed green salad to start, the ten-ounce strip, medium well, and a sweet potato, no butter, no sugar, just a little cinnamon, and the house red wine."

"*You* ordered steak?" Tonya asked.

Abigail gave her, her best grin. "A girl's gotta eat."

"My, how things have changed."

The server slid away discreetly.

"Nothing has changed. Not that much."

"On the contrary," Tonya said. "We've both changed. A lot. If only Clara could see us now. Sitting here, sharing a meal. Not arguing over the food…much."

"With jobs we love," Abigail said.

"Friends," Tonya said.

"Yes."

"Lovers." She waggled her eyebrows at Abigail in what Abigail suspected she thought was a suggestive manner.

"Still incorrigible."

"But you love me."

Abigail nodded. "Yes." She took a sip of her water.

"It's been a crazy six months, hasn't it?"

"Yes, it most certainly has, but not all of it has been bad."

"I don't think much of it has been bad," Tonya said, "just busy."

The server returned with their drinks. When he left again, Abigail raised her glass. "Cheers, and congratulations."

"Thanks," Tonya said as she tapped her big glass lightly to Abigail's. "To us"

"Mmm. Yes."

"So, now what?" Tonya asked. "We've got the holidays coming up, winter, snow—"

"And then softball season, again."

"Are you going to keep playing with us?"

Abigail took a sip of her wine. "Do you think that's wise? The girlfriend of the first sergeant?"

"We're not the only gay players on the team."

"But you're the senior enlisted person in your unit."

"And I'm allowed to have a personal life, though I admit, it's been one on the run lately. Baines plays. She's a spouse, not military."

"Spouse is the key word there, and her relationship is heterosexual."

"If it makes you uncomfortable, Abigail, you don't have to play. It might be easier now with your fellowship position, though. You can make most of our practices and the games."

"I was thinking about you, not me."

"I love having you out there. I was skeptical, I admit, that first time out, but you're all the athlete you've said you are."

"Thanks, I think…"

"I just mean that I'm obsessed, where you've been a lot more reserved about it, hiding some serious talent. And, you're young yet. You could probably play fast pitch, if you wanted to."

"I don't want to. I left those days behind me in high school."

The server came back with their salads.

As she dipped a fork into hers, Tonya asked again, "So, softball? In or out?"

"Let's say I'm in; do I have to call you First Sergeant?"

"No. You can call me Coach."

"How about Tonya?"

"How about Coach?"

"How about wife?"

"Coach is fine…wait. What?"

Abigail pulled a box out of her blazer pocket. "I was going to wait until dessert to do this, but now is good. Tonya Trube, will you marry me?"

"You didn't seriously buy me a diamond, did you? Me? Stone butch me?"

"Open it." She slid the box over to her.

Tonya picked up the ring box, opened it a crack, and peeked inside. She chuckled, opened it wide, pulled out the gold-plated dog tag inside, and read the inscription aloud. "Property of Abigail Ross."

"There's a rainbow tag silencer in there, too."

Tonya pulled the silencer out and fitted it around the tag, then she reached around her neck and pulled her set of Army issued dog tags off. She added the new tag to the two existing ones.

"So, is that a yes?" Abigail asked.

"Yes," Tonya said. "I'll marry you."

"We can talk about the details some time in the future. There's no rush. Life is going to be topsy-turvy for me for a couple more years, yet at RHS until I'm board certified."

"And there's me, and there are the families," Tonya said. "As rough as it's been with my mother, I want you to meet her."

"I want to meet her, and I want you to meet my family…take some of the heat off me."

"Hey!"

"Relax. They're going to love you."

"Speaking of families, what will we do about surnames? Will you keep Ross at least professionally?"

"Maybe we hyphenate," Abigail suggested. "Trube-Ross."

"Or Ross-Trube."

"I asked you to marry me. Trube-Ross."

"I take back my yes then, and I'm asking you. Ross-Trube."

"Uh, uh, Abigail said. No take backs."

MILITARY ACRONYM/TERM GLOSSARY

1LT—First Lieutenant

1SG–First Sergeant, typically the ranking NCO in a unit/company

AT–Annual Training for a National Guard or Reserve unit. Usually 2 weeks in the summer, but it can vary.

Battalion – Army organization that oversees 4 to 6 line units or companies

Buck Sergeant–A newly promoted SGT, Army rank E5

CO–Commanding Officer–In charge of a unit, company, or battalion

CPT–Captain–Outranks a 1LT–typically the ranking person in a line unit or company that falls under a battalion

Drill—Weekend military training for national guard members and reservists

HMMWV–Hummer or Humvee–High Mobility Multipurpose Wheeled Vehicle

LT–Nickname for a first or second lieutenant

Mess–A unit's food preparation section/personnel

MRE–Meal, Ready to Eat–field rations

MSG–Master Sergeant–The rank Tonya wants.

MILITARY ACRONYM/TERM GLOSSARY

NCO–Non-Commissioned Officer–Made up of the Corporal and sergeant ranks in the Army, Marines, and Air Force (no corporals). The Navy does not use a structure with sergeants.

NCOIC–Non-Commissioned Officer in Charge

PLDC–Primary Leadership Development Course for Army soldiers who want to be NCOs

PM–Preventative Maintenance

ROWPU–Reverse Osmosis Water Purification Unit

SFC–Sergeant First Class–Tonya's rank

SGT–The lowest sergeant rank. In the Army, it's pay grade E5.

SPC–Specialist, Army pay grade E4 (not an NCO rank like a Corporal/CPL E4 is, but the last remaining technical track rank)

STRAC–Skilled, Trained, Ready Around the Clock

Top–Nickname for the First Sergeant, the 'top' NCO in a company sized Army unit

UA–Unit Administrator–Atlee's position

XO–Executive Officer–2nd in command of a unit

AFTERWORD

In the spring and summer of 1993, the US State of Iowa experienced flooding unheard of in the state in modern times. I was a 26ish-year-old soldier, doing annual training (AT) with my unit, the 135th Military Police Company of the Ohio Army National Guard, at Camp Grayling Michigan that July.

The 641st Water Purification Unit, a sister unit in our battalion, was at AT along with us and the rest of the battalion when real world duty called for them. They packed up their troops and their ROWPUs, and they trucked from Michigan to Iowa with us and many other units in garrison at Grayling lining the streets cheering them on as they departed.

I was about nine years into my military career, but it was the first full unit mobilization for a real-world mission I'd ever experienced, and it made a lasting impression on me. The members of the 641st (later renamed the 641st Quartermaster Detachment) deployed a lot to disaster zones and war zones in the years after that. Wherever clean water was needed, they went.

AFTERWORD

The character of Atlee, the full-time unit administrator (UA) for Tonya's unit, is a compilation of myself, as I was the UA for the 135th at that time, and of two other UA's in the battalion including the one for the 641st. The three of us were tight. We lived under the reign of a battalion Personnel Staff Non-commissioned Officer (PSNCO) whom we all thought was the definition of an ice queen…had the term been in our lexicon back then. We watched each other's backs because she was one tough cookie.

It wasn't unusual for her to call one or the other of us daily to do her morning checks and reminders, and then for the first one to call the other two to give them a heads up about anything weird, unusual, time sensitive, or labor intensive she brought up. She would get annoyed that she'd annotate whom she called, then try to call another of us to find the line busy at 0730 or so in the morning. This was back in the days before cell phones, when money was tight, and most units only had one line with no call waiting!

It's hard to believe that was nearly 30 years ago. Now, as I look back on those days, I can see that sergeant for what she really was, a woman working in a man's world, who was damn good at her job, trying to climb the military career ladder at a time when being 'out' could get you and everything you worked for kicked out of the military with no recourse. There wasn't even 'Don't ask, don't tell,' then. Those years of being allowed to serve as an LGBTQ person as long as you kept that to yourself would be a few more years down the road.

Tonya doesn't resemble my former PSNCO entirely, only her best qualities. I dedicate this book to that sergeant.

~Anne

ABOUT THE AUTHOR

Anne Hagan is the author of over twenty full-length works of fiction in the mystery, romance, and thriller genres. She writes of family, friends, love, murder, and mayhem in no particular order and often all in the same story. She's a half owner of the weekly discount eBook newsletter, MyLesfic, a wife, parent, foster parent, and an Army veteran. When she writes, she draws from her experiences because truth is often stranger than fiction.

CHECK ANNE OUT ON THE WEB, ON FACEBOOK OR ON TWITTER

For the latest information about upcoming releases, other projects, sample chapters and everything personal, check out Anne's **site** at https://AnneHaganAuthor.com/ or like Anne on **Facebook** at https://www.facebook.com/AuthorAnneHagan. You can also connect with Anne on **Twitter** @AuthorAnneHagan.

JOIN ANNE'S EMAIL LIST

Are you interested in **free books**? How about **free short stories**? For those and all the latest news on new releases, **opportunities to get review copies of all of her new releases** and more, please consider joining Anne's email list at: https://www.AnneHagan-Author.com by filling in the pop up or using the brief form in the sidebar.

ALSO WRITTEN BY THE AUTHOR

Sapphic Sweets Romantic short stories – Some sweet. Some with a little heat.
   Misfit Christmas – A Colorado Holiday Romance
   Broken Women
   Can two women, unlucky in love, find solace in each other?
   Healing Embrace–The stand-alone sequel to Broken Women
   Barb and Janet were a couple... and then they weren't. What now?
   Steamboat Reunion–the third and final book in the Barb and Janet series
   Can you go home again?
   Loving Blue in Red States
   A lesfic romance *short story* series that kicks off with a visit to the little town of Sweetwater, Texas. It's followed by stops in Birmingham, Alabama, Jackson Hole, Wyoming, Perryville, Missouri, Salt Lake City, Utah, Savannah, Georgia, Wall, South Dakota and East Tennessee. There's also an international contribution to the series, Kilbirnie Scotland authored by Kitty McIntosh.

ALSO WRITTEN BY THE AUTHOR

A Sweetwater Christmas
Traditional and progressive meet in ruby red west-central Texas...
This novella is a significant expansion of the short story, Loving Blue in Red States: Sweetwater Texas.
Christmas Cakes and Kisses
Two different worlds brought together by cake...

* * *

The books of the Morelville Mysteries series Anne's Sapphic/Women Loving Women themed mystery/romance series:
Relic: The Morelville Mysteries–Book 1–The first Dana and Sheriff Mel mystery and the first book in the Morelville saga.
Cases collide for two star crossed ladies of law enforcement!
Busy Bees: The Morelville Mysteries–Book 2
Romance and Murder Mix in the Latest Story Featuring Sheriff Mel Crane and Special Agent Dana Rossi!
Dana's Dilemma: The Morelville Mysteries–Book 3–The relationship matures between Mel and Dana in an installment that features a breaking Amish character, an ex-girlfriend, a conniving politician, and murder.
Elections and Old Loves Combine with Deadly Results in a Romantic Mystery Featuring Sheriff Mel Crane and Special Agent Dana Rossi!
Hitched and Tied: The Morelville Mysteries–Book 4
Mel and Dana attempt to bring their growing romantic relationship full circle, but family, duty, and family duties all conspire to get in the way.
Viva Mama Rossi!: The Morelville Mysteries–Book 5–The 5th tale in the Morelville Mysteries and the book that gives fans a full introduction to future Morelville Cozies series sleuths Faye Crane (Mel's mom) and Chloe Rossi (Dana's Mama). The two series stand-alone, but they're certainly better together.

ALSO WRITTEN BY THE AUTHOR

A delayed honeymoon getaway takes a deadly turn for newlyweds Mel and Dana; meanwhile, two meddling mothers won't let sleeping fisherman lie in the latest Morelville Mystery.

A Crane Christmas: The Morelville Mysteries–Book 6
Is it the Christmas season or the 'silly season'?

Mad for Mel: The Morelville Mysteries–Book 7
Rival gangs will stop at nothing to gain sole control of the drug trade in Muskingum County, and they've picked Valentine's week to create a firestorm of murder and mayhem as they battle each other for supremacy.

Hannah's Hope: The Morelville Mysteries–Book 8
A young mother with a troubled past seeks help from Mel and Dana, but is their effort to assist her too little, too late?

The Turkey Tussle: The Morelville Mysteries–Book 9
The old-fashioned country village of Morelville holds a secret.

Sullied Sally: The Morelville Mysteries–Book 10
An unsolved murder, over 40 years in the past, leads to the discovery of a new victim and the return of an old stalker.

Finding Sheila: The Morelville Mysteries–Book 11
A woman, imprisoned for manslaughter, disappears without a trace during transport between states, and it's all up to Dana to find her.

Tennessee Bound: The Morelville Mysteries–Book 12
The politics and the paper-pushing are wearing on Sheriff Mel. Will she chuck it all?

* * *

A spinoff of Anne's Morelville Mysteries series, The Morelville Cozies series features meddling mother sleuths Faye Crane and Chloe Rossi getting mixed up in mysteries all their own.

The Passed Prop: The Morelville Cozies–Book 1
Chloe Rossi wants to retire with her husband and move away

ALSO WRITTEN BY THE AUTHOR

from suburban sprawl to bucolic Morelville; the only trouble is, Morelville is experiencing its worst crime wave ever, and Marco Rossi wants no part of a move there. What to do?

Opera House Ops: The Morelville Cozies–Book 2

Murder and other sinister goings-on at a vacant 1800s era opera house in Morelville and a modern-day property developer who wants to raze the historic building for his own gain have the village residents all tied up in knots and Faye Crane trying to play savior to history.

The Conjuring Commedienne: The Morelville Cozies–Book 3

Faye thinks Hattie's a suspect. Chloe thinks she's a kindred soul. Only Hattie knows for sure!

* * *

Steel City Confidential–Anne's first legal thriller (AKA The Thelma and Louise Book)

Clients hide things from their lawyers all the time. Pam Wilson makes it an art form.

Printed in Great Britain
by Amazon